F
CAR

Carcaterra, Lorenzo.

Apaches.

$25.00

DATE			

APACHES

ALSO BY LORENZO CARCATERRA

A SAFE PLACE: *The True Story of a Father, a Son, a Murder*

SLEEPERS

APACHES

LORENZO CARCATERRA

Ballantine Books

New York

Grateful acknowledgment is made to Alfred A. Knopf, Inc. and Harold Ober Associates Incorporated for permission to reprint "Fantasy in Purple" from *The Collected Poems of Langston Hughes* by Langston Hughes. Copyright © 1994 by the Estate of Langston Hughes. Reprinted by permission of Alfred A. Knopf, Inc. and Harold Ober Associates Incorporated.

http://www.randomhouse.com

ISBN: 0-345-40101-8

Manufactured in the United States of America

First Edition: July 1997
10 9 8 7 6 5 4 3 2 1

For the fallen.

Acknowledgments

None of what follows would have happened without the help and guidance of many. Here are a few:

Peter Gethers, who proved once again to be a great editor and, as I learned with the writing of this book, a patient one. The jokes aren't bad either. No writer could hope to have a better publisher or friend than Clare Ferraro. A tip of the hat to the rest of my Ballantine gang: Linda Grey, Alberto Vitale, Sally Marvin (no more Big Macs), and Nate Penn.

Loretta Fidel has always had my respect and this time around, she earned her stripes; Amy Schiffman, Rob Carlson, and Carol Yumkas are great agents and good friends. A big thank-you also to Arnold Rifkin. Thanks to Jake Bloom and Robert Offer for taking me along for the ride. And to Barry Kingham for being there.

A warm thanks to Jerry Bruckheimer, Susan Lyne, Jordi Ros, Donald De Line, and Joe Roth for their passion. And to Christy Callahan and Christian McLaughlin for their help.

To John Manniel for all he did for my family. A heartfelt thank-you to Steve Collura. I'll see you at Toscana's. And to Sonny Grosso, the best cop ever to pin on an NYPD badge and a friend for life. The next Fernet's on me.

To my phone circle: Liz Wagner, Leah Rozen, William Diehl, Stan Pottinger, Mr. G., Brother Anthony, Hank Gallo, and Joe Lisi. Thanks for listening.

To Vincent, Ida, and Anthony—for the great meals and the happy nights.

To Susan, who makes what I write read better than it should. In return, I can only give my heart. And to my two best accomplishments: Kate, who lets me steal her great plot ideas without complaints, and Nick, who keeps me laughing.

They have taught me how to love.

APACHES

Prologue

My mother groan'd, my father wept,
Into the dangerous world I leapt;
Helpless, naked, piping loud,
Like a fiend hid in a cloud.

—William Blake, "Infant Sorrow"

February 18, 1982

CARLO AND ANNE Santori wanted nothing more than to be alone.

They had planned this weekend getaway for six months, their first one in fifteen years. No kids, no phones, no work, nothing but music, dance, and a little bit of romance at the Jersey shore.

They left behind their fifteen-year-old son, Anthony, to care for the house and his twelve-year-old sister, Jennifer. They felt that both children were old enough to be trusted, allowing them to enjoy a short respite from the daily grind of parental responsibility. Carlo handed Anthony the house keys and three simple instructions—don't stray from the neighborhood, set the burglar alarm and lock the house, and never let Jennifer out of your sight. The boy stared at his father and swore to obey all three.

Anthony, however, had his own plans for the weekend.

His parents were no less than ten minutes out of the driveway when Anthony woke Jennifer from a sound sleep, yelling for her to get ready. They had two hours to catch a bus for a ride into Manhattan, to spend a Saturday in the city his parents had always told him was not to be trusted.

Anthony needed to get away almost as much as Carlo and Anne. He was a teenager eager for the taste of a day without parents, without rules, and with pockets jammed with allowance money. All of it out there waiting less than an hour's ride from the safety of a New Jersey colonial. His only obstacle had been to convince Jennifer.

She balked when she first heard the plan, and it was all he could do to keep her from spilling the secret. Jennifer was afraid something would go wrong, believing all the horror stories she had heard. But she stayed silent, her arms always wrapped around a Kermit the Frog doll, confident Anthony would protect her and allow nothing bad to happen.

Confident that he would be the one to keep her safe.

Jennifer was a frail girl, with a thin, freckled face, eager to cross the bridge from preteen to young adult. She wore a long-sleeved Gap denim shirt over a white pocket T. The jeans were tight and bleached, bottoms scraping a pair of red hightops. Black bangs brushed the corners of her eyes.

"Should we really do this?"

"Stay home if you're scared," Anthony said, walking from her room.

"I'm not scared," Jennifer said right back.

"Then get ready," Anthony told her. "And don't forget to bring your own money."

They walked down a sloping hill, ice, dirt, and moldy leaves brushing against their shoes. Jennifer kept her hands inside her coat pockets. On her shoulders was a backpack filled with a change purse, Kermit, and a hairbrush. Anthony kept his face away from the arctic blasts of wind bouncing past trees and houses. They moved in silence, each excited at the prospect of doing something forbidden.

Anthony held the door to the 7-Eleven across the two-lane street from the bus shelter. He checked his watch as his sister walked past.

"Ten minutes," he said. "Get what you want and meet me by the stop."

They boarded the 11:04.

Anthony paid for the one-way tickets with exact change. They walked down the center aisle toward the back of the bus, taking two empty seats four rows from an old couple bundled into down coats. Anthony unzipped his black leather jacket and leaned back, thick black curls resting against the torn edge of the seat. He closed his eyes as the bus swung past a series of mini-mart shops, fast-food outlets, and used car dealerships, heading for the speed lane of a congested thruway and the streets of New York City.

"I can't wait to see the stores," Jenny said, her Styrofoam cup of tea now cold in her hand.

"We'll walk around a bit," Anthony said, eyes still closed. "Get a feel for the place."

"Will it be crowded?"

"It's New York." Anthony turned his head toward the window. "It's *always* crowded."

"We gonna be home before dark?"

Anthony didn't answer, rocked to sleep by the motion of the bus.

"I hope we're home before dark," Jennifer Santori whispered to herself.

. . .

THE BUS PULLED into the top level of New York's Port Authority terminal at 11:56 A.M., three minutes past its projected arrival. Jennifer put a hand on her brother's shoulder and woke him.

"What will we do first?" Jennifer asked, zipping her parka.

"Find a bathroom," Anthony said.

They walked among thick crowds, Anthony holding Jennifer's hand. He repeated his warnings not to leave him. To wait where he left her.

To speak to no one.

To look at no one.

Anthony pushed open the men's room door, the one directly across from the Papaya King. He left Jennifer against the wall next to the door, pointed a finger in her face, and again told her not to move.

She answered with a nod.

He was out in less than five minutes.

He looked to his left and swallowed hard, feeling the sweat and the chill. Anthony Santori stood there and did the only thing he could think to do. He shouted his sister's name. Again and again and again and again. He shouted it as loud and as strong and as often as he could.

But there never was a response.

His ears were filled with the din of passing conversations. People stopped to stare at him now, curious about the panicked boy shouting out a girl's name. But he didn't care. Not about them. Not about what they thought. Not about what they were saying.

There was only one truth that mattered.

Jennifer had disappeared.

His only sister was gone.

Swallowed by a city not her own.

BOOK ONE

No hero without a wound.

—Bulgarian proverb

1

Boomer

GIOVANNI "BOOMER" FRONTIERI never wanted to be a cop. He was a three-letter athlete during his school years at St. Bernard's Academy, a private high school in downtown Manhattan his parents insisted he attend. He would leave their cold-water railroad apartment each morning before sunup and return each evening after dark, eating dinner and doing homework at the kitchen table facing the fire escape. He was a model student, never complained about his packed schedule, and kept the friends he trusted to a minimum.

He had two younger sisters, Angela and Maria, whom he would either dote on or ignore, depending on his mood. His older brother, Carmine, had already dropped out of school and followed their father, John, into the heavy-lifting, well-paying labor of the meat market. Their relationship was reserved, at best.

John Frontieri was a stern man who commanded respect and demanded his family's full attention. His upper body, conditioned by years of lugging 250-pound hindquarters off the backs of refrigerated trucks, was a weight lifter's dream. He was quick to give a slap of the hand to one of the children if he felt they were out of line, but never hit or screamed at his wife, Theresa, a homely, chunky woman whose face displayed a weariness far greater than her years.

On spring and summer Sunday mornings, after the nine o'clock mass, Johnny Frontieri would change quickly out of his blue dress suit and into work pants, construction shoes, and a sweatshirt. He and little Giovanni would then take their fishing poles and tackle down from the living room closet and rush out of the apartment for a twenty-minute subway ride downtown. There, after a brisk walk, the two would spend the day, feet brushing the sand on the edges of the East River, their backs to the Manhattan Bridge, fishing for whatever could survive the currents.

It was their time together.

"If I catch a shark, can I stay home from school tomorrow?" Giovanni, then nine, asked his father.

"You catch a shark," John said, "and you can stay home from school for a *month*."

"What about if I catch an eel?"

"You reel an eel and I'll make you go to school on weekends," John said.

The two looked at one another and laughed, the morning sun creeping past the expanse of the bridge and onto their faces.

"You're always lookin' to get outta school, Giovanni," his father said. "Why is that?"

"I *hate* it," Giovanni said.

"Then quit." His father shrugged. "Quit right now. Today."

"You mean it?" Giovanni asked, his face beaming.

"You should always walk from somethin' you hate doin'," his father said. "Turn your eye to somethin' else."

"Like what?"

"You can come work with me if you want. Put in your ten, twelve hours a day, help bring some table money home. Or maybe go down to the docks to work with your cousins. Do a full four-day shift with them and get locked into the union. How's that feel to you?"

"I don't know, Dad," Giovanni said, swaying his fishing line to the right of a swirl, pulling on the reel. "None of it sounds like fun."

"If you're gonna forget about school, then you can forget about fun," John said, sitting down on wet sand, gripping his fishing rod with both hands.

Giovanni stared down at his father and then back across at the water, concentrating on a nibble. "*You* have fun," he said after a long stretch of silence. "And you didn't go to any school."

"Working man's fun," John said. "It's not the same."

"Mama thinks I should become a dentist," Giovanni said. "I don't know why."

"I think she's got a thing for Dr. Tovaldi," John said, lifting his face to the sun. "She always dresses up nice when she goes to him and gets her teeth cleaned."

"What do you want me to be?" Giovanni asked. "You never say, one way or another."

"What you end up becomin' is up to you," John said. "I can't lead you down any road. But whatever it is you do, don't go into it half-assed. You'll only wind up hatin' yourself. Give it everything, the full shot. This way, at the end of the day, when the sun's down and you *know* you put in a hundred percent, you'll feel good about yourself. Maybe even feel proud."

"You proud of me now?" Giovanni asked.

"You goin' back to school tomorrow?" his father asked, standing up, dusting off the back of his pants.

"Yeah," Giovanni said.

"Then I'm proud of you," Johnny Frontieri said. "And if you end up catchin' a fish we can all eat, I'll be even prouder."

· · ·

AS HE GOT OLDER, Giovanni would often dream of a career designing great structures in cities around the world. His would be a life far removed from one confined to tenements and churches, a life in which a hard day's labor was rewarded only by a solid meal. As a young man, he looked with disdain upon the fabric of his neighborhood—the old women longing for dead men, street hoods living off the gambling habits of the working poor, the church offering solace and peace to the faithful, demanding silent suffering in return. As an adult, he would pine for that lost world, but in his early years in the New York City of 1955, Giovanni Frontieri was intent on hitting the fast lane out of his East Harlem ghetto.

The murder of his father brought those plans to a halt.

· · ·

IT RAINED THE day Giovanni's father died. His legs crossed, John was leaning back in a two-seater in the third car of a near-empty IRT train, on his way to work. It was nearly three in the morning when they passed the Twenty-third Street station. The passengers were either heading to a working man's job or coming back from an uptown night of drink and dance. Three of the latter, two loud men and one giggling woman, sat in the middle of the car, to the left of John Frontieri. The men were drunk and unsteady, the taller of the two drinking from a pint of Jack Daniel's, free hand resting on the woman's knee. The train was stifling, heat hissing from open vents under the seats.

John Frontieri shook his head as he read his Italian newspaper. He was more concerned about Naples losing a title game to Florence than about the hard looks exchanged by the two men across the aisle. He didn't see one of the men stand and reach for an overhead strap handle. John was reading about an open net goal scored on an inept Naples defense when the man standing pulled a gun and aimed it at the other man, who, five hours earlier, had been his best friend.

In a hard city, a man's life is often decided by the actions of a simple moment. For Johnny Frontieri that moment arrived in the form of a train engineer who hit the brakes too hard coming into the Fourteenth Street subway stop. The squealing halt turned the man with the gun away from his friend and toward Johnny. The man stared at Frontieri, knowing, even through the haze, that it was too late to stop what had been done.

Frontieri looked up from his paper and knew he was about to die.

He was forty-one years old and had never missed a day's work in his life. In the spark of an instant, the images of his wife and children meshed into one warm thought.

The doors to the train opened.

The bullet from the cocked gun hit John Frontieri in the forehead. The back of his skull spread across a subway map behind him as his newspaper fell to the floor.

The woman stared up at the standing man and the thin line of smoke from the fired gun in his hand. She then turned to look at the man in the corner of the train, slumped in his seat, blood thick as mud dripping down his chest. She shook her head, tears frozen to her eyes, and screamed.

A scream Johnny Frontieri never heard.

. . .

GIOVANNI WAS DRIVEN downtown with his older brother to identify their father's body. He looked with impassive eyes as the white sheet was lifted to reveal the dead man whom he loved more than any other. There had been few words between the two, fewer smiles, no middle-American fantasies of touch football games in the yard, camping trips in the summer, or boisterous talks around a dinner table. There was just a love and respect built around a solid wall of silence. A love built on trust.

Giovanni Frontieri reached down, grabbed his father's cold hand, and kissed it. He then turned away and never looked back. He never cried for the man on the icy slab, not then, not at the well-attended funeral, not at the cemetery. Giovanni would shed his tears in another way, one which his father would appreciate.

He would get even.

That night, riding in the back of a quiet squad car, heading home to a crying mother and two hysterical sisters, his slow breathing clouding the sides of the window, Giovanni Frontieri decided to become a cop. He was sixteen years old.

He raced from high school to the army to the Police Academy with a boxer's fury. On the streets, he hated the uniform but liked the taste left in his mouth from being a cop. He stayed clear of neighborhood tags, choosing instead to go for the big arrests. He never wrote up a parking violation, hassled a bookie, or shook down a numbers runner. He saw the working poor not as the enemy, but as important allies to be used against the larger fish that floated in the nearby swamps of drugs, murder, and shakedowns.

In November 1964, the same week Lyndon B. Johnson won a land-slide presidential election, Giovanni Frontieri was moved out of uniform and into plainclothes. He was assigned to buy-and-bust opera-tions in Harlem, a neighborhood he had watched change all too quickly from a haven of hardworking families living in well-kept apart-ments to the central headquarters for desperate men hungry for heroin. He ignored skin color, age, sex, and language. If you moved drugs on his streets, regardless of who you were or who you knew, Gio-vanni Frontieri made it a point to move you.

Three weeks into plainclothes duty, Frontieri scored his first major case. He brought down three members of Little Nicky Matthews's drug crew, costing the gang $250,000 in cash profit and eventually earning them double-decade stretches behind bars. The junkies on the streets were hungry for their score, and the dealers were sour over the lost money. It didn't help anybody's image that the bust was orchestrated by a street cop who was as green as a dollar.

Four days after the bust went down, one dealer, Sammy "Dwarf" Rodgers, decided it was time to teach the young cop a lesson. He offered $25,000, a same-day cash payout, to anyone who would bring him one of Giovanni Frontieri's eyes.

"Ain't nothin' personal against the boy," Rodgers said to members of his Black Satin gang. "I just need me a new key chain. Besides, I like the color of his eyes. They match my car."

. . .

SAMMY RODGERS WAS tall, well over six feet, with a big stomach, wide chest, and full Afro. The street called him Dwarf because he em-ployed half a dozen dwarfs as drug couriers, sending them from house to house, door-to-door, pockets crammed with nickel bags of junk and rubber band rolls of cash.

"I love watching the fuckers walk," he once said. "Move down my streets like fuckin' robots. Time you see 'em, they already past you. Cops hate bustin' 'em too. Makes 'em feel cheap."

Dwarf was standing in front of his bar, La Grande, on the corner of 123rd Street and Amsterdam, when Giovanni Frontieri pulled his car up to the corner. Giovanni had grown solid, muscular like his father, his hair thick and black, his face sharp, handsome, and unmarked except for a thin scar above his right eye. He spoke in a strong but low voice, never shouted, not even during the heat of a bust. His first partner called him "Boomer" because of it, and the name stuck.

He stepped out of the car and walked over to the dealer, stopping when he was only inches from the man's face.

"Hey, Dwarf," Boomer said. "I hear you're looking for me."

Dwarf looked around at his men and then back at Boomer. He had to keep his street-cool facade or lose face. Any sign of a backdown to a young cop could easily give the gunmen behind him ideas, any one of which could end with Dwarf packed in ice.

"What I need with you?" Dwarf said. "I ain't lonely."

"Twenty-five large," Boomer said. "That's a lot to pay out for one eye."

"Got me a business," Dwarf said, "and you startin' to cost me."

Boomer reached a hand into the side pocket of his leather jacket, his eyes on Dwarf. The hand came out holding a black switchblade. Boomer clicked it open with his thumb and tossed it to Dwarf, who caught it awkwardly with both hands.

"You take it," Boomer said.

"Take what?"

"My eye," Boomer said. "You got the knife, so, take it. Right here. Right in front of your crew."

"You crazy," Dwarf said, inching two steps back. "Pull a move on me like this, you got to be fuckin' crazy."

"Take the eye now," Boomer said, pulling a cigarette from his shirt pocket, his voice steady and controlled. "'Cause it's your only chance."

"And if I don't?"

"Then your business is shut." Boomer lit his cigarette with his father's silver clip. "I don't care where you go or what part of town you move your shit to. But if I see you on this corner ever again, I drop you and leave you dead."

Dwarf held his ground, not a move, not a sound.

Boomer smiled and nodded, as if they'd just been exchanging pleasantries about the weather, then put both hands in his pockets and turned. He walked to the driver's side of his jet black Plymouth and took another look at Dwarf.

"Keep the blade," he said, smiling, cigarette still in his mouth. "And enjoy what's left of your life."

Boomer Frontieri got behind the wheel of the Plymouth, kicked over the .427-liter engine, shifted into first, and pulled out into the Harlem street traffic, radio tuned to Sam Cooke singing "It's All Right."

. . .

HE SPENT EIGHTEEN years on the force, rising to the highest rank he sought, gold-shield detective, faster than anyone in the history of the department. In his career, working with a variety of partners, Boomer Frontieri was credited with more felony arrests and convictions than any other New York City cop. The job consumed him; he lived it and loved it. He never married and had no desire for a family. A bullet had killed his father, had left his mother alone at night, crying herself to sleep. He was a cop and he knew his bullet could arrive at any moment. He didn't want to leave anyone behind.

Boomer kept his pleasures to a minimum. He worked out regularly, running as many as twelve miles each morning, long before it became fashionable. He would allow nothing to get in the way of the run. During all-day stakeouts, Boomer would, at some point, jump into the backseat, change into sweats, bolt from the car, and hit the pavement.

"What do I do if they come out while you're gone?" a stunned new partner once asked.

"That's why they gave you a badge and a gun too," Boomer told him.

"They're gonna know you're a cop," his partner whined. "The minute you step outta the car, they're gonna know."

"They already know I'm a cop," Boomer said. "I've been sitting in front of their house all day."

"I ain't takin' 'em down alone."

"I'll be back if you need me," Boomer said, starting his run.

"How you gonna know if I need you?" his partner asked. "You'll be miles away."

"I'll hear you scream," Boomer said, turning a corner, eager to break a sweat.

. . .

THE DARK WEIGHT Boomer Frontieri carried into his work grew heavier through the years. He felt surrounded by the face and smell of death. It had touched many of those around him, from partners to family members to street friends, but had merely toyed with him, hanging him from the brink before returning him to the safety net of a dangerous life.

When his mother died from a stroke in a New York Hospital bed, Boomer was asleep on his stomach in a crosstown hospital as a nervous intern sewed thirty-six stitches down his back, closing up a razor slash, courtesy of a pimp riding a cocaine high. His baby sister Maria, a month shy of her thirtieth birthday, was killed crossing a Jackson Heights street; the hit from a drunk driver's front end sent her through the window of a shuttered bar. Boomer had to go to her funeral on crutches, his ankles shattered from a two-story fall off a fire escape. His brother, Carmine, suffered a severe heart attack when he was thirty-one years old and sat home in Bellmore, Long Island, living hand-to-mouth on a small disability pension. Boomer would spend time with him, the emptiness of his brother's life further fueling his own thirst for action.

Three of Boomer's seven partners died in the line of duty, each working by his side.

The majority of cops go through their entire careers never pulling gun from holster. Boomer was not one of those. He viewed his job under a bright, unmistakable moral light. To him, it was all a battle for turf. The dealers were foreign invaders. The more of them who went down, the safer it would be for a man heading to work, looking to keep a family fed and warm.

The truth be known, he enjoyed his dance with death. And that made him the deadliest type of cop to have on the street, the kind who never thinks he will live long enough to see a pension. In his years on the force, plainclothes and detective, Boomer had been involved in fourteen serious shootouts, half a dozen knifings, and hundreds of street fights. Once, his car was machine-gunned to pieces while he sat in his favorite Italian restaurant, eating a plate of pasta with red clam sauce.

"You just going to sit there and let them do that to your car?" asked his date, Andrea, a dark-haired detective working out of a Brooklyn fingerprint unit.

"It *was* my car," Boomer said, wiping his pasta plate with a chunk of Italian bread. "Sold it to Pete Lucas over in Vice a couple of days ago."

"What are you going to tell him?"

Boomer sipped from a glass of red wine and looked through the window at the shell of what had started the evening as a shiny Impala.

"To keep up his insurance payments," Boomer said.

. . .

BOOMER FRONTIERI NEVER stopped working. Maybe it was because he had nothing else in his life. Maybe it was the feeling of power he got when he walked into a dark bar and every criminal eye turned his way. It could also have been the nods and smiles he garnered from the working people of the tough, put-upon neighborhoods he made it his business to clean up. Whatever it was, Boomer Frontieri was never far removed from the streets, always minutes from his next bust, doing all he could to cause havoc in the pursuit of civil peace.

In between, he always managed to make time for a little fun.

. . .

"I DON'T KNOW if I can do this," the informant said, standing in the darkened vestibule, Boomer by his side.

"Do what?" Boomer said, his eyes farther up the corner, checking out a small circle of dealers. "Point out a friend?"

"They find out it's me that whispered them out and they gonna smoke me for sure," the informant said.

"You showing up at that job I got you?" Boomer asked, eyes still searching faces.

"That job sucks," the informant said. "It's long and hard and don't pay for shit."

"It puts money in your pockets and keeps you out of Rikers," Boomer said. "That's all your mother gives a shit about. Now, cut the chatter and let me have the dealer."

The informant hesitated, his feet shifting nervously back and forth.

"Guy in black," he finally said.

"They're *all* in black," Boomer pointed out.

"One with the panama hat," the informant said. "He's always got pockets full of change. Jiggles 'em all the time. Thinks it's funny."

"He got a name?"

"His boys call him Padrone," the informant said. "Don't know his real catch."

"Disappear," Boomer said, leaving the vestibule and heading down the front steps.

He walked down the street, one hand at his side, the other holding an old New York Telephone meter. It was thick, black, and heavy. It had a reading on it, running from green to red, with a white button at its center. A squeeze of the button and a thin black needle would move from the green area to the red.

The six men, huddled in a circle, turned still as stone the minute they spotted him.

"Five-O on the block," one said. *Five-O* was the current street code for narc, derived from the Jack Lord TV series *Hawaii Five-O*.

All of the men except for one carried .9-millimeter semis tucked inside their stonewashed jeans. The one they called Padrone, short and heavyset, a pockmarked face ringed with stubble, was clean. A nail clipper in his shirt pocket was his only brush with a weapon.

"What's the matter, guys, library closed?" Boomer asked as he came up to them.

"We did our reading," Padrone said. "Now we thinking about it."

"Anything I might like?"

"I don't know what you like," Padrone said. "Don't give a fuck either."

The men around him snickered, and one, the tallest of the bunch, laughed out loud, baseball cap tilted over his eyes, the Rikers cut of his arms gleaming in the afternoon sun.

"So let's forget books," Boomer said, "and let's talk drugs."

"Got any on you?" Padrone said.

This time the laughter grew louder. Even Boomer smiled.

"Nope," Boomer said. "But I know one of you does. The question is, which one."

"That's a good question," Padrone said. "You gonna give us three guesses?"

"I thought you might just want to tell me."

"Think again, badge," Padrone said. "Even if we had the shit, which we ain't, we gotta be dumber than sand to tell you."

"Then I've got no choice," Boomer said, lifting the old New York Telephone meter. "Gotta use the machine on you."

All eyes shifted down to the box in Boomer's hand.

"Fuck is that thing?" one of the men asked.

"It's a drug detector," Boomer said. "New. FBI brought it out. There's a sensor in it picks up a drug scent. When that happens, the needle here starts to move. Tell you the truth, I'm not all that sure myself how it works. All I know is that it *does* work."

"That's bullshit," Padrone said, one hand in his pants pocket, nervously jiggling coins.

"You got nothin' to worry about either way," Boomer said, staring directly at Padrone. "You're clean."

Boomer turned to face the man closest to him and pointed the box directly at his torso. Staring intently, he kept his finger away from the white button.

"Back off," Boomer finally said. "You're just a dope without dope."

Boomer moved through the next two in the circle in the same manner.

Then he came up to Padrone.

"Mr. Clean," Boomer said, smiling. "Time to read your fortune."

Boomer held the box to Padrone's face, slowly moved his finger to the white button, then pressed down. The needle jumped from green to red. Padrone, sweat already pouring down the sides of his face, swallowed hard, coins in his pocket jiggling at a trotter's pace.

Boomer's smile widened.

"Bingo," Boomer said.

"It's the change," Padrone said, looking around to his men, desperation filling his eyes. "Like at the airport. They make noise, that's all. Empty your pockets and they stop."

"I'll bite," Boomer said. "Empty your pockets."

Padrone hesitated, running a beefy hand across the stubble.

"Like you ain't got all the fuckin' cards in your hands already," Padrone finally said, lifting the back of his flowered shirt and handing two five-pound heroin bags over to Boomer. "Now you got yourself a fuckin' machine too. What am I gonna do?"

"Three-to-five," Boomer said, taking the drugs in one hand and pulling Padrone away from his cronies.

. . .

BOOMER LIVED in a well-kept two-bedroom apartment on the second floor of a four-story brownstone on West Eighty-fourth Street, between Columbus and Amsterdam. The living room furnishings were simple, boiled down to one frayed blue couch, two dusty-gold wing chairs, and a marble coffee table. He kept his twenty-one-inch Zenith in the bedroom and had small stereo speakers in every room. His extensive record collection, jazz, blues, and Sam Cooke mostly, filled the left side of the living room. A framed photo of Rocky Marciano landing the knock-out blow to Jersey Joe Walcott's chin in their 1952 heavyweight title bout hung over the mantel of the shuttered fireplace. A small statue of the Blessed Mother rested on a bureau in the hall, left to him by his mother.

The kitchen was well stocked, although Boomer was hardly ever home long enough to make himself a meal. He picked up fresh fruits and vegetables from the nearby Fairway market. But for fish he traveled all the way down to the Fulton market and for meat to Murray's on Fourteenth Street. There, old man Hirsch himself would cut up the rib steaks and chops, wrapping them tight in butcher paper. Murray Hirsch had been his father's employer and closest friend. Two immigrants from two different cultures, trying to make a go of it in a new country. Whenever Boomer saw Murray, he always came away with the feeling that Hirsch missed his father as much as he did.

Boomer dated an assortment of women, staying with them long enough for companionship but never long enough to fall in love. Some were cops, a couple worked in bars he scouted, one was an ex-hooker now earning a living as a meter maid. There was even a college professor he helped clear on a marijuana bust. Of them all, the only woman Boomer Frontieri ever gave any thought of marrying was Theresa.

They met at a cookout at his sister's home in Queens. She was tall and thin, had red hair flowing long down her back, and hazel eyes that twinkled mischievously from an unlined face. She worked in the check reconcilement department of a Wall Street branch of the Chase Manhattan Bank while taking night courses at St. John's, crawling her way toward a business degree. They both spoke Italian, drank coffee with their pizza, and loved music but hated to dance.

She never asked about his work, or complained when he disappeared for days or canceled long-standing dates with last-minute calls. From the go, she understood the nature of his job. Boomer could relax around Theresa, put down his guard as easily as he would slide his gun inside a desk drawer. He felt safe, instinctively knowing she would never betray him and would always be honest with him, tell him what was in her heart whether he wanted to hear it or not. He knew life for a cop's wife was, at best, difficult and lonely. But he trusted Theresa could handle that part. It was the other end of the table that troubled him, the steady gaze of death that hovered above him, the chill of a late night ringing phone or doorbell. It was there that his doubts rested.

· · ·

"It looks bad," Theresa said to him, sitting on a plastic chair across from his hospital bed. Boomer looked back at her and smiled. His hands were bandaged, his chest wrapped tight, and his face marked with bruises, welts, and stitches, the results of a drug raid gone sour.

"Feels worse," he said.

"Who'd you piss off?"

"My aunt Gracie," Boomer said, still smiling. "You ever meet her? She's got some kind of a temper."

"She's got a knife too," Theresa said, sadness touching her voice.

"It's nothing," Boomer reassured her. "Doctor says I can be out of here in two, maybe three days."

"They arrest the guy who did it?"

Boomer stared at her through blurry eyes.

"They didn't have to," he said.

She nodded and didn't talk about it anymore. But Boomer saw the look and knew that it was over. It lasted less than a second, and most men wouldn't have noticed, but Boomer stayed alive reading faces, and he knew what this one reflected.

Theresa could handle the parts of the job that most women couldn't, even his dying. But she could not get used to the fact that he would have to kill in order to stay alive. That would haunt her, keep her awake when he wasn't there, make her shudder in her sleep on empty nights.

"It's late," he said to her. "You should get home. One of us has to get up early in the morning, and I know it's not me."

"Will it hurt if I kiss you?" she asked, standing. The force of her beauty now struck him as she stared down at him, less than a foot away. He knew he would never be this close to love again.

"It'll hurt more if you don't," Boomer said.

She leaned down and they kissed for the last time.

. . .

IN 1978, a small but effective group of radical black extremists bent on overthrowing the government declared war on the cops of New York City. In a span of four weeks, six officers were chosen at random, then shot and killed in cold blood. It was open season on anyone in a blue uniform. Boomer Frontieri, taken off narcotics and assigned to a special unit of the NYPD set up to go after the radicals, quickly and quietly declared his own war.

Boomer squeezed his street informants. He spread out photos of the suspects to all the hookers who trusted him, the ones he kept off the paddy wagon in return for a tip. He had coffee with organized crime members, mutual respect spread across the table, both sides calling a temporary halt to their separate struggles. He went to see the ministers of the black churches in the neighborhoods he worked, banking on their friendship for answers to a horror that plagued all.

He hit the streets and banged around dealers and pimps, roughed up the chicken hawks and seedy flesh peddlers, tossed Miranda out a nearby window, and let fists and fear take him to where he needed to go.

It was his search for the black extremists that, in 1980, led Boomer to a Brooklyn tenement, where his back was to the wall, gun drawn, flak vest under his black leather jacket. He had a .38 caliber cocked in one hand and a .44 semiautomatic in the other. He tilted his head toward a red wooden door only inches away. Across from him was another detective, Davis "Dead-Eye" Winthrop. Boomer nodded at his partner and smiled. Winthrop smiled back. Boomer didn't know much about the man other than that Winthrop was twenty-seven, black, had lost a partner two years earlier in a botched buy-and-bust, had won the NYPD marksmanship award three years running, and was always eager to go through the door first. In Boomer's book, that gave Winthrop points for guts and incentive, but shooting at wooden targets on a grassy field wasn't the same as a shoot-out in a one-bedroom apartment, lights blown out, six gunmen with nothing to lose on the other side.

A normal cop would have been on the talkie asking for backup. Boomer hated backup. He felt it lessened the odds in his favor. Cops are usually the worst shooters around, most of them lucky enough to get off a couple of rounds in the general direction of the perp. More likely to kill those with badges than the guys without. If Winthrop was as good a shot as they said, he would be all that Boomer needed.

Behind the locked red door, Skeeter Jackson sat at a poker table filled with cash. The apartment was well furnished, with two of Skeeter's men sleeping on a soft leather couch, guns resting across their chests. Three others were in the kitchen off the main room, one smoking dope, two munching on cold heros and drinking from bottles of Bud. Guns were spread across the table next to the cold cuts.

Skeeter was a dope courier working for Jimmy Hash's gang in Bed-Stuy. His take alone was $15,000 a day. Seven days a week. Skeeter hadn't even hit his twenty-first birthday and was already looking at a million-dollar haul.

In his free time, Skeeter Jackson shot young cops in the back, charging $500 for each bullet that pierced flesh. Boomer had known his name and reputation for a long time. A hooker on Nostrand Avenue had given him what he didn't have — an address.

Boomer leaned across the door and crawled toward Dead-Eye.

"You want to put in a call for help, I understand," Boomer whispered. "How many in there?"

"They tell me six, all heavy," Boomer said. "Probably got more bullets in their pockets than we've got in our guns."

"So, what's the problem?" Dead-Eye asked with a smile.

"Talk to you after the dance," Boomer said.

He crawled back to his position against the wall, checked his watch, and signaled over to Dead-Eye.

One minute till the Fourth of July.

They went in with their guns drawn. Boomer came in high, his shoulder against the door, running right toward Skeeter, who stared back at him, stunned. In his hand was a wad of cash. Dead-Eye came in low, took a short roll into the foyer, and popped up on both legs, guns aimed at the two men on the couch. The three in the kitchen came out running, bites of sandwiches still crammed in their mouths. Their semis were pointed straight at the two cops.

Everyone held his place for what seemed like hours but measured no more than ten seconds. Skeeter was the first to speak.

"Hope you got money on you," he said in a high-pitched voice that bordered on feminine. " 'Cause I'm takin' it after you're dead. Pay for the fuckin' door you just busted up."

"Take my watch," Boomer said. "I'd want you to have it anyway."

"You here for the cash?" Skeeter pointed to the money spread across his table. "If you ain't, then you gonna be dead for the dumbest of fuckin' reasons."

"You really seem serious about us dyin'," Boomer said.

"All I gots to do is nod my head."

"Your head'll be off before you finish the shake," Boomer said.

"Which makes it easy for me to die happy. And you see my partner behind me?"

"Spook with a badge." Skeeter's voice quivered with contempt. "What tree you shake him off of?"

"He takes two of yours before he buys the plot," Boomer said. "That means only three walk out. We can save ourselves all that shit and make it easy for you and me."

"I got ears," Skeeter said.

"You let us lead you out of the building," Boomer said. "The manpower walks. It's only you we want."

"Don't think so, white," Skeeter said. "I was born in this fuckin' building. Just as soon die in it."

"Well, you can't shoot a guy for trying," Boomer said.

Boomer heard the click of the semi before he saw the flash. He jumped to his right, landed on one knee, and fired four quick rounds toward the men by the kitchen door. Behind him, Dead-Eye laid out the two on the couch, fast-pumped them from head to heart without so much as a twitch. It all happened so quickly, Skeeter had no choice but to remain frozen in place, still holding the handful of bills.

Dead-Eye flipped over a coffee table, landed on his feet, and fired three shots into one of the men near the kitchen. He aimed his other gun at a crouched man coming out of the bathroom, had him in his sights, when Skeeter threw the money in the air and came up shooting. His first shot split the wall. His second got Dead-Eye in the shoulder.

"I'm hit, Boom," he said, falling to the ground, shooting his gun at anyone without a badge that could still move.

"Stay down," Boomer shouted through the smoke, gunfire, and moans. "Reload and stay down."

Skeeter jumped over the table and made a run for the door, slipping over the thousands of dollars that were now raining on the faces of dead men.

Boomer followed him out.

"I'm on him," he shouted back to Dead-Eye. "There's two more in the kitchen."

"They're either gonna stay in there or die out here," Dead-Eye said. "Either way, they're mine."

. . .

BOOMER CAUGHT SKEETER in the middle of the third-floor landing. He threw him against the wall and swung a hard left that found the thin man's stomach. Skeeter gave out a grunt loud enough to echo through the halls. He came back with a right hand of his own, grazing the side of Boomer's temple. Then he went for the throat, both hands wrapped tight around Boomer, pushing him hard against a shaky railing. Boomer's hands went up against Skeeter's jaw, pushing the dope dealer's head back, causing his eyes to flutter toward the ceiling.

"You gonna die, you fucker," Skeeter said, tightening his grip. "Gonna die right here. In front of me."

Boomer pulled one hand away from Skeeter's chin, moving it down his chest, trying to reach the .22 Special he kept in a crotch holster. As his hand found his pants, he heard the wood of the railing behind him start to give way. Skeeter's eyes were bulging now, spittle coming down the sides of his mouth, the strength of his hands cutting the air from Boomer's throat, forcing him to take short breaths through his nose.

Boomer had his hand around the gun when the railing gave way.

The two of them fell together down through the next railing, linked like dancers, wood and rusty iron flying through the air, one shard slashing the right side of Boomer's face. The muzzle of Boomer's gun was flush against Skeeter's stomach.

Boomer felt a sharp pain in his right side the instant his gun went off. He looked at Skeeter's face and knew the man was dead. If it wasn't the bullet that did him, it had to be the iron rail lodged through his throat. Boomer turned his head and saw half a rail hanging through the right side of his own chest, blood flowing out of the hole in his jacket.

He and Skeeter had fallen down three stories, taking every railing with them. There had been a fifteen-minute firefight only minutes earlier. He could still hear Dead-Eye and the kitchen help exchanging shots. Sirens wailed in the distance. Yet despite that, not one apartment door had opened.

Boomer sat there, unmoving, blood oozing from his wound, Skeeter's dead body stretched across his chest. He closed his eyes, willing himself to another place.

The growl of a dog shook him from his dream.

Boomer turned his head to his left and saw a dark gray pit bull. Boomer hated dogs, big or small. But he especially hated pit bulls.

"Let me take a wild guess," he said, pointing to the body on top of him. "This guy belongs to you."

The dog stared and continued to growl and sniff for a minute or two, then turned and walked out of the building.

"Doesn't say much about you, does it, Skeeter?" Boomer said to the dead man. "When your own dog doesn't give a shit whether you live or die."

· · ·

Boomer stared at the retirement papers in his hands, thick triplicate forms filled with numbers and statistics. They were all one big blur, none of the information making any sense. All that was clear to him was the reality of a fall down a set of tenement banisters and half a lung now missing from his chest. That one rusty iron rail had landed him what the beat cops liked to call "the policeman's lotto." A nifty three-quarter, tax-free disability pension doled out for the rest of his life.

Based on his 1980 earnings, complete with overtime and vacation days due him, Boomer's yearly take averaged out to a clean $38,500 a year. Plus full health coverage. Boomer Frontieri was only thirty-eight years old, and there should have been a smile as wide as a canyon on his face. Instead, on that drab early December morning in 1980, all Boomer wanted to do was find someplace quiet and cry.

Boomer had survived dozens of other wounds, healed up and returned to wear the shield once again. Not this time. Not with half a lung slowing his breath and a right leg that couldn't give him more than a quarter of a mile's run without crumbling in pain. Not even

Boomer Frontieri could make it on the streets spotting the shooters those handicaps.

He could never be a cop again.

He took three weeks off and traveled to Italy, visiting his father's hometown of Reggio Calabria, talking to the old men and women who remembered the young John Frontieri. He spent his afternoons walking through the nearby hills as the towns below him slept through the heat. He briefly toyed with the notion of moving there full-time, but let the thought escape, knowing it was not truly the place where he belonged.

His first six months of retirement were spent fitfully and without much sleep. He went to movies, plays, museums, read books, even caught an opera at the Met, something he hadn't done since his father was killed. None of it seemed to shake him from his mental slumber. None of what he saw, read, or heard brought him peace. He still jumped with anticipation whenever he heard a police siren off in the distance. His instincts still told him which of the faces he passed on crowded streets were dirty, which were looking for the easy score. He still carried a gun, his old police revolver, which he bought from the department, and he carried a replica of his detective's badge in his back pocket. He even kept his cuffs, tossed in a desk drawer in his apartment. He often looked at them in the sad way a middle-aged man looks upon a photo of an old girlfriend.

He stayed away from other cops. They would only serve as a reminder of what he so desperately missed. He avoided the bars they drank in and the restaurants he knew they frequented. He limited his nights of eating and drinking to one place, Nunzio's, a small, out-of-the-way Italian restaurant on West Ninety-sixth Street, near the entrance to the Henry Hudson Parkway. The food was excellent, the drink plentiful, and the company just what he wanted it to be—quiet and distant.

Most of the regulars at Nunzio's were made mob guys near the end of their criminal careers. They had taken all the money they could, killed most of their enemies, and done their time. Now they were left alone to watch ball games, argue over old scores and cold feuds. They knew who Boomer was, and there was a time when they would have shunned him. Yet now, in a strange way, the cop was one of them, cast adrift, not a threat to anyone. On occasion they would even send a drink to his table.

The restaurant was owned and managed by an old family friend, Nunzio Goldman. Boomer's father first worked in the meat market for Nunzio's Jewish father, Al, the Fourteenth Street boss who split his proceeds with the uptown Italian mob. On the streets, Al was known as the Rabbi, a man who would kill if he caught a dirty look. At home he was Anna Pasqualini's husband, a quiet, reserved businessman who doted on his family. When the kids were older and Anna got restless, he opened Nunzio's and put her in charge. After she died, their oldest son took over.

"How come you're the only one in the family who's got an Italian name?" Boomer once asked Nunzio, whose two brothers were named Daniel and Jacob.

"Spite," Nunzio said. "My father took one look down at me and said I had too much Italian blood to be Jewish. It was bad enough he fell in love with an Italian woman. Now this. So he let my mother name me. My other brothers, they got lucky. They were given names that fit. But I came out ahead of the game. They don't have a restaurant. They gotta eat the slop their wives cook. You're better off at Frank E. Campbell's than at their dinner table."

Nunzio could always bring a smile to Boomer's face. Make him forget the emptiness that gnawed at his insides. The old man made sure Boomer didn't get too fond of the drink or spend too much time alone. He cared about his friend and didn't want him to fall into the bars and cars cycle he'd seen other cops pursue. A man doesn't have to die to end a life. Nunzio knew that.

· · ·

BOOMER FRONTIERI WAS retired for two years before he was able to shake the ghosts that haunted his soul. For most retired cops, the wake-up call never comes. But Boomer Frontieri wasn't just any cop. He was one of the best detectives the city of New York had ever seen. In his eighteen years on the job, he had made a lot of enemies. Many of them were in jail. Many others were dead. Many more walked the streets. Boomer was well aware of who they were and, more important, where they were.

But, in the course of those eighteen years, Boomer Frontieri had also made a lot of friends. The helpless victims of those he dragged away in cuffs, the anonymous faces of their neighborhoods. Old or young, they all remembered a cop named Boomer Frontieri.

It was a phone call from one who remembered that changed Boomer's life. A call from a man he hadn't talked to in years. About a little girl he had never met.

Though he didn't know it then, from the moment Boomer's hand took the receiver from Nunzio, his course was set.

2

Dead-Eye

HIS MOTHER CRIED when she heard the news. His father didn't speak to him for three months. His two older brothers and younger sister avoided any contact. His friends in the Brooklyn neighborhood where he was born and raised couldn't put together the words to ask him why. His girlfriend turned her back on him and his favorite high school teacher told him he was throwing the promise of a young life into a corner of a room.

All this because Davis Winthrop decided to become a cop.

On the streets he called home, a man walking by in a blue uniform or driving past in an unmarked sedan was seen not as friend but as foe. The skin behind that uniform or that wheel was more often than not pasty white. The eyes behind the badges were filled with anger, hate, or, worse, indifference. On the streets of Brownsville, Brooklyn, a policeman was anything but a friend.

But Davis Winthrop didn't feel that way. Never. He saw everything the others had seen. He had a number of friends who died mysteriously after being taken into custody for a minor offense. He heard the verbal abuse heaped on those around him from those protected by the law. He was aware of the looks of scorn, the snide comments mumbled under warm coffee breath, all meant to deride and keep the listener locked in place.

To many people, those sights and sounds built up a well of hate. In Davis Winthrop, it fueled an eagerness to change. Unlike many in his neighborhood, Davis Winthrop wasn't blinded by the abuse of power. He saw the other side as well—the street dealers turning the promise of childhood into the emptiness of a junkie's life; the young men slain by stray bullets in the dark. He saw the abandoned mothers, many wasted by the ravages of white powder, their men nowhere to be found, dragging their children down the streets, too burnt to know that it was more than their own lives they were tossing into the garbage heap.

It wasn't lost on Davis Winthrop that the source of such sadness shared his skin color. That while white might be the enemy, it would often be black that betrayed the trust.

He vowed to do all he could to change that.

And he would do it in the place he knew best—the hard-edged streets of Brownsville.

Davis Winthrop went from uniform to undercover in less than a year. He was put on the street, posing as a gun runner for a South American outfit. He didn't go into the job blind. He made sure no one knew more about guns, from make and caliber to crate price and street value. He studied the weapons most in demand and learned the habits of the big-time buyers. He also realized that if he was going to be selling guns to people in the killing game, he needed to be an expert in handling them. He took classes to improve his marksmanship, working not only on accuracy but on speed, control, and range. He read all he could about the guns he sold, and was soon able to tear apart and put together any make or model in a matter of minutes.

Soon enough, to both cops and criminals, Davis Winthrop became the man to see. He was a walking edition of *Guns and Ammo*, his knowledge so detailed, even the feds called him in for advice. His shooting was so proficient, it earned him the well-deserved nickname "Dead-Eye." Put a scope on a rifle and he could split a cantaloupe from 150 yards out. In the dark. Give him a .44 caliber and he could put six through a man's chest as he slid across a bare floor. With a .22 in hand, Dead-Eye could land a clean head shot in the quiet of a darkened room.

Dead-Eye Winthrop was himself a weapon, coiled and let loose. And he loved working the danger zones most other cops avoided. It was where he felt most in control.

. . .

DEAD-EYE STOOD in the center of the bar, lit a cigarette, and looked over at the man with the thick mustache and yellow teeth. Dead-Eye was tall, standing close to six feet three inches, and he towered over the man whose Porkpie was tilted up.

"You know what it is I want," the man said, his accent cartoon thick. "Correct?"

"I look like fuckin' Carnac to you?" Dead-Eye said, his eyes making mental notes. "No, I don't know what you want. I don't even know who you are."

"Magoo tell you I'm good for the money?"

"Only reason why I'm here," Dead-Eye said.

Two men were behind him at a table, playing cards, semis tucked tight against their rib cages. A guy too young to be as fat as he was polished glasses over by the cash register, his hands no doubt within easy reach of a weapon. Dead-Eye heard Spanish voices coming from the kitchen, all male, all loaded.

The man poured vodka into an open can of Coke, then took a long sip. He smiled over at Dead-Eye.

"You drink?" he asked.

"With friends," Dead-Eye said. "Now, why don't you take this where it's going."

"I need magnums," the man said. "At least fifty."

"Bulldogs do you right?" Dead-Eye asked.

"If those are the best," the man said.

"Best I can get."

"How soon?" the man asked.

"You skipped a spot," Dead-Eye said. "You're supposed to say how much."

"The guns are important," the man said. "Not the price."

"Just so you know, it's five hundred a gun, more if you want ammo," Dead-Eye said. "You give half now. I take the other half when you open the crate."

"What guarantees do my people get?"

Dead-Eye put his cigarette out on the floor, twisting it with the tip of his work boot.

"Delivery of the guns," Dead-Eye said. "They'll be here on the date and time I say."

"That's it?"

"You want more, shop at Sears. I just hand you guns. Straight up for cash. They don't work, don't mean shit to me. Trigger falls off in a shoot-out, bullet goes backward 'stead of forward, barrel melts before your eyes, any of that happens, don't call me. Complain to the Better Business Bureau. Write your congressman. I don't give a fuck what you do. Just don't call me."

"I hope these guns work as well as your mouth," the man said, eyes moving off Dead-Eye to the two behind him.

"And I hope it's true you got the kind of money Magoo says you do," Dead-Eye said. "You don't, I'm a walker."

"Magoo told me something about you," the man said, his voice armed with an edge. "Something I hope is not true."

Dead-Eye felt the tension in the room notch up a few degrees. The fat guy behind the bar had his hands flat across the wood surface. The two behind him let their cards drop to the table. The voices in the kitchen were stilled.

"I'm gonna hate it if you make me guess," Dead-Eye said.

"Magoo thinks you're a cop," the man said with a smile. "He thinks that's a problem. And he wants that problem to go away. That's why he gave me this."

The man reached into his jacket pocket and pulled out a thick wad of cash, $25,000 easy, cut green and fresh, white wrapper still around it. The man dropped it on the table and looked up at Dead-Eye.

"He must be pretty serious about this problem," the man said. "Put up money like this for one man. What do you think?"

"I'm touched," Dead-Eye said.

"I get more later," the man said. "When I bring him your heart."

"Magoo always was a romantic son of a bitch," Dead-Eye said. "Too soft for this kind of work."

"Tell me, before you die, my friend," the man said. "Are you what Magoo says? Are you a cop?"

Dead-Eye looked around the room, kept the faces in their places, and turned back to the man.

"Yes," Dead-Eye said.

. . .

THE FIRST GUN was in Dead-Eye's right hand, aimed at the man's chest. The second gun, his favorite .38 Special, took out the fat guy behind the bar. The two at the table hadn't even had a chance to move.

"They can live if you let them," Dead-Eye said to the man, nodding his head toward the two behind him. He saw three men stop at the kitchen entrance, guns drawn.

"I'm not armed," the man said.

"That could be a problem," Dead-Eye said. "For you."

Dead-Eye was impressed. The man kept his cool, unfazed by the gun aimed several inches from his heart.

"I know your country," the man said. "Your ways. The police don't kill unarmed people. You are too civilized. It's a shame, but it's true."

"I bet your fat friend behind the bar believed that too," Dead-Eye said.

"He was stupid," the man said. "You won't be."

"That's right, compadre," Dead-Eye said. "I won't be. I just drop you and then take my chances with the rest of your buddies. If I make it out—and, believe me, the odds are in my favor—then I put a drop gun in your hand and walk away clean. Nobody's gonna give a shit."

The man nodded, his eyes finally glancing down to the gun.

"May I light a cigarette?" he asked.

"It won't kill you," Dead-Eye said.

The man took a cigarette from a pack on the table, put one in his mouth, and lit it. He took a deep drag, let out the smoke through his nose, and smiled.

"It would be an insult to offer you money," the man said. "Cop like you don't care about such things."

"I like money," Dead-Eye said. "Just not your money."

"But you want something," the man said. "And I don't think killing a room full of runners is what you want."

"I wouldn't throw myself over your coffins either," Dead-Eye said.

"We can settle this," the man said. "Just tell me what it is you want."

"Magoo," Dead-Eye said. "I want you to set him up. Deliver him to me."

"That could get me killed faster than the gun in your hand."

"Your kind of work doesn't come with a pension plan," Dead-Eye said. "Die now, die later, it all works out the same to me."

"And if I give you that?" the man asked. "If I give you Magoo?"

"Then it won't be my bullet that kills you," Dead-Eye told him. "Least not today."

The man stared into Dead-Eye's face, looking for signs of weakness. He came away empty.

"I will give you Magoo," the man said after a few minutes, sending his men back to their places with a quick brush of his hand. "On one condition."

"Let's hear it."

"Have a drink with me," the man said. "Now that we're friends."

. . .

EDDIE WINTHROP WAS a bigger man than his son, the onslaught of age having shaved only half an inch from his powerful six-foot-five frame. He walked with a slight limp, the arthritis having settled in his left knee, the payback for twenty-five years spent working for Con Ed, days and nights in darkness and dampness under the city streets.

An El Producto cigar was jammed into the corner of his mouth as he sat on the third step of the stoop leading to the four-story Brownsville brownstone he had bought with a G.I. loan and a $2,000 inheritance from his grandmother. He put thirty years into the house, paying off one mortgage and picking up another as soon as a son or daughter was old enough to head for college. He spent his happiest days there, tending his backyard garden, enjoying quiet Sunday afternoons with his wife, Elma.

His saddest days were spent there too.

It was on the second floor, in the back bedroom, where Elma died on a warm June day in 1977, three years ago this month, the heart attack stripping her of the smile he loved, taking away the best friend he would ever have.

A year later, Eddie was in his finished basement, shooting a quiet game of pool. Count Basie was on the turntable, and a cool drink was in his hand, when he got the call about his youngest son, Albert, shot dead on a tree-lined street in a Westchester town whose name he had never heard before.

Now he sat there, his days winding down, the cancer in his stomach spreading, content that he had done the best he could to raise his family. He looked across at his son Davis and wondered if Davis would someday feel the same. Eddie Winthrop had made his peace with the fact that his son had become a cop. He had never warmed to the idea, but he did like the way the neighborhood kids looked up to his boy.

"You want to go sit inside?" Dead-Eye asked his father, buttoning his baseball jacket.

"No," Eddie said. "I always liked the cold. You know that. It was your mother couldn't take it. Thirty years, every winter, had to hear her scream about how we would all be better off in North Carolina. Like it don't get cold there."

Dead-Eye reached into a paper bag by his left leg and pulled out two containers of hot chocolate. He handed one to his father.

"There any sugar in this?" Eddie asked.

"Ain't supposed to be."

"Says who?"

"Your doctor," Dead-Eye said.

"What's he know?" Eddie said.

"Your blood count, your sugar and cholesterol levels," Dead-Eye said. "Want me to go on?"

"Only if you want to bore me to sleep," Eddie said, sipping his hot chocolate. "Only doctor I know puts a dyin' man on a diet."

The two sat silently together, eyes on the passing traffic, ears numbed by heavy blasts of music coming off car radios.

"Still like your job?" Eddie asked his son, eyes focused straight ahead.

"It fits me, Pop," Dead-Eye said. "Don't really know why. But it always has."

"I know," Eddie said. "I was the one wastin' breath tryin' to talk you out of doing it."

"Sorry you didn't?"

"Sometimes," Eddie said. "Whenever I hear about a white cop shooting another black kid. Everybody rushin' in, from mayor to priest, lookin' to clear the shooter's name. Then they all go on the TV and talk about how killing a black teenager who might have had a gun was justified."

"It's not always murder," Dead-Eye said.

"Most times it is," Eddie said, turning to face his son. "You think about it at all?"

"About what?" Dead-Eye asked. "Getting shot?"

"They put you in these places alone," Eddie said. "Then, if there's any trouble, they supposed to be there for you. Back you up. Make sure you don't die. Am I right so far?"

"Pretty much," Dead-Eye said.

"You ever wonder what if they don't show?" Eddie said. "What if they don't want to risk their own white ass for some young black cop."

Dead-Eye sipped his hot chocolate and stayed quiet.

"It's a white man's badge," Eddie said. "Just because they let you have one don't change that."

"Times change, Pop," Dead-Eye said. "Old men like you forget that."

"But people never change, Davis," Eddie said, standing up and putting the spent cigar back in his mouth. "And that's something a young man like you should never forget. Not if you want to stay alive."

. . .

THE OFFER FROM the Spanish man in the funny hat made Magoo smile.

Magoo was only twenty-six years old, but he already had control of all the illegal gun shipments moving in and out of New York City. In six years, starting as a street runner in a Queens housing project, Magoo had worked his way up the criminal ladder with bullet speed, killing anyone in his way, often with the very guns he sold them. He had a street force of more than four hundred men and women, each reporting to district subs who, in turn, handed over orders and proceeds to borough commanders.

They then handed everything over to Magoo.

Magoo had been raised in a series of foster homes, where he learned to trust no one. He especially hated cops and openly bragged about the three he himself had brought down, one of them a young undercover he made crawl on his knees and sing the theme from *Shaft* before putting three bullets in the back of his head.

He knew very little about guns other than that they were in great demand and the right people on the wrong side of the law would pay any amount to get them. He hired only blacks and put a permanent price on loyalty. He stayed clear of drugs and drink, figuring his line of income was risky enough without supervising it through hazy eyes. He banked his cash past a laundering system that was run out of Toronto, flowed into Europe, and eased back into his private Manhattan account. Money meant everything to Magoo, and he made it his business to remove any threat to the cash flow.

Davis "Dead-Eye" Winthrop was such a threat.

. . .

DEAD-EYE WAS a different man at home, caring for his wife, doting on his son.

On many evenings before he hit the streets, Dead-Eye would make it a point to rock and cradle the four-month-old baby to sleep, then lay him in his crib, belly side down.

He watched him sleep, the baby's eyes twitching to a dream, his lips pursed, hands balled into fists. The boy, Eddie, had his mother's pleasant smile and his grandmother's sweet nature. Dead-Eye looked around the room, the stuffed toys bunched up on a corner window seat, soft dolls strewn around the floor. A warm room in a warm house. The house his father bought and paid for with hard work and now shared with his son and his family, keeping his own apartment two stories below.

It was well into the middle of the night.

Dead-Eye's wife, Grace, was sound asleep in the bedroom next door. Dead-Eye moved away from his son's crib and sat on the floor, legs folded, taking in the creaks and moans of the quiet house. All that he loved took breath between its walls. Memories, pleasant and sad, lived within the curves, nooks, and cracks of a house built five years before the start of the First World War. There was no violence in this house, only love.

In there, the price of a gun had no history and a life had meaning and respect. If death did arrive, it came by way of disease or destiny, not in the form of late-night bullets. If only Dead-Eye could seal the contents of this house and keep everyone inside it safe and warm.

But he knew that was a dream.

Reality was waiting for Dead-Eye on the streets of Brooklyn. He had a meeting with Magoo in less than two hours, and one of them would die.

Dead-Eye looked over at his son, asleep in this safe house of peace, and prayed that his guns would not betray him on this night.

. . .

DEAD-EYE KNEW it was a setup the minute he stepped out of his car.

Four men stood around Magoo, each wearing a long leather coat, standard designer wear for the heavily armed.

The Spanish man was behind Magoo, nodding his head as Dead-Eye approached.

"Hello, my friend," he said. "You are here."

"I'm here," Dead-Eye answered, looking over at Magoo.

"Now we can do business," the man told Dead-Eye. "Enough of this silly talk between us. We have to trust each other. You can't do business without trust. And I trust you. It's what I told Magoo. If you are a cop, then I am a cop. Then we are all cops."

"Chatty motherfucker, ain't he?" Magoo said, smiling over at Dead-Eye.

"Too chatty to be a cop," Dead-Eye said.

"It's cold out here," Magoo said. "Let's take it upstairs. I think better when my teeth ain't chatterin'.'"

They walked around the corner in a group, past graffiti-strewn walls, Magoo holding the middle, the Spanish man next to him, four leather coats filling out the huddle. Dead-Eye stayed in step behind Magoo.

"Lips here tells me you pretty good with a gun," Magoo said, looking over his shoulder. "Took out one of his boys before he could even blink. That true?"

"Pays to advertise," Dead-Eye said.

Magoo stopped, bringing the entire caravan to a halt. He turned to face Dead-Eye.

"I ain't too bad myself," Magoo said. "In case you was wonderin'.'"

"I wasn't," Dead-Eye said.

They stood before the entrance to a large housing complex. The benches around them were filled with sleeping homeless and users eyeing their next score. The few patches of grass at their feet were littered with bottles, used condoms, and split needles.

"What sort of piece you carryin'?" Magoo asked Dead-Eye.

"Askin' to buy?" Dead-Eye answered with a smile. "If you are, it's gonna cost you."

"I ain't askin'," Magoo said.

Dead-Eye heard one of the leather coats to his left click a chamber into a semi. He looked over at the Spanish man, who smiled back at him and shrugged his shoulders.

Dead-Eye unzipped his pea-green army surplus and reached into a side pocket. Magoo put a hand on top of his arm.

"Do it slow," Magoo said.

Dead-Eye nodded and pulled out a .44 semiautomatic, showing it to Magoo.

"Release the clip," Magoo said, looking at Dead-Eye and not the gun.

"You ever do anything for yourself?" Dead-Eye asked, staring back, letting the silver cylinder slide from the gun to his cupped palm.

"Only what I need to," Magoo said, turning away.

. . .

THEY MOVED AS ONE, past a flurry of curious eyes. One of the leather coats held the heavy green door to unit number six open with one hand. The other stayed in his pocket, cradling a cocked gun.

Dead-Eye walked with his head bowed, mind racing. He had just made the biggest mistake an undercover could make—he had trusted a marked man. He had bet his life that the Spanish man feared him more than he did Magoo. Moving down the urine-stenched hallway of the project, Dead-Eye knew he had wagered wrong. Worse, he had told no one about his meeting, stubborn in his belief that he could bring Magoo down alone.

Now he had less than five minutes to figure out a way to save his life.

"You ever seen my place?" Magoo asked, the group stopped in front of the double doors of the elevator.

"Don't think so," Dead-Eye said, scanning the faces of the men he was up against.

Except for the Spanish man, they were heavily armed and, considering the odds, confident enough to take him out at close range. Dead-Eye was down to one gun, a .9-millimeter Hauser, jammed in the back of his jeans. It might be good enough to drop two, maybe three. But in a large space, like Magoo's apartment, Dead-Eye had no chance. Too open, too vulnerable. It left him with only one choice, one place to make his move.

The elevator doors creaked open. The group got in and turned forward, one of the leather coats pressing the button for the fourth floor. Squeezed into the twenty-by-twenty space, they watched the doors close, then trained their eyes on the numbers above. The only light was a forty-watt bulb wrapped inside an iron basket.

Dead-Eye had inched his right arm out of his coat pocket and moved it to where his hand could feel the handle of the Hauser. He closed his eyes, took a deep breath, swallowed hard, and was ready.

"These things are so fuckin' slow," the Spanish man said, watching the number move from one to two. "Be faster if we walked it."

"Healthier too," Dead-Eye said, a smile on his face now.

"What's the rush?" Magoo said, looking over at the Spanish man and giving him a wink. "We got ourselves all night."

The elevator eased its way slowly from two to three.

"I can't stay that long," Dead-Eye said. "I made some plans."

"Such as?" Magoo asked, still looking up at the numbers.

Dead-Eye came out with his Hauser, coat slipping off his shoulder, and put one into the back of Magoo's head. He then aimed up and shot out the forty-watt bulb, plunging the elevator into pitch darkness. Within a fraction of a second, all guns were drawn and fired, sparks setting off steady flashes of light. The noise was deafening, screams and shouts as loud as the steady fusilage.

It lasted less than thirty seconds.

More than sixty rounds were exchanged.

. . .

THE DOOR to the fourth floor slowly slid open. An old woman pulling a shopping cart stood by the entrance, a look of horror across her face. The light from the hallway entered the elevator with a sudden jolt. Blood dripped down the sides of the walls. Magoo's body slumped forward and fell onto the hallway floor. Two of the leather coats were piled on top of one another in a corner of the elevator. The other two lay wounded on the ground.

The Spanish man had taken three in the chest, yet stood with his back against the elevator buttons, a sly smile still on his face.

Dead-Eye was against the far wall of the elevator, facing the old woman. He was shot in the leg, chest, and both arms. His empty gun was still in his hand, blood pouring down his fingers. His face was splattered with other men's blood, thick enough to blur his vision. The pain was so intense, he could barely speak. He knew he couldn't move.

"My God!" the old woman said, shaking where she stood.

"Maybe you should wait for the next one," Dead-Eye said to her, trying to manage a smile.

"I'll call the police," she said through quivering lips.

"Doctor be better," Dead-Eye whispered.

Dead-Eye fell to his knees and tossed the empty gun to the side, watching it land in a large circle of thick blood. He rested his head against the wall and closed his eyes, waiting for whatever help would arrive.

Dead-Eye wasn't in any rush. Not anymore.

It was March 8, 1981.

His last day as a cop.

3

Mrs. Columbo

MARY SILVESTRI STARED at her husband across the kitchen table. He had his head down, forking apart a chicken leg, trying to avoid another night of arguing. Their fourteen-year-old son, Frank, sat between them, immune to his parents' squabbles.

"Are you going to answer me or not, Joe?" Mary asked with an edge she usually reserved for work.

"Can we give it a rest?" Joe looked up from his plate. "One night. That's all I ask. One night when we don't have to talk about it."

"I *need* to talk about it," Mary said, hands resting flat on the pine surface. "And I need to talk about it *now.*"

"You *always* need to talk about somethin' *now,*" Joe Silvestri said, pushing his chair back and folding his arms across his chest. "You ask your questions and then you want your answers. And you don't ask them like a wife or a mother. You ask them like a cop. You treat me and Frankie like we're two suspects. Well, not tonight, Detective. You want any answers outta me, you're gonna have to arrest me."

Joe Silvestri walked out of the kitchen, turning his back on his wife and son, and grabbed a jacket from a hook in the mud room. He slammed the door behind him.

Frank looked over at his mother and managed a meager smile, fork poised against the side of his plate.

"It's like an episode of *The Honeymooners* in here every night," he said, shaking his head.

"Keep your facts straight, honey," Mary said, taking a long sip from a can of Dr. Brown's cream soda. "Ralph and Alice didn't have a kid."

Frank stood up, walked over to his mother, and kissed the top of her head. He took a step back, looked down at the .38-caliber revolver in her hip holster, and smiled.

"Alice didn't pack heat either," Frank said, leaving the kitchen for the sanctuary of the den.

Mary Silvestri watched her son disappear around the corner. She rested her soda on a napkin and lit a Kool.

"Alice *should've* had a gun," she whispered to herself, clutching the cigarette between her teeth. "She would've shot him dead for damn sure."

. . .

Mary Silvestri was thirty-six years old and for a dozen of those years had been a member of the New York Police Department. As a rookie, she'd started working out of the Ozone Park section of Queens, moved to Brooklyn and plainclothes, and from there to her true calling, a homicide unit in the Wakefield section of the Bronx.

She had an affinity for the death detail and, each year, her conviction rate placed her in the top tier of detectives across the five boroughs. She never tossed a folder into the unsolved pile. The fewer the clues, the less the logic behind each murder, the more fascinated Mary Silvestri became.

She exploited her talents.

Silvestri studied forensics at the John Jay College for Criminal Justice and then spent three months working alongside the chief medical examiner, trying to understand what he looked for at a crime scene, what crucial information could be picked up from a cold body. She took courses in abnormal psychology at Queens College, wanting to know as much about the killer as she would end up knowing about the deceased. In her free time, Mary Silvestri read mystery novels and true crime accounts of sensational cases. She made ample use of all the available technology and was one of the few NYPD detectives familiar with the Violent Criminal Apprehension Program, then in its infancy. VICAP, when effective, searched for patterns among at-large serial killers and would then draw up psychological profiles. Most street cops scoffed at such notions. Mary Silvestri used one profile to capture a car salesman on Tremont Avenue who had razor-slashed to death four teen-age prostitutes.

Mary was an attractive woman but paid little attention to keeping up her appearance. She was tall, close to five-ten on the few occasions she wore pumps, and svelte despite a steady cop diet of pizza, deli, and coffee. Her long red hair was often unruly and hastily brushed, held in place most mornings with clips. She dressed in a nondescript mix of L. L. Bean outdoor and S. Klein's indoor, favoring short skirts and sneakers, blouses open at the collar. She seldom carried her gun and always had a pack of saltines in her purse.

The homicide cops in her detail, all of them male, took delight in her flakiness. When Mary worked a case, she was so focused, so zeroed in on the most minute aspects of the murder, she would forget everything and everyone around her. The more disheveled she grew, the more foglike she walked around the office, the closer, they knew, she was to cracking the case.

Homicide detectives see themselves as elite members of the department. They carry themselves with confidence and arrogance. Many wear their motto on a T-shirt under their shirts and sweaters. The shirt has a chalk outline of a dead body. Above the sketch are the words OUR DAY BEGINS WHEN YOURS ENDS. HOMICIDE.

Among such a group, Silvestri was considered the best, and her skill earned her the street name "Mrs. Columbo," the female version of the rumpled TV detective.

Mary was the badge others turned to when the case seemed beyond solving. She was also the one that other detectives trusted the most in the interrogation room. She could crack a suspect in less time than it took to play a regulation hockey game. Once again, she used everything at her disposal—from sex appeal to physical force—to break down the man in the bare-back chair. She never came out of that cold room without a tired look and a signed confession.

The only thing Mary Silvestri wasn't good at was marriage.

She hated housework and cooking and had little patience for family gatherings. She had no siblings and both her parents were dead. Her husband was a mechanic who owned two Bronx Mobil gas stations and from day one groused about not having a stay-at-home wife. It was a lament encouraged by her in-laws, none of whom ever resigned themselves to having a cop in the family—let alone a female cop.

Mary loved her son and would sometimes take him out of school and bring him on the job with her, sitting surveillance in unmarked sedans. It was her version of bonding, and Frank ate up every minute.

"You want me to be a cop?" Frank asked one day as her police car sat in a Taco Bell lot.

"Not unless you want to be," Mary said between bites.

"Then why bring me along?" Frank asked.

Mary looked out the window, took a sip of coffee, then turned to her son. "So you understand what I do," she said. "And maybe why I am the way I am."

"When are you and Dad gonna get a divorce?"

Mary was surprised at the question. "Who says we are?"

"Somehow I don't think I have to worry about throwin' a surprise fiftieth anniversary party," Frank said, finishing off a chicken burrito.

"We were kids when we married," Mary said. "Too stupid to know better. I finished high school and he pumped gas. I went to the Academy and he pumped gas. I was pregnant with you and there he was, still pumping gas."

"And this is better?" Frank asked. "Sitting in cold cars, waiting for some guy to make a mistake?"

"For me it is," Mary said. "Putting cuffs on a guy that iced somebody who should still be alive beats a ten-dollar fill-up in my book."

"Dad likes what he does," Frank said. "He's good at it."

"I like what I do," Mary said. "And *I'm* good at it."

"You still love him?"

"In my own way," Mary said. "I do. It's just that my own way may not be good enough for him anymore. If it ever was."

"Would you be happier married to a cop?" Frank asked.

"I don't think so." Mary smiled at her son. "They're good to have around at work, but a waste of time otherwise. Just like me. Given a choice, I'd stick with the guy pumping gas."

"That's good, Mom," Frank said, smiling back.

"And speaking of gas," Mary said, holding her stomach. "Why the hell do you always make me eat these damn tacos?"

"Don't forget," Frank said. "You're the one went in there once and asked for their recipe."

"Had to flash my badge to get it too," Mary said with a full laugh.

. . .

THE BODY OF the thirty-two-year-old bookkeeper had been hanging from a closet door for three days. The skin on his face was ash white, his limbs were stiff, eyes open and bulging. His feet had been cut off at the ankles and tossed on top of a nearby bed. There were puncture wounds, large and small, up and down the front and back of the semi-nude corpse. His hands were tied behind his back, held together by black leather straps, and his throat was slashed. Rats had feasted on the remains and maggots were starting to fester.

"Did a knife do that to the throat, Doc?" Silvestri asked the M.E. on the scene.

"Worse," the medical examiner said in a weary voice. He was short, bald, and looked older than his forty-eight years. Three years on a job that averaged close to two thousand homicides a year, and he was already looking for the fastest way out.

"What's worse, Jerry?" Mary asked.

"Corkscrew," the doctor said. "Same one that was used to open the bottle of wine over on the bureau."

"How long's something like that take?" Tony Russo, Mary's partner on the case, asked.

"As long as the killer wants it to," the doctor said with a shrug, walking with head bowed away from the crime scene.

"You wanna get some coffee?" Russo asked Mary. He watched as the forensic team went about their business of taking photos, dusting for prints, bagging evidence, sealing up the cramped one-bedroom second-floor apartment that overlooked the Bronx River Parkway.

"You have to really enjoy killing to end a life like that," Mary said, eyes focused on the young man hanging from the closet door. "How else do you explain it?"

"You can't," Russo said. "Not until we have ourselves a cup of coffee. And maybe a sweet roll."

. . .

THE BOOKKEEPER, Jamie Sinclair, was single and unemployed. He had held one job over the last two years, working freelance on and off for a Manhattan firm specializing in TV commercials. He ran three miles a day, and, when he did work, attended an aerobics class four nights a week. He had a brother who lived in Jackson Heights and worked for the city in the marriage license bureau. His mother died in 1980 after a long battle with a brain disorder, and his father shared a two-bedroom Co-op City apartment with a twice-divorced mother of two. In a life that had spanned thirty-two years, there wasn't much else for Silvestri and Russo to go on. There were no known girlfriends *or* boyfriends. There were few friends of any kind. All indications were that Jamie Sinclair preferred to spend his time alone.

Except on the night he died.

"Uniform on the scene saw no sign of a break-in," Russo said, taking a huge bite from an apple turnover. "Whoever sliced and diced him was let in."

"Or was already there when Sinclair came home," Mary said, hands wrapped around a container of black coffee.

"Either way, the victim knew the perp," Russo said.

The detectives looked down the street, neat row houses mingling with three-story apartment buildings. Two blocks up, the el rumbled over White Plains Road. A squad car blocked off traffic access, and yellow crime-scene tape was spread across the front of the murder building. Onlookers stared from stoops and the tops of parked cars.

"Where you wanna start?" Russo asked her, finishing off the turnover.

"Let uniform do the first pass around the neighborhood," Mary said. "We'll follow up later. Let them look for the usual. Make sure they ask about anyone not from the area hanging around. Especially these past couple of days and especially if it's a woman."

"You kiddin' me?" Russo put one hand on Mary's elbow. "You know somethin' already? You were up there only, what, ten minutes."

"Relax, Sweet Tooth," Mary said, pulling her arm away. "When I know, you'll know."

"Tell you one thing, Mrs. Columbo," Russo said. "I hang around you, I'll be a captain before I lose my hair."

Mary looked at Russo's thin strands of dark hair rising in the mild spring wind. "Then we better work fast," she said.

. . .

BY THE TIME Jamie Sinclair's body was toe-tagged and put in a freezer drawer, BCCI, the fingerprint unit of the department, had found three sets of prints in the apartment not belonging to him. One set belonged to his brother, who had a key and said he'd let himself in to leave some family documents for Sinclair to sign. Another belonged to the building's landlord, who also had a key and would occasionally let himself in to drop off books and other packages. The third set belonged to Alison Walker, a fifty-eight-year-old woman with a bad heart, hefty trust fund, and Upper West Side brownstone in her name.

Her name shot its way to the top of Silvestri and Russo's interview list.

"Why's a rich Manhattan chick hangin' with a loser from the Bronx?" Russo wondered, dodging Manhattan traffic as he drove crosstown on Park Drive.

"She's fifty-eight years old," Mary said, trying to read her notes. "She passed the chick stage when Kennedy beat Nixon."

"Think she's the one opened him like a can of soup?"

"*And* cut his feet off? I doubt it."

"What, women don't kill?"

"Women don't kill brutal. A gun maybe. A knife if they're really determined. But no, not like that. Not vicious."

Mary put her notebook in her purse and opened a paper bag resting against her hip. She took out a container of coffee, popped the lid, and poured in three packs of sugar.

"You had to ice somebody," Russo said, swerving past a yellow cab. "A guy. Husband. Boyfriend. Whoever. We're just talkin' now. What would you use, gun or knife?"

"Neither," Mary said, stirring the sugar in the coffee.

"What then, a bomb?" Russo said. "Put a timer in and crack his car?"

"Strychnine," Mary said. "Five drops in a clear drink and the muscles hit adenosine triphosphate stage. Guy'd be dead in a few minutes. It's also hard to trace, unless you hit the scene within three hours, because rigor sets in as soon as the body's dead, not when the temp is down."

"You've given this some fuckin' thought, I see," Russo said, looking away from the traffic and at his partner.

"Here's your coffee," Mary said, handing Russo the cup and smiling. "Fixed it the way you liked it."

"You drink it," Russo said. "I ain't thirsty."

"I was hoping that's what you'd say," Mary said, taking a long sip.

. . .

ALISON WALKER LED the two detectives into the living room and offered them cups of tea and a platter filled with an assortment of fresh-baked cookies. Alison was short, wiry, and, despite the skin lifted tight around her jaw and neck, quite attractive. She had on a peach-colored blouse, tan skirt cut at the knee, and brown pumps. A double string of white pearls wrapped around her collar, and a set of earrings matching her blouse hung under golden-brown hair that was brushed and curled.

Mary Silvestri sat on a thick cream-colored couch that from feel and texture cost double any piece of furniture in her own home. The room was large and immaculately kept, the many antiques chosen with a sharp sense of style and concern for detail. The window behind the pale gray silk curtains was open, letting in a soft spring breeze.

Silvestri looked at the older woman and smiled.

"It's a beautiful home you have here," Mary said. "Really. I wouldn't even know how to begin to keep up with a place like this."

"It takes a great deal of time and work," Alison Walker said in an accent so bland and flat, one would never know she was the only child of a New Jersey fisherman.

"And money too, right?" Mary said.

"That goes without saying," Walker said, her manner finishing-school calm, her clear blue eyes devoid of emotion. "There isn't much one *can* do without money."

"Mind if I light one up?" Russo asked from the other end of the couch, trying hard not to polish off the entire tray of cookies.

"Yes," Walker said, eyes never moving from Mary. "I do mind."

"Thanks for nothin', then," Russo muttered, tucking his smokes into a shirt pocket.

"Did you know a man named Jamie Sinclair?" Mary asked.

"What do you mean, did?" Walker asked.

"He's dead," Russo said. "Someone used him as a coat hanger a couple of days ago. Other than the cookies, that's why we're here."

A hand went over Walker's mouth and her eyes did a slow, calculated twitch.

Mary glared at Russo. "I'm sorry," she said, turning to Walker. "Did you know him?" she asked again.

Alison Walker stood from her chair and walked toward the front door of her brownstone. She kept her head up as the sounds of her heels echoed on the polished wood floors.

"You both must leave," Walker said without turning, the door now open to outside sunlight. "Immediately."

"We'll only have to come back again," Russo said, tossing two cookies into his jacket pocket. "Or have somebody bring you down to us."

Mary took a napkin off a pile next to the teapot, filled it with cookies, and folded it. She handed the napkin to Russo.

"Wait for me in the car, Sweet Tooth," Mary said to him. "I'll be there before you polish these off."

"You sure?"

"What, you want milk too?" Mary said. "Now, go."

"You gonna be okay here with her?" Russo asked. "Alone, I mean."

"She whips out a corkscrew, I'll scream for you to come get me,"

Mary whispered. "Until that happens, be a good boy and go eat your cookies."

"If she made these," Russo said. "She ain't that bad a cook."

"Lizzie Borden liked to bake too," Mary said, watching as her partner walked out the door and down the front steps of the brownstone, his pockets lined with cookies. Then she turned back to the older woman.

"You knew him," Mary said, now sitting next to Alison on the couch. "You didn't kill him, but you did know him."

The woman nodded her head slowly and took in a deep breath. "Yes," Walker said, avoiding eye contact, staring instead at a crystal vase in the center of the coffee table, a fresh rose dangling off its edge. "We were friends."

"And you knew he was dead," Mary said, her voice soft and warm, two women talking about the demise of a mutual friend and not a cold-blooded murder. "Even before we knocked on your door."

"How do you know that?" Walker asked, moist eyes now looking over at Mary.

"Most people are surprised when two cops show up at their door," Mary said. "They go against normal behavior. You almost seemed happy to see us. You let us in without even asking what we wanted."

"Next time I'll know better," Walker said, trying to manage a smile.

"Were you and Sinclair lovers?" Mary asked, leaning closer.

"No," Walker said. "Jamie wasn't interested in the physical. At least he wasn't with me."

"Sounds like any other husband," Mary said with a smile.

"I wouldn't know," Walker said. "I've never married. Jamie was my last chance for that. At my age and in my position, most men are interested in only one thing. And it isn't sex."

"How much money were you giving him?"

"I gave what I wanted to give," Walker said, a hint of defiance to her words.

"And how much was that?" Mary asked, pressing the issue.

"Two, sometimes three thousand dollars," Walker said.

"A week?"

"He earned it," Walker said.

"Doing what?" Mary asked, looking around the room. "You've got a housekeeper, you do all the cooking, and the place doesn't look like it needs a paint job."

"Jamie was very good with numbers," Walker said. "He helped me with my investments, paid my bills, arranged my taxes. I trusted him. And he never gave me reason to think I shouldn't."

"How long was he helping you?"

"Almost three years."

"And you were paying him that kind of money all that time?" Mary asked. "Three thousand a week?"

"Yes."

"How did you pay him?" Mary asked. "Check or cash?"

"Cash," Walker said. "As organized as Jamie may have been for me, that's how disorganized he was with his own life. He didn't even have a checking account."

"Where'd he keep the money?"

"I never asked," Walker said. "I just know he never spent much of it, if any. Jamie didn't seem at all interested in money."

"Interested enough to charge a few thousand a week to cook your books," Mary said, standing and folding her notepad.

"Will I have to answer any more questions?" Walker asked, tilting her head toward the detective.

"Just one more for now," Mary said.

"What?"

"Who else knew about you and Jamie?" Mary asked.

"I never told any of my friends," Walker said. "People gossip about me as it is. They always have. And I wanted to keep what Jamie and I had special and private."

"What about him?" Mary asked. "Did he tell anybody?"

"Just his brother," Walker said. "They were very close."

"Did he tell his brother about the money too?" Mary asked.

"No," Walker said. "I don't think so. It's not the sort of thing Jamie would talk about. With anyone."

"You take care of yourself," Mary said, heading for the front door. "I'll be in touch."

"Is there anything I can do?" Walker asked, sadness breaking through the solid shield. "For Jamie, I mean."

"How'd you find out he was dead?" Mary asked. "It barely got a mention in the tabloids. And they don't seem your kind of reading anyway."

"His brother, Albert, told me," Walker said. "He called and told me when and how Jamie died."

"Did Albert tell you anything else?" Mary asked.

"Not to talk to anyone," Walker said, head bowed.

When Walker looked up again, she found herself staring at a closed door.

. . .

THE BAR WAS CROWDED despite the hour and the heavy rain pelting the streets and causing the windows to steam. They sat at a circular table in the back, away from the jukebox. The table was crammed with beer bottles, shot glasses, crumpled napkins, and bowls of salt pretzels. The place was dark, like most cop bars, scattered overhead lights giving off more shadow than glow. The four men and one woman around the table, members of the North Bronx Homicide Unit, were in a festive mood, their work for this day brought to a successful end.

Mrs. Columbo had solved another homicide.

"Took less than a week," Russo said, washing down a Snickers bar with a slurp of Bud. "Mary spots the bottle of wine, squeezes the spinster, and nabs the brother. We coulda called this one in from home."

"I like the *we* part," Stanley Johnson, senior detective on the squad, said to Russo. "What'd you do? Drive?"

"Brother break easy?" John Rodriguez asked. He was the new badge, working Homicide less than a month, promoted from the pickpocket division in Midtown South.

"He cracked in the car," Mary said, sipping from a scotch straight. "Cried all the way to the station."

"You gotta really hate your brother to slice him like that," Captain Jo Jo Haynes, precinct commander, said. "Corkscrew the throat and *then* cut his feet off. Christ! And I thought my family was fucked up."

"If I got a fuckin' nickel, I'm not lettin' my brother know about it," Russo said. "And I *like* the guy."

"It wasn't just the money," Mary said.

"What else?" Rodriguez asked.

"The brother, Albert, has some sort of muscular disease," Mary said. "And his insurance doesn't pick up all the costs. So he's always behind the financial eight-ball."

"He know this Jamie's pullin' in a few thou a week?" Johnson asked.

"No," Mary said. "Thinks the guy's on the balls of his ass. In fact, Albert lends him money. Feels sorry for him."

"What a prick," Jo Jo Haynes said.

"Albert's over at the apartment," Mary said, finishing her scotch. "Sees a bottle of wine and looks for a corkscrew."

"He finds it," Russo said. "In a cabinet drawer next to a folded-up paper bag. Albie, curious as well as thirsty, pops open the bag."

"And finds the money," Johnson said.

"He sat on the bed for three hours," Mary said. "Holding the corkscrew and staring at all that cash."

"Jamie walks in," Russo said. "Sees poor little Albie sittin' next to his stash and starts yellin' at the guy."

"Albert snaps," Mary said. "All those years being suckered by Jamie melt down into a couple of bloody minutes."

"He sliced and diced the fucker," Russo said. "Left him hangin', took the money, and walked out."

"And he never got to drink the wine," Johnson said.

"That's the sad part," Rodriguez said. "Guy comes in thirsty. Goes out the same way."

"Except this time with a murder rap," Russo said. "And Mrs. Columbo here smellin' his ass out in no time flat."

"What happens to the old lady?" Haynes asked. "What's her name? Walker?"

"Who gives a fuck, Cap," Russo said. "She still got her feet and can swallow anything she chews."

"She'll die alone," Mary said in a low voice. "Jamie was her only real friend. After this, she'll never let herself get close to anyone. She'll be warm in the winter and cool in the summer. And she'll die alone."

"Think Albert cops an insanity?" Johnson said.

"Wouldn't you?" Russo said. "He comes up Mr. Clean on the sheets. Not even a parking ticket. One of those jaboes goes through life nobody notices."

"Two lives ruined and one ended," Mary said. "All for a glass of wine."

"Let this be a lesson," Russo said, holding up a bottle of Bud. "Drink beer. You don't need a fuckin' weapon to open a bottle, and anybody who drinks it sure as shit don't have a paper bag filled with cash."

"I guess this means you're not buying," Mary said.

"Not unless one of you got a corkscrew in your pocket," Russo said, standing up from the table.

"Hey, Cap," Johnson said with a smile. "Whatta we get if we each put a bullet into Russo right here and now?"

"A raise," Jo Jo Haynes said.

Mrs. Columbo and the detectives ended their night of victory over death on a loud laugh.

. . .

MARY PARKED HER CAR four blocks from her Whitestone row house. The rain had stopped and the air was cool and clean, early morning smells wafting down from the trees. Overhead lights cast broken shadows across cars and patches of lawn. It was closing in on three A.M. and the streets were empty as she walked with a slow step, head down, her purse hanging from a strap off her shoulder. Sated with drink, she let her mind ease past the events of the day.

The emptiness of Alison Walker's life had rubbed a nerve. The woman had money, comfort, and a certain status. But none of those could fill the vacuum of years built around set routines and nights spent alone. Alison wouldn't die broke, but the odds were strong she would die bitter.

Mary lacked all the luxuries of Alison's life. Her status came courtesy of the gold shield in her purse. Her money traveled on a biweekly spin cycle and her comfort was a small house with a leaky roof, bad plumbing, and two bedroom windows long painted shut. But Mary knew, as she walked down the cracked sidewalk of Thirty-seventh Avenue, that she had Alison beat by a record mile. She had what the other woman would give everything to attain—a husband in her bed and a son in the next room.

Maybe her marriage wasn't such an uneasy fallback after all, and watching Frankie grow had given her plenty of reasons to smile. It was far better than sitting in a room alone, staring at an antique vase filled with a single red rose, knowing no phone would ever ring to a voice that cared and no door would ever open to let in a warm hug.

Mary Silvestri crossed against a flashing red light and picked up the speed of her pace, suddenly eager to get home. She never saw the man with the knife hunkered down in the alley, alongside the shuttered gates of Sergio's Deli. He stood perched on the balls of his feet, watching as she approached, waiting to time his leap and score the purse dangling against her hip.

When she was directly in front of him, he jumped.

The man, wiry and muscular, wrapped his right arm around Mary's throat and wedged the blade of a six-inch knife between her shoulders, hard against the soft wool of her camel's hair J. C. Penney blazer.

"You breathe, you die," the man said. His breath against her neck reeked of alcohol.

He tightened his grip around Mary's throat and gave the edge of the knife a rough twist. He took backward steps, dragging Mary with him, pulling her away from the light and into the blind darkness of the alley.

Mary relaxed her body and let the man's strength do all the work. She kept her hands free, loose, waiting to make her move. The arm around her throat was wrapped in bandages, blood flowing through the white gauze as his fingers gripped thick clumps of her hair. She shifted her face away from him, brushing against the rough skin of his cheek as she moved.

They were in the alley now.

"What you got for me?" the man asked, leaning her face forward against the red brick wall. "How much?"

"Take it all," Mary said, forcing the words out. "In the purse. Take it."

He yanked her head back with a forceful grip of her hair and slammed her face against the wall.

"Don't tell me what to take, bitch. I take what I want. Understand me?"

"Yes," Mary said, tasting the blood dripping down from her forehead.

He moved his arm from her throat and ripped the purse off her shoulder. He leaned her hard against the wall, the blade of the knife keeping her in place. Mary closed her eyes, took in a few deep breaths, and tried to think with a clear head. She knew she didn't have much time and was angry at herself for leaving her gun in the office, something she always did when she went out drinking with the squad.

She heard the man rifle through the purse and knew exactly what he would find—sixty dollars in cash, Visa and MasterCards, one overdue and the other at its limit, a few coins, her father's pocket watch, and an NYPD gold-shield detective's badge.

The man took the cash, missed the badge, and tossed the purse into a corner of the alley. He shoved the money into a front pocket of a pair of soiled jeans and leaned closer to Mary. He rested his head on her shoulder and put his lips to her ear, the knife still in its place.

"Like the way you smell," he said, his tongue stroking the edges of her ear.

"You got what you wanted," Mary said, fighting to keep her voice calm. "You got enough to get a fix and make it through the night."

She heard the man slide his zipper down and push himself closer.

"You gonna be my fix," he said. "You and me, we gonna make it through the night."

The man was rubbing himself against her leg, free hand pawing at her skirt and panties, trying to reach flesh. Mary struggled to free herself from his grip, using the wall as a brace, balancing her feet for leverage.

"That's it, baby," the man said. "Fight me. C'mon, trim, fight me."

Mary turned her face from the wall, moving the man's arm away from her thigh. She looked in his eyes, brown, glazed, and empty, and saw in them what she had seen in the faces of so many killers over so many years. It was in that fragment of a second that she knew what awaited her. It wasn't just sex he wanted. Or drugs he needed.

It was blood.

Her blood.

The man with the knife needed a fix that only the blade could bring him. He was laughing as he stood and watched her blood flow past his legs like melted Jell-O, moving down the cracked path of a dark alley on an empty street in Queens. Laughing and staring into Mary's eyes, watching as the life ebbed out of them.

It was the rush of the killer.

No one understood that feeling better than Mary Silvestri.

. . .

SHE WOKE UP three days later in the intensive care unit of Mission Hospital. Doctors had removed a portion of her lung, sliced beyond use by the man's knife. Her stomach had also been slashed, requiring forty-seven stitches to close. There were welts and bruises up and down her body, and her right arm and left foot were broken and in casts. One eye was closed shut, and the side of her right cheek was bandaged.

Mary looked around the room, pale blue walls floating like waves, shards of sunlight warming the left side of her face. She saw an IV hanging off to the side, fluid slow-dripping into her arm. The inside of her mouth felt crusted, and there were two small plastic oxygen tubes in her nose. A set of rosary beads was wrapped around the fingers of her left hand.

She turned to her left, past the glare of the sun, and saw her son, Frank, sitting in a chair, wearing a New York Yankee jacket and cap, hands folded in his lap, staring back at her. She gazed at him for several seconds, read the concern etched on his youthful face, saw the tense way he leaned his body forward, and studied the eyes of a teenage boy terrified that his mother would die.

"Shouldn't you be in school?" she said, each word weighed down with a pain that reached into her chest.

"It's Sunday," Frank said, surprised to hear her speak.

"Church, then," Mary said, managing a slight smile. "I could use a couple of prayers thrown my way."

"Went this morning," Frank said. "With Dad."

"Here alone?"

"No," Frank said. "Dad went down to the cafeteria. To get some coffee."

"How's he doin'?"

"Scared," Frank said. "Stays here all day. Sleeps in the bed next to you at night. Leaves just to check on work and pick me up from school."

"How about you?" Mary asked, wishing she could sit up, lean over, and, for the first time in many years, take her son in her arms.

"I'm not as scared," Frank said.

"Why's that?"

"Dad forgets how tough you are," Frank said. "I don't."

"I'm not as tough as the guy I ran into," Mary said. "Otherwise, we'd be sending him flowers."

"They caught him," Frank said.

"Who made the collar?" Mary asked.

"Not sure," Frank said. "Russo and some of the other guys started chasin' him down while you were in surgery. By the time you were in recovery, they had him."

"I can't wait to see him in court," Mary said. Her throat was dry and raw, and her jaw ached whenever she spoke.

"He won't be in court," Frank said.

She didn't have to say anything. She just looked at him, first curiously, then knowingly.

"Russo told me and Dad the guy put up a fight." Frank went on in a matter-of-fact tone that would have made any seasoned cop proud. "Came at them with the same knife he used on you. Russo and Johnson stopped him."

Mary nodded and turned from her son. She lifted her head slowly, eyes scanning the flowers and baskets that filled the room.

"I'm glad you're alive, Mom," Frank said, standing up and moving closer to the bed.

"I am too, sweetie," Mary said.

"Dad says now things are gonna be different," Frank said. "Better, you know, than they used to be."

"Because I can't be a cop anymore?" Mary asked. The sound of the words hurt more than saying them. A tear formed at the side of her good eye.

"You'll always be a cop, Mom," Frank said, touching her hand.

. . .

WHEN SHE WAS finally alone, she leaned her head back against the pillow, closed her eyes, and, for the first time since she was a child, began to cry. Her tears went beyond pain and past anger. They were filled with a sense of loss and a knowledge that something besides blood had been left back in that narrow alley.

The man with the knife had ripped away at more than just her body. He had torn into the deepest parts of her soul and walked out into the darkness holding what mattered most to the woman who loved being called Mrs. Columbo.

He had stripped off her badge.

Mary Silvestri was no longer a cop.

4

Geronimo

DELGALDO LOPEZ SAT under the altar of the church, staring at twelve sticks of dynamite. They were taped to a marble slab and set to a one-hour timer that was wound around a blasting cap. All about him, members of the Brooklyn Bomb Squad raced through the church, laying down heavy detainable mats and moving aside statues and votive lights. The front and back doors to the church had been sealed minutes before, and a dozen uniform cops in heavy vests and pith helmets stood guard.

Lopez ran his index finger alongside the dynamite sticks, checking their moisture level, careful as hell not to nudge the array of red, green, and blue wires wound around the hardware store timer.

"How much time?" Gerry Dumane, the Bomb Squad commander, asked as he knelt down next to Lopez.

"Not enough," Lopez said, eyes never moving from the device. "Closing down to twelve minutes."

"How strong?"

"Could take out half a block. Maybe more. Depends how fresh the dyno is and what else he packed in there."

"Jesus," Dumane said.

Lopez turned away from the bomb and looked over at his commander.

"Don't have to look too far," Lopez said, pointing to a large crucifix hanging above the altar. "He's right behind you."

. . .

AT AGE THIRTY, Delgaldo Lopez had already put in six years of service on the Bomb Squad. He joined the PD after an eighteen-month tour of army duty, where he earned his Special Forces stripes as a munitions expert. Delgaldo had always been fascinated by explosives, from his earliest years. His father, Carlos, a Puerto Rican merchant seaman, would help satisfy his son's curiosity by bringing home books and different forms of fireworks from his various travels. His mother, Gloria, a half-Cherokee, would keep her only son up past the midnight hour, telling him folk stories and battle tales passed down by her grandfather.

When he was ten, Delgaldo built his first explosive device out of rubber bands, baking soda, the face of his father's old Timex, powder from two boxes of firecrackers, and blue strands of wool from his mother's knitting basket. He brought it into science class, set the timer at two minutes, and dismantled the piece in less than thirty seconds. His teacher gave him an A for the project and two days of detention for frightening the entire class into silence.

In his teens, Delgaldo gave some thought to going on to college and studying to be a chemist. But a laboratory was too tame a place to spend a life. It wouldn't be enough for him just to know all there was about bombs and devices. Delgaldo was not meant to be a bystander. He had warrior blood and felt a desire to carry on what his mother had always called a family tradition.

He also needed to see the bombs in action. He wanted to be there when the ticking was down to the quick, where one slip of a cutter would mean victory for the bomber and destruction for everyone else. It made Delgaldo Lopez, a tall, muscular young man with thick black hair and eyes so dark that staring into them was like looking at a blank screen, the perfect candidate for the Bomb Squad. He was the one who took the danger calls, who didn't sweat the risks, who never flinched as the final ticks of a timer echoed through an empty room.

To the other members of the Bomb Squad, Delgaldo Lopez, the cop they called Geronimo, was indeed a warrior.

. . .

"How you wanna play it?" Dumane asked, rubbing the back of his neck, looking around the boarded-up church.

"It's a simple mech," Geronimo said, still studying the bomb. "Won't take more than two minutes, three at the outside, to shut down."

"So what's the problem?" Dumane said. "Do it and let's get the hell outta here."

"It's too easy," Geronimo said. "Guy goes to all the trouble of putting one in a church. Even calls it in, lets us know where it is and how much time is left. Then he leaves this, something a kid with a scope and scissors could take down?"

"Whatta ya sayin', G?" Dumane asked. "Maybe he's just not that good."

"Or maybe he's better than we think."

Geronimo was on his feet now, scanning the empty church, searching for the shape of a bomb, the scent of the powder, his mind no longer that of a cop, but of a lone man bent on destruction.

"The crew peel through the church?" Geronimo asked, eyes looking up at a silver organ in the balcony.

"They stopped when they found the device," Dumane said. "Why?"

"I'll take this one down," Geronimo said. "But have them check everything else while I do."

"You make me so fuckin' nervous when I hear you talk like this," Dumane said. "Whatta ya tellin' me?"

"He laid in two, Commander," Geronimo said, looking at Dumane. "The other one's the blaster. This one's just here to keep us busy."

"You sure about this?"

"We could take a vote," Geronimo said. "If you think we got the time."

"Dummy this one," Dumane said, running from the altar. "I'll send for you if we find another."

"If I'm not here, I'll be up there," Geronimo said, pointing to the balcony. "Up by the organ."

"Why there?" Dumane shouted over his shoulder.

"I like organs," Geronimo said with a smile.

. . .

GERONIMO WOULD SPEND vacations losing himself in the hills of Arizona, hiking and horseback riding through the ragged terrain of the Sedona red rock region. He went for weeks at a time, alone, seeking to keep alive the ways of his Indian ancestors and to hold on to a promise made to his mother the year he first became a member of the Bomb Squad.

"You now live among the violent," his mother told him on that day, her voice a lyrical mix of Ponce and prairie. "Your mind and body travel in their circle. Keep your spirit strong and alive. Put it in a place it cannot be touched by evil hands."

"I will, Mama," Geronimo said, gently stroking the thick skin of the old woman's face. He looked in her eyes, dancing to their own flame, and saw in them the beauty of her youth. He didn't need the strength of the spirit world to know how easy it must have been for his father to fall in love with her.

"You visit the lands where the spirit still roams," she said, holding his hand to her face. "Let them show you the way. It is what will keep you safe. And make me know that I will not lose a son as I have lost a husband."

"I miss him too," Geronimo said. His father had suffered a stroke and died halfway through what would have been his last voyage on a merchant ship. It took three weeks for the body to make its way back home. As he had requested, Carlos Lopez was cremated and his ashes scattered about the family farm in the tropical hills of Puerto Rico.

"You have your memories," his mother said. "And I have his heart."

"I should go," Geronimo said. "Won't look good to be late on my first day."

"Before you go, take this," Gloria Lopez said, opening the hand that rested on her knee. Curled up in her palm was a medallion in the shape of a horse hung from a thin gold chain.

"What is it?" Geronimo asked, holding it up to the dim light of the shuttered apartment.

"Put it on," his mother said. "And never take it off. Promise me."

Geronimo took the medallion from his mother and hung it around his neck, tucking it inside his sweater collar. He leaned over, kissed her cheek, and held her close. It was the body of an old woman, and he would not have her for much longer.

"Promise, Delgaldo," his mother said. "You will never take it off."

"I promise," Geronimo said. "Till the day I die."

. . .

THE SECOND BOMB was packed in solid, wedged between a foot pedal and the base of the organ. Thick strips of retainer tape were wrapped around its center, insulated rows of coiled wiring folded over the sides. At its base were thirty-six pieces of heavy dynamite, the flex timer at the center surrounded by a six-pack of nitro vials. Six different-colored wires were all meshed together, each inserted into the silver lid toppings of the nitro.

Geronimo was on his back, under the organ, staring at the device. He followed the paths of the wires, each embedded in a batch of dynamite sticks, each alone holding enough power to destroy several city blocks. He admired the sheer simplicity of its design and wondered about the caliber of man he was dealing with, someone whose only pleasure came from turning loose such a force on the innocent.

He closed his eyes, both hands feeling for the medallion hidden under his bomb-resistant vest. He heard Commander Dumane squeeze in alongside him, stripped down to a T-shirt and bomb gear.

"Whatta ya need, G?" Dumane said. "I'm here."

Geronimo opened his eyes and looked at the timer.

He had eleven minutes to defuse the bomb.

"I need a miracle," Geronimo said. "Got any handy?"

"What's the main contact—the nitro or the dynamite?" Dumane asked.

"Both," Geronimo said. "One feeds into the other."

"You could clip the wires at the center. Defuse both at once."

Geronimo shook his head. "Timer's connected only to one. And there's too many wires to tell which."

"Shit. I ain't seen a job like this in all the years I been snappin' bombs."

"It's a copycat," Geronimo said. "Been used before."

"Where?"

"German terrorist outfit, Baader-Meinhoff gang, used to plant them," Geronimo said. "Back in the early seventies."

"How'd they take them down?" Dumane asked.

"Best I know, no one ever capped their bombs," Geronimo said. "German police just killed all the gang members."

"Why don't we ever think of shit like that?" Dumane said.

Geronimo looked at the timer, now down to six minutes, and pulled a small pair of pliers from his kit. He wiped thick beads of sweat from his upper lip and forehead and took in a long, deep breath.

"How much of the neighborhood is clear?" Geronimo wanted to know, holding the pliers in his right hand.

"Three blocks up and down, both sides," Dumane said. "Every building and store's emptied out."

"This'd be a good time for you to split too," Geronimo said, giving him a meaningful look. "In case I fuck up."

"You selfish bastard," Dumane said, smiling. "All you care about is glory. Well, Chief, I got bad news. This bomb you're gonna have to share."

"I'm gonna click the blue wires first," Geronimo said.

"Why blue?"

"Just a hunch," Geronimo said. "After that, if you and me are still here, I'll move the nitro off the timer and hand them over."

"I need a place to put 'em," Dumane said, looking around. "Where they won't move."

"Up on the altar," Geronimo said. "Might be a chalice. Should be wide enough to hold the bottles."

"I ever tell you I hate bombs," Commander Dumane said, crawling out from under the organ. "Only took the damn job 'cause they told me it was a temporary transfer. Ten fuckin' years later, I'm still here, waitin' for some out-of-work psycho's erector set to blow me to pieces."

"I ever tell you I love bombs?" Geronimo said, more to himself than to Dumane. "Nothin' but me and the device. You can never beat a bomb. You just stop it. Till the next time."

Geronimo put the pliers on the first part of the blue wires, waited a second, and then clipped them apart. Dumane was next to him, hands wrapped around a chalice, eyes on the bomb.

"Two sets of reds, two blues, and two whites," Dumane said. "The guy's a regular George M. fuckin' Cohan."

"Blues are dead," Geronimo said. "Gonna clip the white next."

"Another hunch?"

"It's all I got to go on, Commander," Geronimo said. "Unless you got a thing for red."

"Your call, G," Dumane said.

Geronimo rested the pliers on a long strand of white wire. His hand was steady, eyes were calm. All the tension was internal, buried inside nerve endings, heart beating at such a furious pace, he could feel it pounding against his vest.

He snapped the white wire and held his breath.

"It's the red," Geronimo said. "That's the main hookup. Once I give you all the nitro, take it to the truck. I'll meet you outside."

"There you go, tryin' to get rid of me again."

Geronimo turned to look at his commander, less than three minutes left on the timer, and smiled. "I'm trusting you with the hard part," he said. "I don't like nitro. Makes me nervous."

"I'll try not to trip down the steps," Dumane said.

"Ready?" Geronimo asked, setting the pliers down on his chest and reaching for the first bottle of nitro.

"No." Dumane removed the lid from the chalice and gripped its base with his left hand. "But don't let that stop you."

Geronimo's hands were steady as he lifted the first thimble-size bottle of nitro from its sleeve with two index fingers. He handed the bottle to Dumane without looking at him, his eyes never veering from the device, afraid to turn away. Dumane took the bottle with one hand, slowly rested it inside the chalice, and readied for the next.

Geronimo lifted the second nitro bottle, had it halfway removed, and then stopped. There was a thin copper wire attached to the base of the bottle, the other end connected to a sixty-second timer that started ticking down as soon as he touched the bottle.

"Shit!" Geronimo said, nearly dropping the bottle in his anger. "Smartass little fuck!"

"Please God tell me I'm the one did something wrong," Dumane breathed.

"The whole bomb's a setup. Everything's here, on this nitro bottle. The rest is all bullshit. Only one fuse, one bottle, and all the dynamite."

"How much time?"

"Just enough to get lucky." Geronimo held the bottle between his two index fingers, watching the clock tick down to forty-five seconds.

"Cut the wire," Dumane said. "It's your only move."

"It's the move I'm *supposed* to make," Geronimo said. "Every move's been the one I'm *supposed* to make."

"What ain't you supposed to do?" Dumane asked. "Or maybe I don't wanna know this part."

The clock was down to thirty seconds.

Geronimo could feel his pulse pounding against the sides of his wrists, sweat running down his forehead, into his eyes, stinging his vision. He took a slow breath and swallowed hard, throat dry as stone. He eased two more fingers around the center of the nitro bottle, tightened his grip, and then waited for the timer to tick down to ten seconds.

"You sure about this, G?" Dumane asked, gritting his teeth as he held the chalice tight and steady.

Geronimo pulled the nitro bottle from its slot. The short tug snapped both the nitro and the sticks of dynamite linked to it from the cord.

No sound came out of the dark and empty church.

The timer stopped at six seconds.

"Call in the cavalry, Commander," Geronimo said, resting the back of his wet head against cold marble. "We're done here."

"Now, that's a funny request," Dumane said, inching his way slowly from under the organ. "You being an Indian and all."

"Redskin humor," Geronimo said. "Works all the time." He placed the nitro bottle back in its slot, unsnapped his vest, and folded his hands across his chest. His fingers felt for the medallion and squeezed it through the cold wetness of his shirt. He closed his eyes and said a silent prayer of thanks to his God for helping him save the house of another.

. . .

GERONIMO SAT WITH legs crossed inside the large tent, facing the old man in the buckskin jacket. There was a full fire flaring between them, heat casting both faces in its auburn glow. The old man smoked tobacco from a thin wooden pipe and drank coffee out of a cracked black cup. Outside, heavy flakes of snow fell to the hard ground.

"Do you wish to smoke?" the man asked in a voice as lived-in as an old sweater.

"I'm okay with just the coffee," Geronimo said, the flames dancing like lit matches in his eyes.

"Your face is a tired one," the old man observed, the base of the pipe wedged in between his gums, eyes staring at some unknown distant point. "You are much too young a man to feel as old as me."

"My mother thinks it's the work," Geronimo told him. "Each day can be my last."

"That is true of all men," the old man said. "No matter the job. Only with yours, the fear cannot be hidden."

Geronimo sipped from a cup of coffee and nodded. "That's what I like about it," he said. "I like knowing that any day could be my last. I *like* facing the fear."

"Have you ever surrendered to it?" the old man asked as he tossed the remains of his coffee into the fire, causing flames to spit higher. "Allowed the fear to win?"

"No," Geronimo said.

"Fear waits for us all," the old man said. "And when your day comes, you will know the heart of your strength."

"I'm not afraid of a bomb killing me," Geronimo said.

"What then?" the old man asked.

"I'm afraid of a bomb *not* killing me," Geronimo said. "It's my only fear."

"A warrior is meant to die in battle," the old man said, nodding in agreement. "Not left behind for other men to pity."

"I see some of the guys who used to work Bomb Squad," Geronimo said. "They come around once in a while, looking lost and empty. Legs missing, arms gone, eyes blown out. Acting as if they want to go on with their lives. But in their hearts they curse that bomb for not taking them when it went."

"Then pray, Delgaldo," the old man said. "Pray for death."

. . .

GERONIMO WAS STUCK in traffic near the Williamsburg Bridge and a half hour late for an appointment with his mother's doctor when he heard the call over his police scanner. The radio was calling the Brooklyn Bomb Squad to an abandoned warehouse in the Flatbush section to scan a suspicious device on the third floor. Geronimo looked at the clock on the dashboard and at the clogged cars in front of him. The morning papers were tossed on the seat across from him, each folded open to the sports section. Geronimo loved basketball nearly as much as he loved taking down bombs. In between stop-and-go traffic moves, he clocked the scores from the previous night's playoffs.

It was a sunny April morning in 1980, and Geronimo was only a few hours into his first Saturday off in three months.

The female voice over the scanner called the bomb unit for a second time, confirming the device and requesting backup patrol to seal off the area. Geronimo looked at the rows of cars ahead of him, snarled in four roads to nowhere, and slapped a red cherry cop light on the roof of his Chevy Impala.

He was on the scene in ten minutes.

He got out of the car, flipped his shield over the collar of a light tan sweater, and nodded to two officers holding back a row of onlookers.

"What's the word?" he asked.

"Bomb guys just went in," one cop, the younger of the two, said. "Must be serious shit. They came in three trucks."

"Only way we know what goes down is when the guys walk out

of the building," the other cop, older, more seasoned, said. "Or if we hear a blast."

"You in on this?" the young cop asked.

"No," Geronimo said, shaking his head and eyeballing the crowd. "Just waiting for rush hour to thin."

"Bar be a better place to wait," the older cop said.

"I don't drink," Geronimo said, walking past a police barricade and into the gathered crowd.

. . .

HE CHECKED THE EYES and body language of the bystanders. Bombers plant devices for two reasons. They like the rush of the blast, relishing the fact that it was their handiwork that caused panic and destruction. The other reason is more basic.

They crave attention.

Geronimo had seen the statistics. More than three-quarters of bombers are cop buffs who make regular calls into the hot lines set up after a blast. Twenty-seven percent of all potential bomb suspects in the New York City area have, at one time in their lives, taken the police exam.

And 65 percent stay on the scene.

The bomber waits quietly among the crowd, wanting to see if the bomb unit can beat him at what he does best. If there is a blast, the bomber is among the first to volunteer his help. If the device is defeated, he's there to lead the cheers.

Geronimo, hands buried inside front pockets of his faded jeans, walked through this throng, trying to find the guilty lurking among the curious.

It didn't take long.

The man was young and well dressed, gray slacks tailored, brown loafers buffed, blue button-down shirt visible under a navy blazer. His brown hair was combed straight back and gelled, the clear complexion of his freshly shaven face shining in the glow of the morning sun. He resembled what he wanted those around him to think he was: a young executive derailed on his way to work.

But the eyes betrayed him.

Geronimo kept his distance, half hidden by a trio of schoolgirls lugging large L. L. Bean backpacks on their shoulders. He saw the man's eyes scan the empty warehouse, knowing which window to peer at and which door the bomb unit needed to enter. There was a bomber's hunger to those eyes, a sense of anticipation, a confidence that maybe on this day the police would be a poor match for his expertise.

They were eyes waiting for blood.

Geronimo stepped around the three girls and edged closer to the wooden barricade. With his back to the bomber, he glanced at the ground, checking only the motion of the stranger's shadow. He heard a lighter click behind him and watched a thin stream of tobacco smoke as it filtered past. Geronimo turned his head toward the man, and the two exchanged looks.

The man saw the badge dangling around Geronimo's neck.

Geronimo saw the man's right hand bunched up in the folds of his jacket pocket, cigarette gritted between teeth, sly smile across his face.

A cool breeze brushed past the cop. His body relaxed, the way it did instinctively when he was left in a room alone with a device. He took his hands from his pockets and moved closer to the suspect.

They were surrounded by two dozen people—old women on their way to the deli, workers on morning break, mothers taking toddlers out for a stroll. All attention was focused on the building and the commotion in front of it. The children gleefully watched the squad cars parked at odd angles, bright red lights twirling. The duty cops, backs turned to the crowd, talked about logged overtime, unconcerned about the gawking bodies.

"Hello, Bomb Man," the man in the jacket said to Geronimo. "I thought you'd be in on this."

"You know me?" Geronimo asked.

"I know what you do," the man said, still holding the grin. "And you know what I do."

"How much time?" Geronimo asked.

"Five minutes." The man directed his eyes toward the building. "Not one of my better works. They should be able to dismantle without much effort. Even without you."

"Gonna be the last one you plant," Geronimo said. "Should have given it your best."

"I'm not finished yet," the man said.

Geronimo reached behind his sweater, pulled out a .45 Colt, and aimed it at the man. He spread his legs apart and cocked the trigger.

"Hands high," Geronimo said, ignoring the cries of the people around him. "Where I can see 'em."

"Anything you say, Bomb Man," the man said.

He raised his free hand first and then slowly took the other out of the jacket pocket. Geronimo looked at the hand and raised the scope of the Colt a half inch higher, toward the center of the man's head.

The man's fingers were wrapped around an unpinned grenade.

"I drop this and we all die," the man said gleefully and in a voice loud enough to be heard by the people around him.

"You're dead before it touches ground," Geronimo said.

"I hope so," the man said.

A woman screamed.

Two men knocked over the wooden barricade, trying to get out of the way.

A young woman in a sweat suit pulled her baby from the stroller and stood there, shivering with fear, inches from the man and the grenade.

Two cops were up behind Geronimo, guns drawn, aimed at the man.

"They say you're the best, Bomb Man," the man said. "You think that's true?"

"Let the people go," Geronimo said. "Then we'll talk."

"There isn't a bomb you can't beat," the man said. "That's what I've read."

"Let them go," Geronimo said. "Make it you and me. That's the only way for you to find out."

"If they go, you'll shoot me," the man said. "And I still won't have my answer."

"I'm gonna shoot you no matter what," Geronimo said. "But I promise you'll have an answer before you die. If you let them go."

"I want it now," the man said. "I want to see for myself if you're as good as they say."

Geronimo knew the man was without fear. In the madness of his dark world, that feeling had been stripped away. More than the grenade in his hand, it was the lack of fear that gave the man the advantage.

With a smile, the man made his move.

He tossed the grenade toward the woman clutching her child.

Geronimo moved as he fired. Three quick 250-grain bullets flying at 860 feet per second landed in the man's forehead and chest.

He was dead before his head hit concrete.

The grenade bounced off the screaming woman and fell to the ground.

Geronimo, in full leap, landed on top of it, one hand holding the metal tight, the other slapped against the medallion hanging around his chest.

Four seconds later, the grenade exploded across his body.

For Delgaldo "Geronimo" Lopez, the dream he feared the most had come true.

He lost to a bomb and he lived.

5

Pins

J IMMY R YAN SAT in the backseat of an idling black Ford van and watched the woman in the red patent-leather pumps cross Madison Avenue against the light. Her tight black skirt stopped at mid-thigh; her black blouse was covered by a red Lagerfeld jacket, double-breasted and snug. Her thick hair, black and curled, fell across her shoulders, swinging past a set of pearl earrings that dangled near her neck. She strolled with confidence and her figure matched her style.

Augie Calise, the young detective behind the wheel, muttered, "I'm fallin' in love. Just sittin' here and lookin' at her, I'm fallin' in love."

Andy Fitz, the detective sitting on the passenger side, slowly shook his head. "You're married, shmoe."

"Your point?" Calise asked, still looking at the woman as she sauntered through the entrance of a doorman building.

Ryan snapped open an attaché case on his lap. Inside was a Sony SRS-P3 recorder, its high-frequency tape spooling from one end of the machine to the other. He turned the volume to high, sat back, and listened to the clicking sounds the woman's heels made as she walked across the lobby toward the elevator bank.

"Great sound," Fitz said. "It's like we're right next to her."

"I'd feel better if we *were* right next to her," Calise said. "These guys smell a mistake, they're gonna take everything but her teeth."

"They won't know she's wired," Ryan said. "Unless they strip her naked."

"I'd do that even if I *didn't* think she was wired," Calise said.

"Where'd you lay the wire?" Fitz wanted to know.

"Inside her right bra cup," Ryan told him. "They'll never find it."

"Her bra cup?" Calise turned his head, staring at Ryan with awe. "How the hell did you get it in there?"

"Secrets of the trade," Ryan said, smiling. "If I told you, Andy here would have to pump two into the back of your ears."

Calise refused to smile back. "Least you could do is let me take the wire out."

"Sorry, Augie," Ryan said, snapping a cord into a set of earphones and resting them around his neck. "I'm the only one who can touch her. My hands've got a priority one clearance."

"Who the hell gave you that?" Calise asked, checking the traffic in front of the building.

"I was born with it," Jimmy Ryan said.

. . .

JIMMY RYAN WAS ORPHANED at birth, abandoned in an upstate New York hospital by frightened teenage parents. His childhood memories revolved around a series of loveless foster homes inhabited by faceless adults, too anonymous to call parents, too familiar to call strangers. He grew up quiet and alone, confiding in no one, reluctant to form bonds, knowing they could soon be severed by the sudden shrill ring of a telephone.

The calls always came at night.

They would soon be followed by the mad rush to pack secondhand clothes into a worn valise and the false warmth of hurried good-byes. The car rides to each new family were always silent. Jimmy would sit in the back, scrunched down in his seat, eyes peering out at the passing landscape, feeling empty and lost.

He never stayed with any one family for more than a year. His plight was similar to thousands of other unwanted youngsters his age, all pawns in a statewide bureaucracy shuffle that revolved around cash payments. Children locked inside the state's foster care system were peddled off to applicant families who agreed to take them into their homes for a maximum twelve-month period. In return, they would receive average monthly checks of $78 per child, money meant to cover food and clothing expenses. More often than not, the checks helped cover gambling habits and drink binges. At any time, either the child, foster parent, or a system representative could rescind the deal, trucking the orphan off to still another foreign place to call home.

In one eight-month period, between fourth and fifth grades, Jimmy was moved three separate times, each new set of parents welcoming him to his new home and then just as eagerly seeing him off only a few weeks later.

Jimmy's way of life didn't leave much room for hobbies. There were no baseball card collections to hoard or comic books hidden on dusty shelves to be read in the dead of night. There weren't any kittens to hold or fish tanks to tend. Though Jimmy loved to read, he owned few books of his own. Anything to make packing easier.

Jimmy did have one passion, and he fell back on it to help get him through those early dark years. With a magical talent for anything electrical, he welcomed the secondhand toys his array of foster parents would send his way. Plug-in remote-control robots that had smashed into too many walls, chewed-up tape recorders, acid-stained transistor radios: They all found their way into Jimmy Ryan's hands.

Slowly and with great care, Jimmy would take a gadget apart, reconfigure the wiring, and emerge with something virtually new. If he had the time and the tools, he would even add a few fresh dimensions to his re-creation.

In his empty hours, Jimmy pored through the electronics magazines he found in local libraries and carted out as many books on the subject as he had time to read. He absorbed all the knowledge available, stored it, and shared it with no one. Then, when that knowledge would do him the most good, Jimmy Ryan would figure a way to put it to use.

Ryan planted his first bug when he was twelve.

He was living with a plumber, George Richards, who had a short-fuse temper and a wife with a flirtatious eye. They both drank heavily and often took the frustrations of a night's drunk out on the boy. The wife, Elaine, began her assaults with an angry voice and ended them with an even louder flurry of slaps, leaving Jimmy with a series of welts and bruises hidden under his shirts and sweaters. Afterward, she scolded him into silence and backed the warnings with hard hits across already reddened flesh.

Jimmy Ryan never uttered a word.

Instead, he laid a wire inside the main bedroom of the Richardses' two-story stucco house in Peekskill, New York. The wire was wrapped around a wooden board under the queen-size mattress. It connected to a remote mini-recorder taped under a bureau next to the bed. On those tapes, Jimmy listened and learned about the couple he was told to call Mom and Dad.

He heard about their mounting debts and backed-up loans. He laughed as George boasted about customers he double-billed and how Elaine had her doctor file false medical claims in return for half the insurance check. But the best tapes of all, and the ones that would extract the sweetest justice, involved Elaine and her lover, Carl, a real estate attorney who also happened to be her brother-in-law. They shared two passionate afternoons a week, finishing their lovemaking just before Jimmy got home from school. All of it, from moans of pleasure to rants against George, was picked up by Jimmy's spool of tape.

On the night he was sent away, packed valise in his left hand, Jimmy stood before George and Elaine.

"We're sorry it didn't work out," Elaine told him, already on her third gin and tonic.

Jimmy nodded, checking the inside pocket of his tattered hunting jacket, making sure the dozen tapes were safely tucked away.

"Gonna miss having you here," George said, holding a longneck bottle of beer.

"I have a gift for you," Jimmy told George. "To thank you for what you did for me."

"You kiddin'?" George rested a hand on the boy's shoulder. "You got me a gift?" He turned to Elaine, hitting her with a scornful gaze, then looked back at Jimmy with a smile.

Jimmy reached into his pocket and took out the set of tapes, neatly wrapped in flowered tissue paper and held together with a ribbon.

"Want me to open it now?" George asked, taking the package and holding it in both hands.

"Maybe you should wait," Jimmy said, looking over at Elaine. "Until you're by yourself."

"Thank you," George said, nodding his head. "I'll never forget you doin' this."

Jimmy buttoned his coat and picked up his valise. "I know," he said.

He walked past George and Elaine for the last time, toward the front door, a waiting car, and another set of parents.

. . .

THE WOMAN in the red pumps knocked on the door to Room 1211, silver bracelet jangling against her wrist.

"It's like she's knockin' on the front hood of the car," Calise said. "It's so damn clear."

"Narcotics have their guys in place?" Jimmy asked, head down, fingers adjusting a series of sound dials.

"They got four in the next suite," Fitz said. "And three more in a stairwell down the hall. She gets jammed up, should take less than a minute to get to her."

"Unless they're asleep," Calise said. "Which is always fuckin' possible with those dimrods."

The door handle snapped open and a man's voice warmly greeted the woman. He spoke in a thick Spanish accent.

"She's in," Jimmy said, sitting straight up and flipping a red switch on to full volume.

"How long you givin' her?" Fitz said.

"All she needs," Jimmy said. "These guys are top line. They're gonna play her first. Make sure she's legit before they close the deal."

"What about her?" Calise asked. "How good is she?"

"I'll let you know in about half an hour," Jimmy said, putting the earphones back over his head.

. . .

AT SEVENTEEN, Jimmy Ryan did a two-year tour of duty with another foster family of sorts, the U.S. Army. While stationed in Germany, the dark-haired, coal-eyed Ryan was allowed to fuel his passion by working as an electronic surveillance trainee. The army brass was impressed with his ability to handle their most sophisticated equipment and asked him to stay on for an additional four years, promising him tours of Mexico and the Middle East. Ryan, bored and unimpressed with the military regimen and tired of spending weeks without being able to cast his electric gaze on a beautiful woman, took a pass and signed out.

He was in New York City, taking a two-week seminar on wiretapping at the John Jay College for Criminal Justice, when he spotted a civil service flyer posted on a hall bulletin board. He ripped it down and signed up to take the New York Police Department exam. Six months later, working as a clerk for a small electronics firm on Queens Boulevard, Ryan got the letter that paved his way to becoming a cop.

He spent a dull sixteen months in uniform and then was transferred to the Manhattan Drug Task Force, working undercover, doing what he had prepared all his life to do—lay down wires, plant devices, and listen to the secrets of others. The assignment also freed Ryan from the uneasy potential for gunplay, the area of police work he cared for the least. He was a listener, content to skirt the perimeters of other people's worlds, but never eager to enter any one of them.

There were more than enough guys on the squad who had become cops looking to play cowboy, feeding off the nerve rush of the split-second shoot-out. Jimmy Ryan, rugged and catalogue handsome, with a head of thick curly hair and a John Garfield smile, liked living on the outside, doing his police work from a safe distance. He carried only the one gun, the .38 Special, and had never fired it in the line of duty. His danger zone rested in the mining of the wire and the spinning of the spool. Not in the spilling of blood.

. . .

WITH THE MONEY he'd saved from the army, plus his heavy overtime earnings as a cop, Ryan bought his first home, a single-family wood frame on Staten Island, six miles from lower Manhattan. It was the first place he could ever call his own, and he stocked it with books, electronic equipment, stereos, radios—all the toys of a childhood he was never allowed to have.

He worked constantly; his expertise was sought out by every undercover operation team leader throughout the five boroughs. Ryan linked his affinity for computers to his electrical magic show and turned the tedious routine of police surveillance into a state-of-the-art experience. He could tap on anyone, from mob bosses to drug rollers to politicians bagging payoffs. He could lay a wire anywhere, from a car bumper to the hull of a yacht, the sound always clear, the reams of information the tapes generated almost always enough to put away the voice. He was the best bug the NYPD ever had.

The respect the other cops showed him was comforting to Jimmy Ryan. It was his first taste of family.

The cops on the job called him Pins.

Ryan loved bowling and was captain of the Manhattan Task Force team. Every Thursday and Sunday night, he could be found pounding lanes at alleys throughout New York, competing against other squads from around the city. He was the police league's MVP three years running, holding a steady 201 average and walking off with an armful of trophies.

As much as he loved what he was doing, he had his life beyond the police force planned out.

He would open a small electronics store within walking distance of his home and think about doing six-month tours as a professional bowler. Neither job would be done for the money, but for the pleasure.

They were simple dreams.

Ryan had spent a childhood locked away in silent places where faces and names blended together. It taught him not to stray far from the cold glare of reality and to trust only what he found comfort in, what he knew would never betray him. The cold, sterile world of electronic surveillance was all Jimmy Ryan ever counted on. The shiny brown lanes of smoke-filled bowling alleys were his sanctuary.

And like his home and the police department, the rare places he could call his own.

• • •

THE MAN WITH the heavy Spanish accent sounded agitated.

"You were supposed to bring the cash yourself," he told the woman in the red pumps.

"It couldn't be worked out," the woman answered coolly, traces of a southern accent hidden by a dozen New York winters. "So I had a friend arrange it. He should be here in a few minutes."

"We didn't ask your friend to bring the money," the man said. "We asked *you*."

"I've known him all my life," she said, still cool. "I trust him. So can you."

"I trust no one," he said. "It is what's kept me alive."

"Sad way to live," the woman said.

"In my business, it's the only way to live," the man said. "Trust ends with a bullet."

• • •

"HE'S ON TO HER, Pins," Calise said. "You can hear it in his voice."

"It's too early to move," Fitz said. "We don't know if he's got the shit with him. We bust in and he don't have the drugs, he walks away clean. And we can't touch that fucker ever again."

"You can send Steve in earlier," Jimmy said. "Once he sees the cash, he'll be calm."

"I don't wanna spook the narcs," Calise said. "They always look to end these things with guns."

"Then, I'll go in," Jimmy said.

"*You?*" Fitz scoffed. "Since when do *you* go in?"

"You guys handle the equipment and I'll go up."

"As *what?*" Calise said, turning to face Jimmy.

"Hotel's got computerized phone lines," Jimmy said. "It'll take me about two minutes to find the basement and short-circuit the phones in the suite. Then I go up, knock on the door, and ask to check the phones."

"Dressed in a bowling jacket with your name on the chest and jeans," Fitz said. "What'd you do last night, take a bowling ball to the head?"

"We need the kilos and we need him," Jimmy said, resting the attaché case on the seat next to him and opening the car's rear door. "And we need time to get both. This buys it for us."

"What about the machine?" Calise said. "You're the only one knows how to run the fuckin' thing."

"It'll run itself," Jimmy said, looking at the two cops. "All you gotta do is listen. And be there if I need you."

"Have I ever let you down?" Calise asked.

"Yes," Jimmy said.

"When?"

"Every time I've needed you," Jimmy said, stepping out of the car.

"Maybe today I'll fuck up and you'll get lucky," Calise said.

"I'm counting on it," Jimmy Ryan breathed.

He slammed the car door behind him, zippered the front of his black bowling jacket, and raced across the street toward the entrance of the luxury high rise.

· · ·

PINS WAS ON HIS BACK, in the basement of the high rise, staring up at a thick cluster of phone lines. He held apart the dozen wires connecting the twelfth floor to the mainframe and followed their flow until he found the one leading to Room 1211. He gave the wire a slight tug and unclipped it from the board, killing the line. He checked his watch and clicked on his radio ban.

"How we doin'?" Pins said, holding down the red transmit button.

"Stevie's in the room," Calise said, the machine giving his words a grainy weight. "They cleaned him for weapons. Now they're scopin' out the bag of cash."

"How's our girl?" Pins asked.

"Like ice in winter," Calise said. "This broad don't sweat. Dealer tells her about some guy he smoked in Miami just 'cause he felt like it. Know what she tells him?"

"What?" Pins said, scooting out from under the wires and closing the phone system lid.

"She did the same to a guy in a motel in Ohio," Calise said. "For keepin' her waitin'. That jammed his balls back in his shorts."

"I'll be up there in less than five," Pins said, heading down a dark corridor toward the dim light of a basement elevator.

"Check in before you go in," Calise said. "I need you safe, sound, and alive."

"Didn't know you cared so much," Pins said, walking into the empty elevator and pressing the button for the twelfth floor.

"I don't," Calise said. "But I put a hundred on you in Sunday's bowling tournament."

Pins turned off the transmitter and slid it into a side pocket of his jacket. "Easy money," he whispered to himself.

. . .

THE EIGHTEEN LARGE PACKETS of cocaine were piled in two neat rows on top of a glass coffee table. The woman in red sat on a couch, lit cigarette in her right hand, bemused look on her face, watching the man with the accent take the bag from the undercover cop to her right. She watched the man's manicured fingers slowly unzip the black duffel and saw his brown eyes gleam when he flipped it over, emptying a dozen thick pads of cash over the kilos.

"I'm gonna go take a piss," the undercover, Steve Rinaldi, said. "While you and your boys busy yourselves countin' out the cash."

"We don't need to count it," the man said, his eyes on the woman, his voice soft. "We trust you."

"I still gotta piss," Rinaldi said. "Trust me on *that*."

There were three other men in the room.

Two sat at the bar, elbows stretched out, facing the group around the coffee table. The third man stood with his back to the bedroom door, hands hidden behind the folds of a white silk jacket, heavy lids covering albino blues. The man with the accent turned to him, a smile Krazy-glued to his face, and nodded.

The albino whipped his right arm free, a .44 S&W Special in his hand, silencer screwed tight over the smoke end. He fired off three quick rounds, each finding flesh. The first hit Rinaldi in the neck, spraying blood across the blue fabric of the three-cushion couch. The second hit his right shoulder and shattered bone. The third bullet killed him, entering at the temple and lodging at the base of his skull. The force of the bullets jolted Rinaldi's body forward, his arms dangling at his sides, his face smearing blood and bone over the cocaine packets.

The woman in the red pumps finally lost her cool demeanor, the color fading from her tanned face, eyelids twitching, her expensive suit splotched with the undercover's blood. She sat straight up on the couch, cigarette still in her hand, staring down at the body next to her, the man's jeans soiled through with urine and excrement, the smell reaching down into her throat.

"He really did have to go to the bathroom," the man with the accent said. "I thought he was only joking."

"You kill everybody you do business with?" the woman asked, taking several deep breaths, fighting to regain any semblance of composure.

"Only the ones with badges," the man said.

"You think my friend was a cop?" she said, trying to sound credible.

"No," the man said, moving closer to her. "I *know* he was a cop. What I don't know is, who are you?"

The woman crushed her cigarette out in an ashtray and stood, ignoring the blood droppings on her hands and clothes, staring straight at the man with the accent.

"I was here to make a deal," she said, her voice regaining strength. "It looks to me like that's not going to happen."

"We made a deal," the man said, pointing to the coffee table next to his leg. "We have the money. And you have your drugs. I will even have Ramon pack it for you."

The beefier of the two men at the bar walked over to the table, lifted the undercover by the hair, and tossed his body to the ground. He picked up the black duffel and started to lay in the cocaine packets.

"Before Ramon finishes, there is something I would like you to do for me," the man said. "A small favor."

"Do I have a choice?" the woman asked.

"No," the man said.

"Then just tell me what it is," she sighed.

"Take off your clothes," the man with the accent said.

. . .

PINS WAS at the door, poised to knock.

Calise and Fitz were in the elevator, out of the van, and into the high rise as soon as they heard the undercover take the hit. The narcs in the stairwell held their position, lead man with one hand gripped around the doorknob. The three detectives in the suite next door snapped on their vests and clicked their .44 semiautomatics into readiness.

The albino opened the door on the second knock.

"Who the fuck are you?" he said, staring down at the much shorter Pins.

"Telephone repair," Pins said, catching a glimpse of the undercover's body behind the albino's left shoulder. "Your lines are down."

"We didn't call nobody," the albino said, large hand on the edge of the door, ready to slam it shut. "Go play with somebody else's phones."

Pins had his gun in the albino's chest before he had a chance to breathe. "You don't understand," Pins said, his gun hand visibly shaking. "I take my job very seriously. Now, let me in."

The albino took two steps back, hands at his sides, palms out. "Two phones. Bedroom and out here."

"There's three, putz," Pins said, walking into the suite, looking at the dead undercover and the woman in the red pumps, stripped down to her bra. "You forgot about the one in the bathroom."

"You walk in here, you don't walk out," the albino said. "I make sure of that."

"Hey, fixing phones is a risky business," Pins said, backing the albino against a wall. "But the benefits can't be beat."

Ramon tossed the duffel bag back on top of the coffee table and turned to the man with the accent for a signal. The man put an arm around the woman in the red pumps and held her close to his side, rubbing against the lines of sweat running down her back. The albino slid an open blade down the side of his sleeve and cupped it in his palm.

They held position as the cops flowed into the suite.

Calise and Fitz were in the doorway, short of breath and guns drawn. The three narcs from the stairwell were in vests and shotguns, crouched down behind them. The four detectives from the adjacent suite had poured out and were braced two apiece on both sides of the hall.

"Looks like a lot of people want to use your phone," Pins said, turning his head slightly toward the cops covering the room.

The albino saw the opening and took it.

He wrapped his fingers around the knife handle and swung it. The blade slashed open the sleeve of Jimmy's bowling jacket, drawing blood and knocking him to the ground.

Calise turned into the room, stepped over Jimmy, and fired four .38-caliber rounds deep into the albino's chest. The force slammed him against the wall, knife rattling to the floor. He slid down the side of the pink stucco wall, staining it with streaks of red.

The second dead man in the room.

"I hope that's not your bowling arm," Calise said to Pins, looking down at him between his legs.

Then before Pins could say "You're all heart," the bullet came out of Ramon's .41 Remington Magnum and traveled into Calise's brain at a speed of 1,300 feet per second. Calise fell into a heap, the smile on his face frozen in death, crashing down on top of Ryan.

Ryan felt the breath ease out of Calise's body, his friend's blood pouring down the side of his face and onto his bowling jacket. Pins looked beyond Calise and over at the narcs by the door, hearing them curse and then empty their chambers into Ramon's white suit. He lifted his head and watched the dealer flip across the room, knocking over a chair and landing on top of a dinette table near the bar.

The man with the accent held his place next to the woman in the red pumps, his right arm still wrapped around her waist, his left hand holding a .32 short Colt to her head. The narcs and the detectives pointed guns and rifles at him.

"I walk out with her," the man said. "Or I die with her."

The man with the accent tightened his grip around the handle of the gun and swallowed hard. The cops around him held their aim. Pins stayed still, blood still pouring down on him from Calise's wound.

Pins looked over at the woman in the red pumps. She ran a hand slowly up her leg, lifting the skirt until it showed the top of her stockings. Tucked inside the sheer frill was a white-barreled .22 Remington Jet. The man with the accent was sweating. Wavering. He jiggled the gun nervously, moving it from the woman's head to flash it menacingly at the cops lined up before him, then back to the woman. When he flashed his gun around the room a second time, the woman moved. She pulled out her gun, put it to the man's head, and fired off two rounds.

He fell to her feet, dead.

The woman tossed the gun to the floor, bent down, picked up her jacket and blouse, and walked out the open door, well aware of her fellow cops' stares.

Pins didn't move from the carpeted floor, now darkened by his friend's blood. He put his arms around the dead cop, still too afraid to let him go, waiting for the hard faces with the body bags to come take him away.

. . .

FOR PINS there were few friends. Women were there when he wanted them, which was not often and never for long. He didn't sleep much and spent free nights roaming bowling alleys, looking for a fast game for quick cash, quietly excelling in a sport meant to be played alone. He had the house and the car to call his own. And he had the wires.

With his bugs in place, Pins could enter any number of private worlds and listen to the planned deceits of others, free from their treachery, exempt from the harm they sought to cause. It was the center of the safe world he had built from the rubble of youth.

He should have known it was not meant to last.

. . .

THE BUILDING WAS on the Upper West Side, in the high seventies, prewar, seven stories high, with an Otis elevator creaking up and down. Surveillance photos taken by an undercover unit scouting the area led them to believe that a three-bedroom unit on the sixth floor was being used to launder drug dollars. The apartment was always empty between nine A.M. and noon every day; the young couple renting it for $3,000 a month worked out at the Jack Lalanne on Broadway during that time. The undercovers needed Pins to drop a bug near the bed and a video camera somewhere close to the bureau.

It was less than an hour's work.

Pins pressed the two dozen black buzzers dotting the entry wall, waiting for some frazzled tenant to ring him in.

He moved to the elevator, watched the thick black door slowly close, and leaned on the button that had the number six on it. Pins was dressed in jeans and a thick blue baseball jacket, topped by a Yankee cap. In his left hand he held a thin leather briefcase. He popped two slices of red hot cinnamon gum in his mouth and got out of the elevator when it stopped at the sixth floor. He pulled a folded sheet from his back pocket to double-check the apartment number. He found it scrawled in black ink across the top of the wire sheet, 6F, and moved on down the hall.

It took less than thirty seconds for Pins to pick the lock and enter the apartment.

He moved down a long corridor, a large living room and two bedrooms to his left, a bathroom facing straight ahead. There was little in the way of furniture. A scrawny black cat hissed at him from behind a radiator pipe.

At the end of the corridor Pins turned right and walked into the master bedroom. The walls were painted dark blue, photographers' flashlights stood in each corner, and a Sony twenty-five-inch color TV rested on the bureau. In the middle: a king-size four-poster.

Pins tossed his case on the bed, zipped it open, and started to work. He laid a bug inside the thin pole of one of the lights, running it from the bottom up, past the wires and into the main fuse connector.

He grabbed a Minicam out of the briefcase and walked to the back of the television, planning to rest it alongside the main tube.

It was then he heard the footsteps coming down the hall.

They were heavy, a man's step rather than a woman's, wooden slats creaking with each imprint. Pins rested the back of the TV on the floor and moved toward the bed, looking for the radio that would link him with backup.

He had his back to the door.

A young man, thin brown hair disheveled, vacant look in his eyes, stood at the edge of the bedroom entrance. His entire body shook with anger.

"I knew I'd find you here," he said.

Pins turned around, radio in his hand, and faced the man.

"You live here?" Pins asked.

"I'm Sheila's husband," the man said. "And you're standing in my bedroom."

"I don't know anybody named Sheila," Pins said, pressing down on the black transmitter button.

"You *should* know her," the man said. "You've been fucking her for almost a year now."

"There's a mistake here," Pins said, his voice steady. He stayed focused on the man's eyes, looking to talk his way out of this strange situation.

"I love her," the man said. "Can you understand that, you bastard? I love her."

"Listen to me," Pins said quietly. "I'm a cop. I'm gonna take out my shield and show you. Okay?"

The man lifted his right arm and pointed it straight at Pins. There was a .22 caliber clutched in his hand.

"You're not gonna show me anything," the man said, clicking back the trigger. "And you're not gonna see Sheila ever again."

"You don't know what you're doin'." Pins was surprised at how level his voice was. He wasn't even yelling. "I'm not the guy. I'm a cop."

One look at the man and Pins knew he had moved beyond reason to reside in madness.

In a lifetime constructed around caution, Jimmy Ryan had made a mistake. He had misread the scrawled handwriting on the wire sheet. He had walked through the wrong door, 6F instead of 6E, and there he stood, inches from a jealous husband's rage, accused of having an affair with a woman he had never met.

The first bullet hit Pins in the right shoulder. The second shattered bone above the right elbow. The final two hit him in the chest and sent him to the ground, pain rushing through his body like a river.

The young man hovered over him, two more shells left in the chamber.

"You'll never see her again," he said to Jimmy Ryan.

"It's sure startin' to look that way," Pins said.

He heard the undercovers before he saw them, guns drawn, ready to fire. He looked up at the young man and watched him drop the gun back down to his side. He saw two undercovers rush over, yank the man's arms back, cuff him, and pull him away. Through it all, the man kept his eyes on Pins, a small smirk etched across his face.

A third undercover, Gennaro, ran over, leaned down, and lifted Pins's head, holding it in the crook of his right arm.

"We got an ambulance comin'," Gennaro told him.

"Think I need it?" Pins wanted to know, looking down at the blood flowing out of his bowling arm.

"Who's the shooter?" Gennaro asked.

"Just a kid," Pins said.

Pins looked away from Gennaro. He turned to the photo lamp in the corner. He tried to take a deep breath and smiled.

The small bugging device he planted in the neck of the lamp had picked up everything he said and did during his final moments as a cop.

It was the last bug Jimmy Ryan would plant as a member of the New York City Police Department.

6

Rev. Jim

BOBBY SCARPONI WAS a drug addict and an alcoholic.

He was twelve when he had his first taste of scotch; two weeks later he lit his first joint. Besides his ability to consume large quantities of any illegal substance, Scarponi was known for his chronic truancy and violent streak. He stole bikes and toys from his South Jamaica neighbors to help feed his expensive habits. His parents couldn't exert any control over the boy, finding it easier to ignore, as much as they could, the whispers that followed their troubled son.

Bobby never dealt drugs, but was a steady customer for a number of local dealers. If he got in too deep financially and couldn't make the payoff from what he could steal, he could bank on a discreet parental bailout. As a result, he was stripping the Scarponis of their security, slapping away at their pride, and digging into their future, which for them embodied nothing more ambitious than a two-bedroom Laguna Beach condo built around Albert Scarponi's construction foreman's pension.

Despite his problems and frequent run-ins with the police, Bobby Scarponi was a well-liked kid. In the pattern of the users and abusers he associated with, Scarponi learned early in his addiction to be a performer, to adjust his demeanor, hide the tracks, clear the eyes, and pretend to be normal. He had an easy way, blending natural charm with rugged features that managed to withstand the ravages of the drugs he ingested.

By the time he reached sixteen, Bobby had been in and out of four rehab clinics and undergone three years of ineffective counseling. He had worked his way up the pharmaceutical ladder from pot to glue to crystal meth to acid to cocaine. Then, on a cloudy April afternoon in 1966, Bobby put a thin needle to a fat vein and felt the hot rush of heroin for the first time.

He was now traveling on a narrow strip of road that often led its passengers to a head-on with death.

Bobby Scarponi was no exception.

. . .

Bobby sat next to his mother, Beatrice, on a park bench across from the empty playground. It was cold and late, deep into a Monday night. His mother turned up the collar of her brown parka against the chill wind, shoved her hands deep inside the front pockets, and stared down at the withered grass by her feet. She was a short woman, slender, with a thick head of prematurely graying hair and sorrowful dark eyes. She spoke with a slight trace of an accent, remnants of her years growing up in the Italian seaside village of Panza.

"I never lied to your father, Roberto," she said. "Tonight was the first time."

"Relax, Mom," Bobby said. "It's gonna be over soon. We pay them the money and then we go home."

"It's never over, *figlio*," Beatrice said. "As long as you buy what they sell."

"Mom, please," Bobby said, zipping up his green army jacket. "No lectures, okay? It's bad enough we gotta sit in the cold and pay these dirtbags off."

"You took your father's heart," Beatrice said, looking at her son, a hand on his right leg, which was jiggling nervously from the cold and the need for a fix. "You kill him a little bit each day. Every time you put that stuff inside your arms."

"It's my life, Mom," Bobby said, throwing a glance up and down the street, concern etched on his face.

"It's *our* life," Beatrice said. "And it's a wrong life right now."

"I'm gonna quit," Bobby said, turning to look at his mother, seeing the tears welling in her eyes. "I promise you. I don't like this any more than you do."

"You know, I was sixteen when I first met your father," she said. "I looked and I fell in love. I love him even more now. And I can't let him die and leave behind a junkie for a son. I can't live with that shame."

"What about me?" Bobby asked, sadness wrapped around the question. "You still love me?"

"I'm here, no?" Beatrice said. "To give strangers money your father works in a hole to earn."

"I'll pay you back," Bobby said. "I swear it."

"Don't pay me with money," Beatrice said.

"What, then?"

"Walk away from this life for good," she said. "From the drugs and these bums who sell them to you."

"I said I was gonna quit," Bobby said. "This'll be my last payoff."

"If you can't do that," Beatrice said, cupping his chin, "then take enough to kill yourself."

"You want me to die?" Bobby said slowly. "That's what you're tellin' me you want?"

"You're dead now, Roberto," Beatrice said. "You walk and talk, eat and drink, but inside you're dead. So, make it simple. For everybody. Stop what you're doing or let me have a grave to pray over."

The dealer came up out of the shadows to stand by Bobby's left, a long, dark raincoat buttoned to his neck. The thin brim of a gray fedora shielded his eyes and hid his face; his hands were covered by thick black gloves. He was in his mid-twenties, long blond hair rubber-banded into a ponytail.

"Hey, Ray," Bobby said in a startled tone, standing when he saw the dealer. "I didn't hear you coming."

"You got my money?" Ray asked, his tired voice sprinkled with venom.

"This is my mom," Bobby said, pointing down toward Beatrice, who stayed in her seat, staring at the dealer with contempt.

"I don't give a fuck who she is," Ray said. "You got my money?"

"Most of it," Bobby said, looking over Ray's shoulders, spotting the car waiting by a fire hydrant, smoke filtering out of the exhaust.

"I didn't ask for *most* of it," Ray said. "I want *all* of it. *Now.*"

"I brought five hundred," Beatrice said to the dealer in the strongest voice she could muster. "It is all we have left."

"You're a thousand short," Ray said.

"I'll have the rest in about a week," Bobby told him.

"How you gonna do that, High School?" Ray said. "Mama already gave you everything she's got, and she's all you know that's got money."

"It's my problem," Bobby said. "I'll figure it out."

Ray jumped off his stance and pounced on Bobby. His two gloved hands grabbed hold of the front of the zippered army jacket, lifting Bobby several inches off his feet.

"It ain't just *your* problem," Ray said. "It's *my* problem now. And I gotta solve it."

He let Bobby go, pushing him back toward his mother, who sat rigid in fear, her hands locked across her face. Ray walked past the boy, stopping in front of Beatrice. He crouched down, his eyes meeting hers, two hands on her knees, and smiled.

"You tellin' the truth?" he asked her. "Five hundred's all you got left?"

Beatrice nodded, too frightened to speak.

Ray took a hand off her knee and put it in his pocket. He leaned closer to Beatrice as the hand came out holding a black Indian-point switchblade. He pressed on a thin button at the bottom edge of the handle, releasing a seven-inch knife, sharp enough to cut through wood.

"I want all my money, Bobby," Ray said, his eyes still on Beatrice, his face close enough for her to smell his drink-stained breath. "So I'm gonna ask you again. You got it for me?"

"Give me one more day." Bobby moved two steps closer, trying not to sound as panicked as he felt. "I'll get you the rest tomorrow. I swear it."

"When tomorrow?" Ray ran the edge of the blade up the front of Beatrice's coat.

"I'll meet you here," Bobby said. "Same time."

"You think your little junkie's tellin' me the truth?" Ray asked Beatrice.

"My son is a junkie," Beatrice said, putting a hand on Ray's raincoat, bunching a small corner into a ball. "But you are much worse. You live off junkies. And that makes you nothing but an animal."

"This is between us, Ray," Bobby said. "Keep her out of this. Please."

"You're the one that brought her," Ray said.

"Take your blood money." Beatrice pulled out the envelope with the five hundred dollars from her coat pocket, then shoved it against Ray's chest. "And go."

Ray took the envelope with his free hand, stood up, put it in his pocket, and turned to look at Bobby.

"Forget the rest of the money," Ray told him. "After tonight we're even, you and me. You want any fresh shit, you hustle it someplace else. Anyplace but me. Deal?"

"Deal," Bobby said, nodding his head. "Thanks, Ray. I appreciate it."

Ray smiled at Bobby, turned back to Beatrice, grabbed her hair, and pulled it back with a hard snap, waiting until he saw her neckline under the glimmer of the overhead light.

He brought the blade down next to Beatrice's throat, his eyes gleaming, a relaxed smile on his face. He ran the blade against her neck, one long cut from the edge of the left ear across to the bottom of her right jaw. He watched the blood gush out in thick rolls and held on to her hair until he saw the life float from her body. He watched Beatrice slump down the side of the park bench.

Ray Monte cleaned the sides of the knife against his victim's coat, snapped it closed, and walked off into the night.

"My pleasure," Ray said to Bobby, leaving the young boy with his dying mother.

Bobby cradled Beatrice in his arms, letting her blood flow over him. He didn't cry, didn't speak, just held her close, head against her heart, rocking slowly back and forth. He hadn't touched her in years and couldn't remember the last time he told her he loved her. And yet he knew she would forgive him anything, even her own death.

He put his head down against the side of hers, his lips close to her ears and whispered the words to *"Partira,"* the Italian ballad she had sung him to sleep with when he was a little boy.

They stayed that way until the dawn broke and the police arrived.

. . .

Bobby Scarponi buried his drug habit alongside his mother. He stayed clear of the streets and worked hard in school. He fought off the nighttime urges when he hungered for a needle bubbling with heroin, for an escape from the life around him.

He lived with his father in a silent house. Albert Scarponi said good-bye to the only woman he ever loved, then turned his back on his only child. They shared a home but never spoke, the older man living quietly with his grief and anger, unable to forgive Bobby for leading his mother into the path of a dealer's knife. Albert's hatred was further fueled by his son's refusal to identify his mother's killer.

Ray Monte had walked free.

"Don't get any ideas about doing this on your own, Bobby," one of the detectives told him. "He'll kill you just like he did your mom."

"The dealer didn't kill my wife," Albert said, looking up at the detective. "He only held the knife. She was brought there by her son. Her own blood."

"You get a change of heart," the other detective told Bobby, placing a card in the napkin holder in the center of the table, "give us a call. Day or night."

The two detectives left through the back door of the wood-shingled house, leaving Albert and Bobby Scarponi behind, alone in their two separate worlds.

. . .

FROM THEN ON, Bobby Scarponi kept track of Ray Monte.

He would see him occasionally walking the streets of his Queens neighborhood, drinking coffee and pushing drugs, never far from a new car with a running engine. Bobby finished a two-year army tour while Ray sat out the calendar in a Comstock cell, doing three to five on an assault charge. They were discharged two weeks apart.

Ray Monte returned to the streets, ready to move back into the prime arena of the drug trade. He teamed up with an Irish crew working out of Forest Hills and set up shop on 168th Street in Jamaica, handling heroin and cocaine for the posses wresting control of the drug action from the old-time Italians. He took a cut from all the pot and illegal prescription sales generated in the area, and contracted out members of his outfit for hits on anyone who objected.

And he never carried a gun. Only a knife.

. . .

BOBBY SCARPONI SAT across the desk from a detective with a long scar across his face, its edges brushing the lid of his right eye. The detective lit a cigarette and sat back in a creaky wooden swivel chair.

"Why you telling me all this now?" the detective, Sal Albano, asked. "Why didn't you say anything before?"

"I wanted to see if I could make it through the Academy," Bobby said. "If I didn't, nobody needed to know."

"How long've you been off the shit?"

"Eight years this March," Bobby said. "Shot three speedballs on my sixteenth birthday. Two nights later, my mom got killed."

"You ain't the first cop that ever took a hit on the hard stuff," Albano said. "Shit, these days, I think half the fuckin' guys in uniform are buzzed out of their skulls."

"So I don't get booted?" Bobby asked.

"You're the best pure cop I ever trained," Albano said, "and I've been doing this long enough to know good when I see it. You stay clean, you've got no beef with me."

"I asked to be put in a precinct in my old neighborhood," Bobby said, sitting back in his chair, muscular frame relaxed, the once-dead eyes now clear and lucid. "Any chance of that?"

"I'll make some calls," Albano said. "Shouldn't be a problem. But don't get used to it. Guy like you ain't gonna be in uniform long. An old friend of mine in Brooklyn needs a good young cop to work decoy. Told him about you. Expect a call in about six months."

"I won't need that long to do what I have to do," Bobby said, standing and reaching over to shake Albano's hand.

"Which is what?" Albano asked.

"Look up an old friend," Bobby Scarponi of the New York City Police Department said.

. . .

THE HEAVY APRIL RAIN pounded the squad car as it circled the empty South Jamaica streets, fog lights on, wipers slapping aside thick streams of water. Bobby Scarponi kicked up the sound on the police radio and turned the window defogger knob down. He was starting his fourth month as a street cop and had already made a dent in cleaning up his old neighborhood. He had nailed four mid-level drug dealers and had taken down an armed felon hiding in a public school science lab. He reintroduced himself to the local merchants, many of whom remembered him as the drug-crazed teen who shoplifted from their stores. Now he was there to protect them.

The street kids, aware of Scarponi's past, called him Rev. Jim, after the brain-frazzled character portrayed on the hit television series *Taxi*. The name made its way into the halls of Bobby's precinct and stuck. Scarponi didn't mind. It helped give him a street ID, a name they would remember, a key first step toward being a cop they would turn to for help.

The passing years had failed to soften the frost between Bobby and his father. They still shared a roof, but nothing more. Not even the first sight of Bobby in a policeman's uniform could shake loose his father's hate.

Bobby Scarponi understood.

He had resigned himself to his culpability in his mother's death, fighting daily to control the emotions boiling beneath his calm exterior. He knew those emotions would eventually need to be set free to exact their toll. Only then, perhaps, could he work toward building a peace with the man whose house he occupied but whose love he long ago lost.

Bobby Scarponi also knew that when the day came for him to open that emotional cage, the beast it unleashed would be aimed at Ray Monte.

. . .

BOBBY PULLED THE SQUAD CAR directly behind the parked Mercedes and shoved the gear stick into park, letting the motor idle. He put on a pair of thin black gloves and grabbed a brown nightstick, twisting the cord around his knuckles.

There were four men around the Mercedes, all dressed in long gray coats and brown fedoras, brims folded down to catch the rain. They separated when they saw Bobby approach, smiles on their faces but menace in their eyes.

Ray Monte stood in the middle, right leg up against a rear hubcap, thin cigar in his mouth.

"You know the world's a fucked-up place," Ray said, "when they go and give a junkie a gun and a badge."

Bobby walked closer, taking small steps, measuring the men, knowing they were all armed and backed up by a small crew drinking in the dimly lit bar behind him.

"Rain like this must cut into business," Bobby said, his eyes on Ray.

"A junkie ain't no weatherman," Ray said. "All he cares about is the fix. Shouldn't have to be tellin' you that."

"I remember," Bobby said.

Bobby and Ray had not talked in the years since the murder, but they were keenly aware of each other's activities. Bobby watched as Ray grew his drug business, earning thousands a day as he fed the increasing neighborhood demand for cocaine and heroin. For his part, Ray Monte knew enough about Bobby Scarponi to understand he was not the type to let a blood murder sit. He watched him clean up his life, kick his habit, and then wait for his opportunity, patience his only partner.

The day Bobby Scarponi pinned on a policeman's badge, Ray Monte knew their moment was close enough to touch.

"You here to pick up the payoffs?" the chubby man to Ray's left asked, laughing through the question. "They always send the new guys for the pickups. Breaks them in good that way."

"You got it goin' pretty good, Ray," Bobby said. "I figure six blocks in the one-sixties, all kickin' in to you."

"I eat," Ray said, shrugging his shoulders, cigar smoke filtering up past the lid of his fedora.

"What happens if you go down?" Bobby asked. "Who moves in on your take?"

"That's somethin' I wouldn't know or care about. Seein' as I ain't goin' any fuckin' place."

"I figure Uncle Angie." Water dripped down from the peak of Bobby's policeman's hat. "He'll give your corners to one of the Jamaican gangs. Walk away from it with a bigger cut than he's getting from you."

"By the time that happens, I'll have enough money to buy Florida," Ray said, taking the cigar from his mouth and tossing it over his shoulder into a puddle. "And you'll still be walkin' in the rain, bustin' joint-rollers."

"You still carry that blade?" Bobby asked, moving in closer to Ray, watching the three men by his side stiffen.

"Always," Ray said. "You wanna see it?"

"I saw it once," Bobby said. "It's enough to hold me."

"When your mother died, she didn't make a sound," Ray said. "She just went. Think you'll go the same?"

"You did her alone," Bobby said. "Didn't need anybody else. Now you got three. Maybe all that money makes you scared."

Ray Monte smiled and looked over at his men. "Go dry off inside and get a drink," he told them. "Pour me one too. I won't be long."

Bobby and Ray stared at one another, waiting as the three men brushed past, heading for the dark warmth of an old bar.

"You gonna draw down on me, Officer Bob?" Ray asked. "I don't have a gun."

"She wasn't carrying anything," Bobby said, the rain coming down in heavier doses.

"She had her son to protect her." Ray's voice was cold, heavy with hate. "Except he didn't do nothin' but watch her bleed."

"I've watched her die every day since then," Bobby said, the blade of a knife slipping down the side of his police jacket. "And every night."

Ray Monte pulled the switchblade from his pants pocket and snapped it open, its familiar sound echoing like a drum, as it had so often down through the years. All Bobby heard was his laugh.

The knife went in chest deep, past muscle and bone, through vein and artery. Two hands reached for it, holding it tight, burying it deeper into flesh. The two men stared at each other, the rain around them mixing with the thick flow of blood, one set of eyes welled with sadness and tears, the other losing their grasp on life. The two leaned against the rear door of the Mercedes, wet bodies clinging together, low gurgles coming from the throat of the dying man.

"You didn't make any noise either," Bobby Scarponi said to Ray Monte, letting his body go, watching it slide down the side of the Mercedes and crumple to the curb, head against a Firestone all-weather tire.

Bobby walked to his squad car, got in, put it in gear, and drove off, heading back to the station house.

His tour of duty done.

· · ·

THREE MONTHS AFTER Ray Monte's death, Bobby Scarponi was transferred out of uniform and assigned to the Brooklyn Decoy Unit. At twenty-five, he was the youngest member of a team that roamed the borough posing as potential criminal targets. They were a traveling troupe of actors whose successful performance ended with an attempted mugging and an arrest. Bobby, who loved acting, took to the detail as easily as he once took to drugs. More important, he cherished the risk involved, the chance of exposure, of being taken down by desperate hands.

For the cop they called Rev. Jim, it was just another way to get high.

In no time, he mastered the disguises of the job—from the drunken Wall Street executive asleep at a subway stop to the tattered rummy sleeping one off on a heat grate to the unruly drug addict hustling street corners for throwaway change. He was the best performer on the street, pushing his talents to dangerous limits as he lulled his suspects into action.

It was as a member of the Decoy Unit that Bobby Scarponi found himself leaning against a railing in Brooklyn Heights, looking out across the still river at the diamond glimmer of the Manhattan night. His hair was caked, clothes torn and soiled, black plastic garbage bags wrapped around his feet. He took a fast swig from an iced-tea-filled pint of Four Roses and turned to look at the two young girls on the park bench behind him, both drinking from cups of hot chocolate. The elder of the two, running about sixteen, held a cigarette between the fingers of a gloved hand. They giggled as they talked.

He moved a few steps down, dragging his feet, one hand on the rail, eyes catching a glimpse of his target, hidden behind a tree, a quick jump from the girls on the bench.

"We got company," Bobby Scarponi said into the top button of his torn coat. A wire transmitter was attached to a band clipped to his waist. "About five feet from the marks."

The two backups were in a black Plymouth hidden behind a Parks Department shack a quarter of a mile away, guns on their laps, empty coffee containers strewn about their feet.

"You sure it's him?" the one behind the wheel, T. J. Turner, asked. "Might just be a bum takin' a piss."

"Bums piss *in* their pants," Bobby whispered into his coat. "It's part of what makes them bums."

"You would know, Rev. Jim," Tommy Mackens said from the passenger seat. "Never met a decoy liked to wear pissed-in clothes as much as you."

"It's not what you wear," Rev. Jim said, "but how you wear it."

"Be careful with this guy," T.J. told him. "He's into the pain more than the takeoff."

"He found two soft ones tonight," Rev. Jim said. "Not gonna get much of a fight out of these kids."

"Hates bums too," Tommy said, laughing. "Might come beat the shit out of you."

"I'll be ready," Bobby Scarponi said.

He moved away from the railing, staggering his walk, singing "Bye Bye Blackbird" in a soft voice marked by a drunken tilt. He kept his eyes away from the girls, ignoring their chatter, his ears tuned only to the rustle of leaves and the rush of feet.

He was twenty yards from the two girls when the man behind the tree made his move, rushing out to stand in front of the girls, their voices silenced by the sight of a gun. He was tall and solid, a wall of muscle packed under a black set of sweats. He had a ski mask over his face and gloves to hide his fingerprints.

"Don't hurt us," one of the girls begged. Her thin face was hidden by thick curls of brown hair.

"Kind of hurt I got, you might like," the man answered, his voice hard and low. "You both stand up slow and get behind that tree."

The girls were shaking too hard to move, tears running down their faces, gloved hands gripping the sides of the bench. The man stepped closer and stroked the barrel of the gun against the side of one girl's temple, nudging the blond hair tucked beneath the flap of her pink wool hat. She didn't turn her face.

"I can put it inside any kind of trim," the man said with a small boy's giggle. "Dead or alive, don't mean shit. Now, you two gonna walk or be dragged?"

" 'Here I go singing low, Bye bye blackbird.' Everybody!" Bobby was up behind them now, his voice loud, the pint of Four Roses held high, a big smile on his face. "C'mon, girls, let's hear it. You, with the mask, I *know* you can do it."

The man turned to Bobby, gun in hand, eyes lit with anger.

"Take your shit down the road, bum," he said. "Before I put you to sleep for good."

"I look like a bum to you?" Bobby said, dragging his garbage bag–covered feet closer. "You blind? I'm a *singer*, man. And you're steppin' on my stage."

The man raised the .38 Special, placing it inches from Bobby's chest, and tightened his grip around the trigger.

"Hear me out, *singer*," the man said. "I kill you and there ain't nobody out there gonna give a fuck."

"I tell jokes too." Bobby planted his feet, his right hand clutching the Four Roses pint. "Make the girls smile nice and pretty."

"Last chance," the man said, pressing the gun against Bobby's cheek.

"I'll take it," Bobby said.

He slapped the gun away with his left hand and smashed the pint of Four Roses on the side of the man's head. As the glass broke against bone, the ski mask was drenched in iced tea.

But the blow only dazed the larger man.

As he hurled his body on top of Bobby, both falling to the ground, he landed two solid punches to Bobby's temple and one to his lip.

"Gonna kill you, bum," the man said, wrapping a large gloved hand around Bobby's throat and pressing down hard. "Gonna fuckin' kill you."

"I keep tellin' you," Bobby managed to say, his words garbled. "I ain't no bum."

The two girls sat frozen in place, staring at the struggle in front of them. T.J. and Tommy started the Plymouth and roared out from behind the park station, rear tires kicking up dust and leaves, the red cherry on top of the unmarked car twirling.

Bobby turned his head slightly to the right and spotted the .38 Special on the ground, inches from his hand. His legs were wrapped tight around the man's waist. Bobby landed two quick punches to the man's face, both with little effect. He was having trouble breathing, lungs searing with pain, his throat clutching. The glare of T.J.'s headlights illuminated the man's large frame. His weight sat like a boulder on Bobby's chest.

Bobby closed his eyes, took a short breath through his nose, and stretched the fingers of his right hand, tearing the back of his coat as it scraped across the black concrete. But he reached the .38.

T.J. and Tommy were out of the Plymouth, their guns drawn.

"Let him go," T.J. said in a relaxed voice. "Don't even think."

"You can't stop me," the man said, eyes glowing as he pressed down tighter on Bobby's throat.

"I can," Bobby said in a raspy whisper.

He had the gun barrel inside the man's mouth.

The man looked at Bobby, whose gaze was focused and determined.

It was the look Ray Monte had seen before he died.

It was the look of a man ready to kill.

The man slowly released his grip on Bobby's throat, holding his hands out to his sides. T.J. and Tommy came up next to him, cocked guns aimed at his head. Tommy snapped a cuff around one of the man's thick wrists and clamped it shut. He swung the arm down to the man's back, took the other hand, and locked it in cuffs.

"Okay, Rev.," T.J. said, still holding the gun on the man. "Take the jammer outta his mouth."

"This piece of shit," Bobby said between coughs, gun rocking in and out against the man's teeth. "You see what he did to me?"

"He almost killed you," Tommy said in a soothing tone. "But he didn't. Now let him go so we can drop him off at the station, take the girls' statements, and then go grab us a bite."

"And if there's time," T.J. said, a firm grip on the back of the cuffed man's jacket, "we'll come back here and see if we can find somebody else who might wanna kill you."

"Forget killing me," Bobby said, his voice cracking with anger. "The fucking bastard pissed all over me!"

. . .

BOBBY SAT on the living room couch, nursing a Dr Pepper, TV tuned to a late fall Giants-Eagles football game, the sound muted. Ronnie Earl and the Broadcasters were playing on the corner stereo, halfway through a rendition of "Drown in My Own Tears." Outside, heavy snow blanketed the streets.

Albert Scarponi walked into the room and sat on the far end of the couch, a large tumbler of red wine mixed with water and ice in his right hand. He was wearing a white sweatshirt and black jeans, his feet covered by fur-lined moccasins. He had a three-day gray stubble across his face, and his left hand was slightly swollen, a winter bout with rheumatism starting early.

They sat, as they usually did, in silence, absorbed by the game and the music.

Albert looked away from the screen and stared at his son, as if noticing him for the first time.

"Tomorrow's the memorial," Albert said, watching Harry Carson wrap an arm around the Eagles quarterback. "If you want, we can go together. No sense us taking two cars. Not in this weather."

The sound of his father's voice startled Bobby. He had grown comfortable with the wall of silence that surrounded them, not quite sure how to react to the sudden cracks conversation brought.

"You sure?" Bobby asked, lifting his legs from the coffee table, eyes on his father.

His father turned his head from the television, strong hands stretched across the tops of his legs. "I think it's time for us to go together."

"I usually stop off and pick up some flowers first," Bobby said.

"Pink roses," Albert said, nodding.

"I'm sorry, Pop," Bobby said. "I'm sorry I took her away from you."

Albert stared at his son, tears flowing from the corners of his eyes. "All these years I blamed you for what happened," he said. "Now I think, maybe it needed to happen for things to right themselves. Maybe she put herself there thinkin' it was the only way to get her son back."

"The man that killed Mama," Bobby said. "He's dead."

"I know," Albert said.

"I killed him," Bobby said.

"I know that too," Albert said. "I don't know how your mother would have felt about you doing somethin' like that."

"How do you feel about it?"

"I'm proud of you, Bobby," Albert said, speaking his son's name for the first time since his wife's death.

. . .

THE CARDBOARD BOXES were torn and piled high in a corner, up against the step wall of the tenement, mounds of dirty snow and torn plastic garbage bags lodged near their edges. A cold wind, whipping off corners and side streets, blew across their flaps.

Bobby Scarponi sat shivering under the mound of boxes, his back crunched against cold bricks. He had his hands wrapped around a coffee thermos and his legs were folded to his chest. He was wearing black jeans, two pullovers, and a thick blue windbreaker. A Red Sox baseball cap rested backward on his head. A hand radio sat by his side.

"You see anything yet?" From the warmth of a parked car around the corner, Detective Tony Clifton's voice came crackling over the radio.

"Just my life flashing before my eyes," Bobby muttered into the box, stretching out his legs and resting the warm thermos between them. "It's early still. These guys never come out till the soap operas are done."

"Caddy still parked down front?" Clifton asked.

"Empty and with the windows down." Bobby stared across the deserted street at the late-model pea-green Cadillac with the Florida plates. "Been there all day."

"That car sticks out like a set of tits," Clifton said. "You'd think these guys would show some sense."

"It ain't a Mensa reunion, Tony," Bobby said into the radio. "It's a drug deal. Unless your stool gave us the wrong feed time."

"My guy's never been wrong," Clifton said. "Just sit tight, Rev., and let the deal go down."

"Must be warm where you are," Bobby said, rubbing his hands across the tops of his legs.

"Like Miami in July," Clifton said.

"Can't wait till I'm old and slow like you, Tony. Then I can sit in a ratty car, breathing in hot, shitty air, while a real cop does all the work."

"Tell you what, Rev. Jim," Clifton said. "If it gets any colder, I'll stop over at the liquor store and pick up some more boxes. Come around and toss 'em on your pile."

"I got only two words for you, Tony," Bobby said, his lower lip shaking. "Carbon monoxide." Then his eyes shifted across the street. "We got movement," he said into the radio.

Three men stood in a narrow doorway, hands inside their coat pockets, eyes scanning the silent street. The pea-green Cadillac was parked directly in front of them. The man in the middle, short and bald with a thick black mustache, stepped out of the shadows, moved to the car, opened the passenger door, and got in. He put a cigar with a plastic tip in his mouth and lit it.

Bobby kneeled down on a box, watching.

"Any civilians out with them?" Clifton asked.

"I wouldn't worry too much," Bobby said. "Everybody in this neighborhood's a phone call away from an indictment."

"Let's keep it clear," Clifton said. "Just in case."

"Money man's already in the car," Bobby reported.

"His connect can't be too far away," Clifton said. "Dealers hate being out in the cold."

"Tell me something I don't know," Bobby whispered to himself, resting the radio by his leg.

A tan Buick ragtop, lightning bolts painted on its doors, pulled up behind the Cadillac and cut its engine. Five men sat squeezed inside, windows rolled up, breath and smoke clouding the interior.

"Elvis is in the building," Bobby said into the radio, moving his .38 Special out of its holster and into his right hand.

"Sit tight, Rev.," Clifton said. "And let it happen. Won't be long."

The two men in coats stepped out from the litter of the doorway and walked toward the parked cars. The one on the left, head down against the cold, dug a key from his pocket and opened the trunk of the Cadillac. The one on the right, unbuttoned coat flapping in the wind, stood next to the trunk of the Buick, his hand reaching out to lift it up when the driver popped it from the inside.

Bobby pushed aside one of the box lids, watching as the two men each pulled out identical leather briefcases, walked toward one another, and made the transfer.

"Houston, we have liftoff," Bobby said into the radio. "Come and get 'em."

"Hold on to your boxes, Rev.," Clifton said, slamming a red cherry light on top of his unmarked sedan and jamming the car into gear. "We're just a phone call away."

"Try not to hit any innocent bystanders before you get here," Bobby said, turning the baseball cap brim forward.

"Too late," Clifton said with a laugh, tossing the radio onto the dashboard.

Bobby Scarponi didn't see the two teenagers.

Blanketed in the seclusion of his cardboard complex, his only focus was on the two cars, the drug deal, and the bust about to happen. He didn't see the boys carry the red canisters of gasoline down from the corner Mobil station, lids off, their brains pan-fried with an angel dust and glue omelette, looking to torch the cardboard shanty and the bum who lived inside. They moved quiet as cats, first dousing the edges and then the sides of the tenement wall.

One lit a match and the other leaned over the side of the shaky banister and poured gasoline into the small opening Rev. Jim had cleared for a view.

Then they both laughed.

Bobby knew it the second he tasted the gas and smelled the fumes, his body locked in place, a steady calm engulfing him. He watched the match float down past his shoulder and then felt the sudden rush of heat and saw the blue and yellow of the flames.

He jumped out of his inferno, clothes burning, body torched. He was all smoke and light as he rolled onto the sidewalk, leaving shreds of melted skin and burning fabric in his wake.

He heard the sound of sirens, a steady round of gunshots and shouts coming at him from all directions. He caught a glimpse of Tony Clifton running toward him, gun drawn, his mouth forming words, his weary face burdened with fear.

Then Bobby Scarponi stopped his roll and lay still on the streets of a

Brooklyn ghetto, less than a hundred feet from a leather bag filled with a drug he once would have killed someone to snort.

The ex-junkie-turned-cop was sprawled on a sidewalk, charred head hanging over a cracked curb, his partner kneeling beside him, holding a gun on his lap and crying in anger to the heavens.

Rev. Jim heard and saw none of it.

He was once again living inside a dark world.

BOOK TWO

I love war and responsibility and excitement. Peace is going to be hell on me.

—General George S. Patton

7

February 21, 1982

HOLDING A FELT HAT with both hands, the man walked through the double wood front doors of Nunzio's. He squinted, his eyes adjusting to the candlelit room. He stood next to the bar, scanned the empty stools, and turned to the ten small tables lined in rows of five to his left. He looked past the young couple sharing a cold antipasto platter and the three middle-aged women shoulder-hunched over large glasses of red wine.

The face he was looking for belonged to the man at the last table, whose back was to the wall. Framed pictures of Rocky Marciano, Jersey Joe Walcott, and Carmen Basilio hung just above his head. Steam from a large bowl of lentils and sausage filtered past a set of intense eyes, right hand holding a glass half-filled with San Pellegrino.

The man at the table lifted his left hand to wave him over.

"You look like you could use something to drink, Carlo," Boomer Frontieri said.

Carlo Santori rested his hat on the counter separating table from window, took off his overcoat, and folded it over the back of a wooden chair. Boomer signaled a waiter with two fingers and a pouring gesture, and the waiter appeared immediately with a bottle of Chianti.

Boomer was happy to see his old friend and was about to make a joke, but the expression on Carlo's face stopped him. The man had come a long way from Jersey to see him, so all Boomer said, very quietly, was "What's the favor?"

"Jenny's gone," Carlo said, his voice cracking, words bursting out, hands gripping the table edge for support.

Boomer put his soup spoon down and took a deep breath, feeling the tinge of pain from the piece of metal still embedded inside a partial lung. Then he stretched out and rubbed the side of his right leg, the one with the scars from three surgeries.

"Tell me what 'gone' means," he said.

"We went away, me and Annie, for the weekend," Carlo told him, eyes welling up. "Down the shore. We left Jenny and Tony alone at the house. I didn't think about anything going wrong. I mean, Jesus, we were only a phone call away. One call, Boomer, that's all."

"What *did* go wrong?" Boomer asked. A cop's edge still colored the question and his eyes never left his friend's face.

"They took a bus into the city," Carlo said, forcing the words out. He struggled now to lift a glass of wine to his lips. "Tony's idea. You know the routine. Check out the city, have a little fun. Not have parents on your back all the time."

"How far'd they get?" Boomer sipped the Pellegrino, ignoring the wine.

"Port Authority," Carlo said. "Tony went in to use a bathroom. Told Jenny not to move from her spot. When he got out, she was gone."

"How long ago?"

"Three days," Carlo said, biting his lower lip. "Tony raced all over the terminal lookin' for her. When he gave up, he called me. I could barely make him out. Kept screamin' into the phone, 'Daddy, I lost her. I lost her.'"

"Who called the cops?" Boomer asked, finishing off the water. "You or Tony?"

"He did," Carlo said. "By the time we got back, Tony was already over at the midtown precinct. We took him home, sat by the phone, and waited. We were still waiting when Annie told me to call you."

"Who's on it?"

"Maloney's the lead guy," Carlo said. "Somebody you know?"

Boomer shook his head. "But I've been away awhile."

Carlo drained his glass of wine and sat in silence, his eyes lost in the distance. He looked over at Boomer, his face flushed. "Tell me she's not dead, Boomer," he managed to say. "Please, I beg you. Tell me my baby's not dead."

"I can't tell you what I don't know," Boomer said, reaching a hand across the table and gripping Carlo's forearm. "I'd only be guessing."

"Take the guess," Carlo said, tears sliding down his face.

"You don't have the kind of money that screams ransom." Boomer tightened his grip around Carlo. "And Jenny's not the runaway type. Not from what I remember."

"Which leaves us what?" Carlo wiped his eyes with the back of a sweater sleeve. "The truth, Boomer. I want bullshit, I can get it from any other cop."

"Raped and left for dead." Boomer's eyes were like hot magnets burning through Carlo's skin. "Or waiting to be sold to a flesh buyer."

Carlo didn't flinch. He almost looked thankful. "I want you to find out which it is," he said quietly. "I don't want to find out from some fuckin' stranger."

"I'm a retired cop with half a lung and a limp," Boomer said, releasing his grip. "And I've been off the job closing in on two years. There's not much I can do except put out a few calls, make sure there's the right kind of follow-up."

"She's just another name to them," Carlo said, his sadness bolstered by defiance. "But she's a face to you. I've known you all my life, Boomer. I don't think you'll be happy just making a few phone calls."

Carlo stood, reached for his hat and coat, and looked down at Boomer. "I'll be home with Annie," he said. "She's counting on you too."

"You're betting on an old horse, Carlo." Boomer sighed. "That's not a smart thing to do."

"I'm betting on a friend," Carlo said. Then he turned and left Nunzio's, tables now filled with cold and hungry customers.

Boomer looked away, staring out at the windy streets of a frigid winter night. He rubbed at his leg again, the pain always sharper when the temperature dipped below thirty. He thought back to that day in the hospital bed, his small room at Metropolitan shrouded in darkness. The chief of detectives standing above him, smile on his face, a gold shield and a small medal clutched in his hands. "It's over, Boomer," the chief whispered. "You can rest now."

Resting was all he'd been doing these last two years. There were no more doors for him to kick in, no more junkies to roust, no more dealers to take down. And he missed all of it. The stakeouts, the dives into dark rooms, the split-second walk between life and death. They were now only memories.

Boomer was forty but had enough scars and twisted bones to add another ten years to his body. Carlo had walked in and asked him to go back into a game he might not be able to play anymore. A game he shouldn't be playing. The smart move would be to call his friend and tell him the truth, admit that he was too beat up, in too much pain to do the job he needed done. That he was now a runner who could barely walk.

Admit to his friend, and to himself, that he just wasn't a cop anymore.

Boomer wasn't afraid to die. But he was afraid to fail. He had come to terms with being crippled and tossed from a job he loved. He could never come to terms with being a failure.

He looked up at a night sky filled with rumbling gray clouds and watched the snowflakes start to fall.

. . .

DAVIS "DEAD-EYE" WINTHROP stood behind the glass doors and watched the man from apartment 17B double-park a pea-green Jeep in front of the building. He saw him run from the driver's side, slip and dodge his way through slush and ice, then wait as Dead-Eye held the door open. The man was in his early twenties, dressed more for a safari hunt than life on the Upper East Side. He handed Dead-Eye the keys to the Jeep.

"There are a few boxes in the back," he said in a voice that dripped with privilege. "Get them out for me, would you? I'll be waiting upstairs."

"I can't leave the door," Dead-Eye said, watching the man disappear around a wall and toward the elevators.

He lifted the collar of the brown doorman's coat, pushed down his hat, and pulled on a pair of brown gloves. Dead-Eye opened the door and stepped into the cold air. He stared inside the back of the Jeep, crammed with six heavily taped packing boxes. Car horns blared as he swung the trunk lid past his face and reached for the nearest box.

No one cared anymore about who he used to be; they knew him only for what he was. It had taken eight months for Dead-Eye's wounds to heal after the elevator shoot-out. Doctors were forced to remove half his stomach and a kidney. There would always be a numbness in his throat, from a bullet fragment that had shredded pieces of his vocal cords. He had caught two shots to his right hip, which made running painful and walking a chore. The muscles on his right arm would never be the same.

Dead-Eye was no longer a cop, the disability check sent to his home twice a month a constant reminder of that. His only action now was opening and closing doors and reminding old ladies to button their coats against the winter weather. He never talked about being a doorman, not to anyone, he just did it. He handed out packages and dry cleaning to smiling faces who didn't need to know his name, buzzed in delivery men dropping off take-out Chinese and pizza boxes and complained about the Knicks and Yankees to the UPS and FedEx drivers on his route. Then he went home to his family and tried to forget it all.

He managed to get the first box to the door, straining for breath, the muscles in his back tight against his coat. Dead-Eye went for physical therapy three times a week, fighting to keep his body in one piece. He still worked out, ignoring the pain it caused, and he ate what little he could hold in what was left of his stomach. He was a cripple, but a damn stubborn one.

It took him a full hour to get the boxes up to the front door of 17B. He was sweating and his breath came out in a wheeze as he pressed the buzzer. The man opened the door holding a glass of white wine.

"I thought you forgot about me," he said. He pointed to the den. "Put them in there. Gently, please."

Dead-Eye did as he was told, refusing to let the man see his struggle, closing his eyes to the pain. He put the last box in the den and walked out the door, tipping the lip of his cap to the man.

"Wait," the man said.

Dead-Eye turned and watched the man reach a hand into his pocket. He pulled out a thick roll of bills, peeled off a dollar, and handed it to Dead-Eye. "This is for your troubles."

The man closed the door. Dead-Eye stood there, sweat running down his face, his right arm trembling, his stomach cramped with pain, holding a dollar bill in a gloved hand.

He crumpled the bill, tossed it on the mat in front of the door, and walked into the elevator for the ride back down. To finish off his shift.

. . .

Boomer slid his Cadillac into an open spot next to a fire hydrant, shifted the gear to park, and let the engine idle. The windshield wipers were still on low, slowly clearing away heavy streaks of rain. He put five slices of Wrigley's spearmint gum into his mouth and watched the man walk toward him, his head down against the rain, collar of a brown leather jacket turned up to brace the wind. The sounds of Ry Cooder's rendition of "Little Sister" filled the car's interior.

The man was less than ten feet from the car when Boomer leaned across the front and flipped open the passenger side door. He smiled when the man drew a .44 semiautomatic from the sleeve of his leather jacket and aimed it at the steering wheel.

"Thought you'd lost your touch," Boomer said, watching the man shove the gun back up his sleeve and slide into the car, slamming the door shut.

"Lucky for you I'm in a good mood," Dead-Eye said, lowering his collar with one hand, rainwater dripping on the brown interior. "Spotted you at the corner. Could have taken you out before the light turned green."

Boomer looked over at his ex-partner and smiled. The two had remained friendly in the years since their retirement, each helping the other through the dark days of therapy and inactivity.

Dead-Eye's father had lost his battle with cancer less than six months after his son was shot in the elevator. They spent those months together, the father dying, the son often wishing he were dying too. The two men talked, cried, sometimes laughed, tightening their already strong bond. It was during those precious months that Dead-Eye's father learned how much being a cop meant to his son and how a crippled future opening doors for blank faces could bury him faster than a bullet.

It was difficult for the other cops to understand. For many of them, getting *out* was the goal. Pocketing the pension and working an easy second job the ideal way to leave the department. But to Boomer and Dead-Eye, a life void of action was a death sentence. Unwillingly dragged from a front-row seat to what they considered the greatest show on earth, the red gauge on their adrenaline tanks was brushing on empty. They lived to pin a badge to their chest. Now, left to tend to their wounds, stripped of the work they loved, they felt abandoned, living out the remains of a still-youthful existence in silence.

Dead-Eye at least had a job to fill his idle time. Boomer's plate was empty. He refused to take any of the standard ex-cop details, passing on offers to work security, tend bar, bodyguard the rich, or turn private investigator and chase deadbeats for short money. For Boomer it was either be a cop or have nothing, and right now he was standing up against a blank wall.

Boomer and Dead-Eye could look at one another and sense the pain of what each had lost. They wore a mask of anger alongside the rigged scars of battle, frustrated to be pulled from the game at such an early stage, fearful of journeying toward that final step taken by many disabled cops. The one where a single bullet was all that was needed to free them of their misery.

A bullet fired from their own gun.

"You didn't bring me any coffee," Boomer said to Dead-Eye. "I had my heart set on a black."

"The only black you gonna see in this car is me," Dead-Eye said. "Besides which, I don't drink that shit anymore."

"Suppose you don't have any smokes either."

"Cigarette's just the thing for a guy with one kidney and a scarred lung," Dead-Eye said. "Got a mint. Would that do you?"

"I'll stick with the gum." Boomer shifted the Caddy into drive and pulled away from the hydrant.

"Where we going?" Dead-Eye asked, popping the mint into his mouth.

Boomer ignored the question and stopped at a red light. "You working door detail tonight?"

"Start in two hours," Dead-Eye said.

"Can you call in sick?"

"Depends."

"On what?"

"On what you need," Dead-Eye said.

Boomer put his right hand into his jacket pocket, pulled out a photo of Jennifer Santori, and handed it to Dead-Eye.

"She's twelve years old and I need to find her," Boomer said.

"Snatched?" Dead-Eye asked, staring down at the smiling girl.

"Three days ago," Boomer said. "Over at Port Authority. Cops working it got nothing. Father's an old friend. Called me to see what I could do, and I called you."

"Pull over by that phone booth on the next corner," Dead-Eye said. "Next to the deli."

Boomer eased the car between a dented Chevy Caprice and a VW with Met and Yankee stickers covering the front and back fenders. Dead-Eye searched his pockets for loose change, found it, and opened the passenger door.

"While you're out there," Boomer said, "would you get me a coffee?"

"Fuck no," Dead-Eye said, and slammed the door behind him.

. . .

BOOMER AND DEAD-EYE worked the city streets for two full days and nights. They walked into old haunts looking to scare up some familiar faces, only to end up staring at blank eyes. They drove past familiar corners and saw new players in control, players who didn't even bother to give the two ex-cops a second look. Two years away from the action is a lifetime in the underbelly, and the names Boomer and Dead-Eye dredged from their memory banks were now either dead or doing hard time upstate. They felt old and rusty and were in constant pain. But the more they came up empty, the more determined they grew.

They were in the final hour of their second day when they spotted the reed-thin pimp in the black leather raincoat and purple felt hat. He smiled when he saw the two ex-cops walk up to his Times Square station. The rain had let up, replaced by a soft mist.

"Didn't know you two had any taste for the deuce," the pimp said, his smile exposing a long bottom row of silver teeth.

"Cleve, that tinfoil look you got is gonna catch on," Dead-Eye said, patting the pimp on the shoulder and pointing to his mouth. "Let 'em laugh much as they want. You stick with it."

"Be hostile, bitches," Cleve said. "I'm still happy to see your asses."

"We're lookin' for a girl," Boomer said, reaching his hand into his jacket pocket.

Cleve held his smile. "Don't know what your action is, Boom-Man, but I'm sure I got the muff to cover it."

"A *missing* girl, asswipe," Boomer said, jabbing Jenny's photo against the lip of Cleve's leather flaps. "Dropped out three days ago off a Jersey bus."

"I don't buy runaways, Boom," Cleve said. "My birds fly pro. Any trim I break in, I marry."

"She's not a runaway," Dead-Eye said. "She's lifted."

"To sell or snuff?" Cleve asked, eyes searching the street beyond the ex-cops' shoulders, making sure his ladies were walking their beat.

"You play the market," Boomer said. "Not us."

"Street ain't the same as you left it," Cleve said, shaking his head, voice almost nostalgic. "This crack shit that's movin' got everybody flyin' in crazy ways."

"Save it for Mike Wallace," Dead-Eye said. "All we wanna hear is you spit up some names."

"Don't have to give you shit, Super Fly." The smile was back on Cleve's face. "You can't arrest me. Your badges been stamped out."

"I never shot a pimp on the job," Boomer said, looking away from

Cleve and checking the two hookers in hot pants and fake fur standing by a pink Lincoln, shivering in their six-inch heels. "How about you, Dead-Eye?"

"Fleshed one once in the shoulder," Dead-Eye said. "Up in Spanish Harlem. He ran off down the avenue, screaming like an old woman."

"There's a hundred wacks, easy, out here movin' kids," Cleve said. "I ain't no fuckin' yellow pages. Can't know them all."

Boomer looked away from the hookers and stepped in closer to Cleve, lips inches from the pimp's left ear. "Be a pal," Boomer whispered, "and give us your three best names."

"I only go by their street names," Cleve said, eyes moving from Boomer to Dead-Eye.

"We'll take what you can give," Dead-Eye said.

"I'd peek at a lowball PR calls himself Crow," Cleve said, toning down his voice. "Works the terminal, lifting boys for the chicken hawks, sometimes takes a chippie home for himself."

"You're riding a wave, Cleve," Boomer said. "Don't stop it now."

"There's this white dude rides around the deuce in out-of-state wheels," Cleve said, lifting the front flap of his coat and pulling out a filter-tip Kool. "Nasty piece of business. Got more tattoos than skin. Couldn't miss him if you were blind and tied to a tree."

"We get the idea," Dead-Eye said.

"He deals in runaways," Cleve said, putting a lit match to the cigarette, talking as he puffed. "Hangs on to them for a week or so, chillin' his bones, then sells 'em off to an outside shipper."

"Nice set of friends," Boomer said. "I should shoot you just for knowin' 'em."

"We only walk on the same streets, Boom," Cleve said. "I don't ever chop wood with shit like that. I aim my end simple and clean. Keeps my pockets filled with cash, my dick covered with pussy, and my soft ass outta jail."

"You should have your own talk show," Boomer said. "Now, get back on track, Romeo. Give us up another name."

"There's a brother calls himself X," Cleve said, tossing the butt end of the Kool out toward the curb. "You know, like Malcolm X?"

"Minus the religion," Dead-Eye said.

"He's as close to Malcolm as me to the Pope," Cleve said. "This fucker's out there, pulls in runaways and sells them over to some uptown crew that takes 'em, fucks 'em till they're knocked up, then deals them *and* the baby. Like a two for one."

"Jesus Christ," Dead-Eye muttered.

"He work the area steady?" Boomer asked.

"I see him enough to make me nervous," Cleve said. "He don't always sell what he picks up."

"Why's that?" Dead-Eye asked.

"Sometimes the goods are too damaged," Cleve said. "Buyers take a pass, if you read what I mean. He ain't happy just gettin' his rocks soft. He's into the pain."

"He have a regular spot?" Boomer said. "A hang place."

"I hear he scores his dope off a dealer works the Eighth Avenue end of the Port," Cleve said. "That'd be where I would gaze. But then, I ain't no shot-up super cops like you two."

"Appreciate the info, Cleve," Boomer said. "You ever end up doin' a stretch, we promise to visit."

"Bring you and your prison chick some home cookin'," Dead-Eye said.

"Like being in the can ain't bad enough," Cleve said, silver teeth gleaming under the glow of the overhead streetlight.

"Just one more thing," Boomer said, nodding over toward Dead-Eye.

"I gave up the three." Cleve was annoyed. "That's all I can do for free."

"This one won't cost," Boomer said, smiling. "It's just a favor, Cleve."

"What you need?" Cleve started to slow-step it toward the parked car and the waiting hookers. "But make it quick."

"The name of your dentist," Boomer said.

. . .

BOOMER PLACED THE sharp end of a pocket knife in the dealer's ear. He had his left hand wrapped around the man's throat, force-lifting him inches from the floor. The dealer was thin and bug-eyed with long, greasy black hair covering half his face.

They were inside an empty Port Authority men's room, Dead-Eye leaning his back against the front door. The dealer's glassy eyes veered from Boomer to Dead-Eye, trying to place the faces of the men who had yanked him without warning from the street and dragged him into the first open door they found.

"I *know* you guys ain't dealers," he said. "And I don't *think* you're cops."

"We're priests," Dead-Eye said.

"And we're willing to save your fucking soul," Boomer said, lifting the dealer higher up against the side of the grimy wall. "So the only thinkin' for you right now should be about how can I make these guys happy."

"Take my works," the dealer said, fear kicking his voice into a higher gear. "Got enough for ten, maybe twelve, easy, on the street."

"You sell smack to a low-end run chaser calls himself X," Dead-Eye said, pointing a finger toward the knife inside the dealer's ear. "Give us his name, unless you want to spend the rest of your life reading lips."

"You guys lookin' for chicks, no problem, I can help you out," the dealer said. "X is the best. He can find a fresh piece of fur in the desert."

Boomer slid the edge of the knife across the side of the dealer's ear, bringing a thin row of blood drops flowing down his neck. "You guys ain't fuckin' priests," the dealer muttered.

Boomer squeezed his hand tighter against the man's throat, muffling the sounds of pain, causing his eyes to bulge. "The name is all I wanna hear from you," Boomer said. "We understand each other?"

The dealer nodded and Boomer lightened his grip. "Malcolm Juniper," the dealer said. "We did a spin together up at Attica."

"Where's he sleep?" Dead-Eye asked, popping four Maalox tablets into his mouth.

"Here and there," the dealer said. "No place steady. He's only been loose a few weeks."

"Where's he sleeping tonight?" Boomer asked, wiping the knife blade on the sleeve of the dealer's torn velvet jacket. Then he took a handkerchief from his pants pocket and handed it to the dealer. "Clean that blood off your ear," he told him. "*After* you answer the question."

"He's been stayin' at a park-and-lock on Thirty-ninth Street," he said, putting the handkerchief next to his ear. "Put down enough for a four-day stay."

"When?" Dead-Eye asked.

"Yesterday," the dealer said. "Day before, maybe."

"Don't be wrong," Boomer said.

He turned away from the dealer and walked toward Dead-Eye and the exit door, slipping the closed knife into his back pocket.

"You think I'm gonna need stitches for this cut?" the dealer asked, jabbing the blood-soaked handkerchief against his wound. "It feels pretty deep."

"We ain't doctors either," Dead-Eye said as he closed the door behind him.

. . .

MALCOLM JUNIPER WAS twenty-seven years old and four weeks removed from a three-year spin at Attica prison on a rape and molestation conviction when he had spotted the teary-eyed girl from across the street. He smiled, took a hit off a joint, and turned the engine over on his cherry-red Chrysler Imperial. Ramming the gear stick into drive, he angled his way across the busy intersection, his glassy eyes barely aware of the traffic, smelling his prey.

"You look like you could use some help, sugar" were Malcolm's first words to Jennifer Santori. He was leaning across the front seat, talking through an open window.

"I'm okay," she managed to say. Jennifer stared at his scarred and chapped lips and the fingers of one hand that gripped the steering wheel.

"You okay, you wouldn't be standing out in the rain," Malcolm said with a laugh. "Be somewhere safe. Warm. Be with family."

"I am with family," Jennifer said.

"All I see is you," Malcolm said.

"My brother," Jennifer said, turning away to look past the car, down the distant streets. "I'm here with my brother. He had to use a bathroom. Told me to wait for him here."

Jennifer was lying. She was lost and looked it. It was so stupid of her not to wait for Anthony outside the bathroom door as he had asked. But he had taken such a long time, like he always did at home, and she just couldn't wait anymore. Not with all those people rushing past, some looking at her and smiling, others staring with empty eyes, dirty clothes held together by rope and cloth. Then there was the horrible smell, strong as a punch, of dried urine sprayed across walls and stuck to the floor. Jennifer clasped a gloved hand to her mouth and swallowed the urge to vomit.

She needed to get out. Just for a few minutes.

She rode an escalator up toward fresh air, which she welcomed with a deep breath. The ride was slow and creaky, and the guttural shouts of eager newsboys hawking morning papers filtered down toward her. She stepped carefully off the escalator, turned left, and was soon washed into a swarm of people moving with concerted speed to a variety of destinations. There was a smile on her face, and her curiosity overwhelmed, for the briefest moment, her fear of the unknown.

She was walking the streets of a city she had always heard about and seen perhaps ten times in her life. It was the city her brother talked about with a sense of wonder. The same city her father faced daily with dread and unease and her mother reserved for special occasions. She was in it alone, at pace with the people who called it home, in step with the hungry and the moneyed, the desperate and the dreamers.

She had crossed three streets before the warmth of adventure was replaced by cold awareness. She turned and tried to make her way back. It took a few moments, two wrong turns, and a quick run against a flashing light before she knew the truth.

The dream weekend she and her brother had planned had turned a dark corner.

And on that corner lurked Malcolm Juniper.

"Be better for you to wait in a dry place," Malcolm said to her, reaching across to the passenger side door.

The light facing Jennifer turned from red to green, but she didn't move. "He must have stopped to get something to eat," she said.

"I can help you find him," Malcolm told her.

Jennifer hesitated before stepping into the car, too frightened to recall her father's constant litany of caution. She slammed the car door shut and disappeared into a world of darkness.

. . .

MALCOLM JUNIPER WALKED out of the deli entrance and spotted Boomer and Dead-Eye coming toward him from across the street. Even from a distance, the two men, one favoring his right leg, the other breathing through his mouth, smelled like cop. Malcolm gripped the large paper bag filled with a six-pack of Colt .45 malt and turned the corner, trying to hold on to his calm, knowing the two men would be fast on him. Even if they grabbed him, they didn't have much. He wasn't armed, had clocked in regular with his parole officer, and had applied for work at three fast-food outfits. The very model of a parolee and the last man any cop could finger for a street kidnapping.

But Malcolm Juniper was a career criminal who had spent the better part of his adult years behind the cold bars of a lockup. His ex-con's survival instinct told him that the two men tracking him had no interest in probable cause or Miranda rights. These two looked serious, so they either wanted a snitch out, which would put Malcolm in street trouble, or they knew about the girl, which could land him behind bars until coffin time. Either way, Malcolm Juniper wasn't going in. Not on this day.

He crossed against the light, moving up to Fortieth and Eighth. The street was filled with early morning stiffs heading out of the terminal and into work. Side streets were clogged with traffic, Jersey plates trying to squeeze into twelve-buck-a-day garage slots. The two men had drawn closer, walking less than twenty feet behind him, the white guy sure to be the first one to make the move, the brother not looking to be one to jump and tear on the street. But then, the worst beatings Malcolm Juniper ever took were from black badges and, if anything, the one stalking him looked fit to hand out the punishment.

Malcolm was straight enough to know not to outfight them, and he wasn't in the mood to deal with their shakedown shit, and he sure as sin wasn't going to be dragged to the house to be fingered on something he didn't do. It left him only one viable option, and he took it as soon as he crossed Forty-first and turned right, heading down Ninth Avenue toward less congested streets.

Malcolm tossed the bag filled with the Colts over his shoulder and started to run, heading for the rummy shacks down by the West Side Highway.

"Rabbit's on the go, Boom," Dead-Eye shouted, starting to take chase.

"Let's try and keep him alive," Boomer said, running alongside. "For a change."

"You're talking like a civilian now," Dead-Eye said, ignoring the pain in his chest as he ran.

"He's makin' for the highway," Boomer said, wincing from the pressure the hard concrete was putting on his bad leg. "We gotta cut him off by the time he gets to Tenth."

"If *we* make it to Tenth," Dead-Eye said, starting to slow his pace, the burn in his chest growing with every deep breath.

"We're makin' him look like Jesse Owens," Boomer said, the frustration in his voice spiking as high as the pain.

"With us chasin', *everybody's* Jesse Owens," Dead-Eye said, wiping a hand across his forehead, brushing away cold drops of sweat.

They stopped next to a cab stand, both gasping for air, bent over, hands to knees, faces twisted in pain, Malcolm Juniper long gone from their sights.

Dead-Eye took a step back and leaned his aching body against a taxi. "What are we doin'?" he said angrily. "We're finished, man. This shit ain't for us anymore. We're done, you and me, and we got the papers to prove it."

"It's just a little rust," Boomer wheezed, walking in small circles, willing the pain in his chest and leg to flee from him as fast as Malcolm had. "We've just gotta get our timing back."

"We got all the timing we need," Dead-Eye said, his voice wistful. "Me for being a doorman and you for lifting a pasta fork."

"You can't walk away from this," Boomer said, grabbing Dead-Eye's jacket. "It's all you know. And it's all I got."

"I'm sorry about your friend's kid," Dead-Eye said, slowly easing Boomer's hand away. "And I wanted to help. But she don't need me.

She needs a *cop* to help her. A *real* cop. Not some guy trying to remember what it was to be one."

Dead-Eye patted Boomer's arm, braced his jacket against the cold, and headed toward Eighth Avenue. Boomer stood and watched him, his breath still coming hard, the pain fading, tears rolling down the side of his nose. He walked over toward the front steps of a tenement, ignoring the stares of the cabdrivers on break. There were three garbage cans lined in front of the basement apartment. He flipped the lid off the nearest packed can, picked it up, lifted it to chest level, and heaved it into the street. He stared at the bags of waste as they weaved into the wind, loose strips of greasy foil and paper towels slapping against the sides of parked cars. He saw the dented can rumble down the sharp incline and come banging to a stop next to a no parking sign.

Boomer Frontieri looked over at the drivers, who stared back at him in silence. He took a deep breath and walked away, hands inside his pockets, leg still burning from the run, moving slowly down the quiet street, nothing ahead of him but time.

8

MALCOLM JUNIPER STOOD in a dark corner of the one-room apartment and stared over at Jennifer Santori. The girl's face was tear-lined and bruised; her bare arms were extended, wrists locked in a set of cuffs attached to the top of a radiator pipe. She was naked from the waist up, thin legs bunched against the side of her hips, her frail body shivering in the cold emptiness of the room.

"You must be somebody special," Malcolm said, eyes glaring down at the unformed breasts, "cops be chasin' me way they did."

Jennifer looked at the man she once believed would help her find her brother and tried to form the words to beg for her release. She forced her eyes to wipe away the blurry images and bring Malcolm Juniper into a clear focus. Her throat burned and her damaged body ached and she wanted more than anything to be back in the safe womb of the New Jersey home she so often used to think of as a dull prison.

It seemed like months since he had driven her around the Port

Authority area for the better part of an hour, a concerned look etched across his brow, playing the role of Good Samaritan. He parked and ran out to buy her a Pepsi and a hot dog from an all-night stand, returning with the food, a smile, and a sincere reassurance that her brother would be found.

Jennifer grew tired, eyelids itching and burning from lack of sleep. Long bus rides tended to make her groggy, and that, coupled with the anxiety over losing Anthony, made it all the easier for her to ease into the backseat of the car, as Malcolm suggested, and curl up to nap while he continued his search, looking for a boy he had no intention of finding.

She woke up with his mouth over her lips, his hands sliding up and down her body, both their pants down around the ankles, a sharp burning pain between her legs. Her eyes bubbled over with fear; his were lit by contempt.

He forced himself on her for the better part of three hours, slapping her face and arms, running lit matches down the sides of her thighs and across her breasts during his restful moments. He poured cheap whiskey down her throat, laughing with glee when she coughed up the foul taste. He lit a crack pipe and forced the smoke of the cooked cocaine into her lungs, holding her head back, pushing her down deep into the rear cushion of the car.

They were parked in an abandoned lot near the Fourteenth Street meat market, the windows rolled up and steamed with breath and smoke, an overhead streetlight casting the car in its cloudy glow. He cuffed her hand to one door handle and her foot to another and forced a handkerchief into her mouth while he went out for cigarettes. He came back a short time later with another man, stoop-shouldered, haggard, and crazed, and let him have at her for the price of a Big Mac and a large Coke.

She blacked out during the final rape, letting the pain, the drugs, and the drink whisk her away on a blanket of dreams.

When she woke, she was handcuffed to a radiator, head pounding, dried blood and semen caked to her body. She opened her eyes slowly, the room revealing itself in an array of shadows as streams of light flashed in from the streets outside. Her legs felt weighed down and her arms were cold and numb, dangling from the pipe above her head. She had trouble breathing, the insides of her lungs and nostrils scorched from their cocaine and whiskey diet.

Malcolm Juniper stood above her, wearing only a pair of brown socks, a crazed smile on his face, crack pipe in his right hand, kitchen knife dangling from his left.

"We're low," Malcolm said, running the crack pipe past her eyes. "More's on the way. Junior's gettin' over a fresh load that'll turn your eyes. Won't be long."

Jennifer stared up at him, biting down on her lower lip, her teeth breaking through the cracked and sore exterior, droplets of blood forming on the edges.

"Are you going to kill me?" she asked.

The words pressed themselves out slowly, each one enclosed in layers of pain and embarrassment. She wanted so much to cry, to shout out for help, but couldn't muster the strength required. Instead, she took in another long, painful breath and asked him again, "Are you going to kill me?"

Malcolm Juniper crouched down and rested the crack pipe on the floor between them. He brought the sharp end of the knife up across the side of Jennifer's neck and pressed it tight against her skin. He reached up and rubbed her arms with his free hand.

"Killin' you be like burnin' money," Malcolm said in as soothing a voice as he could muster. "You worth way too much. I'm gonna make me a killin' all right. But it ain't the kind you be thinkin'."

"I just want to go home," Jennifer said to him, the rush of his acid breath warm on her cheeks. "I won't say anything about this. Or about you. I'll just say I got lost."

"You gonna be goin' home, baby," Malcolm said, still in his seductive voice. "Be a different home, is all. But that's down the road a ways. Right now you and me got to be thinkin' about Junior and how we need to make him a happy man."

"Why are you doing this to me?" Jennifer wailed, more with confusion than with anger.

"You pay the good price for good smoke," Malcolm said, looking past Jennifer, eyes and mind adrift on their own. "And nobody's got better smoke than Junior. It's worth it. Whatever the price, it's gonna be worth it."

"Why? Tell me why?" Jennifer begged in the soundless room, her upper body trembling from the sharp wind creeping through the cracked walls.

"Junior ain't normal like you and me," Malcolm said, easing the knife away from Jennifer's throat. "He don't give a five-cent fuck about money. So you can't just up and pay him out for the smoke. Cares even less about pussy, so there ain't no sense askin' him to a slow dance with you."

Jennifer closed her mouth and eyes, rushing breath through her nose, choking back a violent need to vomit.

"Junior's religious," Malcolm said, standing now, brushing the knife against the sides of Jennifer's arms. "Fucker walks around prayin' all the time. He's into that voodoo shit, where you kill a cat or a dog, drink the blood, burn the bodies. But he always keeps somethin' for himself. Bone, tooth, nail, eyes. Hangs them on a gold chain around his neck. Keeps away what looks to do him in."

Jennifer coughed up a mouthful of thick bile and spit it out on the floor, inches from the crack pipe resting on its side. Malcolm ignored it, running the knife slowly between the fingers of the girl's hands.

"So I'm thinkin' you and me, we gotta give Junior a little present," Malcolm said. "Somethin' he's gonna wanna have hangin' around that chain. You know what that present's gonna be, don't you, baby?"

Jennifer's eyes widened, the sudden rush of fear forcing her back to push against the wall and her hands to clench into tight fists. Malcolm whistled Otis Redding's "Sittin' by the Dock of the Bay" as he undid the fingers of Jennifer's left hand. She kicked her legs at his side and tried to get close enough to bite, but he shouldered her head away and pried loose the index finger.

"Don't fight me, baby," he said in a vacant voice. "It's only a gift."

She saw the sheer look of insanity mixed with glee that filled Malcolm Juniper's eyes and knew she was in an unholy place that promised her no avenue short of torment and death.

She looked up and watched the sharp edge of the knife close in on the soft flesh of her finger, Malcolm's staccato laughter cutting through her cries.

Outside, on the cold streets of a cold city, a young girl's screams cascaded down past a silent army of empty cars and distant faces.

. . .

BOOMER STOOD HALFWAY DOWN the alley, back resting against a Jimi Hendrix poster, eating a cold slice of anchovy pizza and holding a cup of hot black coffee. He was wearing an unzipped black leather jacket, crisp jeans, work boots, and a blue Yankee cap. He had a .22 in the front pocket of the leather and a .44 semiautomatic tucked in the back of the jeans. He chewed the pizza, sipped the coffee, and studied the early morning Harlem street, filled with blue collars on their way to union jobs, and on-the-nods half hanging near tenement doorways, dreaming of the next place to score.

Boomer took a final bite of the pizza, dropped the crust into the coffee container, and tossed them both into an open garbage can.

He took a deep breath and walked out of the alley.

He hadn't slept all night, sitting straight up in a lounge chair in his silent apartment, staring out into the cold air of an open window. For the first time in memory, Boomer Frontieri was a frightened man. He had adjusted to living with the pain of his disability, soaking the throbbing aches in his leg and chest not with pills doctors prescribed but with daily doses of the homemade red wine Nunzio had stored in his basement. It was the vague discontent that ate away at Boomer and ground his insides into thick masses of bubbly tension. He felt adrift and helpless.

Boomer wasn't expecting much when he retired from the job, and he wasn't disappointed. There were no official notices, no members of the top brass walking up to shake his hand and thank him for all the long hours he put in and for all the years he spent crouched in danger, waiting to give or take a bullet. He had made more than eight thousand arrests in his career with a conviction rate that needled out at 94 percent, and that didn't even get him so much as a nod from the file clerk behind the mesh cage who took his retirement papers, stamped them, and turned back to her coffee and soap opera.

It was a sad way to end a career, but not an unusual one. Some took it in stride, shrugging it off to departmental indifference. Others brought the parting home with a bitter taste, letting it simmer beneath the surface as they mentally relived their great moments. For these men, both past and future eventually melded inside the dark haven of a local bar.

Boomer was facing a long and shaky break in his road.

Retirement didn't suit him as well as it might have a less complicated man. He didn't have enough money to live well and travel, but he had too much just to sit and lounge around a table in the only restaurant he trusted enough to relax in. It was not his way to mix it up with everyday life, to settle into and find comfort within the confines of a routine. He set his own clock as a cop and resented having the timepiece snatched from his grasp at a time when he was too young for the early-bird special and too old for the after-hours clubs.

It was one of the reasons he was on the Jennifer Santori case. He knew it was a crazy notion. How could he chase down a missing girl when he was better suited to sit in a lounge chair and let the sun soak his wounds while he listened to a ball game on the radio? Bringing in Jennifer was a risk, and Boomer knew the smart thing for him to do would be to walk from it. But Boomer had always lived for the risk. And now risk was all that he had left.

Common sense told him that the girl was either dead or long gone from the area. But the cop inside shoved common sense aside and let the power and ego of the shield take charge. If she was alive, and if she was to be found, then Boomer Frontieri was the only cop, disabled or not, who could bring her home. He believed it with all the strength left in a body that had so recently betrayed him during that futile chase down a Manhattan side street.

It was why he had stayed up all night and why he was back there now, coming out of an alley off a Harlem corner, heading for a brownstone brothel run by a 350-pound madam with a glass eye.

If Boomer Frontieri's ride as a cop was going to come to an end, he wasn't going to let it be with him leaning against the side of a yellow cab, clutching at the cold air for breath, a circle of foreign drivers mingling around him, as indifferent to his plight as the pencil stubs down at One Police Plaza. After all the years and busts and chases and gun-fights, Boomer needed to stamp a better ending to it all.

The ending required him to find Jennifer Santori. And maybe, if luck traveled down the same path, he would die in the triumph.

. . .

BOOMER CROSSED THE INTERSECTION, ignoring the light and walking against oncoming clusters of gypsy cabs on the prowl for downtown passengers, and headed toward the well-kept brownstone. He had his hands in his jeans pockets and his head down from the wind, lost in a whirl of thought. He heard the footsteps of the man coming up behind him, and saw the shape of the large shadow start to overtake his own.

He stopped walking and turned.

"Don't tell me," Boomer said. "You could have taken me out any-time you wanted."

"Back in the alley," Dead-Eye agreed. "Head shot right into the garbage can."

"I thought you were too old and shot up for this shit," Boomer said, looking over at him. "Or am I going deaf too?"

"I *am* too old and shot up," Dead-Eye said. "And so are you."

"But you're here," Boomer said.

"You and me broke every case we ever worked on," Dead-Eye said. "They took us off the job because we were *wounded.* Not because we couldn't solve cases."

"I'm goin' up to see Bel," Boomer said, nodding toward the brown-stone. "You want in?"

"Just to talk?" Dead-Eye said, stepping up alongside Boomer. "Any-thing more, I'll wait for you here."

"I *never* need to do anything with Bel that doesn't involve talk," Boomer said, walking up the brownstone steps. "When that day comes, then I'll *want* you to take me out."

"You wake up next to Bel," Dead-Eye said, "and it'll be my pleasure."

. . .

BEL STIRRED A large cup of black coffee with a thick wooden spoon, her glass eye gleaming under the glare of the dining room chandelier. Boomer and Dead-Eye sat across from her, squeezed in together on a red velvet love seat. The five-room railroad apartment was well furnished and clean, its windows covered by red satin drapes, the wood floors hidden beneath thick shag carpets. Ornate lights, shaded by low-watt bulbs and starched white handkerchiefs, hung from every ceiling. A blanket of incense filtered through the halls, blending easily with varied scents of perfume and lingering marijuana smoke.

Bel sat on an overstuffed lounge chair, arms and hips resting against a variety of soft fluffed pillows. She was a large woman with an easy manner, round folds of black skin barely hidden by a sheer nightgown and a flowered purple robe. Her fingernails were long, each painted a different shade. Her chubby, unlined face was free of makeup, and her large feet were curled comfortably beneath her robe.

She flicked a gold-plated lighter and lit the end of a filter-tipped Lord cigarette. As she took in a deep drag, smoke curled up in small clouds in front of her damaged right eye. She kept stirring her coffee and smiled at the two former detectives.

"You boys looking for some security work?" Bel asked in a voice treacherous as an ocean wave. "Help me protect my girls against bad company?"

"We're not here for work, Bel," Boomer said. "We're looking for a girl."

"Used to throw them at you for free back when you were badges," Bel said, holding up her cup with a large paw of a hand, fat hiding any traces of knuckles, smile still on her face. "You weren't interested then. Maybe now that you're both older, a piece of the triangle isn't as easy to come by."

"We don't want one of yours," Dead-Eye said. "No offense."

"None taken, sweetskin," Bel said, swallowing down two large gulps of coffee. "But just so you understand, I don't feed off another table. You want somebody else's girl, you got to go talk to somebody else."

Boomer stood, took a picture of Jennifer Santori out of the front pocket of his leather jacket, and placed it on the circular table next to Bel's ashtray. He turned and returned to his place next to Dead-Eye.

"She was lifted out of the Port Authority a couple of days ago," Dead-Eye said. "We caught a bead on the lifter, a street rodent calls himself X. Real name's Malcolm and he deals in young trade, selling runaways and lost girls on the market."

"Sounds like you know as much about this Malcolm as I could tell you," Bel said. "Besides, you know my trade is clean. I deal only in pros. I don't buy fresh meat."

"We need you to tell us who does, Bel," Boomer said. "We've been off the loop the last few years."

Bel picked up Jennifer's picture and studied it with her one good eye.

"Pretty girl," Bel said. "Twelve, maybe thirteen. And she's white. People be willing to pay extra for that."

"Those are the people we want to meet," Boomer said.

"The sort of business you're hunting has never been lacking for a crowd," Bel said, placing the picture back against the ashtray, a fresh cigarette in her mouth. "It's like selling a car. Once you sign over the papers, you pocket the money and never see the car again. It's the same with flesh. Except there's more money and no papers to sign."

"If you were Malcolm, who'd you be lookin' to sell the girl to?" Dead-Eye asked.

"If I was Malcolm, honey, I'd swallow rat poison." A look of disdain creased the rolls around Bel's face.

"Let's go one better, then," Boomer said. "Who's the last guy you'd like to see one of your girls end up with?"

Bel stared across the table at Boomer and Dead-Eye, the cigarette dangling from a corner of her lower lip, the glass eye locked on them in a dead gaze. She took in a deep breath, lungs filling with smoke, and rested the back of her large neck against the side of one of the soft pillows.

"Walt Billings," she said. "They call him Junior on the outside. He's a white guy with a rich daddy and a pretty sick sense of what passes for jewelry."

"How sick?" Dead-Eye asked.

Bel lowered her voice to a near whisper. "He collects body parts.

Hangs them around his neck, wrists, ankles. God only knows where else. When Junior feels the need to add to his collection, he trades a lifter some dope for a girl. Usually a girl the cops have given up for dead. If that child in that picture ends up with Junior, you both pray for her to die."

"Where's he shop?" Boomer asked, standing again, lifting the collar on his jacket and slipping a hand into his front jeans pocket.

"Manhattan mostly," Bel said, finishing off the last of her coffee. "Steers himself clear of the outside boroughs. I'm surprised you two never ran into him all those years you were out busting heads with the sinners."

"If we'd run into him, we wouldn't be talkin' about him now," Dead-Eye said, nodding his head toward Bel and walking over to the double-latched front door.

"Thanks for the news, Bel," Boomer said. "Anything I can throw your way?"

"Label it as a favor for an old friend," Bel said, pursing her thick lips and tossing a kiss at Boomer. "Tell you what, though. If I hear that Junior somehow landed faceup in a pine box, I wouldn't be short of smiles."

"I just love it when I can make a woman smile," Boomer said.

. . .

MALCOLM AND JUNIOR both ordered large papaya drinks, leaning forward against the counter of a Times Square food stand, watching a thin black teen with a shaved head reach for two paper cups.

"Squeeze it out right, little man," Malcolm said to the teen. "I'm lookin' to drink juice, not foam."

The teen looked blankly back at Malcolm and nodded.

"How come you didn't bring the girl down?" Junior asked. "You know I hate payin' for what I haven't seen."

"Can't risk it out here," Malcolm said with a flashy smile. "Minute your eyeballs touch, you gonna by lookin' to chop her up like an onion on a stove and start prayin' over her bones. That's how fine a little one I got me. But I did bring you a taste."

Junior's eyes widened as Malcolm slipped a hand into a side pocket and came out holding a thick roll of toilet paper. He handed the wad to Junior.

"What's in it?" Junior said, his voice filled with Christmas morning excitement.

"A gift," Malcolm said. "Just to show my heart's in the right place."

Junior carefully unrolled the toilet paper, turning his back on Malcolm and the teen. He giggled when he saw Jennifer's severed finger, stroking it and nodding his head with approval. He covered it back up and put it inside his shirt pocket. "Thank you," he said, turning back to Malcolm. "I really do thank you."

"No sweat," Malcolm said.

Junior took his cup of papaya from the teen. "How much you want for this fine little one?" he asked, taking a long drink, ignoring the thin line of orange foam it left across his upper lip.

"A week's worth," Malcolm said. "I need off the street for a few days. Get lost inside of some good shit, but I don't wanna end up dead doin' it. That's why I come to see Junior. You always deal me the best."

"A week's expensive, Malcolm," Junior said, shaking his head and finishing off his drink. "I don't know what you think I am, but I'm not here to be taken."

"I *know* what you are." Malcolm stared back at Junior, holding his half-empty cup at chest level.

Junior's eyes turned to rocks and the muscles around his jaw clenched. "What is that?" he said, his voice cold, his body taut. "What do you think I am, Malcolm?"

Malcolm was quick to sense the abrupt change in Junior's body temperature, and he had heard enough street talk about his flash temper to know that he could easily be left for dead with a half-finished papaya cup in his hand.

"You a businessman, Junior," Malcolm said, showing off his sweetest smile. "That's what you are. A businessman. One of the smartest around."

Junior tossed his empty cup into a trash bin to his left. The tension in his body eased, his shoulders relaxed, and a soft look returned to his eyes. "Okay, then," Junior said. "Let's you and me do us some business."

"What time?"

Junior flicked his wrist and checked his Rolex. He was tall and solid, his body pumped by a personal trainer three morning's a week in a chic downtown gym. He was in his early twenties and had a handsome, unlined face topped by a mane of thick, blond, designer-cut hair, gelled straight back. He wore only expensive imported clothes bought and paid for by an indulgent mother he saw less than five times a year.

"You in a hurry to make the drop?" Junior asked Malcolm, resting a five on the countertop. "Or you want some more time to be with your girl?"

"Can't ever have enough time with somethin' as sweet as I found," Malcolm said, watching the teen replace the five with two-fifty in change and Junior turn his back on it.

"Anytime after seven, then," Junior said over his shoulder as he walked slowly toward the stairs that would take him out of the Times Square station and into the street. "And clean her up before you bring her over."

"I'll scrub the soap on her myself, Junior," Malcolm said, smiling at the teen and pocketing the change that was left behind. "Bring her by clean and fresh as a newborn baby."

. . .

BOOMER SHOVED HIS SHIELD into the doorman's face and put an index finger to his shaky lips.

"Billings," Boomer said. "Floor and number."

"Sixteen A," the doorman said, sweat starting to form around the edges of his cap. "But he's not there. He's out."

"Got a key?" Boomer asked.

"Super has all the keys," the doorman said. "He lives around the corner, first apartment after the mailboxes."

"Go tell him you need the key to 16A," Boomer said. "Tell him the tenant locked himself out, you'll have it back to him in a few minutes."

"What if he doesn't believe me?" the doorman asked.

"Then you tell him there's a crazy cop out here with a gun just burnin' to put a hole in his chest," Dead-Eye said.

"Go ahead, kid," Boomer told the still-shaking doorman, putting his shield back in his pocket. "Convince him. We'll watch the desk while you're gone. My friend here's in the business."

· · ·

Boomer and Dead-Eye stood behind a circular mahogany desk, staring down at a series of camera banks covering the building and elevators from all angles and a three-unit computerized phone system.

"Most of the doorman buildings have setups like this?" Boomer asked, clicking the cameras on at different locations.

Dead-Eye nodded. "The ones with money do. This system's pretty new. Can't be more than a year old. Guy working the desk controls the elevator. You tell him the floor, he hits the button from here."

"So you can get off only at the floor he presses," Boomer said.

"Cuts down on break-ins," Dead-Eye said. "And you can clock who went to what floor at what time."

"It work both ways?" Boomer asked. "Up and down?"

"Just coming in. When you leave the apartment is still your business. It's when you enter that everybody knows."

"What the guy at the desk doesn't know, these cameras do," Boomer said, running a hand across the monitors. "Every corner's covered."

"It's like that in the building I work," Dead-Eye said. "I can tell you who throws out his trash and when they do it."

"Anything happens up there with Junior," Boomer said. "We make sure it happens *inside* the apartment. Last thing we want is our mugs on these camera reels."

"They'll catch us going in," Dead-Eye said.

"Then we make our play out on the street," Boomer said, looking up and seeing the doorman walk toward them. "Or at a safer drop. For the record, we're here just to talk to the man."

"You talk," Dead-Eye said. "I'll listen."

"Don't matter if you talk or not," Boomer said, slapping Dead-Eye on the back and smiling. "We get pinched, you're the one's going to be put away."

"How you figure?"

"White guy always walks," Boomer said. "Black guy takes the fall."

"You sound exactly like my father," Dead-Eye said as he shut down the cameras that covered the perimeter and hallways on the sixteenth floor.

"And mine," Boomer said.

They walked out from behind the counter, nodded at the doorman, took the set of keys from his hand, and headed for the open elevator door.

. . .

THEY STOOD in the center of the two-bedroom apartment overlooking the Manhattan skyline, surrounded by a blend of leather and chrome furniture, six-figure paintings, sculptures resting on antique surfaces, and religious artifacts, all of which highlighted human and animal sacrifice.

"We don't need to take a poll to figure out how fucked up Junior is," Boomer said.

"A goat head on the wall is always a giveaway," Dead-Eye pointed out. "And you can't afford to miss the view over by the fireplace."

Boomer turned and stared at a circular pattern of various animal and human body parts nailed to the wall above the center fireplace, dried blood lining the sides like thin streak prints. Below them was a round oak-wood table covered by an assortment of candles of different sizes.

"A lot of what's up there's only a few days old," Boomer said, taking a few steps closer, eyes studying the wall. "This guy likes his kill fresh."

"All the cuts are from a ragged-edged knife," Dead-Eye said. "We look hard enough, we'll find it in here somewhere. Give us something to use to put him away with."

"I'd just as soon go with plan B," Boomer said, turning his head toward the door just as Junior's key jangled in the latch.

"Which is what?"

"I'll let you know soon as I think of it," Boomer said, watching the door open and Junior's body fill the entryway.

. . .

IF JUNIOR WAS surprised, he didn't show it.

He took the key from the lock, slid it back into his pocket, and closed the door softly behind him. He gave them an arrogant smirk as he walked into the living room, a lit cigarette cupped in his right hand, and tossed his Bill Blass lamb's wool coat onto the back of a dining room chair. He was wearing cuffed tan slacks, brown loafers with tassels, a button-down cream-colored Calvin Klein shirt, and a brown Hickey-Freeman jacket. Everything about Junior smelled of money and upbringing.

And everything about his apartment smelled of a depravity that would elude any rational explanation.

"You two look too stupid to be burglars," Junior said, smiling and sitting down in a leather recliner. "So I figure you must be cops. Am I right?"

Boomer walked over to Junior and stared down at him for several seconds before he slapped him across the face with the back of his hand, the hard crack echoing through the room. A red finger welt covered Junior's face from the side of his head to his jawline.

"I have a few questions I need to ask," Boomer said in a calm voice, feeling the cop gears clicking back in. "And I want the answers I'm expecting."

"And if I decide to tell you shit?" Junior said, his arrogance only slightly tempered. "What then, assholes?"

Boomer reared back and landed another slap across the same side of the face, only this one was harder. A thin line of blood formed on Junior's lower lip.

"I ask the questions," Boomer said. "You're here only to give the answers."

Junior wiped the blood from his mouth with the back of his hand. He looked past Boomer and over to Dead-Eye. "And what's the nigger here to do?" Junior asked with a smirk. "Take notes?"

This time Boomer punched him flush to the forehead, sending

Junior's head snapping against the back of the recliner, a large red blotch forming in the center of his head, just above his nose, which was now flowing blood down to his mouth.

"Be polite," Boomer said. "It counts toward your final grade."

"You two have no idea who you're playing with," Junior said, trying to sound tough, blood running past his chin and down onto his shirt collar. "None at all. If my father knew any of this, he would have the both of you in jail before dark."

"Pop ever been up here?" Dead-Eye asked. "Check out your collection? Or he just pays out whenever psycho son gets jammed up?"

"You're gonna be a dot on the sidewalk outside before your father even knows where the fuck you are," Boomer said. "So save the my-daddy's-rich routine for people who scare easy. Now, I wanna know names and places and I'm gonna get them from you. If I don't, I start putting *your* body parts up there on the wall. Nod if you're starting to understand."

Junior nodded, blood streaming down the front of his shirt, his arrogance giving way to uneasiness.

Boomer snapped open the top two buttons of Junior's shirt, exposing a gold chain around his neck. Boomer's fingers slowly began to scan the items hanging down from it. They were dried animal parts mostly—teeth, nails, stretched skin.

Boomer stopped when he saw the finger.

It was human and the cut was fresh, pink polish still gleaming on the nail. The flesh around the finger was unlined, free of scars and the bruises of age. It belonged to someone young, and the lack of calluses told Boomer that someone was a girl.

A hard look filled Boomer's eyes and Junior was quick to catch it. Fear started to creep into his voice.

"I don't know where that came from," Junior said. "I swear to you. It was a gift."

"Hey, Dead-Eye," Boomer said, his eyes not moving away from Junior.

"Yeah, Boom?" Disgust etched across the angles of Dead-Eye's face.

"I think I just came up with plan B," Boomer said.

. . .

MALCOLM PUT A LIGHT to the top end of the sheer plastic pipe and closed his eyes, letting the thin vapors of smoke fill his lungs and jolt his brain. His lips curled into a smile as he rested the hot pipe on his lap and looked across at the man with the long scar running down the right side of his face. The man sat with his legs crossed, staring out onto the empty side street.

They were in the back of a new four-door Cadillac that had plush leather seats and a well-stocked bar. A driver in a dark blue suit sat up front, keeping the engine on idle and the car warm.

"I never smoked rock was this clean," Malcolm said, the smile on his face growing wider, his words coming out slow and slurred.

The man turned from the window and looked at Malcolm, eyes hidden by a pair of dark, wraparound ski shades. "You supply what I need, Malcolm," the man said, his lips barely moving as he spoke, "and you'll die with a clean pipe in your hand."

"A man can't ask for more," Malcolm said with a nervous laugh.

"A man like you shouldn't," the man said.

He had jumped out in front of Malcolm by the Eighth Avenue side of the Lincoln Tunnel entrance. A smart man in a smart suit, standing by a new car, wanting to talk over a little business. He said he got Malcolm's name from Smiley Glimmer and was waiting there, ready to offer him all the free smoke he could handle. All Malcolm had to do in return was sit back in the car, get high, and listen.

Malcolm was in a hurry, rushing to get back to his room and do the girl a few more times before handing her over to Junior so he could start shredding her up. Then he planned to wash down the taste of the girl with a week's supply of smoke Junior was going to dish as payoff. But the promise of a taste of rock, a taste that cost more than Malcolm would see in a year, was too strong for him to pass up. Besides, taking a couple of slides off the pipe would put him in a better mood, make him enjoy the girl even more.

The driver never spoke and the man only in short sentences. The man put a hand into his coat pocket and handed Malcolm two more cocaine rocks.

"These are for later," the man said. "Help you get to sleep the right way."

"What's your market?" Malcolm asked, shoving the rocks into his shirt pocket.

"Girls," the man said, lifting the crack pipe back to Malcolm's lips and lighting it with a flick of a gold butane. "The younger the better."

"Only kind I know to deal in," Malcolm said, drawing in a deep breath. The smoke turned the soft skin behind his eyes a cloudy shade of gray.

"And there's one other thing," the man said, smiling for the first time.

"What's that gonna be?" Malcolm asked.

"Babies," the man said.

"Babies?" Malcolm held the pipe inches away from his mouth. "What kind of babies?"

"The kind that cry till you rock them," the man said, turning his attention back to the street. "The ones that make men smile and women want to hold."

"These babies for you?" Malcolm asked, still confused by the request.

The man turned back and looked at Malcolm. He removed the shades, dark eyes cutting a sharp path past the crack smoke and Malcolm's dulled senses. He reached a hand into his shirt pocket and slid out a black business card.

"For my boss," the man said. He handed the card to Malcolm, who stared down at it, glassy eyes unable to read the name and Arizona address stenciled across the front in white letters.

"Keep it," the man told Malcolm. "And remember the name. When you have something, you call that number and someone will find you."

"How much?" Malcolm asked, slipping the card into his jeans.

"Ten thousand for a baby," the man said, putting the shades back on. "Five thousand for a girl who can give us one. Twenty for both."

"I always liked babies," Malcolm said, nodding, a wide smile on his face. "Now I like 'em even more."

"They can help make you rich," the man said. "If you're smart."

"I'm a doper," Malcolm said, "not a dummy."

"The card in your pocket will decide that." The man now leaned over and placed a Polaroid snapshot between the fingers of Malcolm's right hand. Malcolm brought the picture to eye level, squinting, trying to focus.

The photo was of a male body, charred beyond recognition, washed ashore on a desolate strand of beach.

"What's this?" Malcolm asked.

"It's not a what," the man said. "It's a who. He lost the card and let someone else see the name. That forced me to come get him. It took a long time to find him and it took him a long time to die."

"What's on that card stays with me," Malcolm said, seeing the photo in his hand with a clear eye. "Bet your life on it."

"I'll do one better, Malcolm," the man said. "I'm going to bet yours."

. . .

JUNIOR MOVED SLOWLY down the street, sandwiched between Boomer and Dead-Eye, two blocks away from where they had parked the car. Cold blasts of air hit against his sweat-stained clothes, causing him to shiver and bury his hands deeper into his pockets.

"I told you the address," Junior said, turning his head from the wind. "Why do you still need me?"

"In case you lied to me," Boomer said. "I don't wanna have to go all the way back uptown just to kill you."

"You aren't fooling anybody," Junior said. "You're gonna kill me no matter what."

"Don't know about him," Dead-Eye said. "But I'm sure leaning that way."

"Work with me on this one," Boomer said. "You come up with us and finger old pal Malcolm. He takes a ride in a patrol car and kills a few months down at Rikers. He's got nothing but time to tell all the brothers that you were the one stooled him out."

"That's not right," Junior said, shifting his head from Boomer to Dead-Eye. "You said all I had to do was point out the building and give you the apartment number. You didn't say anything about me going up. You promised." His voice degenerated into a whine.

"Here's a lesson for you, Junior," Boomer said, gripping his arm to prevent a bolt. "Never believe what a cop tells you."

"Your daddy's got enough money to buy himself a judge or maybe pay off a family too scared to know better," Dead-Eye said. "But not enough money's been made can keep a street stool alive."

"Like walking around with a loaded gun to your head," Boomer agreed. "Sooner or later, the trigger's gonna click."

"You don't have to do this." Junior's voice had risen to full-throttle panic. "And who says I have to show you the right building. I could keep you two walking all fucking night if I wanted."

"We better get there before my leg starts to ache," Dead-Eye said. "My mood turns ugly when that happens."

"Does your father know?" Boomer asked, hand still wrapped around Junior's arm. "About your little hobbies?"

"Who you think I learned them from?" Junior said, a heavy dose of sarcasm moving in beside the fear. "Some kids play catch in the backyard with their dad. And some don't."

"And I was pissed at my dad for making me collect stamps." Dead-Eye shook his head.

"You missed out on the big-time," Boomer said. "Coulda been out on the cannibal circuit with Junior here and his old man, making finger neckties and toe necklaces instead of getting glue on your tongue."

"Yeah. And even money says his collection's worth more than mine," Dead-Eye said.

"But at least you can always send somebody a letter," Boomer said. "That's gotta count for something."

. . .

MALCOLM WAS ON his knees, naked, a knife in one hand, his other gripping Jennifer Santori's waist. The force of his thrusts banged the top of her head against the side of the wall, but his mind was too clouded by drugs and drink to hear her screams and moans. With the knife he slashed thin lines across her bare shoulders. Her blood ran down her body and splattered up onto Malcolm's face and chest.

She was naked, numb, and ready to die.

Jennifer wanted Malcolm to kill her. She mentally begged him to free her from the torrent of sexual assaults and abuse. She had lost all sense of time, but felt as if she had been cuffed to the pipe forever, held captive to a madman's demons. The blood over her severed finger had caked, but it still ached from the pain. The cuts down her back felt like sharp pinches, the kind she'd given her brother when he teased her too much about the way she combed her hair. Only the pinches from Malcolm's blade drew blood and left scars.

As if from afar, she heard Malcolm groan with pleasure, then he eased out of her, falling face down on the floor.

"I'm gonna miss you, baby," he said, out of breath and drenched with sweat, right hand clutching the bloody blade. "You one of my favorite catches."

Jennifer stared at him, her mind darting with quick, brutal snaps of all that had been done to her. She took a deep breath, felt the sting settle in her lungs and the dryness coat her throat. She leaned closer, stretching her arm as far down as the radiator pipe would allow.

"Whatta ya need, baby?" Malcolm asked, still breathing hard, watching her move closer. "Ain't no time for any more lovin'. We gotta get you ready for Junior. Coupla hours from now you be playin' in his house and you gonna be beggin' for me to come save you. That's a fact."

Jennifer closed her eyes, her legs cut and scraped, inching along the wooden floor, smelling the foul mixture of urine, semen, blood, and drug residue. She stopped when the cuff cut deeper into her wrist, the skin already sliced away, white bone exposed. She brought her head down and could smell Malcolm's breath. She opened her eyes, looked at him one more time, holding the stare, wishing she could reach over and pounce on the face she would never be able to erase from her memory.

She knew that if she lived, if she somehow escaped from Malcolm's hold, she would always be his prisoner. The days and nights spent captive in this room had ensured that he would always be alive inside her, crawling to the surface at any moment, bringing with him the visions and the pain, resurrecting the horror and misery she had suffered.

She knew that smiling face would be as much a part of the rest of her life as her own skin. And as young as she was, as innocent as she'd been, she realized that if, in some way, she survived this nightmare and was set free, she would wait for the moment and then commit the one act that would break his hold on her.

At that moment Jennifer Santori knew that if Malcolm did not kill her, she would one day take her own life.

Malcolm stuck the edge of the knife into a floor panel and used it to help lift his face up. He inched closer to Jennifer, always with the smile, his brain still reeling from the smoked rock and the Four Roses pint he'd lifted from a street rummy.

"Why you lookin' at Malcolm like that?" he asked her. "There something you want to say? Is there, baby?"

Jennifer nodded her head.

"What, baby?" Malcolm said in a voice that for him passed as soft and concerned. "Tell me."

Jennifer drew up all that was left of her strength, took in one more long breath, and then spoke her very first words since Malcolm had taken her finger.

"Fuck you," she said.

Malcolm reacted with a rage not even Jennifer could have imagined. He jumped to his feet, dropped the knife to the floor, and began punching her, his two closed fists balled into stone. He forgot all about Junior and cleaning Jennifer up for his approval. His fury was unleashed now, and there was no reeling it back.

His punches landed hard, heavy, and often, smashing bone and breaking skin. Within minutes there wasn't a part of Jennifer's body that wasn't bruised, bleeding, or broken. When he tired of throwing punches and landing kicks, Malcolm grabbed her hair and slammed the front of her head against the base of the cold radiator.

"Talk to me like that?" Malcolm shouted. "After all I done for you. You bitch! You spoiled, rich, fuckin' bitch! You gonna die here. You gonna die for talkin' to me like that."

Malcolm's words were heard by no one.

Jennifer was long past hearing him, her mind having entered a warm room surrounded by familiar sounds, smells, and features. A room where she would be loved and trusted. A room where no intruder would ever be allowed in to cause her harm.

A room far away, removed from blood, pain, and misery.

A room that would always remain unknown to a crazed man named Malcolm Juniper.

And a room where the shadows of Boomer Frontieri and Dead-Eye Winthrop would soon loom large.

. . .

JUNIOR CAME CRASHING and flailing through the wooden front door, crying out in pain as he landed on his hands and knees, his right hand inches from the handle of Malcolm's bloody knife. Boomer and Dead-Eye stood in the entryway behind him, arms out straight, guns cocked and drawn, aimed at Malcolm's head.

"Move away from the girl," Boomer told Malcolm, looking down at the still body. "I want you with your back to the wall and your hands out flat."

Malcolm let go of Jennifer's hair, took two steps back, and pressed his body against the wall. He was breathing through his mouth, his body tense and coated with a foul-smelling sweat.

Boomer stepped over Junior, sliding the gun back into his hip holster as he walked over to his friend's daughter. He crouched down and held her battered face, wiped away strands of hair and brushed off lines of blood and mucus. He slid his hand down to her neck and felt for a pulse. It was beating at a low rate, just enough to keep her alive.

"She needs a doctor fast." Boomer cradled Jennifer's head with both hands. Fighting both the impulse to cry and the desire to kill, he turned to Malcolm. "Where are the keys to the cuffs? And I don't wanna hear anything more outta you than the fuckin' answer."

Malcolm kept his eyes square on the barrel of Dead-Eye's gun. "Front pocket of my jeans."

Boomer rested Jennifer's head against the wall and took four quick steps over to Malcolm's jeans, which were crumpled in the center of the room. He picked them up and took out a tiny set of silver keys. Along with the keys, Boomer pulled out a business card, black with white lettering. He pocketed the card and walked back to Jennifer. It was then that he noticed the missing finger.

Malcolm ran a dry tongue over an even drier set of lips. Sweat dripped down the small of his back and he couldn't stop the right side of his face from twitching.

Boomer uncuffed Jennifer, brought her arm down gently to her side. He pulled a handkerchief from his back pocket and wrapped it around the top of her hand. As the girl let out a soft whimper of pain, he held Jennifer in his arms and lifted her up.

"It got a little crazy," Malcolm said. "That happens sometimes."

Boomer made no attempt to hide his revulsion. He'd seen a lot in the years since he first pinned on his shield and he knew about the ugliness that filtered down the streets of his beat: men who killed the women they loved over the last hit on a pipe; dealers who sold poison to junkies, caring little that they would die within seconds of the rush; hitters who murdered strangers for cash and walked off into the night without care or concern; radicals so filled with hate they butchered the innocent in honor of some indefinite principle. All those he had seen and, over the years, had slowly come to understand.

But what he had seen over the past several days was a new form of evil. The man he stood across from and the other on his knees behind him were alien creatures to Boomer, each so willing to drop into the depths of an inhumanity he found terrifying.

There had been many criminals who'd crossed paths with Boomer whom he'd found pleasure in arresting. There were a handful he had killed because of the situation and the moment. But there had never been anyone he had wanted to kill for the pure emotional need to eliminate him.

Not until he crossed paths with Junior and Malcolm.

"I'm taking the girl," Boomer said quietly. "The police'll be here soon and take you and your friend away." He took two steps back, and for a moment closed his eyes.

"Learn to pray, Malcolm," Boomer said. "Pray for a long prison sentence and for me to die the day before you get out."

. . .

DEAD-EYE HAD HIS gun back down by his side, the heat of anger swelling within him as well. It was fueled by the bleakness of the room, the thick smell of blood and body fluids that filtered into his lungs. He fought back a desire to scream, trying to erase from his head images of his own wife and son caught in the grips of such men. His eyes were fixed on the girl in Boomer's arms, so different now from the open, smiling face on the picture that was hidden inside the fold of his jacket pocket.

It takes a great deal to touch a hardened man, to penetrate the defensive shield and reach down and press his vulnerable core. Dead-Eye always felt he had made himself strong enough to escape such pressure.

He knew now that he was wrong.

Dead-Eye took his eyes away from the girl and looked down at Junior, who had inched closer to Malcolm's knife. His fingers were stretching to reach it, only a quick grab away from the handle. Junior had stayed silent, making himself easy to ignore. He had glanced behind him and was aware that Dead-Eye's gun was at rest, no longer pointed at him. Besides, the rich, pampered Junior was arrogant enough to think no cop would ever shoot him and expect to walk away.

It was the perfect time to make his move.

Malcolm saw it first, saw Junior standing behind Boomer, the blade of the knife held high, ready to come down hard into the cop's back, the gleeful look of a vengeful killer fulfilling his fate.

Malcolm curled a half-smile over at Boomer and shook his head slowly. "Maybe," he said, "I don't have to pray so hard as you think."

Boomer looked into Malcolm's eyes, saw the confidence suddenly show itself. He held his ground, gripping Jennifer's slight body closer to him, burying her head deeper into his chest, sensing what was about to happen.

One shot brought it to an end.

It came out of Dead-Eye's .44 and flew past the center of Junior's brain.

A low, guttural moan came from deep inside Junior's body. Thick, dark gushes of blood sprayed across Malcolm's face and over the back of Boomer's head and neck. Boomer turned to see Junior fall face first to the floor, the hole in his head large enough to shine a spotlight through, the knife held loose in the curve of his right hand. Behind them, Dead-Eye stood in a crouch position, his legs spread, right arm extended, smoke filtering off the barrel of his gun.

"You're not supposed to shoot a suspect in the back," Boomer said. "Or is that one of the classes you missed?"

"He wasn't a suspect," Dead-Eye said, holstering his gun and walking toward Boomer, ignoring the body on the floor. "And I didn't shoot him in the back. I shot him in the head."

"Give the uniforms your statement," Boomer said. "I'll call in from the hospital to back it up. Then we'll take it all from there."

"I'll tell 'em what I saw," Malcolm said, his upper body starting to shiver. "Swear to God, tell 'em everything. Unless you let me go. Now."

"Look down at that big hole in Junior's head," Dead-Eye said to Malcolm, turning his back on him long enough to close the door behind Boomer and the little girl in his arms. "Then remember I've still got five more bullets in my gun."

Dead-Eye rested his back against a far wall, his legs stretched out, arms folded across his chest. In the distance, he heard police sirens drawing closer.

"I don't see you puttin' down a brother," Malcolm said. "You don't look the type to kill your own blood."

Dead-Eye pushed himself away from the wall, the siren wails growing louder, and headed straight for Malcolm. He pulled the gun from his holster, cocked it, and jammed it right under the naked man's chin.

"We don't have the same blood," Dead-Eye said, barely moving his lips, shoving the gun in harder against the fleshy part of Malcolm's jaw. "And, believe me, I would kill any brother who was scum like you. Even my own."

He pulled the gun away, stepped over Junior's body, and walked to the apartment door. He opened the door, leaned his shoulders against the cracked hinges, rested his head on the wood, and stared up at a bare bulb hanging from a ceiling wire.

A cop waiting to be rescued.

9

BOOMER SAT AT his usual corner table at Nunzio's, hovering over a large bowl of penne with pesto. Across from him, Dead-Eye quietly cut into a thick char-broiled veal chop. Nunzio Goldman watched as they both ate, his back to a closed window, a large glass of red wine in front of him.

Nunzio knew his two friends had been through an ordeal these past few days. He could read it in their faces. Reading people was one of the things that came as second nature to Nunzio Goldman. He had spent his life on both sides of the law and managed to avoid any problems from either end. The good cops, like Boomer and Dead-Eye, trusted him. They knew that bets came in steady over his phone and that the sporting spreads for the Upper West Side were set behind his bar, but that kind of action didn't interest them. Boomer's mother bet a dollar on a number every day of her life, even hit one on a few occasions. Dead-Eye's father had ten dollars riding every week on his beloved Giants during football season, with or without points. It didn't make it right, it just didn't make it a crime, not in their eyes. Not when off-track betting in New York State was legal, enticing people as easily as any street hustler to lay down money they could ill afford to lose. To Boomer and Dead-Eye's way of thinking, they were all bookies.

Dirty cops periodically tried to shake Nunzio down and were always sent away empty-handed. Nunzio made it his business to get as much information on them as could be dug up. If they were too dirty for his hands, he passed the folders on to the right people. If they were just looking to do some light skimming, he told the cops what he knew about their business and threw down a simple choice—either disappear from his line of vision or prepare to deal with Internal Affairs.

In Nunzio's world there was no black and white, only shades of gray, and he lived with ease within that cloudy area. He was a criminal who hated drugs and all that their sale embodied, but was comfortable in the company of hired killers who contracted out murders as easily as he sliced off strips of prosciutto. He ran an honest restaurant, treating customers with respect and serving only the finest foods he could afford. At the same time, he and his accountant devoted hours to cooking the books, keeping two sets of ledgers, reporting only the false set to the Internal Revenue Service. In the midst of a complicated universe, Nunzio Goldman kept his life and his ways as simple as he could manage.

"What kind of fallout did you guys get from taking out Junior?" Nunzio asked Boomer and Dead-Eye.

"His father says he's gonna sue the department." Boomer paused, filling his mouth with pasta. "He's put a team of six-figure lawyers on the case."

"He know you were in on it?" Nunzio asked.

"He knows what he was told," Dead-Eye said. "Two retired detectives heard a rumor about a young girl being held against her will in an abandoned building."

"When we went in, Junior panicked and came after me with a knife," Boomer added. "And Dead-Eye iced him."

"That's not gonna be enough for Pop," Nunzio said. "He's gonna want the ones buried his son."

"They can take my pension if they want it," Boomer said, breaking off a hunk of bread from a basket. "I don't give a fuck. Nothing can take back what they did to that kid."

"Pop's gonna use his money to talk for him against the two of you. I'll use mine to talk against him. End of the day, we'll see whose money talks louder." Nunzio sipped his wine.

"How's Jennifer?"

Boomer put down his fork, took a sip from a glass of mineral water, and looked over at Nunzio, sadness easing its way across his face. "The doctors, with all their fucking diplomas, told her parents that kids can rebound out of these kinds of things."

"She say anything?" Nunzio said. "Can she talk at all?"

"I was carryin' her down the street to my car." Boomer's voice betrayed the weight of his emotions. "I still couldn't get over the shape she was in. So much blood, so many bruises, you had to look to find skin. I was cursin' to myself, sick about the whole fuckin' business. Then she opens one eye, looks at me, and says 'thank you.' " Boomer put his head down and picked up his fork.

"I'm only sorry I didn't leave Malcolm's body on top of Junior's," Dead-Eye said. "Cancel out both their checking accounts."

"What happens to him now?" Nunzio asked.

"Malcolm?" Dead-Eye said. "He's looking at a hard ten. Even with a soft judge and a kind wacko report."

"Doesn't seem like it's enough," Nunzio said.

"It's never enough," Boomer said. "No matter what they end up with, it's never enough."

"The family needs anything," Nunzio said, finishing off his wine and getting up from the table, "let 'em know I'll do all I can."

They watched the restaurant owner walk toward the bar, giving quick greetings to diners along the way.

"How much juice does Nunzio really have?" Dead-Eye asked, leaning back in his chair.

"About as much as he needs," Boomer said.

He paused for a moment and then reached inside the pocket of his blue button-down J. Crew shirt. He pulled out the card he had taken from Malcolm's jeans and slid it across the table.

"Lucia Carney," Dead-Eye said, reading the name printed on it. "Should that mean something to me?"

"She's got four names." Boomer picked up the card and placed it back in his shirt pocket. "Been married three times. All three husbands ended up dead."

"Everything comes in threes," Dead-Eye said. "Good things and bad."

"She works out of Arizona," Boomer said. "Runs a day care center. One of those drop-off-at-seven, pick-up-at-six places. Takes in about fifteen, maybe twenty thousand a year."

"Any kids of her own?" Dead-Eye said.

"Can't have any," Boomer said. "She had a botched abortion when she was twenty. Messed up her insides. She was either living with or spending quality time with a drug runner down south. Beyond that, her early background's sketchy."

"I'm ready for another Pepsi," Dead-Eye said. "You set with your water?"

"Get yourself two and a large bottle of Pellegrino for the table," Boomer said, pushing his chair back and walking off toward the men's room. "I'll pick it up from there when everybody else gets here."

"Who's everybody else?" Dead-Eye asked, wondering where Boomer was taking all this, why he had devoted so much time to digging into the life of a three-time widow who spent her days watching other people's kids.

"Don't worry," Boomer said, stopping between two empty tables. "You'll like 'em. They're a bunch of cripples. Like you and me."

· · ·

BOOMER FRONTIERI HAD STOPPED being a cop physically but not emotionally. His every action, every movement, every glance smelled of cop. He would regularly pass on tips he picked up from old street stools to the beat units and was one of the few retired cops brazen enough to make citizen's arrests. Once, not long after he'd been pensioned off, he spotted two teens mugging an elderly woman on Sixty-sixth Street, over near Central Park. He cornered the two, confiscated their pocket knives, and yanked them face forward against a black stone wall. He needed to keep them in place while he phoned for two uniforms. After helping the woman to her feet and resting her against a parked car, he stopped a young student heading home from a nearby private school.

"What's your name?" he said to the startled boy.

"Joshua," the kid said.

Boomer pulled the service revolver from his hip holster and handed it to Joshua. "Make sure they don't move" was all he said, pointing to the two teens over by the wall.

"What if they do?" Joshua said, holding the gun toward the pair, both hands shaking.

"Then shoot 'em," Boomer said, limping off to the corner phone booth to call the local precinct.

The rescue of Jennifer Santori had brought Boomer back to life. He was angered and repulsed by all that he had witnessed, but it also made him feel like a cop again. His mind was back on red alert, and the adrenaline rush was nearly strong enough to drown out the pain of his wounds. The eventual capture was worth the risk of being hit with a fatal bullet. He knew now that was all he had to keep him going.

The risk.

After finding her card in Malcolm's pocket, Boomer spent three full days gathering information on Lucia Carney. His first meeting was with DEA Special Agent Tony Malazante, a head banger from his days working buys and busts in Alphabet City. Over two cups of coffee in a downtown diner, Malazante told him about a new brand of cocaine that was just hitting the streets. The dealers called it crack, the junkies called it heaven, and the narcs called it their biggest problem since the Golden Triangle glory days of heroin. New York got its first taste in late 1981. Since then, arrests had multiplied and demand for the drug quadrupled.

"What's the difference between that and regular blow?" Boomer asked.

"The hits are cheaper," Malazante said. "Five bucks gets you high for five minutes. Don't need a lot of cash to stay on the wire all day. You can pick it up stealing petty."

"Who's in on it?"

"Everybody so far but the Italians," Malazante said, sipping from a large cup of mocha. "The demand's so high that a street dealer can set up shop on a Monday and have a full crew of twenty working for him by Friday."

"Where's it coming from?" Boomer wanted to know, holding Lucia's card in his right hand.

"Same place all this shit comes from," Malazante said. "South America. Southeast Asia. And it's landing heavy on the streets. The rock comes in and the cash goes out, usually on the same day."

"That's where Lucia comes in," Boomer said. "How big a hitter is she?"

"She started out small-time." Malazante leaned his large frame against the back of a torn plastic booth. "Now I'd say she's in the top three, easy. She's got a big outfit that's well run and, I guess you could say, unique."

"What's unique about it?"

Malazante finished the rest of his coffee and leaned closer to his friend. "I can help you with this, Boomer," he said. "But only up to a point. I don't know what you're thinking and I don't want to know. You and me didn't talk about this and I didn't leave this folder behind on my seat. If anybody asks, we met, had coffee, and talked about my kids."

"You don't have any kids," Boomer said.

"Then we didn't talk," Malazante said, squeezing his girth out of the booth.

An old girlfriend from the FBI gave Boomer the statistics he needed about crack and a confidential printout on Lucia Carney. She promised to help in the future as well, in return for anonymity and the occasional dinner at Nunzio's. He spent a day working the computers at One Police Plaza, cross-referencing Lucia's name with known cartel bosses and seven-figure dealers. In between, Boomer ate a quiet office lunch with Deputy Chief Ken Wolfson, a bright, personable man who collected rare comic books and was known on the streets as a cop who liked to see jobs done with as few questions asked as possible. He agreed to be Boomer's inside man so long as his involvement was that of a silent partner. Boomer would assume all the risks. Wolfson's cops would get the credit for any busts. Once that was agreed upon, the deputy chief opened a file drawer and laid out all the NYPD background information on Lucia Carney.

A connection from the Bureau of Alcohol, Tobacco and Firearms then gave Boomer a stat sheet filled with her known lift-and-drop locations. A neighborhood friend now working for a Secret Service unit in Maryland gave him a detailed report on her money-laundering capabilities and how the fast cash was washed overnight between one flight and the next.

In seventy-two hours, using the sources available to him, Boomer Frontieri knew as much about Lucia Carney as any cop in the country. He studied up on crack and read assorted medical documents detailing its instant addiction. He learned about mules and smurfs and the women who carried drugs and cash for Lucia and the men who killed at her whim. The more he read, heard, and learned, the more determined Boomer Frontieri grew. His anger wasn't fueled by the fact that she was a drug queen. He had heard about other such women working the distribution end of the drug business.

It wasn't even the amount of money involved, even though it totaled out to a numbing multibillion-dollar-a-year network.

It was the way she did it.

Lucia Carney was as cold and as heartless as any drug runner Boomer Frontieri had ever seen. Life meant nothing to her, especially an innocent life that had yet to begin.

That's why he read and reread the folders until his vision blurred, quietly steeling himself toward making the most difficult decision of his life.

. . .

DR. CAROLYN BARTLETT sat on a gray folding chair, her legs crossed, blond hair combed back into a tight bun. The room was filtered with shadows, lit only by a fluorescent bulb attached to the center of the wall, just above the roll-away bed. She read over the contents of a yellow folder which was clutched in her hands, crammed with the detailed notes and observations she had made over the previous four days.

Dr. Bartlett, though only thirty-six, was in charge of the hospital's rape and trauma psychiatric unit. In her four years at the hospital, she had seen all the horror imaginable.

Until the afternoon they wheeled in Jennifer Santori.

The sight of the young girl, the condition of her body, the sunken look on the face of the man who had brought her in, made Bartlett, for the first time, truly question what it was she did and what, if any, difference it made.

She closed the folder, resting it on the ground next to her Cuban-heeled black Ferragamo shoes, and ran her hands across the starched white sheets of the bed. She took a deep breath and touched the soft hand of the young girl asleep beneath those sheets.

She studied the silent, bandaged face. The girl's rest was disturbed only by the occasional twitch and moan. There were three IV pouches draining off into her right arm and bandages covering a multitude of wounds. Her left hand was in a cast that brushed up to her elbow, an empty space where the index finger should have been.

Dr. Bartlett leaned closer and touched each of the wounds with a gentle hand. She had clear blue eyes, a taut athlete's body, and a face that had not begun to betray her years. She had seen a great deal of abuse in her four years at Metro, but never anything close to this. It had taken nurses and interns two full days to wash off the caked blood and three days for Bartlett to get the child to give her anything more than a nod.

She had paid a visit to the suspect. She always made a point of doing that, even though some doctors in the department frowned on the idea. But it was important to her, allowing a rare glimpse into the other side of the room, in an invariably futile attempt to understand why such men—and they were always men—did what they did to their victims.

She didn't get much out of Malcolm Juniper, about as much as she got out of any of them. He smiled, asked for some coffee, even asked her how Jennifer was doing. She turned her back on him when he asked for her phone number, leaving him with a smile on his face and a look in his eyes that told her all she really needed to know. She walked out of the holding room thinking about her father, Richie Bartlett, a twenty-year veteran of the NYPD who had killed two men in the line of duty and who died working three jobs so his dream of a daughter with a medical degree could become a reality. She wondered how long Malcolm Juniper would have survived in a locked room with Richie Bartlett.

Dr. Bartlett sat back in her chair, her eyes locked on Jennifer's face. It was early for the dreams and nightmares to begin, but she knew they would soon be there for the girl who had seen so much darkness in such a short period of time. She knew that the girl's parents would turn to her for answers, for pleas to bring the nightmares to a halt, but all her years of training, all the books and files and reports, now boiled down to one horrible fact: She couldn't make those nightmares stop. They would be a part of Jennifer Santori for the rest of her days.

Helping Jennifer cope with the night visions was the best Dr. Bartlett could do. In truth, it was the only hope she could offer.

There was a bigger problem facing Dr. Bartlett, one she had wrestled with since she was first handed the file folder less than three days before. She knew that the police, the district attorney's office, every prosecutor assigned to her case, would need Jennifer's testimony, demand it, in order to secure a prison space for Malcolm Juniper. Without Jennifer Santori in the courtroom, there would be no conviction. There wouldn't even be a case. But having Jennifer testify would mean reliving the nightmare. It would mean sitting next to a judge and, worse, across from Malcolm Juniper, telling all in attendance what had been done to her, in full detail, with as many follow-up questions as the defense team could muster. Questions meant to rattle a teenager and release the shackles from a man without remorse.

Dr. Bartlett stood and leaned closer to Jennifer. She stroked her hair, careful not to touch the thick bandages surrounding it, gently

10

THEY SAT CROWDED around a table in a rear room off the main bar. Boomer held the head, his back against a wood-paneled wall, just below a framed photo of Nino Benvenuti and Emile Griffith slugging it out for the middleweight title. Dead-Eye sat to Boomer's left, a large wine glass filled with ice and Pepsi in his hand, a puzzled look on his face.

There were four others gathered around the table, three men and an attractive woman in tight jeans, white crew neck, and soft leather jacket. Dead-Eye knew that they were all cops. They had the look and the attitude, each coming into the room with a swagger, greeting Boomer with only a handshake and a cautious nod.

If they were all cripples, like Boomer said, then they managed to hide their handicaps successfully. You couldn't tell much by looking at them, except for the guy hanging loose in the far corner, a young, dark-haired man in a hooded sweatshirt that couldn't hide the reddened, burnt skin around his neck, hands, and along the right side of his face.

Dead-Eye also had the guy across from him figured, more or less. He was tall and muscular, sitting with his hands spread flat across the tablecloth, a large glass of skim milk in front of him, a bowl of ice cubes off to the side. The others had asked for beer, wine, or booze. Generally, only two kinds of cops order milk in a restaurant: those trying to stay on the wagon—and this guy didn't look shaky enough to be walking down that street—and those who'd been shot in the gut. Dead-Eye was even willing to bet that a pat-down of the quiet guy in the bombadier jacket would shake out several packets of Maalox and a half-empty bottle of Zantac.

There was little in the way of small talk. Everyone waited for Boomer to open the conversation. But Boomer just sat there, sizing up each cop. The glasses were close to empty and the chunky guy in the bowling jacket was already on his third cigarette, when Nunzio came in with a fresh tray. He rested it in the center of the table, closed the door behind him, and sat on a corner stool.

"The place is closed, Boom," Nunzio said. "I just checked the last couple out."

"You got any pretzels to go with this?" the guy in the bowling jacket, Jimmy "Pins" Ryan, asked, lifting a long-neck Bud from the tray and taking a swig.

"We'll eat later," Boomer said. "After we talk."

"Talk about what?" Delgaldo "Geronimo" Lopez, the man nursing the glass of milk, said.

"A lot of things, Geronimo. We're going to start it off with a story about a lady. After that, if you're still interested, I'll tell you one about us."

"Did Boomer just call you Geronimo?" the guy in the scruffy sweat-shirt, Bobby "Rev. Jim" Scarponi, asked. "I mean, like the Indian?"

"You bothered by it or just curious?" Geronimo looked at Rev. Jim with a hard set of eyes.

"Neither one, Chief," the Rev. said. "And I mean that with respect."

"Just so we're all on the same page and nobody steps on the wrong foot," Boomer began, "know this. Everybody in this room was once a cop. Each top of the line, best in the department. I'm including myself in there. And now we're all disabled, all of us collecting tax-free checks every two weeks. Everybody except for Nunzio over in the corner."

"And he is what?" the woman, Mary "Mrs. Columbo" Silvestri, asked.

"A friend," Boomer said. "And we're gonna need us one of those."

"Does that mean the drinks are on the house?" Rev. Jim asked.

"He said I was a friend," Nunzio told him. "Not an idiot."

"You really know how to warm up a room," Mrs. Columbo said to Rev. Jim.

"I give it my best." The Rev. winked. "That's all you can ask."

"You need us for something, Boomer," Geronimo said. "And it's not to sit here and drink with you. So, let's hear it."

"I just finished something with Dead-Eye," Boomer said. "It started out as a favor for a friend. It ended up taking us to a whole other place."

"I heard about it," Mrs. Columbo said. "A kid got grabbed off the streets. You caught the lifter and somehow his partner managed to walk into your gun."

"The lifter had a business card in his pocket," Boomer went on. "With a woman's name on it. Lucia Carney is what it says on the card, and that's what she likes to be called. At least this week."

"What's her angle?" Rev. Jim asked.

"I told you guys on the phone about her day care center," Boomer said. "That covers her, money-wise, with the IRS."

"So what's her second job?" Geronimo said.

"She moves cocaine into the country," Boomer said. "Cocaine and crack. And then she moves the cash payments out. Guy I know in D.C. tells me she's got herself a crew of at least four hundred spread out across the country. Half of them are smurfs, all of them women. The other half work as muscle."

"What the hell's a smurf?" Nunzio asked.

"Drug and cash couriers," Rev. Jim muttered.

"She calls her smurfs the Babysitter's Club," Boomer said.

"Like the children's books," Mrs. Columbo said. "I just bought a couple of them for my niece."

"Right," Boomer said. "The ladies she uses are all neat and clean. No record, no arrests, no history of drug usage. Half of them don't even know they're movin' shit."

"How do they work the transport?" Dead-Eye asked. "If they don't know they're transporting?"

Boomer took a deep breath before he answered, scanning the faces in the room one more time.

He knew he was going to go after Lucia Carney. That decision was made the minute he ran her aliases through the DEA's BCCI computer. What he didn't know was whether he could get the people in the room to go along with him. He had chosen each of them very carefully, using his instinct but also assessing their individual backgrounds. They were all adrenaline junkies whose daily rush had been taken away long before they were ready to give up the high. Now they were all drifting, living from paycheck to paycheck, working second jobs they couldn't care less about, feeling closer to dead than alive.

They faced a dark future, one crammed with regrets, memories, and could-have-beens.

Boomer knew it.

He was betting they would too.

"Dead babies," Boomer finally said when every face in the room was still enough to focus only on his answer. And his answer got everyone's attention.

"How?" Dead-Eye asked quietly.

"She finds a baby any way she can," Boomer said. "After our experience with Malcolm and Junior, we know there's no shortage of scum out there willing to lift a kid."

"The dealers work the runaways," Rev. Jim said. "Always have. Turn 'em on to the junk, then throw 'em to the streets to earn what they spend on smack. Some of the girls get pregnant, they carry through and sell the kid. But that market's not big enough to supply a whole team of mules."

"This crack shit's changed all the rules," Boomer said, standing and resting his hands on the table. "And Lucia's got every space covered. She's got the runaways, but instead of having 'em turn tricks, she has her crew get them pregnant and hand the babies over to her."

"Probably buys whatever else she needs on the black market," Mrs. Columbo said. "You could move five, maybe ten thousand babies a year that way."

"At the least," Boomer said. "And when all else fails, she lifts them. Home invasions, backseat of a car, front end of a stroller. Anywhere, anyplace, Lucia's crew will make the grab."

"How much she moving?" Geronimo asked. "Cash wise."

"The feds put a rough estimate on it of at least two hundred and fifty million," Boomer said.

"A year?" Pins asked.

"A month," Boomer said.

There was a respectful silence before Dead-Eye asked, "What about the babies? How's she work that angle?"

"She keeps the kids until they're about six, seven months old. Then they kill them."

"I don't know if I want to hear this part," Mrs. Columbo said, downing her scotch and wishing she had another.

"Didn't warm my insides either," Boomer said. "But it's what's out there and what's gotta be stopped."

"They use the dead babies as mules," Rev. Jim said. "Cut 'em open, empty them out, fill them with cocaine for the flight up, and cash for the flight down."

"You knew about this?" Pins asked, putting down his empty bottle of beer.

"I've heard rumors," Rev. Jim said. "Never knew if they were legit."

"They're legit all right," Boomer said. "You get on a plane sitting next to a woman holding a sleeping baby in her arms, you don't even think twice."

"Probably smile and tell her what a beautiful baby she has," Dead-Eye said. "Don't even notice that the baby slept through the entire flight."

"I grew up with hard people," Nunzio said. "Tough people. Some were criminals, ran numbers, owned brothels, couple shot a guy or two. But I don't know any who would turn this way."

"Where are the feds on this?" Mrs. Columbo asked.

"They're on it," Boomer said. "As best they can be. But you can't convict what you can't nail down. And it's not the mules they want. It's Lucia."

"What do we know about her?" Dead-Eye asked. "Besides her little habits of killing babies and burying husbands."

"I've got private access to whatever they have," Boomer said. "And through them, the locals too. Files, surveillance, taps. What I get, I'll pass on to each of you. It's not a lot, but it should be more than enough to get us started."

"Started on what, Boomer?" Geronimo asked. The muscles in his face were rigid.

"On bringing Lucia and her little crew of babysitters down."

There was another silence in the room. Then Mrs. Columbo gave out with a mirthless laugh.

"There are cops out there for this," she said. "*Real* cops. Not ones like us."

"The real cops can't do it," Boomer said.

"Why not?" Geronimo asked.

"Because they're the law and they have to follow it," Boomer said. "We don't."

"Which makes us criminals," Pins said. "Not cops."

"This is a major crew you're talking about," Rev. Jim chimed in. "They've got the money and the muscle. We can't keep up with that. At least I know I can't."

"I can understand some of you being nervous," Boomer said.

"I'm not nervous, Boomer," Mrs. Columbo said. "I'm scared. We probably all are. You were right about what you said before. We were the best in the business. But now we're not. I wake up in pain and go to bed the same way. Just like everybody else in this room. That's no shape to be in when you're chasing down a prime-time queen."

"Six cops, crippled or not, up against a crew of four hundred are pretty steep odds to begin with," Dead-Eye said, wishing for the first time in his life that he smoked.

"You're forgetting someone, Dead-Eye," Nunzio said.

Dead-Eye looked over at him. "Sorry. Six and a half against four hundred."

"That's better." Nunzio nodded, pleased.

"Look, I admit I didn't always go by the book when I was on the job," Geronimo now said. "But this is about more than bending the rules. This is about breaking the law. That's one line I never thought of crossing."

"I'll give you the strongest reason I can think of," Boomer said. "And it's got nothin' to do with Lucia."

"Fuck the suspense, Boomer," Mrs. Columbo said. "Just tell us."

"It'll make us feel alive again." It was Dead-Eye who gave the answer, with a nod toward Boomer. "Make us feel like we used to feel before they took it all away. That's a feeling worth getting back. Even if it kills us. Is that what you were going to say, Boomer?"

"Something like that," Boomer said.

They all sat quietly and digested what they had heard. Each one weighed the task Boomer had laid out before them. It was warm in the room and throats were dry. Pins took off his bowling jacket and tossed it behind his chair. Geronimo leaned back and stretched. Mrs. Columbo kept her eyes on Boomer, both happy and angry that he had called her in. Rev. Jim ran a hand along his scarred neck and kept his head down. Dead-Eye stared into his empty glass.

"Nunzio, do I have to kill somebody to get another drink?" Rev. Jim said, breaking the silence.

"Only on Sundays." Nunzio stood up, opened the door, and headed for the bar.

"You decided already?" Dead-Eye asked Boomer.

"I don't have family like some of you," Boomer said. "I don't have a job I might grow to care about. I've only got the shield. For me, it's an easier decision."

"A shield doesn't cover breaking the law," Pins said.

"I'm still doing what I swore to do," Boomer responded. "Bring the fight to the bad. I'm just doing it a different way, that's all."

"It's a way that can get you killed in a heartbeat," Rev. Jim said.

"Then I exit on my terms. And that's a contract I can follow and not look back on. Now all I'm looking for are a few other signatures."

"And you're recruiting from among the wounded," Dead-Eye said.

Boomer nodded. "That's because they're the most dangerous."

11

THE BRAND-NEW PINK stucco house was large, well lit, and heavily guarded. Motion spots rested behind the dozens of bushes, trees, and large fruit plants that dotted the half acre of property. Two all-terrain vehicles were parked and locked behind thick garage doors and a black Mercedes sat in the circular driveway, shaded by an overhanging palm tree.

The house had been sculpted in the flatbed manner that was so popular with the thousands of fresh faces migrating each year into the rocky terrain of Sedona, Arizona, and its surrounding regions. It had been designed and built on spec by a local company, then sold to a man named Garrison Cross, who paid in full, in cash, and had never once set foot inside. The furnishings had all been ordered through catalogues and department stores, shipped to a Phoenix warehouse, and paid for COD. The wildflowers that circled the exterior had been ordered from a greenery in Scottsdale, prepaid, and shipped, then planted in the middle of the night.

Inside, the rooms were large and spread out, the center hall, living room, and dining room dominating the wood-paneled first floor. A thick oak staircase led to the three bedrooms on the second. There were skylights and gas fireplaces in every room except the kitchen. Wall-clipped surveillance cameras recorded each move, from every possible angle. Two purebred German shepherds walked the rooms with complete freedom. Outside, the morning air was fresh and brisk, with a cool breeze coming down from the cliffs. Less than a mile from the house, tourists, fresh off a fast-food breakfast, were already lined up in front of the Red Rock Jeep Tours waiting area, eager to bounce their way through well-charted terrain.

All the activity was in the kitchen, a large, airy space with bay windows, overhead fans, and a three-screen video display terminal bolted into the granite countertop to the left of the oversized microwave. Two middle-aged women in housecoats and slippers padded quietly across the thick tile floor, carrying cellophane-sealed two-kilo bags of cocaine. They were taking the bags from a large satchel on the kitchen table, then resting them in neat piles next to the sink. Three men in well-tailored suits stood at different ends of the kitchen, eyes hidden by dark shades, arms folded across their chests, silently counting off the piles.

The women were two bags away from emptying the satchel when Lucia Carney walked into the kitchen.

The three men dropped their arms to their sides when they saw her. She stared and smiled at each of them as she passed, the thick aroma of her Chanel perfume filling the air. Her dark hair was combed straight back, hanging down long over the shoulders of a black Karl Lagerfeld dress. She wore four-inch heels and her skirt was slit high on both sides, revealing ample portions of well-sculpted legs. The nails on her fingers and toes were painted dark red, her skin was tanned and unlined, and her brown eyes, while seductive and enticing, conveyed a distant and frightening chill.

Lucia was thirty-eight years old but looked much younger. She maintained her spectacular figure with punishing daily two-hour workouts. She took great pleasure in knowing that men both desired and feared her equally. It was what had helped keep her alive in what was a very dangerous occupation. But for Lucia Carney, surviving was always the priority.

She was born in a clinic in Houston, Texas, the third child of migrant workers with little in the way of money and even less in the way of hope. At seven she was sent to Galveston to live with an aunt and her bedridden husband. They lived in a wood frame house with off-and-on running water and a bathroom hooked up next to the shed. Her aunt, a once-beautiful woman eaten away by hard times, worked as a waitress in a local diner during the day. At night she turned tricks in her bedroom while her husband sat in the kitchen propped next to a hand-cranked turntable, listening to Hank Williams and Patsy Cline.

Lucia was a poor student and found herself skipping more classes than she attended. By the time she was ten, she was helping her aunt serve customers in the diner, handing over the tips but eating as much of the cherry pies as she wanted. Her aunt noticed the way in which the weary men who frequented the diner fawned over the girl and how Lucia was quick to flirt back.

A month past her twelfth birthday, Lucia was moved out of the diner and sent to work in the shed next to the house. There, in the shadow of a twenty-five-watt bulb, sitting on a wooden bench rich with splinters, her back against the creaky shed wall, she gave oral sex to any man who paid her aunt the five-dollar fee. She always wore the same blue-flowered print dress her mother had sent her from Houston for Christmas, white socks trimmed with lace, and black buckled shoes shined daily with spit and water. She always kept her eyes closed and her hands wrapped tightly around the sharp edges of the bench. Tight enough to draw blood.

Lucia left her aunt behind when she was fourteen, traveling with the money she had earned running bets for her uncle and the extra cash given her by grateful customers. She also left behind the blue print dress and the black shoes.

Too many stops and too many wrong men later, she found herself living and partnered with an angel dust and coke dealer in a two-room apartment in Lexington, Kentucky. The gangly, brown-haired young man with the funny smile and the tattoo of Casper the Friendly Ghost floating down the center of his back was the first man in her life she didn't charge for sex. His name was Otis Fraimer, but she always called him Jerry and he never seemed to mind. She knew it wouldn't last, knew they were only one knock on the door or one bad buy away from a jail sentence or a bullet, but she felt comfortable with him. And she never did expect Jerry to die, to end up slumped over the steering wheel of a burning car, two shots through his heart and his throat slashed.

She left herself little time to mourn.

Not when Jerry's rival and the man responsible for his death, a fifty-year-old former gunnery sergeant with a severed leg and an engaging smile, offered to bring her in as a full partner. Harry Corain was intent on expanding his drug business, looking to move beyond the low-end money of downstate Kentucky and head into the fertile terrain of nearby Ohio, where the cities of Cincinnati and Columbus were more than eager to offer a demand equal to his supplies. Lucia, who was by then seventeen and tired of being poor, made the move and, in no short order, reorganized Harry's runners into small teams of movers and packers, insisting on a crew that was free of users and abusers. She left the muscle end of the business to Harry and his younger brother, Terry, a draft dodger as quick with a knife as he was slow with a word.

Lucia handled all the cash and coke transactions.

She gained the loyalty of the mules and sellers by cutting them in on a small percentage of the action, this despite strong protests from the Corain brothers. She hired a cancer-riddled career booster from Canton named Delroy Rumson to teach her all he knew about laundering money and reinvesting clean cash into safe, insured, and tax-free municipal bonds. In return for the knowledge she picked up during his six-month cram course, Lucia promised to keep up the $800-a-month home-care payments for Delroy's retarded daughter, Dorothy, after he died.

It was the first of many promises she didn't keep.

Lucia married Harry Corain on April 18, 1964. It was her twentieth birthday, and a week after the wedding she told him she was pregnant with his child, even though she had no intention of keeping either husband or baby. She was simply buying herself more time and using whatever pull Harry had among other midwestern drug runners to build on what she was already raking in.

Two months into the pregnancy, Lucia drove over the Kentucky state line into Cincinnati during the early morning hours of a soft summer day and had an abortion performed in the basement office of a ramshackle two-story house half a mile off Ezzard Charles Boulevard. Dr. Ranyon B. Travis had long ago lost his medical license to drink, drugs, and bribery, and now found himself earning a living disposing of the unwanted for a three-hundred-dollar-cash-up-front fee. Travis had a modest reputation among the dopers and hookers working the riverfront strip and could be counted on to keep his business quiet, if for no other reason than that the years of booze and drug binges had made it impossible to remember.

Travis had been up all night with an underage co-ed and had already gone through half a pint of gin and two grams of coke when Lucia walked into the foyer leading down to the basement steps. He dressed quickly, splashed water on his face, swallowed two five-hundred-milligram Benzedrine tablets, and prepped Lucia for her abortion. Five minutes into the procedure, she felt a sharp, stinging burn in her pelvic region and immediately knew that the doctor with the shaky hands and shady past had butchered her beyond remedy.

She walked out of the house, leaving three crinkled hundred-dollar bills on the doctor's desk, blood still running down her legs, not answering Travis's apologetic pleas. Her mind forced her body to stride forward and ignore the growing pain that had replaced the curled fetus. Lucia had learned at the earliest age not to cry at the hurt life threw down a person's path, and she did not shed any tears on this night. Instead, she found solace in thoughts of revenge.

Harry found her sprawled face down in the backyard of their house and rushed her to a nearby clinic that excelled at asking few questions. A three-day stay was all it took to heal the external wounds, stop the hemorrhaging, reduce the fever, and quell the infection.

Lucia smiled and kept her focus on the half-empty IV dripping into her arm as she listened to the soft words of a concerned intern tell her she could never have children. She was warmed by the knowledge that at that moment Dr. Ranyon B. Travis, who once headed the OB-GYN wing of a northern Chicago hospital, was hanging from a back alley wall, two thick tire chains wrapped around his hands, his mouth sealed, and his eyes stapled open, being stomach-gutted by the sharp end of Terry's bowie knife. The pain was so intense Dr. Travis chewed off his tongue in the minutes before he died.

Lucia was spending a long weekend in New Orleans in the summer of 1966, looking once again to expand her drug operations, when she met Carlo Porfino sitting by himself at the back table of her friend Anna Cortese's blues bar. She joined him for a drink and then for the night. By midafternoon the next day, Lucia had found her second husband and a fast route out of Kentucky.

Carlo Porfino had affiliations with both the New Orleans and Chicago mobs and was moving heavy quantities of everything imaginable. He was the opposite of Harry in all respects and was not shy about flashing the cash to show Lucia a good time. He also learned quickly in their relationship that she was more than a bar pickup. She had a knack for the drug business, combining a natural ability to make people want to work for her with a ruthlessness that was often necessary in the powder game.

While eager to expand into new territories, Lucia was reluctant to give up what she had built back in Kentucky and Ohio. She turned Carlo's initial indifference into enthusiasm when she told him about the $100,000 a month Harry and Terry were taking in without having totally exploited the burgeoning market. She and Carlo cut a deal. Lucia would get 25 percent of all the Midwest action, plus an additional 10 percent of his southern end, in return for overseeing the operations from her new base in New Orleans. It was a deal a woman like Lucia would never pass up.

She and Carlo were married on the afternoon of July 27, 1967, in a small chapel overlooking a pre–Civil War cemetery. On that same day, Kentucky police found Harry Corain's electrocuted body floating face down in a cast-iron tub, his left arm amputated at the shoulder and hanging loose off the side. He was less than ten feet from his baby brother, Terry, who had taken three Magnum hits to the head, his bowie knife still clutched in his right hand.

Lucia was twenty-three years old and well on her way toward stashing away her first million. She had laid the foundation for a national drug network that in fifteen years and one more husband would blossom into an empire that reached into forty-six states and eight foreign countries. By the time she was standing in the large, airy kitchen in Sedona, Arizona, Lucia Carney was feeding four hundred million a year into the coffers of the international drug cartels and organized crime families that relied on her for safe delivery of their cocaine and guaranteed transfer of funds.

She was their cocaine queen, a beautiful woman with a luscious smile and a cold heart. They called her the Dragon, since she had a tattoo of a small black one breathing flames stenciled over her right shoulder blade, a birthday gift years earlier from Carlo, who had a larger one anchored across his chest. She had grown to like Carlo. They had fun together and he always treated her with respect. He had helped link her up with all his organized crime connections and introduced her to the heads of the South American outfits. He taught her how to wash the coke and still keep it pure. And he was a master on profit skimming, careful to leave behind a trail that always led to a greedier drug dealer.

Lucia often missed Carlo and sometimes regretted that she had had him killed. But he was getting in the way of her business, and Lucia would allow no one to do that.

Especially not a husband.

· · ·

SHE GOT THE idea for using babies one night while watching a Johnson & Johnson TV commercial. In the high-end drug circles in which Lucia traveled, babies were easy to get, easy to transport, and even easier to dispose of. By the mid-1970s, the black market was a bull market for newborns; this back-door, middle-of-the-night, cash-on-receipt business was a multimillion-dollar-a-year operation.

Within six months of watching the commercial, Lucia had made her mark on the baby industry. She opened clinics in eight states, each of them catering to unwed-and-pregnant teenagers on the low end of the income scale. The girls were all looking for good homes for their babies, some cash in their pockets, and the news of their pregnancies to be broadcast to no one. Lucia used third parties to hire only those whose medical credentials were beyond reproach. Once born, the babies were sent to safe homes, where they were fed and nurtured for six months. Then they were picked up by one of Lucia's soldiers, dropped off at a drug transfer center, usually a newly bought condo on quiet resort property, and killed.

The empty cavity of a dead baby could hold as many as six kilos of cocaine on the front end of a long flight and $100,000 in cash on the return. Each baby was good for three round trips and then shipped to local funeral homes, where his or her remains were cremated and tossed in next to the most recent of the dearly departed.

At no time did the horror of her actions ever bother Lucia. For her, the infants were nothing more than a tool, a safe and inexpensive means of transport, allowing her to move large quantities of drugs and cash free and undetected. If what she did made her enemies in the drug trade fear her even more, then that was a dividend.

Over time, as the demand for baby transports began to far outstrip her dependable supply, Lucia began to send her troops out to the streets. There she found hundreds of willing partners unafraid to deal in the hot item of the moment. They kept tabs on runaways and drifters, prime candidates to get pregnant and either abandon or sell their children. They tracked birth records at hospitals located in low-income areas, where record-keeping tended to be as shoddy as the security, helping to make any newborn a perfect target. They secured welfare rolls, scanning the lists for mothers who had a drug problem or record and more than three children. Lucia's emissaries then offered them a better deal than what the state allowed.

The cartel leaders were so pleased with this grisly but safe method of operations that they offered up, free of charge, babies born to their string of prostitutes. A number of other gangs willingly sold Lucia the women with whom they had grown tired, from old girlfriends to older wives, and, in some cases, their own daughters.

All done in the name of profit.

And at the expense of the innocent.

· · ·

LUCIA WALKED AROUND the kitchen of the Sedona house, cradling a six-month-old boy in her arms. She ran a finger softly under the flabs of his chin and got him to smile. She loved the smell of a fresh-washed baby and kissed him on both cheeks before handing him to one of the men in the dark glasses.

"Get him ready," Lucia said to the man, her eyes still on the smiling baby. "The flight leaves in less than two hours."

She stood there as the man walked past her, opening a thick wood door to the basement, where he would perform his assigned task. Lucia watched as the man closed the door behind him, the baby's eyes on hers until he disappeared into the shadows of the basement steps.

Lucia smiled at the baby and waved a final good-bye.

12

THEY HAD EATEN their grilled salmon dinner in silence. Nunzio was the only one who got up during the meal, scurrying back and forth from the kitchen to the table with a large bowl of salad or a fresh bottle of wine. By the time the fruit and coffee were served, most of the cops had absorbed what Boomer had told them. They sat at the large table in the middle of the empty restaurant, the shades drawn down, only three of the overhead lights turned on, lost in their own internal struggle.

Geronimo fingered the medallion around his neck, the one his mother had placed there years earlier to ward off harm. He wondered if the others in the group felt as empty as he did. His days were blanks, working a steady shift at a job he cared little about. His nights were horrors, cold sweats mixing with wasted prayer and cries in the dark, wishing he had not lived through the grenade blast that had left him a whole man on the outside and half of one on the inside.

He had not gone near a device since that day. His retirement papers were put through for him while he was still in a hospital bed, about to endure the sixth of what eventually would grow to fourteen surgical procedures, all fruitless attempts to piece together abdominal muscles and lower intestinal tracts. The daily physical therapy he endured was as constant as the pain he forced himself to ignore. The pills he was prescribed sat in rows on three shelves of a medicine cabinet in a one-bedroom apartment in Ozone Park. Geronimo was surviving on antacids and willpower.

He worked for Unger Electronics on the Lower East Side, reporting to an overweight man with a bad back named Carl Ungerwood. It was a family-owned operation that survived mainly because of the popularity of its computer repair department, which was where Geronimo toiled. That was as close to a set of wires as he was willing to get since the blast. He still kept a cache of dynamite in a closet off the main hall of his apartment, more for the memory of who he used to be than for use.

Carl Ungerwood had a thirty-second temper that was mostly set off by problems with an ex-wife who was suing him for a piece of the business. He often directed his tirades at Geronimo, hurling insults and venom at a man the city had often decorated as a hero. Geronimo sat in silence during those moments, his eyes dark and distant. He saw the abuse as further punishment for what he had lost to the man with the grenade. That the pay from Unger Electronics was steady didn't matter as much to Geronimo as the fact that the work was as far removed from the New York Police Department as he could hope to get.

Unlike Boomer, Geronimo didn't miss being a cop. But he did miss the thrill of taking down a device. He would set time limits for himself when he worked on the computers, doing mental countdowns as he repaired burned-out modems and replaced weak transmission wires. But it just wasn't the same. There was no sense of mystery to a computer, not like with a device, where someone as good as Geronimo could will it, control it, thrive on its energy, or die in the clutches of its power. Alone with a device, Geronimo's life and his possible death took on spiritual weight. It was better than the slow death he was living through now, hunched on a stool in the back room of a dusty electronics store.

Geronimo couldn't speak for the others, but he sensed that their decision about whether or not they would join Boomer in his battle with Lucia was a matter of choice. Not so for him. For a warrior like Geronimo, it was a matter of destiny.

. . .

"It's GETTING LATE," Boomer said, taking a quick glance at his watch, "and it's been a long night, so I'll keep the rest of this short. All I ask is for you to think about what I'm going to say. Think on it hard. And then let me know. Either way, I'll walk away with no problem about your decision."

"How soon do you need our answers?" Mrs. Columbo asked.

"It doesn't have to be an overnight deal," Boomer said. "Come to it when you're ready. But come to it soon."

Mrs. Columbo nodded and smiled. She had known Boomer since he was in uniform and had worked with him on several cases. She knew him well enough to realize that alone or with the group, he was going after Lucia. She saw it on his face, from the way he moved and chose his words. He'd always been an obsessed cop, the one guy with a badge criminals hated to have on their trail. He never gave up, never backed down. He thirsted for the rush of the bust.

The same as Mrs. Columbo.

She missed working homicide. Missed it desperately. At best, she was indifferent to her new job—selling insurance from a bland cubicle in a downtown office building. When she was a cop, she always used to pick up a phone after the first ring, waiting for the voice on the other end to tell her that a body had been found and a killer needed to be caught. Now she often let it ring four or five times, knowing it would only be someone asking about the new rates on their car insurance or looking for a two-week extension on a payment. She had stopped reading mysteries and watching them on television. She no longer followed the crime stories in the papers and on the news. Mrs. Columbo was afraid to do anything that would remind her of how much she loved the puzzle of a case.

She knew she should have been a happy woman. There was a husband at home who loved her and cared about her and a son to watch grow. There were PTA meetings to attend and Little League games to monitor. School plays needed to be put on and cake sale funds had to be raised. And while Mrs. Columbo packaged all these activities into parts of her day, she did it without any emotion. It was the same way she approached her physical therapy sessions, handling the difficult exercises with a cold efficiency, hoping that the feeling would soon return to her lower back and ease the sharp pains running down her legs.

Every Sunday, on a rotating basis, Mrs. Columbo and her family had dinner with relatives. The packed dining rooms all looked and sounded the same to her, whether at her sister-in-law's Mineola ranch in Nassau County or her brother-in-law's Bergen County Tudor. The talk always revolved around family, bills, old squabbles, sports, and retirement. The language of middle-class life. She listened and participated, but her words were empty. Maybe it was because none of the talk was ever about an unidentified male found floating by the edge of the river late into the night. No one at any of the tables cared about what to look for at a crime scene, or how to read a suspect's walk and tell who was the one with the killer's heart.

Mrs. Columbo hated not being a cop. Every pained breath she took reminded her of that. Now Boomer was sitting across from her and offering a chance to be one again. She sipped her coffee and wondered if maybe the wounds she suffered had done more than just scar her body. She worried that they had also stripped away her skill.

· · ·

"YOU STILL HAVEN'T told us what you want us to do," Pins said, washing down his fifth beer of the long night.

"I want us to go after Lucia," Boomer said. "The people at this table up against whatever she's got."

"Six disabled cops and a waiter making a move against an army of drug smackers who like killing cops a lot more than they like selling junk." Rev. Jim leaned across the table, a hand on Boomer's forearm. "I'm not one to give advice, but maybe you should give your idea a little more thought."

Rev. Jim sat back and kept his gaze on Boomer. He still couldn't understand why he was chosen to be at this meeting. Sure, he had once been a great decoy cop and loved working with different disguises and accents, but that was long before the fire burned the skin from his body. He wanted so much to be a part of what Boomer was putting together, but Rev. Jim knew he had nothing left but a smart mouth and an old gun, and that wasn't going to get anybody at the table very far. And it wasn't just the burns, it was the weakened muscles, the charred lungs, the left eye that constantly teared. These other cops didn't know what he needed to do just to get through one day. He gauze-wrapped his body in winter to keep the cold air from touching the raw skin, otherwise it would feel like dry ice on flesh. He wore long-sleeved shirts in the summer to keep away the rays of the sun and the cutting pain that they would bring. Boomer was asking him to be a cop again when there were some mornings he wasn't sure if he could even be a man.

Rev. Jim still needed three more skin-graft operations and many months of physical therapy. Even then there would be no promise of relief. On some nights, long past final call, lying in an empty bed, inside a cold apartment, Rev. Jim would stare up at the ceiling and wonder why he was even alive at all. It would be so easy on those nights to open his desk drawer, take out his .38, and swallow a bullet. Instead, he would reach for the cardboard box he kept under the bed. He would open its flaps and empty its contents on the sweat-stained sheets: his graduation photo from the Police Academy; a replica of his shield; a handful of colored ribbons; three folded citations for bravery; and the knife he had used to kill the dealer who murdered his mother. It wasn't much, but it was enough to keep him alive.

Rev. Jim kept his eyes on Boomer. He realized why the call had been made. Boomer knew he still wanted to be a cop. Still wanted to be a man. Scars and all.

. . .

"WE'RE NOT WALKING into this blind," Boomer said.

"That's the one thing we're missing," Pins said. "A blind guy."

"We've all got the connections," Boomer said. "Federal and local are covered solid. We can pull files, run taps, have computer access. And on the other end Nunzio will hook us into the old wise guys. They hand us what the feds can't. Everything we need is a phone call away."

"Why is everybody going to be so eager to help us?" Mrs. Columbo asked.

"They want Lucia to go down as bad as we do," Boomer said. "But they have to go by the book. Our book was taken away. In their own way, the real cops are just as disabled as we are. Maybe more."

"What if we don't get killed?" Dead-Eye asked. "What if we just get caught?"

"Jail time ain't a sweet time for a cop," Rev. Jim said, taking a match from his mouth and putting it back in his shirt pocket.

"We keep a book," Boomer said. "Fill it with the names of everyone who helps us—from a cop who drops a dime on a guy to an A.D.A. making a few copies of a confidential file."

"We get pinched, we show the district attorney the book," Dead-Eye said.

"We show him a *copy* of the book," Boomer said. "Tell him there are at least six others floating around. That should give him something to worry about."

"It's like Allstate," Nunzio said. "An insurance policy."

Everyone either laughed or smiled at Nunzio's crack.

Except for Pins.

He held his worried look. Pins didn't think he belonged there, just like he didn't belong in many of the places he'd been in his life. He knew why he was asked. That end was easy to figure. The group would need somebody good with a wire, and it wouldn't have taken Boomer long, after asking around, to end up looking his way. But this was a hard group, used to heavy action, not afraid to empty a clip inside a crowded room. And that just wasn't a road Pins traveled down.

The only thing he shared with the cops who sat around the table was a damaged body. He might not have been in as much pain as some of the others, but the confident man who had walked into the wrong apartment less than two years before was long gone. In his place was someone with several vital organs that had been shredded by three bullets. That someone had mended slowly, working his lung capacity to the point where he could once again take deep breaths with only minimal amounts of pain. His right arm was numb from the elbow down, and he suffered from constant migraines, popping as many as five Butalbital tablets a day to ease the pressure. Pins collected his disability pension, paid off the mortgage on his Staten Island home, and invested in a bowling alley. Three afternoons a week, he let the neighborhood kids in free to bowl as many games as they wanted. All he asked in return was for them to clean up after they were done and to put the balls and shoes back in place. Pins enjoyed having the kids around. It gave him a sense of family, which he craved. He wanted so much to fit in, to be part of a group. It was what he had on the job. It was what he had with the kids on the lanes. And he realized it was what Boomer was offering him from across the table.

For a man like Pins, belonging was all that mattered. Mixed with that desire, however, was a deeply hidden fear, one Pins thought he would never have to face again. It was the fear of the gun.

Like the other members of the group, Pins never worried about dying. But he didn't want to have to survive another wounding, didn't think he could walk through that pain and come out of it one more time. He also didn't know if he could complete the one act that seemed second nature to the other cops in the room—Pins didn't know if he could kill a man. His risk was always in laying down the plant, his action was in the wire, his trigger was turning on the tape. That was where he excelled. With this group, it was a talent that just might not be enough.

. . .

"WHEN DO WE go?" Geronimo asked, scanning the faces of the others, trying to detect their levels of interest.

"I start Monday morning," Boomer said. "I'll be working out of Nunzio's basement. We'll keep everything we need down there. Anybody else who shows up that day starts with me."

"This crew of ours," Rev. Jim said. "You gonna give it a name?"

"The Crips would be good," Pins tossed in. "But that L.A. gang beat us to the punch."

"I haven't thought of one," Boomer said. "Is it important?"

"Eventually, Lucia's gonna wanna know who we are," Rev. Jim said. "Who it is fucking up her business. Be nice if we could tell her. Let her know who she's at war with."

"Apaches," Geronimo said in somber tones. "We should call ourselves the Apaches."

"Just because you've got a little Indian blood in you?" Dead-Eye asked. "I've got African blood all through me. Don't hear me layin' any of that *Roots* shit on the rest of you."

"In this case, we all have Indian blood," Geronimo said, turning from one face to the other. "In Apache tradition, when a warrior was wounded in battle, he was left behind by the tribe. Left to fend and care for himself. He had become too much of a burden to the tribe. That's us, Dead-Eye. That's all of us."

"Do we get shirts and hats to go with the name?" Rev. Jim asked. "You know, with our logo?"

"What about Nunzio?" Pins asked. "What do we make him?"

"A scout," Mrs. Columbo said, leaning her head against Nunzio's shoulder.

"Okay, we've got a name," Boomer said, standing, reaching behind him for his jacket. "And by Monday afternoon, based on who's here with me, I'll know if we've got a team."

They all stood, picked up their coats and hats, shook hands, and headed for the door, moving quietly, minds already drifting toward a decision.

Geronimo and Boomer waited for Nunzio, watching as he closed up the restaurant.

"That on the level?" Boomer said.

"What?" Geronimo asked.

"About the Apaches. And leaving their wounded behind."

"How the hell should I know?" Geronimo said, smiling for the first time all night.

Boomer smiled back as he put on his jacket. "Well, as of tonight it's a fact."

"Sure it is," Geronimo said, following Boomer and Nunzio out the door. "First Custer, then Wounded Knee, and now the Apaches."

. . .

FLIGHT 518, the 9:08 A.M. Phoenix to New York direct, was full. Each seat was taken, overhead compartments were stuffed with carry-on luggage, stowaway space was crammed with handbags, briefcases, coats, hats, and sweaters. Signs of a long plane ride were already apparent: tanned passengers in flowered shirts; flustered parents trying to calm anxious children; earnest young businessmen poring over computer printouts; Manhattan-bound tourists underlining passages in their color brochures; flight attendants preparing coffee and drinks and setting out cold turkey sandwiches.

The mule was in seat 14C, on the aisle, her legs crossed, the baby boy cradled firmly in her arms, his eyes closed, a soft blue blanket wrapped around zippered Snoopy pajamas. The mule was in her late thirties, rich brown hair combed in a swirl, unlined face barely touched by makeup.

As she turned to peer down the aisle, she noticed the overweight man next to her rest his paperback on his knees and smile down at the baby.

"I always like flying with babies," the man said. "Makes me think the flight has a better chance of making it."

The mule smiled back and stayed silent.

"Got yourself a beautiful one there," the man said. "He can sleep through this racket, then maybe he'll sleep through the flight."

"He's good that way," the mule said. "Never gives me much trouble."

"That comes when they're older," the man said. "Trust me. Got three of my own. I'd give anything to have them back to when they were as small as your kid."

The mule nodded and turned her head away, watching a young flight attendant chant the procedures to follow in the event of a crash.

"Got family in New York?" the man asked her.

"No," she said, turning back to face him.

"How long are you staying?"

"Not very long," the mule said, looking down at the baby, making sure the blanket concealed a portion of his face.

"New York's a great place for short visits," the man said. "It's living there full-time that's hard. What hotel are you staying at?"

"We'll be with friends," the mule said, bracing herself for takeoff, once again turning away from the man, resting her head on the back of her seat.

"There's a lot there to see," the man said, picking up his paperback and folding it in half. "Lots of great things."

"We won't have much time for any of that," the mule said. "We're only in town for a day. It's a quick business trip."

"That is quick," the man said, shifting his body up higher in the seat. "What sort of business are you involved in?"

The mule leaned closer to the man and smiled, her eyes locking on to his. "Promise you won't tell anyone," she said in a whispered voice.

"I promise," the man said, lowering his head.

"Jason and I are drug dealers," the mule said, lifting her eyebrows, a smile wrapped around her face.

"Who's Jason?" the man asked.

"The baby," the mule said, throwing a look at the boy wrapped in the blanket.

The man had a quizzical look on his face and held it for several moments. Then he heard her start to laugh.

"Yeah, right," the man said, laughing along with the mule. "And me? I'm a hit man. But you've got to keep that one to yourself too."

"It's a deal," the mule said, leaning back again and shutting her eyes.

The man returned to his paperback thriller.

The mule slept through the remainder of the flight into New York's LaGuardia Airport, content and confident.

A dead baby held warm in her arms.

13

BOBBY SCARPONI, SHIRTLESS, a hand towel draped around his neck, stared into the mirror. The exposed bulb just above the hanging glass cast the small bathroom in a series of shadowy contrasts. He ran a hand along the red scars covering the upper part of his chest and running into his neck and cheek. They were hard and crusty to the touch, a constant reminder of the flames that had changed the course of his life.

Rev. Jim lived in Queens, a one-bedroom apartment on the second floor of a private home owned by a carpenter and his wife who seemed to be foolishly too young for him. It was the kind of apartment usually reserved for a young man starting out. It was not meant as a final stop.

Rev. Jim walked out of the bathroom, passed the small kitchen, and stopped by the open window near his bed, thin white drapes flapping in the wind. He stared down at the quiet street below, filled with parked cars and lit by the glow from a series of houses similar to the one in which he lived. It was how he spent most of his nights, his mind crowded with visions of his mother dying by his side, flames and heat surrounding his body, his mouth too seared for him to scream.

He was afraid of lying down to sleep. It only brought the visions to life, causing him to wake up bathed in sweat and tears, having ripped and torn at his sheets and skin. So he rarely slept. Rarely rested. Rarely escaped the hell that was his past, present, and future.

Rev. Jim had often thought of suicide, but knew if he was ever really going to go that route, it would have happened after his mother's death. Rev. Jim was not the kind of man to go out with a note, a bag over his head, and a rope around his neck. He was a fighter and needed to find a better way out.

Boomer's plan seemed just the route he sought.

He turned from the window, went over to the refrigerator, pulled out a cold can of Budweiser, popped it open, and took two long slurps. He leaned his back against a cold wall and reached for the phone, dialing a familiar number with his free hand. He let it ring eight times before he hung up. His father had always been a sound sleeper; age had only made that sleep deeper.

Rev. Jim finished the beer, tossed the empty into a silver trash can near the window, and reached for the phone again. The voice on the other end responded on the third ring. He heard Boomer grumble a hello and waited. He took a deep breath, eyes searching past the houses across the way, gripping the receiver hard enough to crush it.

"I'm in," he finally said. Boomer stayed silent on the other end. "Good night."

Rev. Jim hung up the phone, walked slowly back toward the open window, and waited for the morning sun to arrive and bring with it a small sense of relief.

. . .

THE MULE STEPPED out of the cab and looked up at the four-story Manhattan brownstone, the infant still cradled in her arms. She walked slowly up the front steps as the cab sped off into the New York night. She heard the dead bolt on the front door click open as an icy blast of winter air snapped against the edges of her skirt. A large man in a red silk shirt and black leather pants stood braced next to the door. He nodded a greeting as she went past.

"Which way?" the mule asked, her eyes catching a glimpse of the .44 semiautomatic holstered and exposed under his sleeve.

"Take the hall steps," the man said, locking the door and turning his bulk toward the mule. "The second door on your left."

"Everybody there?" She moved toward the center hall, her heels clacking on the slick hardwood floor.

"Everybody that needs to be," the man said, disappearing around a corner, heading into a game room with a full bar and pool table.

The mule took the steps in a rush, gripping the baby with both hands, eager to get on with her task. She turned a sharp corner at the head of the stairwell and nudged open the second door in the hall. She walked in and rested the still baby on a large wood table, next to six hefty stacks of hundred-dollar bills, each wrapped with thin strips of white twine. Four men, sitting in hard-backed chairs spaced throughout the oak-paneled, book-lined room, stood and joined her by the table.

"Any problems?" Paolo, the smallest of the four men, asked.

"The guy next to me smelled," the mule said. "And the food was horrible. Other than that, no hitches."

"How much time do you have?" Paolo offered a cigarette from a half-empty pack of Marlboros.

"Flight to Atlanta leaves in two hours," the mule said, refusing the cigarette. "I make the exchange at the airport and catch a connecting to L.A."

"Can I have a piece of your frequent flyer miles?" Paolo asked.

"Wish I had some to give," the mule said. "Each flight's under a different name."

"So much for the perks." Paolo turned from the mule and nodded at the three men huddling around the cash. "Ready the baby and the money," he said to them in a rougher tone than he took with the mule. "We'll wait for you downstairs."

"How long?" one of the three asked, already taking off his jacket and rolling back the sleeves of a black shirt.

"Thirty minutes at the most," Paolo said, leading the mule by the arm, walking her out of the room and shutting the door softly.

. . .

Joe Silvestri threw one pillow against the bedroom wall. Another clipped the shuttered windows and fell against a bureau lamp, knocking it harmlessly to its side. "Is this what you been doin' all this fuckin' time?" he shouted. His anger was directed at his wife, Mary, who sat under a pile of blankets, her flannel nightgown buttoned to the collar. "Cookin' up crazy schemes on disability night?"

"Stop yelling, please," Mary said. She kept a tight rein on her reaction and her emotions under control. "You're going to wake up Frankie."

"Almost losin' your life wasn't enough for you?" Joe continued to shout, stomping around the small bedroom in bare feet and red Jockey shorts. "Almost leaving him without a mother wasn't enough to make you wanna turn your back for good? And almost leaving me, not that you give a shit, should at least be worth a little something after all these years."

"All of that *is* important." Mary kept her eyes on her husband, understanding his need to vent, trying not to let her words cut deeper into the frustration he harbored over never having the kind of wife he so much wanted. "Don't think for a minute that it isn't."

"If you do this, Mary, you gotta know it's over between you and me," Joe said, stopping at the edge of the bed. "I've lived through a lot with you, but I won't live with this. You lookin' to get yourself buried, get somebody else to help you do it."

"Look at me, Joe," Mary said, trying not to make her words sound like a plea for help. "I've got scars up and down my body. I can't even look at myself in the shower without crying. I work at a job I hate when I'm there and hate thinking about when I'm not."

"Not many people get shot selling insurance policies." Joe spit the words out and sat on the side of the bed away from his wife. "And they like you there. You're doing good work for good people."

"It's not what I want," Mary said softly. "And it's not what I need."

"Going out on a suicide job, that's what you want? And getting yourself killed and breaking the law while you're at it, that's what you need?"

"I'm dead now, Joe," Mary said, pushing back the covers and sliding across the bed to sit next to him. "You have to be able to see that. To know that. I'm never going to be the kind of wife you want. Especially not the way I am now."

"You don't need to tell me." Joe stared down at the violet carpet. "I learned that a long time ago."

"I need to try and get back to being the kind of cop I was," Mary said. "For no other reason than to feel alive again."

"What about us?" Joe asked, turning to face her. "What about me and Frankie? And what about me and you?"

"I love you both very much," Mary said. "But I love you both for what you are and who you are. That's all I'm asking from you in return. After all these years, you've got to know I'm not someone who keeps house. And I sure as hell am not someone who sells insurance."

"And you're not someone who can cook worth a shit either." Joe shook his head and forced a smile, putting an arm around his wife's shoulders.

"I'm a cop, Joe." Mary rested her head on his chest. "Like it or not, you fell in love with a cop."

"And I'm still in love with one," Joe said. "No matter what you might think."

"Then let me do this," Mary said in a whisper. "Please."

"You want my okay for you to go out and get yourself killed." Joe sighed. "That's an awful lot to ask from *anybody*. Let alone your husband."

"The only person I'd ever ask *is* my husband," Mary said. "I'm asking you to let me go out and feel what it's like to be alive again."

"Who tells Frankie?" Joe asked after a long silence.

"We will," Mary said with a slow smile. "You and me. In the morning, while you're making us all pancakes."

"Looks like I'm back to doing the cooking now too," Joe said.

"And it looks like I'm back to being a cop," Mary said, leaning against her pillow, holding Joe's hand and bringing him along.

"Don't die on me, Mary," Joe said. "That's all I'll ask from you."

"That's a big step over what you used to ask," Mary said, a full smile spread across her face now.

"What was that?" Joe said, slipping under the blankets alongside his wife.

"Not to burn the eggs," Mary said.

In the shadows of the quiet room, they held each other tight, kissed, and slid farther under the blankets, finding warmth and comfort with each touch.

· · ·

THE MULE SPOTTED Erica standing with her back to a newsstand, a small cardboard sign printed with the word STEVENS across it. She walked over, gave the woman a quick smile and a nod, and handed her the baby boy.

"Your plane's at the next terminal," Erica said. "Two stops on the tram." She was dressed in a black pants suit, the jacket with too much shoulder padding. A thin shawl rested around her neck. She wore open-heeled slides and favored her right leg when she walked. She carried the baby in the crook of her left arm, more like a sack than an infant.

"I hate airports like these," the mule said, picking up the pace, scanning the state-of-the-art mall interior of Atlanta/Fulton County with a disdainful look. "It's like being inside a spaceship."

"You get used to it," Erica said, shrugging her shoulders and bouncing the baby higher up against her chest. "And you can shop while you wait for your plane."

"You should go," the mule told her, waiting for the doors to the computerized train to open. "Just in case you get caught in traffic."

"Anything you want me to tell Leo?" Erica asked.

"That I need a vacation," the mule said without a trace of a smile. "They've run me ragged these last three weeks. I can barely stand up."

"We're in the middle of a gold rush," Erica said. "There's too much money to make to let up now."

"We won't be making anything if we slip up," the mule said. "And that's all that can happen when we're this tired."

The train pulled into the stop area and a prerecorded voice alerted passengers as to their destination. The mule stepped aboard, grabbed a handrail, and looked at Erica, giving her a tired smile.

"I'll be back Tuesday," she said. "By then Leo should have a new baby for me. This one's starting to get more than a little ripe."

The mule turned her back as the doors closed, leaving behind two late-arriving passengers.

Erica stayed on the platform and watched her go, holding the baby and the $125,000 in cash sewn into the empty cavity of his body.

. . .

GERONIMO SAT ON a damp block of wood on the deserted beach, listening to a series of ocean waves batter the soft sands of the shoreline. His legs were crossed and his arms folded; his head was tilted up toward the star-packed sky. A rush of cold wind blew through the back of his dark blue sweater and sent thick strands of his hair slapping across the front of his face.

This small strip of land had become Geronimo's favorite spot, a private beach nestled quietly away from the large clapboard homes of Ocean Parkway, down a side ramp from the Brooklyn/Queens Expressway. It was his refuge, a place to come, hole up and clear his head, re-energized by fresh salt air and marsh breezes. A place where he could feel safe and disconnected from the pressures of his life.

Geronimo was slow to recover from the multiple wounds he had suffered at the drop of a grenade from the hands of a madman. On a Brooklyn street, surrounded by caked blood, streams of smoke, and frightened screams, he had left behind a shattered stomach, chunks of his liver and kidney, and all of his small intestine. The months of rehab were painful and frustrating, and a man with less inner strength would have found it easy to quit. But Geronimo had actually thrived under the weight of such a battle, especially one so personal, and he made it his business to come out of it as whole a person as possible.

Barely able to digest even soft foods and cool liquids, he had to learn how to eat all over again. The early surgeries to piece his stomach back together were ineffective and painful. Still Geronimo would not give in, mixing weekly visits to an army of specialists with nightly sessions with a Native American mystic whose form of medicine knew no age.

Geronimo believed in the healing ways of the past and the recuperative powers of long-dormant ghosts. That was one of many reasons he spent so much time sitting in his private corner of beach, alone in darkness, lost in the shadow of the stars.

He took to his healing by walking in small steps and casting his will to the whim of past warriors, gaining from the study of their lives the strength he currently lacked and the force of spirit he had nearly abandoned after his disability.

When he wasn't being probed by technicians or losing himself to the fog of the mystic, he stayed to himself and prayed to the gods of his mother. His prayers were more than pleas for renewed health. They were soulful cries that he be made one again and be allowed to die as he was meant to die, as he was destined to die.

As a warrior.

Down deep in his heart he knew it was an impossible request. His future looked to be as numb and dull as the emptiness he felt in the pit of his stomach. It would be a mournful life devoid of action and confrontation.

He missed those tense moments with the instrument, the precious rare seconds when he was alone, only a slight twitch of the hand away from instant death. Those hours spent in front of a bomb, time slipping before him with each tick of the clock, were the hours Geronimo felt fully alive and in total control. It was the period during which he felt most united with the spirit of his ancestors. And he would give anything to experience that feeling again. That was what he prayed for.

It was a desperate prayer from a lonely man.

It was not until his dinner with Boomer, in a restaurant whose food he couldn't eat, that Geronimo realized his desperate prayer might be answered.

. . .

LUCIA HELD OUT her empty glass and stared across the ocean as a young waiter nervously poured from a stainless-steel pitcher filled with perfectly chilled martinis. She was stretched out on a blue lounge chair on the sun-drenched front deck of the *Maraboo*, a sixty-five-foot yacht her fourth husband, Gerald Carney, had bought for her as a wedding present. A black two-piece bathing suit revealed skin tanned the color of toast. Light beads of sweat dotted her thin arms, shapely legs, and flat, muscular stomach.

The boat was anchored three miles off the Bermuda coast and carried a full working crew of seven—one waiter, one chef, a nanny, and four armed bodyguards. The nanny was there to care for Gerald Carney's eight-year-old daughter from a previous marriage. The girl, Alicia, sat on a white beach towel and played to Lucia's left, dressed in a polka dot swimsuit and surrounded by a gaudy array of Barbie dolls.

Gerald Carney sat across from his wife, legs crossed, white sailor shirt hanging over a plump stomach. Carney was sixty-one years old, a retired investment banker born to money and bred to silence. He met Lucia in the spring of 1980 when she came to his Manhattan office seeking advice on how best to shelter her cash flow. He knew her business was drugs and had heard rumors about the hand she played in disposing of her previous husbands. But Gerald Carney had dealt with all breeds in his four decades of investing, laundering, and skimming money. His nefarious clients had made him a very wealthy man.

Carney and Lucia were quick to move their financial conversation from his office to a nearby bar and then, within weeks, to the bedroom of his Park Avenue penthouse apartment. They married on the same rainy afternoon that Carney's divorce from an East Side socialite was finalized. They chose to keep separate residences, Lucia more comfortable working out of her central bases of Miami and Sedona, while Carney kept to his Manhattan–Los Angeles axis. He asked few questions about her business and she asked none about his. But she grew to trust him in all matters financial. In less than a year's time, Lucia saw her hidden stash of five million dollars nearly double. Her new husband never met any of her associates and she was quick to shun the role of hostess on those rare occasions when they were in the same town. Theirs was a business partnership that made room for occasional moments of passion.

It was the kind of marriage Lucia had always dreamed about.

A fairy tale come true.

. . .

THE CROSS BAY Lanes were shut down for the night, outside lights dimmed, front doors bolted. Inside, the large Bud sign above the bar cast a green glow across the lanes, all of them dark except for one. A corner jukebox sent out a haunting Ry Cooder instrumental.

Pins Ryan stood crouched above the black bowling ball cupped in his hands. His feet were planted firm and balanced. He took three steps forward, arched the ball behind him, and brought it down in one smooth motion. His front foot curved as the ball slammed against the hardwood and buzzed toward the pins, scattering eight of them, leaving behind only the three and four. Pins walked slowly back to the scoring table, took a swig from a bottle of Amstel, and then stood still, enjoying the quiet darkness of his alley.

He had bought a share of the place three months after his shooting, going in as full partner with two retired firemen from Ozone Park. The income from the alley, coupled with his disability pension, made Pins more than comfortable and afforded him the stable environment he had always sought. Besides, he could bowl seven days and nights a week without digging into his pocket.

He had neither a wife nor a family, but since so much of his life had been spent in solitary circumstances, this lack of intimate ties no longer seemed important. He had plenty of friends, most of them bowling buddies. And unlike many of the other disabled cops Pins came across from time to time, he didn't miss the job. On certain occasions, when a special call came in, Pins still laid down some plants for the department, pleased to note his wounds hadn't cost him his skills.

He removed the ball from its base, took his position, and blew out the two standing pins to record a spare. After penciling in his score for the opening frame, he took in a deep breath, relishing the stale smells of the old alley, looking around at the rows of shiny balls glistening in the light off the Bud sign. Behind him, racks of old bowling shoes, each colored uglier than the next, hung in straight rows of twelve across, based on size and use. He loved being in the alley, especially when it was dark and empty, a dozen lanes all to himself.

Pins had left the dinner with Boomer having no answer framed in his mind. Boomer's plan had the ring of a no-win mission. Jail time or death were the only likelihoods. But there had been a feeling to the group, a warmth and spirit emanating from each cop that forced Pins to hold his tongue. He missed that camaraderie in the years since he was shot off the job, that sense of belonging to a special group, of being kidded and teased by others who shared the same passion and dedication.

The alley was his home, a place for him to get away, roll as many games as it took for him to erase from his mind the places he'd been and the faces he wanted to forget.

But being a cop was where he was most needed.

If Pins could no longer fill that large void as a member of the department, he could easily do so as one of the Apaches. He could be their safety net, planting bugs in hidden places. A piece of his life's puzzle that had been missing for years could now be fitted back into its proper place.

Three games, one beer, and two cups of coffee later, Pins had decided to join up with Boomer's team of crippled cops. He would lay down the taps and wires to help the Apaches reel in Lucia Carney. He would ignore his fear of the gun and hide behind the shield of the electronic bug.

Those three games were the best Pins had bowled since before he took the bullets meant for the body and transgressions of another man.

· · ·

BOOMER SAT ACROSS from a gray metal desk stacked high with books, files, and newspapers, hands jammed inside his jacket pockets, gnawing on a thick wad of Spearmint gum. He watched as Dr. Carolyn Bartlett reached down into her briefcase and pulled out a worn manila folder with Jennifer Santori's name written across the front in black felt tip. She placed it on top of a six-deep pile of similar-looking folders, opened it, gave the cover sheet a quick read, then sat back in her tattered black swivel chair. She looked over at Boomer through tired eyes, her face shrouded by tension.

"I appreciate your stopping by," she said, her voice echoing the exhaustion in her eyes.

"I was already in the neighborhood," Boomer said casually, resisting the temptation to blow a bubble with his gum. "I'm going to meet Jenny's folks over by the courthouse. Watch that bastard get arraigned."

"I know," Dr. Bartlett said. "They told me."

"When did you talk to them?" Boomer sat up in his chair, his police radar kicking into alert.

"I called them late last night," she said, pointing a manicured finger toward the brown couch and coffee table next to Boomer. "I don't usually drink, Mr. Frontieri. But I needed one just to be able to make that phone call."

"Call me Boomer." He pulled his hands from his jacket pockets and looked over at the two empty coffee containers, wine glass, and half-empty bottle of warm Chardonnay scattered around the end table. The couch cushions were crumpled and there was a thin brown blanket rolled up in one corner. "It must have been a tough call. Looks like you spent the night here too."

"I need your help with this," Carolyn said. "If you go against me, it will only make it rougher for everyone."

"I don't know what this is, but I'm not going to like it, am I?"

"No," she said, shaking her head, her eyes meeting his. "You're going to hate what's being done and you're going to hate me for doing it. But I'm willing to risk all that if I come out of it having saved a little girl's life."

"You need a drink before you tell me too?" Boomer asked.

"I've asked that the district attorney's office drop all charges against Malcolm Juniper," she said in as firm a voice as she could muster.

"Your reason?" Boomer said, staying tight, keeping control of his temper.

"In order to convict, they'll need to put Jennifer on the witness stand," Carolyn said. "I can't allow that to happen."

"Why not?"

"As it is, it's going to take years of therapy to get Jennifer to the point where what happened will fade to a distance she can live with. If I let her take the stand, let his lawyers have a shot at her, force her to relive every minor detail, I can almost guarantee you she'll be nothing more than a vegetable for the rest of her life. I can't live with that. And I'm hoping you can't either."

Boomer stayed outwardly calm but his hands bunched into fists and his eyes betrayed the anger burning inside. "What about Malcolm? Without Jenny taking the stand, he'll go out on the streets and do the same thing all over again. To some other girl. You ready to live with that, Doc?"

"I've lived with it every day I've been in this damn job," Carolyn said, her frustration rising to the surface. "I've had to help piece back together too many Jennys. And I've had to sit and watch as too many Malcolms walked out of court free men."

"What is it you want from me?" Boomer asked her.

"Talk to the family," Carolyn said. "Convince them it's the right thing to do for their child. If they want me to continue to help her, then this has to be the way."

Boomer took a deep breath and ran a hand across his face. The image of Jennifer hanging from a pipe, seconds from death, her body a beaten and bloody mess, raced through his mind.

"In all my years on the job, I was pretty lucky," Boomer said quietly. "I usually got to see only the bad guys. And I went after them like no one ever has because I always knew that behind the face of a bad guy there was one of an innocent victim. So when I brought that bad guy in, it was my own way of helping out the victim."

"You're still helping out the victim," Carolyn said with sympathy. "More than you will ever know."

"We're helping out Malcolm too," Boomer said. "More than you'll ever know."

"Would you rather I put Jenny on the stand?" Carolyn asked him. "Would you rather torture her more, all for the sake of a conviction?"

Boomer lowered his head and his voice, staring down at thin, frayed strands of industrial carpet. "No," he said in a near whisper. "I don't want that kid to be hurt any more."

"Then talk to her parents," Carolyn said. "You can say things to them in a way that I can't."

"Jenny's father came to me because he knew something I didn't," Boomer said.

"What?"

"He knew that I'd bring in Malcolm and save his kid."

"And you did bring him in," Carolyn said. "You and your partner did save her life. Don't let that get lost in all of this."

"Maybe so," Boomer said, standing up and zippering his jacket. "But we did make one mistake. One very big mistake."

"Which was?" Carolyn also stood. She reached out her hand and placed it in his.

"We brought him in alive," Boomer said.

He shook Carolyn Bartlett's hand, turned, and walked slowly out of her office.

· · ·

DEAD-EYE BANKED A shot against the backboard, took a step back, and watched as the ball fell through the net. He let his son, Eddie, race for the bouncing ball, grab it with both hands, and toss it back to him.

"Your shot," Dead-Eye told him. Both of them were smiling. "Make it count."

Eddie, one month past his third birthday, bounced the ball twice against the concrete court, then stumbled, scraping his hands and falling down to his knees.

"What happened to you?" Dead-Eye asked, lifting him to his feet and dusting off his hands.

"I fell," Eddie said, brushing off the fall with a sad face and a shrug.

"Game's over anyway," Dead-Eye said, reaching down to give his son a quick hug. "I guess you know what that means?"

"Winner buys ice cream." The smile rushed back to Eddie's face.

"I don't remember who won," Dead-Eye said. "Do you?"

"I didn't score, Daddy," Eddie giggled. "You did."

"Looks like it's me buyin' again." Dead-Eye feigned a sigh, lifting his son in the cradle of one arm, bouncing the basketball with his free hand and walking out of the fenced-in playground and toward the ice cream truck parked at the next corner.

They sat with their backs against the black wall of a handball court, their legs stretched out, faces up to the sun, each working over a double-swirl vanilla ice cream cone. Eddie was getting as much on his chin and cheeks as he was in his mouth, occasionally dabbing at his face with a wadded-up ball of napkins. The grounds around them were quiet and empty except for two winos sleeping the night off on a set of park benches to their right.

"Is Mama mad?" Eddie asked, his gaze focused on the melting ice cream in his hands.

"Yes," Dead-Eye said. "She's very mad at me."

"Why?"

"She doesn't want me to do something," Dead-Eye said.

"Why?"

Dead-Eye looked down at his son, washed in ice cream, his innocent face crammed with a natural sweetness, his eyes blazing with curiosity. He reached over, picked him up, and wiped the ice cream from his face. He then sat Eddie between his legs, resting the boy's head against his chest.

"What kind of work does Daddy do?" Dead-Eye asked him, leaning down and kissing the top of his son's head.

"You let people into buildings," Eddie said, looking up at him. "Right?"

"I'm a doorman," Dead-Eye said. "That's right."

"Before that you were a policeman. Mama said you were famous."

"I wasn't famous," Dead-Eye said. "I was good. There's a difference."

"Mama says you don't like opening doors." Then Eddie asked, "That why she's mad at you?"

"Being a doorman is a good job," Dead-Eye said, looking out over the park, past the swings and slides, the backed-up traffic moving into Manhattan. "It's just not the right job for me."

"Mama says you wanna be a policeman again."

"And that's why she's mad," Dead-Eye said. "She's afraid I'll get shot up all over again."

Eddie jumped from his father's lap and turned to face him.

"I don't want you to die, Daddy." There was a lilt of fear in his voice.

Dead-Eye laid his two hands on the sides of his son's face and stared at him for several moments, willing the fear from the boy's body.

"I want you to be proud of me," Dead-Eye said. "Same way that I'm so proud of you. When you grow up, I want you to go out and do what's in your heart to do. What you feel you have to do more than anything else. You'll find what that is, maybe early, maybe late, but you'll find it. Same way I found what I had to do. Then I got shot and I lost it."

"Mama said you and Uncle Boomer are both crazy," Eddie said.

"She's right about that," Dead-Eye said, smiling at his son. "We are crazy. But it's a good crazy, Eddie. The kind you need to have around every once in a while."

"Are the bad people crazy?"

"Bad people are always crazy," Dead-Eye said. "That's why they do what they do. And sometimes it takes crazy guys like me and Uncle Boomer to go out there and stop them."

"Are you going to be a policeman again?" Eddie asked.

"I never really stopped," Dead-Eye said, resting his son back against his chest. "But I won't do this until I know you're okay with it. Until I know you're backing me up. All good cops need a backup. So that's what I'm asking you to be."

"Do I get a badge?" Eddie asked, lifting his head.

"Even better," Dead-Eye said, reaching a hand inside the front pocket of his windbreaker and coming out with a replica of a detective's gold shield closed inside a leather flap. "I made you a copy of my badge. That makes you my partner."

"Uncle Boomer's your partner," Eddie said, taking the badge from his father, his eyes opened wide in amazement.

"Uncle Boomer's my friend," Dead-Eye said. "And you don't have as many bad habits. So what's it gonna be? Are you with me? You gonna cover my back?"

"Yes, Daddy," Eddie said, wrapping both arms around his father's neck, holding him tight, the shield dangling loose from his right hand.

Dead-Eye hugged his son close, his face nestled into the boy's shoulder.

They sat there still and quiet in the chilly winter morning, their backs against a spray-painted wall, surrounded by barren trees, still swings, sleeping drunks, and congested traffic.

Father and son linked in trust and love.

. . .

THE COURTROOM WAS drab and silent. Court officers stood, arms folded, their backs to the few spectators in attendance. Judge Geraldine Waldstein, a thin woman with thick dark hair and sharp features, glared down at the defendant. Malcolm Juniper sat on a wooden chair wearing his only suit, a gray sharkskin, with a white button-down shirt and a thin black tie. Malcolm's lawyer, Jerry Spieglman, sat next to him, eyes gazing at an open folder.

Boomer sat in the third row, directly behind Jennifer's parents, Carlo and Anne. Dead-Eye had decided to wait outside. Like most cops, he felt uncomfortable in a courtroom. It was one of the few traits those inside the law shared with those outside. Boomer kept his eyes on the back of Malcolm's head, but his mind was in another place. He saw himself in uniform again, a rookie walking a Harlem beat with his mentor, Iron Mike Tragatti. Day after day, Tragatti, using his nightstick as a pointer, would hammer home the one lesson he insisted young Boomer learn.

"You see these people?" Iron Mike would say, pointing out the Harlem merchants opening their stores, preparing to serve their customers. "They are the ones we're here to protect. They are the good. The bad are the ones who take from them. And they are the ones we put away. The courts call it justice. The people here call it safety. You and me call it our job. It's as simple as that."

For two decades, Boomer Frontieri believed every one of those words. Believed them because they used to be true. But they weren't true anymore. Not on a day when he had to sit in a barren courtroom and stare helplessly at a mother and father, holding hands and crying as they listened to a new set of words, this time spoken by a judge with two children of her own.

Words that would set their daughter's tormentor free.

Judge Waldstein kept it simple and direct. Her shouts and frustration had been vented behind closed doors.

"You've got *nothing* else?" she had asked Kevin Gilbert, the assistant district attorney assigned to the case.

"Not without the girl, your honor," Gilbert admitted. "Erase her and I've got a room with two retired cops who shouldn't have been there in the first place, staring at one dead man and one naked one."

"You have Dr. Bartlett's testimony," Waldstein said. "And you have photos of the crime scene."

"It's all too cold and clinical," Gilbert said. "I need the jury to see Jennifer. It's the only way I can get a guilty."

"Then we're wasting our breath," Jerry Spieglman said. "It's time to set the innocent free."

"*I'll* decide when it's time, Counselor," Judge Waldstein hissed.

In the courtroom, Judge Waldstein kept her anger masked behind a calm veneer. Her eyes were moist and strained as she uttered the phrase that shattered everyone else's serenity.

"Case dismissed," Judge Waldstein said sadly.

Malcolm Juniper slammed an open hand on the scarred wooden table and clapped. Jerry Spieglman closed the folder and shoved it inside a soiled backpack.

Anne Santori bowed her head and sobbed quietly into the palms of her hands.

Carlo Santori turned and looked at Boomer Frontieri. It was the look of a defeated man.

Boomer took a deep breath, stood, and turned his back on the scales of justice, vowing never to enter a courtroom again.

. . .

Malcolm Juniper, a bounce to his gait, took the cracked concrete steps coming out of the Manhattan Criminal Court Building two at a time. He stopped short as soon as he spotted Boomer and Dead-Eye waiting for him on the sidewalk below, their backs warmed by a winter sun.

Malcolm's smile widened and he began to take the steps at a slower pace. He pulled a cigarette from his jacket pocket, turned his back to Boomer, Dead-Eye, and the wind, and lit up, using a cheap plastic lighter. He crunched the cigarette between his teeth, smoke leaking out one corner of his mouth, and barely disguised his glee from the ex-cops who had gone to such lengths to have him arrested.

"Scopin' out more innocent men?" Malcolm asked. "Or you just come to apologize?"

"The judge and the D.A. cut you loose," Boomer said, looking directly at Malcolm. "Not me."

"I ain't free but two minutes and you shot-up losers start hasslin' me." Malcolm acted indignant, tossing the cigarette to the ground, inches from Dead-Eye's brown boot. "My man Jerry here ain't gonna sit for that kinda shit." Malcolm turned his head, looking over at the lawyer with a thick head of hair and a face layered with red pimples, whiteheads, and acne scars. "That right, Jerry?"

Jerry Spieglman stepped forward, less confident than Malcolm about confronting Boomer and Dead-Eye. He was a low-tier lawyer building a practice from the bottom-feeder end of the pool. "There's no need to further hassle my client," Jerry said in a voice as light as his frame. "He's been cleared by a court of law."

"They got shit that can help that," Dead-Eye said, pointing a finger at Jerry's scarred face. "You let that get any worse, lepers are gonna start takin' a step back."

"The only reason we're not pressing charges against the two of you is that my client wants this put behind him," Jerry went on, trying to sound tough but not getting anywhere close. "However, if you continue, you will force our hand."

"Lemme pass it to you soft," Malcolm added, full of swagger and dare. "You breathe near me and you gonna be the ones in cuffs. That clear enough, Five-O? Or maybe all them bullets you two swallowed fucked up your hearing too."

"Besides, you two guys are in enough trouble as it is," Jerry said, taking his confidence cue from Malcolm, convinced now that he was in no physical danger. "You don't need more. Certainly not from us."

"How do you figure?" Boomer asked, curious. "Us being the ones in trouble, I mean."

"You're being named in the civil suit," Jerry announced matter-of-factly. "Along with the police department, the Santori family, and the city of New York. Malcolm was arrested for no just reason. Someone has to pay for that."

"You're suing?" Dead-Eye asked, incredulous. "*You're* suing?"

"That's right, you crippled, mother-fuckin' losers." Malcolm lit another cigarette. "I don't wanna see you fuckers behind bars. Ain't nothin' in there for me. I want you out on them streets, workin' job after job and handin' that hard-earned green over to me. That's gonna eat you up, kill you quicker than any gun I could buy."

Jerry stood between Boomer and Malcolm, nervously shifting his brown backpack from one hand to the other. Boomer took two steps toward him and put a hand on his shoulder.

"I want a word with your client," Boomer said, squeezing the fingers of his hand tight across the top of Jerry's jacket. "I want that word alone. And I know you're not going to have a problem with that. Am I right?"

"It's a reasonable request," Jerry said, casting a quick glance at Malcolm. "Not even you would be crazy enough to try something in passing view of the public."

"All I see around me are skanks and ambulance chasers," Dead-Eye said, glancing at the faces rushing by. "We ain't exactly talking Vatican City."

"I'll be over by the mailbox if you need my help," Jerry told Malcolm. He lowered his head and slowly walked away.

"I needed your help *inside*, Jerry," Malcolm said, inching closer to Boomer, taking a drag on the cigarette and letting the smoke flow toward the cop's face. "Not out here. Not up against these limpin' fools. I got their shit down nasty."

Boomer ignored the smoke and moved close enough to Malcolm to smell the nicotine and stale coffee on his breath and spot the marijuana seeds dotting his lower teeth.

"The court can give you all my money," Boomer said in a low voice edged with violence. "They can give you every dime I've got. And you can spend it any way that you want. Gamble it, sniff it, screw it. That doesn't mean shit to me. You walk your way, I walk mine, and we both live out our lives. But you even think about touching that girl again or taking one fucking thing from her family after all this and I will kill you in a way you never even knew existed."

Malcolm's eyes widened in mock incredulity. "I just hear a threat from the mouth of a cripple?"

"No," Boomer said, standing as still as stone. "It's no threat. It's a promise."

. . .

NUNZIO POURED BOOMER and Dead-Eye refills of their amaretto on the rocks, then held the bottle perched against his knees.

"*He's* suing," Dead-Eye said. "That motherfucker is suing the city!"

"And the city'll cut a sweet deal with him for sure," Nunzio said, sadly shaking his head. "They'll make sure it's kept under a tight wrap, but they want him out of everybody's picture. The best way to do that is to cut him a check and tell him to take a walk."

"I never had a guy look at me the way Jenny's father did today." Boomer gripped his glass with his right hand. "It was all there on his face. Everything that kid suffered was right there, looking back at me."

"You did your job," Nunzio said. "You both did. But there were other hands in this. You got no control over that. You can live with it or you can forget it. Either way, you gotta make it pass."

Boomer said nothing, just stood and walked toward the bar, the lines on his weary face staring back at him in the large mirror hanging above the wide assortment of liquor bottles.

"He won and we lost," Dead-Eye said. "And when he gets that fat check, we lose all over again. Every fucking day he's alive, he wins all over again."

"Guys like Malcolm don't live all that long," Nunzio said solemnly. "Things happen to people like him. Bad things. It don't take much. A call to the right ear is all you need."

Both Dead-Eye and Boomer stayed still and silent after Nunzio's words. Boomer met Nunzio's eyes in the mirror, watched his face, empty of emotion, understanding the subtle weight of his words. He saw Dead-Eye look away from the window, his eyes catching Boomer's, his head giving a slow nod of approval.

Boomer turned from the bar and walked toward Nunzio, sitting on the edge of a stool. He stopped halfway between the bar and his two friends, picked up a hard-backed wooden chair, swung it over his head, and tossed it with a full force against the mirror above the bar. It landed in the center of the glass and shattered it, pieces large and small crashing to the wood floor and across the countertop.

"I'll pay you for that, Nunz," Boomer said, his hands by his sides, his head hanging low.

"It's my treat, Boom," Nunzio said, unfazed. "I'll just take out for the chair."

Boomer lifted his head and glanced over at Nunzio, his eyes welled with tears, his face flushed red.

"I have to go," Nunzio said. "You two stay as long as you want. Wreck the place if it puts smiles on your faces."

"Where are you going?" Boomer asked, staring at the old man through wet eyes.

"To make a call," Nunzio said. "To find the right ear."

It was a move both Boomer and Dead-Eye wanted to make but couldn't, and Nunzio knew that. They could never order a hit, pick up a phone, whisper a man's name and have him done away with. Even someone as despicable as Malcolm Juniper. They were tough cops but not cold-blooded ones. That's why they needed Nunzio as part of their team. He had made such calls before. He had grown up in the shadows of his father's world, a place where a nod of the head or the flicker of a light signaled the end of a life. Nunzio knew that the ones at the other end of the bullet were rarely innocents whose lives should or could be spared. He had learned at a young age that every time a call went out, it touched someone who was meant to die.

Nunzio stopped at the corner of Ninety-sixth Street and Amsterdam Avenue. He stood in front of a pay phone, the receiver in his right hand, dropped change into the coin slot, and pressed down on seven numbers.

He waited for the three rings and a pickup.

"Yes," the voice on the other end said.

"Malcolm Juniper," Nunzio said. "Tonight."

He hung up the phone and crossed the street against passing traffic, heading for a corner newsstand to buy a late afternoon paper. The cold air felt clean and fresh against his face, and he whistled a show tune as he walked, the phone call now nothing but a memory.

. . .

MALCOLM JUNIPER STUMBLED as he twisted his hand through his pants pocket, looking for the key to the midtown hotel room he had rented for the night.

The room was Jerry's treat, his gift for the sweet victory of the day. He even threw Malcolm three crisp hundred-dollar bills, an advance against their upcoming payday. Jerry told him the city was ready to settle, offering a tax-free six-figure sum if they just agreed to walk away, keep quiet, and forget about any lawsuits. Malcolm was all for the big check, but he wanted more. He wanted the police to hassle Boomer and Dead-Eye, maybe mess with their pensions, come down hard and teach the two cripples a lesson.

Teach them not to touch a player like Malcolm Juniper.

Malcolm had scored enough crack in three hours on the street to float his brain for a solid week. He had ordered up an Asian hooker to be sent to his room in less than an hour, pointedly asking the madam for somebody small, thin, and willing to handle rough action.

Malcolm was hungry for a party.

He dug out the key and with an unsteady hand slid it into the slot. He opened the door to the dark single-bed room and stepped inside, his right hand sliding up and down the wall, searching for a light. He kept the door open with the edge of his foot, allowing the light to filter in from the hall.

He stood on shaky legs, staring into the dark void of a hotel room, took in a deep breath, and gave out a short laugh. The warmth of the crack cocaine that flowed briskly through his body, combined with the sweet smell of the flowered room, had emptied him of all tension, all anger. He had made his score. He was a happy man who was only short weeks away from being a rich one.

Life was going to be good.

. . .

THE MAN STEPPED out of the hallway shadows and stood behind Malcolm Juniper, moving with gentle motions. He was dressed all in black, from the brim of the fedora that hid his forehead and eyes to the desert boots that silenced his walk. He stood behind Malcolm and scanned the hall from left to right, a dark specter on a mission that would tolerate no interruption.

The man pressed the cold metal of a silencer against the nape of Malcolm's neck, feeling Malcolm's body arch and stiffen. He placed a gloved hand on the center of his back and eased him farther into the room. No words were exchanged, no emotions spent, as each man quietly understood the purpose of the visit.

There would be no party for Malcolm Juniper.

Nothing to celebrate. No hooker to stroke and torment through the long night. No big check to cash. No more innocent blood to shed.

Malcolm's journey was at an end.

The man in black closed the door behind him and locked it. The click of the cylinder caused Malcolm's eyes to flutter.

It was now only a matter of time.

The anguished cries of innocent children who suffered under Malcolm Juniper's crazed urges would finally be brought to an end.

They would be avenged.

BOOK THREE

Beat the drums of tragedy for me,
Beat the drums of tragedy and death.
And let the choir sing a stormy song
To drown the rattle of my dying breath.

Beat the drums of tragedy for me,
And let the white violins whir thin and
slow,
But blow one blaring trumpet note of sun
To go with me
       to the darkness
           where I go.

—Langston Hughes, "Fantasy in Purple"

14

April 17, 1982

THE NAKED BABY was placed on a thick white bath towel in the center of the kitchen table, under a large overhead light. Two men hovered over him, both wearing translucent surgical gloves, one gripping an eight-inch butcher knife. Behind these men were two others, standing by the kitchen counter, taping and sealing small packets of cocaine from the kilo sacks resting inside a dry aluminum sink. The rest of the four-room second-floor apartment was a blanket of darkness, the back bedroom windows half open, letting in a soft spring breeze. A portable radio nestled near the baby and lodged against a napkin holder was tuned to an all-news station.

Outside, the narrow Queens street was silent and still, leaves on the trees still damp from a late afternoon shower. Cars were parked tightly on both sides, alarms armed, tires turned in curbside. All were empty except for two, which were parked directly in front of the building.

A middle-aged man sat upright in the lead car, a black four-door Buick LeSabre, smoking a thin cigar, windows rolled up tight.

Periodically, the man checked both his watch and the safety on a .9 millimeter jammed inside the spine of the passenger seat. He was nervous and edgy, concerned that the people at work in the apartment above were leaving him little margin for error. He had chewed the lip of his cigar down to the quick, the smoke from its tip engulfing him in small circles. He was new to the country and even newer to a line of work that could easily end with a bullet to the head or a long prison sentence in a state with a name he couldn't pronounce.

The money made it worth the risk.

Three hundred in cash to drive a mule and a baby to the airport, another two hundred to gas the car and wait in the parking lot for the next pickup, and a final three hundred to wrap up the round trip. Eight hundred cash in less than four hours, three nights a week. Tack that on to the thousand-dollar salary he pulled in working for a private car service on Long Island, and Gregor Stavlav, less than three months in the States and a wanted man in his native Greece, found himself smack in the middle of an American dream.

The car parked behind Gregor was dented, rusty, and dirty. He had given it a quick glance in his rearview mirror, then shrugged it off. It was the kind of car a student working his way through school, or a small-timer years past any chance at a score, might own. It was not the kind of car a man with money would be seen in, let alone call his own.

And it was definitely not a cop car.

That much Gregor, who prided himself on his knowledge of cars and the people who drove them, knew.

He would bet his life on it.

. . .

REV. JIM LOVED his seven-year-old AMC Gremlin, loved the way it handled, even liked the way it looked. He took pride in the polished full-leather interior he had custom made at discount by a friend in Washington Heights and wasn't all that concerned by the ruined condition of the outer body. It was, for him, the perfect car.

He was stretched out across the front seat, head on the door rest, the heels of his construction boots flat against the passenger side jam, two

.38 Police Specials crisscrossed on his chest. He slipped a cassette of Clifton Chenier and the Zodiac Ramblers into the tape deck and listened, at uncharacteristically low volume, as they stomped their way through "The Things I Did for You." Rev. Jim closed his eyes and took several deep breaths.

He wasn't sure if he was ready for what the Apaches had planned. This would be his first bout of heavy action since the fire that had disabled him, and while he could taste the fear, the adrenaline flow he always felt still hadn't kicked in. He knew the other members of the team were out there, positioned in the dark, ready to pounce, each of them probably running through the same emotional checks he was clicking off in his mind. He knew it was every cop's natural instinct to hesitate before going into a bust, but for reasons he couldn't quite pin down he seemed suddenly uncomfortable with those feelings.

Rev. Jim had always loved the rush that came with being a decoy, walking in blind, never knowing when or if the hit would come or if the assigned backup would really be there. It was all part of the play, risk being as important as the takedown. Rather than fear it, he had always welcomed it. Except for now.

Lying down next to the steering wheel of his beat-up Gremlin, Rev. Jim wondered if it was too late for him to be a cop again. Wondered if he had lost too much of what he needed.

He checked the red digital light on his wristwatch.

8:56 P.M.

In less than four minutes he would have his answer.

• • •

BOOMER AND DEAD-EYE sat on opposite ends of the fire escape, backs to the wall, separated by the streaks of light pouring out from the kitchen. Both wore thin black leather jackets, thick black sweaters, and black racer gloves. Boomer had a .38 revolver in his right hand and another pushed into the back of his jeans. Dead-Eye had two .44 semiautomatics, both snug inside their shoulder holsters.

Boomer glanced into the kitchen and saw the man with the knife talking in animated tones with the one whose back was to the window.

Sweat ran down the man's forehead and into his eyes. Boomer knew the layout of the apartment and the backgrounds on the men inside from the sealed packet he had received earlier that morning from One Police Plaza. If everything in the narcotics report held accurate, this would be the first hard slap by the Apaches against Lucia Carney.

"We gotta freeze the guy with the knife," Boomer whispered to Dead-Eye. "Otherwise, he sticks the kid."

"Make that my worry," Dead-Eye said. "You deal with his friend."

"Mrs. Columbo can handle the ones hanging by the sink," Boomer said. "Any other surprises, we've gotta take 'em."

"Two minutes more." Dead-Eye checked his watch, then rested his head against the red brick wall, his eyes closed.

"Let's hope Geronimo hasn't lost the touch," Boomer said. "Otherwise we're in for a tough stretch."

"Ain't Geronimo I'm worried about," Dead-Eye said, still with his eyes closed.

"Who, then?" Boomer asked.

"Me," Dead-Eye said.

. . .

GERONIMO WAS ON HIS KNEES, a short wire in his hand, a thick ball of plastique stuck to the door lock leading into the apartment. Mrs. Columbo and Pins were against the wall on either side of him, guns drawn, eyes on the stairwell and the other apartment doors.

"You going to make this?" Mrs. Columbo asked, looking down, watching Geronimo circle the coil wire into the plastique.

"It's easier taking them apart, that's for sure," Geronimo said, his voice as calm as his manner.

"How long's that fuse gotta burn for?" Pins asked.

"Ten seconds." Geronimo pulled a lighter from his jacket pocket and looked up at Pins. "If I did it right."

"What if you didn't do it right?" Pins said with just a bit of an edge. "And it doesn't blow?"

"Then we knock," Geronimo said, "and hope they let us in."

. . .

INSIDE THE APARTMENT, Albert, the man with the knife, stared down at the cooing infant. The man across from him, the sleeves of his white shirt rolled to the elbows, rubbed a palm full of Johnson's baby oil over the infant's chest. Albert scratched at his chin with the pointed edge of the knife, waiting for the soft skin to finish being coated. The baby's eyes were bright and clear blue and the man with the knife couldn't help but smile at the child he was seconds away from slicing open.

Albert nodded to his partner, Freddie, who pressed an oily hand across the baby's mouth, silencing his coo. The other men in the kitchen continued with the mundane task of wrapping cocaine, taping it shut, and preparing it for transfer.

As the blade of the knife touched the baby's breastbone, Albert's eyes focused, his hands as steady as a surgeon's. He looked up at his partner across from him, felt Freddie's hand press down harder on the baby's mouth, saw him nod and smile with anticipation.

"Do him, Albert," Freddie said. "Do him now."

"I don't know how much more of this I can do," Albert said back. "I'm startin' to see their faces in my dreams."

"*Now*," Freddie said. "Otherwise, we're gonna miss our plane and then somebody's gonna have to fly up here to do *us*. Dream about *that*."

"This is my last one," Albert told him. "I swear to God, it's my last one."

"Then make it your best one," Freddie said.

. . .

THE FRONT DOOR blew out and exploded into six large chunks, taking out parts of the wall on both sides. Plaster, shards of tile, and blasts of dust whirled past the small foyer and out into the kitchen. The shudder of the bomb shook the apartment to its foundation and sent the men by the kitchen sink scrambling for cover.

Albert fell across the table, the front half of his body on top of the baby, the knife slipping from his hand to the floor. Freddie fell over backward, hitting his head against a plate shelf, a thin line of blood coloring the back of his neck.

Sprawled on the floor against cracked walls and toppled tables, the men were still quick enough to recover, drawing and cocking double-action revolvers, holding them out, arms extended.

Albert lifted himself from the table and grabbed the baby with one arm. He turned and looked toward the dust. His eyes made out three figures standing in front of where the door had been thirty seconds earlier. He planted his feet, aimed his gun, and fired off four rounds. The three shadows scattered, hidden by the safety net of dust and debris.

"Shit. I hate this," Pins muttered, crunched down in a corner of the foyer, using the top of a small end table as his shield. "You think they'd want to know who they're shooting at before they start to blast away."

"They know who we are," Geronimo said, flat down on the stained linoleum floor, his .38 Special held forward with both hands. "We're the guys who just blew up half their fuckin' apartment."

"I told you that would only go and make them mad," Mrs. Columbo said. Her back was against the doorjamb, her legs up, gun aimed and pointed through the haze.

"I figure it's too late to apologize," Geronimo said, checking his watch and trying to make out the faces in the smoke and the dark. "So stay ready. Thirty seconds till Boomer."

· · ·

BOOMER AND DEAD-EYE both flinched when they heard the blast. But they held their position on the fire escape, waiting the agreed-upon ninety seconds for the dust to clear and for Geronimo, Pins, and Mrs. Columbo to stake out a solid post. The glass above them had cracked from the explosion, but they could still see into the kitchen to watch the men regroup. Albert held the baby in one arm, clearly more for his own protection than that of the child.

"You feeling young yet?" Boomer asked Dead-Eye, who was pulling his guns from their holsters.

"Young enough to be in love," Dead-Eye told him.

Boomer lifted the kitchen window to waist level with the heel of one hand, letting out gusts of white smoke. He crouched down, pointing his gun into the open window. "Then it's time to show them we're back."

"And find out if anybody gives a shit," Dead-Eye said, following him in.

. . .

REV. JIM HEARD the rumble of the explosion and sat up, waiting for Gregor to bolt from his car. He had both his guns aimed at the back of the man's head, expecting him to jump out and hit the stairs to the house at full pace. Instead, Gregor held his place, cigar still stuck in the corner of his mouth, the interior of his car awash in smoke.

If the explosion didn't faze him, the quick clips of the four shots that came from Albert's gun made Gregor sit bolt upright behind the steering wheel. He rolled his window down, stuck his head out, and looked up at the apartment. His neck was glazed with sweat, his mouth was dry, yet he let the gun on the passenger seat rest there untouched. This was not part of the deal. He hadn't left Greece to be buried in America.

Gregor pulled his head back into the car, tossed the cigar on the sidewalk, rolled up the window, turned the ignition over, and pulled out of his parking spot. Rev. Jim smiled as he watched him speed off into the Queens night. Then he hopped out of the Gremlin, guns in hand, heading for the door of the apartment building. Rev. Jim turned and glanced down the street, the red taillights of Gregor's car still in his line of sight. He wondered if maybe the frightened driver with the hunger for American dollars just didn't have the right idea after all.

At least, this one night, he wasn't going to die.

. . .

BOOMER CAME ROLLING OUT of the window and clicked off two rounds, hitting Freddie in the right shoulder and chest, sending him sprawling back to the floor. Dead-Eye, fast behind Boomer, jumped out of a crouched postion right behind Albert, jamming the barrels of both guns on the sides of his neck.

"That baby gets upset," Dead-Eye whispered in his ear, "your head's gonna roll out the door."

Geronimo and Mrs. Columbo fired eight rounds at the two men by the sink, three of the bullets clipping kitchen cabinets and lodging inside thick wall beams. Five bullets found their mark and sent the men sprawling to the ground.

Rev. Jim stood in the doorway, legs spread, two guns aimed into the apartment, looking for any movement. He exchanged a quick glance with Pins, who still held his position behind the end table, his gun by his side.

"Take the drugs," Albert said in a calm voice, seemingly unfazed by the shooting and the massacred bodies around him. "Take whatever you want."

"You heard the man," Boomer said, nodding to the four Apaches by the door. "Take the drugs."

Mrs. Columbo and Geronimo immediately holstered their guns as they walked toward the sink and the thick piles of cocaine. They took out Swiss Army knives, stepped around the bodies lying faceup on the ground, and sliced the cellophane packs down the center. Then they dumped the kilos into the sink, turned on the faucets, and let cold water take the powder down the drain.

"That's more than two hundred thousand you're throwin' away," Albert said. He sounded more distressed over the disposal of the cocaine than over the loss of the lives around him.

"What's the time?" Boomer asked.

"We got three minutes till the cops show," Pins said, the gun in his hand now replaced by a police scanner that allowed him to pick up all monitored calls. "Maybe a few seconds less."

Boomer walked over to stand across from Albert. He looked into Albert's eyes, then over at the baby, legs wiggling, calm amid a sea of smoke, blood, and death.

"Are there clothes for the baby?" Boomer asked.

"In the bedroom." Albert nodded as Mrs. Columbo headed into the back room.

"Who the hell *are* you?" Albert asked, his eyes focused now on Boomer.

"I got the clothes," Mrs. Columbo said, coming back from the bedroom holding an armful of small blue pajamas, diapers, a T-shirt the size of a handkerchief, and tissue-thin white lace socks. "Now all I need is the baby to put in them."

"You heard the lady." Dead-Eye moved his guns from Albert's neck to the inside of his ears. "She wants the baby."

"One minute," Pins said. "We better motor-out now. You can't count on them being right on time."

Boomer took the baby from Albert's arms and handed him to Mrs. Columbo. "Put him under your jacket," he told her. "You can dress him in the car."

Dead-Eye pulled the guns from Albert's ears and holstered them. Boomer took one last look around the apartment, then nodded to the others. They left through the open window, Geronimo first, followed by Pins, Mrs. Columbo, the baby, and Rev. Jim. Dead-Eye stood with one leg on the fire escape and the other on the kitchen linoleum.

"He lives?" Dead-Eye asked Boomer, nodding toward Albert.

"He lives," Boomer said with a smile, still looking at Albert. "Just long enough to tell Lucia what happened."

For the first time all night, Albert's eyes betrayed him. Hearing Lucia's name washed away the cold facade of the career criminal. Now there was only fear.

"She's going to love to hear how you stood there and watched two strangers flush two hundred thou of her drugs down a kitchen sink," Boomer said, walking away from Albert and putting a leg out through the open window. "I can't figure if she'll have you shot or beaten to death. But, then again, you know her better than I do."

Boomer climbed out the window, but as he started to close it he leaned his head in. "The cops sure as shit aren't gonna believe your story either," Boomer said to Albert. "Whatever that story is gonna be. You have a good night now."

Boomer closed the window behind him and disappeared into the darkness, leaving Albert standing in an apartment filled only with the dead. He listened as police sirens wailed in the distance. His future was now as clear to him as the bodies that lay sprawled by his side.

· · ·

LUCIA PUT THE RECEIVER BACK in its cradle and stared down at the phone for several minutes. The midday Arizona sun filtered through the open screen doors, the gleam off the swimming pool casting her face in its warm glow. Her hair was wet and pulled back tight; gold clips held two curled-up buns in place. She stood in the center of her living room, tanned and glistening with sweat, the straps of her two-piece designer bathing suit hanging loose from her shoulders, a calm woman at peace with herself and her surroundings.

Only her eyes and her shallow breathing betrayed the rage within.

Lucia ran a manicured hand over the smooth surface of the phone as if caressing the arm of a lover. She then reached down with both hands, lifted the phone off the polished wood coffee table, and with four violent tugs yanked it free from its wall socket. She spun around and threw the phone across the room, past the open screen doors. With a splash it landed in the shallow end of her forty-foot swimming pool.

The noise brought in her two bodyguards, who'd been sunning themselves by the edge of the deck.

"Get us on a plane," she told them, her voice eerily quiet. "The next one out."

"Out where?" asked the bodyguard with the trim black goatee and a tattoo of Lucia's face on his right forearm.

"New York." Lucia stood, legs apart, hands folded on her hips, staring out at the pool. "I want to be there by tonight."

"We takin' cargo?" the other bodyguard asked. He was as burly and muscular as the first, with a sharp razor cut and a long, ragged scar running down his hairless chest.

"No." Lucia turned her gaze toward him. "No cargo. But arrange to have some of your tools shipped ahead. We may have to fix a few items."

The two bodyguards nodded and left the room to tend to their tasks. Lucia paced about in bare feet, sun still beaming off her face, forcing herself to regain focus. The raid on the drug den in Queens was the first move ever attempted against her crew, and its wake left much more than a bitter taste. It left behind questions. And in the drug business, questions were as dangerous as a loaded weapon.

The team that made the hit on the apartment were pros. No prints had been left behind. The shell casings came out of the barrels of street guns. They had their timing down, from the bomb latched to the door to the precision shooting. These weren't the actions of either low-level dealers looking to ice a big score or a renegade outfit tied into an existing crew. Albert would have picked up on those. He had been in the drug trade long enough to have done business with everybody working the streets, from first-rate groups to bottom-tier wannabes.

Lucia lit a cigarette and walked out onto the sun-bleached deck, blowing a stream of smoke into the hot desert air. She sat down and placed her feet in the crystal-blue chlorinated water, calmer now than she had been since Albert called her with the news. She lifted her face to the sun and played the heist over in her mind as it was relayed to her.

Other than walking out with the baby, the thieves hadn't stolen anything. They had washed two hundred thousand in cocaine down a sink without even a second's hesitation. So it wasn't money or drugs that piqued their interest. And they certainly didn't need to shoot their way into a Queens apartment to steal a baby she had paid a hooker $600 for three months earlier.

No, there was a professional logic to the attack.

That meant it was personal.

Whoever it was, they were coming after Lucia and they weren't being coy. They wanted her to know. Maybe they were backed by somebody bigger or maybe they were lone wolves out looking for a name to match the bravado. Or maybe it went even deeper.

Maybe someone Lucia had touched, a young girl perhaps, or the relative of a child, now wanted to touch her back.

It didn't really matter to her. She would do all that she could to find them and erase them from sight. Lucia Carney was sitting on the crest of a six-hundred-million-dollar mountaintop and had come too far over too many long nights to let anybody throw her off.

The group that shot up the safe house had come out gunning for a battle.

Lucia was going to give them a war.

She tossed the cigarette into the clean pool, looked down at her reflection, and smiled, once again a happy woman.

The smell of death was in the air.

15

BOOMER LEANED THE back of his chair against the wall and watched Mrs. Columbo feed the baby a bottle of warm formula. The other Apaches sat around a table in the main dining room at Nunzio's, nursing their drinks and replaying the actions of the night over in their minds.

"You look good with a baby in your arms," Boomer said, smiling.

"It's been a long time since I held one this close."

She thought back to when Frankie was the same age as the baby she held, Joe following the two of them everywhere they went, armed with a smile and a camera. It was a happy time for all three, filled only with warm feelings. She wished they could someday get back to that.

Boomer held his smile and stared at Mrs. Columbo and the baby, thinking only about what might have been.

"You make the call to social services yet?" Geronimo asked.

"We don't need social services." Boomer answered the question without looking away from Mrs. Columbo, the baby serene and content in her arms.

"You sure as shit got a full plate planned out for us, Boomer," Rev. Jim said. "We break a drug ring *and* we babysit. You can't find a squad like us anywhere."

"We look like a couple to you guys?" Boomer walked over to Mrs. Columbo and put his arm around her.

"A couple of what?" Pins asked, finishing off a glass of tap beer.

"I'd buy into it," Dead-Eye said, understanding without being told what Boomer was really asking. "Married since high school, two other kids grown and out of the house, money a little short, and then, the last thing you need, a surprise baby."

"Is that what you doormen do with all your days?" Rev. Jim asked him. "Watch soaps?"

"I work nights," Dead-Eye said. "And I listen to the radio."

"Me and the wife here got ourselves a kid we can't afford," Boomer said, walking slowly around the table. "We're way low on cash and there's no way we can keep him. But we wanna make sure our baby has a good home to grow up in and good people to raise him. So where do we go for something like that? Who we gonna turn to?"

"I'll take Lucia for forty, Alex," Rev. Jim said.

"Holy shit," Pins said. "You guys *are* fuckin' crazy."

"Maybe," Boomer said, stopping at the table between Geronimo and Pins. "But I don't see it any other way."

Mrs. Columbo instinctively held the baby tighter to her body. "Are you really going to sell him back to Lucia?" she asked.

"Only way to get our foot in her door," Dead-Eye said.

"There's a lot of layers between her and the sale," Geronimo pointed out. "It's not like walking into J. C. Penney's and finding her behind the counter. Lucia's never near the buy and always far away from the kill."

"We take it one step at a time," Boomer said. "We start at the bottom of her outfit and work our way up."

"Where the hell's the bottom?" Pins asked. "It's not like this crew takes out ads."

"You find a guy named Saldo," Nunzio said, opening a manila folder and sliding out a half dozen head shots of a man with thick dark hair and a long scar running down the right side of his face. "He's the guy who fed Malcolm the lady's business card. He's her main New York line into the baby market. Pays top dollar and asks very few questions."

"What is it you *do*, exactly, Nunzio?" Rev. Jim asked, looking over at the older man with a trace of admiration.

"I listen," Nunzio said.

"Pins, we'll get you an address and a plate number by early tomorrow morning," Boomer said.

"I'll have him wired before lunch," Pins said. "You want him bodied too?"

"How the hell can you body-wire him?" Boomer asked. "You're not gonna be anywhere close to the guy."

"I don't have to be." The confidence in his own abilities overcame Pins's shyness. "I don't even have to meet the man."

"What are ya gonna do?" Rev. Jim asked. "Mail him the wire and ask him to put it on himself?"

"He gets his clothes cleaned somewhere," Pins said. "As soon as I have his address, I'll figure out where. I'll plant the bugs there *before* he puts on his clothes."

Boomer glanced over at Dead-Eye, who looked back at him and smiled. "My hunch is the guy works out of the East Side. We'll have the layout soon enough. I want the building covered in case of trouble."

"If there's a super or a guy at the door, I can talk my way into having them let me do the windows," Rev. Jim said. "I'll look scruffy enough so they won't notice."

"That shouldn't be too hard," Nunzio added.

"Go in on a day there's a garbage pickup," Geronimo said. "Around the time they're working that street."

"Why?" Boomer asked.

"I got a friend in Sanitation," Geronimo told him. "He'll let me work on the truck crew. This way I'm visible but nobody notices me. There's trouble, I'll be there."

"That covers the ground and the outside of the building," Boomer said. "That leaves the roof for you, Dead-Eye. Your gut tells you something's not right, don't even hesitate."

"What about me?" Mrs. Columbo asked. "What am I doing while all this is going on?"

"Nothing," Boomer said with a smile. "You're my wife and no wife of mine's gonna have a job."

Mrs. Columbo looked down at the baby, lifted him to eye level, and kissed his flushed red cheek. "Your father's an asshole," she cooed as she placed him on her shoulder and patted his back. Seconds later, the baby let out a loud burp.

"That's what he thinks of you," Mrs. Columbo said with a laugh.

. . .

LUCIA SAT at the head of the eight-foot dining table, a yellow folder spread open beneath her elbows. A crystal ashtray and wine goblet were off to her left, a 1980 merlot in one, a filter-tipped cigarette smoldering on the edge of the other. She stared across the length of the bare table at the private investigator sitting nervously at the far end. He had on a cheap coffee-colored suit, worn at the cuffs, a brown shirt in need of a wash, and a poorly knotted cream tie. He was thin and balding, the top of his head coated with beads of sweat, his small fingers softly drumming on the top of the table. Three of Lucia's men stood silently behind him, hidden by the shadows of the drawn brocade drapes that kept out the afternoon sunshine. There was a large glass of ice water in front of the man. It sat untouched.

"You're charging me two hundred and fifty dollars an hour plus expenses, Mr. Singleton," Lucia said in a level-toned voice. "I expect you to have something to show for it."

"It's all there in the file," Trace Singleton said. "You can see for yourself."

"I don't want to see for myself," Lucia said in harsher tones. "I want you to tell me."

"That ambush on your apartment was pulled off by a group of cops," Singleton said, wiping a thin line of sweat off his upper lip. "Working on their own."

"How do you know they were cops?" Lucia asked, taking a puff from her cigarette.

"That part's confidential," Singleton said, smirking. "That's one of the reasons I'm so good at what I do. You gotta trust me on it."

"And if I don't trust you on it?" Lucia asked. "What happens then?"

"Then I guess you and me can't do business anymore," he said, glancing behind him at the three large men who never seemed to move.

Lucia pushed back her chair and walked down the length of the table, the fingers of her right hand skimming the dark wood surface. She walked past Singleton and over to one of her men. She looked up at him and smiled, slowly running a hand up the front of his blue silk shirt and down to his side, stopping when she found the handle of the .9-millimeter Luger. She pulled the gun from the man's hip and rested it against her stomach, her back still turned to Singleton.

"Were you telling me the truth?" Lucia asked, her eyes cold and steady, looking at her man, her question aimed at Singleton.

"About what?" Singleton turned slightly in his chair, one arm braced against the curve of the antique wood.

"That everything I need to know is in the file?"

"Everything's there," Singleton said, his arrogance tempered by the oppressive heat in the room. "Like I always say, you bring me in, you bring in the best."

"You were also right about something else," Lucia said, turning away from the man in the silk shirt.

"You get to know me better, you'll find out I'm right about most things." Singleton was full of swagger now, squinting over at Lucia. The dim light in the room kept the gun in her hand hidden from his line of vision. "Now, which thing in particular were you talkin' about?"

Lucia raised the gun and aimed it at Singleton. "You and I can't do business anymore."

Lucia's index finger put pressure on the Luger's quick trigger and clicked off two rounds, both of which landed in Singleton's forehead, cracking open the back of his head, sending blood and bone fragments splashing against the flocked red wallpaper. Singleton's upper body slumped against the back of the chair, resting there as if he were fast asleep.

Lucia handed the Luger back to the man in the blue shirt. He took it by the handle and shoved it into his hip holster.

"Have someone clean up the room," Lucia told the three men. She walked back to the head of the table and picked up the folder. "I've got some reading to do."

· · ·

"Where is your husband now, Mrs. Connors?" the well-dressed man behind the desk asked Mrs. Columbo, flashing a toothy smile.

"He's trying to find a parking spot." Mrs. Columbo shifted one leg over the other. Boomer had made her wear a tight miniskirt and she was showing more than enough thigh to interest the man behind the desk. "That's no easy thing in this neighborhood."

"How did you find out about our agency?" the man asked, still with the smile, his eyes scanning Mrs. Columbo and the baby braced against her right arm.

"My friend Carmella," Mrs. Columbo said. "She told me you guys helped her out about six, maybe seven months ago. You found a good home for her baby and paid her off in cash. No questions. Is that part true?"

"Which part?" the man asked.

"About the questions," Mrs. Columbo said. "When Richie comes in here, if you start asking him a bunch of, you know, personal shit, excuse my French, he's gonna get nasty and walk out."

"That wouldn't be smart," the man said. "He'd be leaving the way he walked in, with no money and a baby he doesn't want."

"That's where you're wrong," Mrs. Columbo said. "I'm sorry, I don't know your name."

"Edward."

"You see, Eddie," Mrs. Columbo said, "my husband wants the baby. I don't. I went through enough with the two I had and I don't need to raise more. What I need is to find me work, something that pays good and brings it in steady."

"What kind of work?"

"Doesn't matter," Mrs. Columbo said, looking around the barren room. "Years ago, before I hooked up with Richie, I did it all, didn't care what it was. 'Course, I was a little better-looking back then, but I'm still willin' to do it all, whatever it is, so long as the money's there at the end. Maybe I shouldn't be telling you all this. But Carmella said—"

Edward interrupted her, his arms spread out in front of him, the smile on his face locked in place. "Does your husband know about any of this?"

"Are you kiddin' me?" Mrs. Columbo said. "Wait till you meet him. I mean, I love the guy and all, but my Richie's lucky if he can find his ass with two hands. There are guys just made that way. I'm sure you met some workin' this job."

"A few," Edward Glistner said, leaning back in his chair, resting his hands on top of his head.

"Then you know what I'm talkin' about," Mrs. Columbo said, running a finger under the folds of the baby's chin.

"I might have a job for you," Edward said, turning his head slightly at the sounds of empty garbage cans being tossed by the sanitation workers outside. "If you really are as interested as you seem."

"Let's hear it." Mrs. Columbo looked over Edward's shoulder to catch a glimpse of Boomer crossing the street. "Make it quick. Before Richie comes inside."

"You don't want him to know?" Edward asked.

"Not till I know," Mrs. Columbo said. "Then, depending on what it is, we'll see if he can handle it."

"It's everything you say you're looking for," Edward said, checking the time on the wall clock. "Steady hours and a pretty good salary."

"What do I have to do?" Mrs. Columbo asked.

"Come back tomorrow," Edward said. "Without Richie. We'll work out the details then."

"How about a hint?" Mrs. Columbo asked, throwing Edward her most alluring smile.

"Do you like to fly?" Edward asked, smiling back at her, then standing to greet Boomer as he walked into the room.

. . .

PINS WAITED OUTSIDE Harry Saben's Cleaners, watching as the blonde in the skintight leggings dropped off three of Saldo's jackets and two of his slacks. He saw Harry, old and hunched from too many years behind a counter, fill out the work slip, his eyes more on the blonde's cleavage than on the cut of Saldo's clothes. The blonde took the slip, gave Harry a smile, and walked out of the store, heading east.

"Good morning," Pins said to Harry, closing the glass door behind him.

"How may I help you?" Harry asked, traces of a childhood spent speaking Russian still in his voice.

"It's really about how I can help you," Pins said. He reached into the side pocket of his windbreaker and flipped his detective's shield.

"You a cop?" Harry asked, squinting down at the badge through thick glasses.

"I'm investigating a ring that's ripping off designer labels," Pins said. "I'm sure someone as experienced as yourself in the business knows the routine. Take a secondhand jacket, tag a designer label on it, sell it on the street for three times the price."

"I've heard of people doing things like that," Harry said, nodding his head.

"Then you know there's a lot of money in it," Pins said.

"I imagine," Harry said. "But what can I do?"

Pins leaned closer to Harry and lowered his voice. "Can the department trust you?"

"Yes," Harry said, lowering his voice right back. "I'm very pro-police. I'd like to see a couple of thousand more of you out there."

Pins nodded. "All right," he said. "I'm going to take a chance."

"It's not a chance," Harry said. "Believe me, I'll go to my grave with what you tell me."

"The blonde that was just here," Pins said. "I'm sure you noticed her."

"Even at my age."

"She's part of the ring," Pins explained. "These clothes she left, they're not designer clothes. They come out of some sweatshop in the Bronx."

Harry reached down and felt Saldo's black Armani jacket. "It looks so real," he said. "It even feels the way it should. The label's in it and everything."

"I can get you a case of labels by this afternoon." Pins reached over and grabbed Saldo's clothes. "That's the easiest part."

"Are you going to take those with you?" Harry asked with some concern.

"Don't worry," Pins asked. "I'll have them back to you by this afternoon, cleaned and pressed. When did you tell her they'd be ready?"

"Six tonight," Harry said.

"Perfect." Pins jammed the clothes under one arm and reached out a hand to Harry. "I appreciate all your help."

"It's been my pleasure," Harry said, smiling and shaking Pins's hand.

"I'll see you in a few hours," Pins said, heading for the door. "Is there anything the department can do for you?"

"Is the place you're having those cleaned a good one?" Harry asked, walking around the counter.

"It's a special cleaner," Pins said. "Like running your clothes through a car wash."

"Then there *is* something you can do," Harry said. "A small favor."

"What?" Pins asked.

"I need to get a stain out of Mrs. Babcock's black cocktail dress. I've put it through the wash three times and it's still there. I don't know what the hell she spilled on it, but I just can't get it to come out. Maybe your place can give it a shot?"

Pins smiled at Harry. "Get the dress," he said. "I'll bring it back to you like new."

"You're the best," Harry said, rushing to the back of the store for the dress.

"I hope so," Pins muttered.

· · ·

GERONIMO WAS LIFTING a large cardboard Zenith television carton filled with wires and a rusty old air conditioner when he spotted the double-parked car. The black, late-model Lincoln was inched alongside a Toyota Corolla and a blue Renault, engine running, tinted windows up.

Geronimo tossed the box into the back of the sanitation truck and shifted the crush gear, his eyes on the Lincoln. The lead man shifted the truck and moved it slowly up to the next hill of garbage. Geronimo walked in the shadows of the truck, his head down, his mouth inches from the collar of his work jacket.

"That double-parked car doesn't look right to me," Geronimo whispered into the tiny microphone wired inside his collar. "You picking up anything from inside?"

"Saldo's in the backseat." Geronimo heard the crisp sound of Pins's crackling words come through his ear mike. The thin wires from the audio devices ran down his neck and into a small box taped to the center of his back. "He's got two shooters with him, both in the front. All three carrying heavy."

Pins was parked on the north corner, dressed in the brown uniform of a Department of Transportation officer, behind the wheel of a battered tow truck.

"Shooters always carry heavy," Rev. Jim's voice said through the mikes. "Why should these two be any different?" He was on his third set of windows, turning slightly to drop a squeegee into a bucket of water and pick up a hand towel.

"Well, these two are out gunning for us," Pins said. "Somebody's tipped them. They know we're sending a plant into the building. They just don't know when or who."

"Do Boomer and Mrs. Columbo know?" Dead-Eye asked, crouched against the iron door leading from the roof to the top floor of the brownstone.

"Their mikes are turned off," Pins said. "It's too risky otherwise."

"It's your play, Dead-Eye," Geronimo said. "We'll walk it any way you want."

"Just make it fast," Rev. Jim said. "I'm runnin' outta water and windows."

"Pins, can you hear me?" Dead-Eye asked.

"Got you," Pins answered.

"Back up into the block and tow that car out of there," Dead-Eye told him. "Geronimo?"

"I'm here," Geronimo said, dragging a thick bag of garbage from the curb.

"Back-up Pins," Dead-Eye said. "Let's try and do this clean. We don't need a gunfight on the street. Rev. Jim?"

"Talk to me."

"Get in here without too much noise," Dead-Eye said. "Just in case I get jammed up."

"What about Boomer and Mrs. Columbo?" Pins asked.

"They've got a job to do," Dead-Eye said, "and so do we."

"And Saldo?" Geronimo asked. "How do we play him?"

"Let him take the ride with the tow truck," Dead-Eye said. "There's a better chance he'll run his mouth sitting in the car. Pins will let us know if he says anything we need to hear."

"Can Saldo's wire pick me up when I get close?" Geronimo asked.

"Don't worry," Pins said. "As soon as you touch the car, I'll turn it off."

"Anything else?" Rev. Jim asked.

"Yeah," Dead-Eye said. "Stay alive."

Pins slammed the truck gears into reverse and backed the hook end close to the bumper of the Lincoln. The driver's side window rolled down and an overweight man in wraparound sunglasses stuck his head out.

"What's up, asshole?" he said in a Spanish accent, watching Pins lift a large wooden slab and place it under the front tires of the Lincoln.

"You're double-parked," Pins said. "That's illegal."

"I'm in the car," the driver said. "I can move it."

"You should have thought of that before," Pins said. "Once the wood's down, the job's a done deal."

"What the fuck are you talking about?" the driver said, his face red with anger. "You don't have to tow anybody anywhere. I'll move the fuckin' car."

"The wood's down," Pins said. "You can't move it once the wood's down."

"Fuck you *and* the wood," the driver said.

The middle of the garbage truck stopped right next to the Lincoln.

Geronimo approached from the passenger end, his hands down by his sides, one holding a .44 semiautomatic, a silencer attached to the muzzle. He gave two hard knuckle taps on the passenger window. The window buzzed halfway down, letting out miniclouds of smoke, most of it wrapped around the face of a man in light-colored clothing.

"We break a garbage law now too?" the man asked with mild irritation.

The man behind the wheel punched the dashboard repeatedly, his anger at full throttle. He had pockmarked cheeks and hair the color of straw hanging down the sides of his face. "I hate this fuckin' city," he shouted. "Take a look at who's giving us shit. A fuckin' tow-truck driver and a garbage man."

"Do you know you have to pass a test to get this job?" Geronimo said.

"I don't give a fuck!" the driver screamed.

Geronimo leaned his head into the car, looking beyond the two men in the front, staring into the darkness of the backseat, where Saldo sat quietly through the commotion.

"You're all going to take a ride to the pound," Geronimo said to Saldo. "Believe me, you'll like it. You can roll down your windows and take in the water view. It's a better place for you to be than here. Have I painted a clear enough picture?"

Saldo nodded, his eyes and manner indifferent.

"You're no fuckin' garbage man," the driver said.

Geronimo shrugged. "I couldn't pass the test."

"What are you then?" the man in the front asked.

"He's a cop," Saldo said. "They're both cops."

"Cops?" the man behind the wheel said. "The tow-truck driver too?"

"A lot of us have to work two jobs," Geronimo said.

"Say the word," the driver said, looking into the rearview at Saldo. "We'll take these fuckers out right here and now."

Geronimo lifted his hand and showed them the .44. "Let's not be stupid," he said to Saldo. "They make a move on me and I move on you and we both know it's not worth it. So stick to the plan and enjoy the ride."

Saldo stared into Geronimo's dark eyes, feeling the front end of the car start to tilt upward.

"We stay with the car," he said to the two men in the front.

"It's been nice talking to you," Geronimo told him.

"I hope we get to do it again," Saldo said. "Soon."

Geronimo backed away from the car, the two men in the front staring angrily at Pins as he lifted the car into tow position.

"Kill the engine, please," Pins said to them.

"I'd like to fuckin' kill you first," the driver said.

"Hey, I'm nervous as it is," Pins said with an innocent smile. "I've never towed a car before. I would hate to lose you guys on the highway."

. . .

THE THICK WOODEN DOOR to the four-story brownstone swung halfway open, the brass knob held by a large man in charcoal-gray slacks and red suspenders draped over a black shirt. His eyes narrowed as he watched the commotion around the Lincoln. He moved his free hand to the small of his back, fingers wrapping themselves around the handle of a .32 short Colt. He saw the DOT man chain the car and lift it. The two men in the front were exchanging angry gestures while Saldo's shadow sat motionless in the back. He eased the Colt out of its holster and released the safety.

"I'm done," Rev. Jim said, jumping down from one of the window ledges to the front of the door well, blocking the man's view. "Now for the fun part. Getting paid."

"Outta my fuckin' eyes," the man hissed at Rev. Jim, the gun held against the side of his right leg.

"You ain't anything special to look at either," Rev. Jim said with a smile, holding his work pail, half filled with water, in his left hand. "You hand me the thirty bucks for the job and I'll turn invisible."

The man looked at Rev. Jim and lifted the gun in his hand to chest level. "Get the fuck outta here," the man told him. "Now."

Rev. Jim held the smile on his face. "They're only windows," he said, turning his back on the man with the gun, still blocking his view with his body. He then swung the pail high above his shoulder and crashed it down against the side of the man's head. The man fell backward into the entryway, out cold, his gun falling to the floor. Rev. Jim stepped into the building and quickly dragged the man into the hall, locking the door behind them.

"We're in," Rev. Jim said into his mike.

"Who the hell's *we?*" Dead-Eye asked.

"Just a friend I bumped into," Rev. Jim said.

. . .

DEAD-EYE STOOD with his back to the flowered paper of the hall wall, his two guns crisscrossed over his chest. He listened as the three men in the room to his right griped about the long hours they were forced to work in return for low pay and small chance for advancement. Dead-Eye took two steps to the side and braced both his feet against the doorway entry, guns now held out at waist level. The men looked up and chose not to move.

"If you're looking for money, you're on the wrong floor," the one with a thick dark beard and shaved head announced.

"I heard," Dead-Eye said.

"This is an adoption agency," said the biggest of the three, a tall, middle-aged man dressed in a long-sleeved olive shirt and tan slacks. "You come here for babies, not for bucks."

"I came for your guns," Dead-Eye said, walking into the room. "Pull 'em out slow and slide them on the floor over to me, butt end first."

"We'll find you, man," the last of the three, young, with a bushy mustache and slight lisp, threatened. "We'll hunt you down and burn you."

"I lead a really boring life," Dead-Eye said. "Sounds like you'd bring a little spark to it. Now the guns."

The men lifted their weapons from their holsters, bent their legs, and slid the guns over. The revolvers scraped against the hardwood floors, coming to rest near Dead-Eye's boots.

"That's only three," Dead-Eye said.

"How many of us do you see?" the one with the beard asked.

"I see pros," Dead-Eye said. "Guys paid salaries to kill on orders. Those guys carry more than one."

"Maybe we ain't as good as you think, spook," the one with the lisp said. "Maybe we're just startin' out. Not as smart as we should be."

Dead-Eye wasn't listening.

He was looking at the eyes of the third man, the one in the dark designer suit and black button-down shirt. The eyes that told him everything he needed to know.

There was someone standing behind him, ready to do some damage.

. . .

BOOMER HELD THE BABY with both hands and watched him as he cooed and smiled. Mrs. Columbo rummaged through a large fake leather handbag open on her lap, looking for a tissue. With one hand she dabbed at her eyes and blew her nose. Her other hand stayed in the purse, holding her .38 caliber.

"I really hate to give up on the little guy," Boomer said. "It's tough knowing I'll never see him again."

Edward responded in the most professional of tones. "He'll be living in a good home. That I can assure you."

Boomer looked down at the baby, then across at Edward. "You're sure about that, right?"

"Our lists are made up of the best people in need of a baby." Edward was growing impatient with Boomer's unending stream of questions. "This child will go to private schools, travel to Europe, and live a life that wouldn't be open to him living with you and your wife."

"Listen to the man, honey," Mrs. Columbo urged Boomer. "He's making sense here."

"All right," Boomer said, handing the baby back to Mrs. Columbo. "Just one more question. You answer that one and we've got ourselves a deal."

"All right, then," Edward said, pleased that they were nearing the end. "One more question."

Boomer leaned across the desk, bracing his knees against its wood exterior, his arms and chest resting close enough to smell traces of Edward's expensive French cologne. "Do I have your word on what you just told me?" Boomer asked.

"Honey, please," Mrs. Columbo said. "You're insulting the man."

"I don't mean it the wrong way," Boomer said to Edward. "I just want to be sure. You can understand the way I feel."

"Yes, of course I understand," Edward said, eager to get them both out of his office. "And you do have my word. Everything I've told you is true."

"Then I guess you got yourself a baby," Boomer said, pushing his chair back and standing.

"What's our next step?" Mrs. Columbo asked.

"It's very simple, really," Edward said, his voice calm and in control. "You hand me the baby and I hand you some money and we all walk away."

"How much?" Mrs. Columbo asked.

"I usually pay six hundred," Edward said. "But you've caught me on a soft day. I'll make it a thousand."

"A thousand dollars?" Mrs. Columbo said, wide smile on her face. "Richie, did you hear? He's giving us a thousand."

"That's great, honey," Boomer said, looking out the window over Edward's shoulder, seeing the Lincoln being towed away.

"That's more than we made all of last month," Mrs. Columbo said. "I can't thank you enough, Eddie."

Edward opened the central drawer of his desk, pulled out an envelope, and counted out ten one-hundred-dollar bills. He handed them to Boomer, who folded them and shoved them into the front pockets of his jeans.

"I left the diapers and clothes in the trunk of my car," Boomer said. "Want me to go and get them?"

"That won't be at all necessary," Edward said. "We're fully stocked."

"Then there's nothing left to do but leave," Boomer said. He leaned down and kissed the baby curled in Mrs. Columbo's arms. "I'll wait outside," he said to her, keeping his head down and walking toward the door. "Don't take too long."

"Won't be more than a minute," Mrs. Columbo said.

She waited for the door to close before she stood and handed the baby over to Edward. He reached for him and held him face forward on his lap.

"You're not going to forget me, now, are you?" she asked Edward.

Edward shook his head no. "I'll call as soon as there's a slot for you."

"Can you make it quick?" Mrs. Columbo asked. "I'm real eager to get started. We really need the money."

"I just gave your husband a thousand dollars," Edward said.

"You kidding me?" Mrs. Columbo said. "With the bills we got, I'm lucky that'll last us through the weekend."

Edward stared at her, smiled, and nodded. "Do you mind working nights?" he asked.

"You're holding the only thing that kept me home," Mrs. Columbo said, pointing to the baby in Edward's arms.

"Take the baby for a moment," Edward said, holding out the child. "I need to look up something on the computer."

Mrs. Columbo took the baby and stood over Edward's shoulder. He clicked on the IBM at the side of his desk and watched it chart down a list of names and destinations. He hit a few buttons, leaned back in his chair, and smiled. "Have you ever been to Maine?" he asked.

"No," Mrs. Columbo said. "But I always wanted to go there."

"You'll be going tomorrow," he said. "I've just logged you in. Someone will call you and tell you what time to be at the airport. You'll be met there by a woman. She'll tell you what to do."

"I don't know how I'll ever thank you," Mrs. Columbo said in a seductive manner, handing Edward back the baby.

Edward picked up on it, gazing at her legs and holding the smile. "I'm sure between the two of us, we'll come up with something interesting," he said.

"I know we will," Mrs. Columbo said. She leaned down and kissed the baby good-bye, resting one hand on Edward's shoulder.

"We'll speak again soon," Edward said.

"I'll be by my phone," Mrs. Columbo said, opening the door leading to the foyer. "Waiting."

. . .

DEAD-EYE SAW THE SHADOW behind him lift a hand holding a gun. He rolled over on the hardwood floors and came up on his knees, surprised to see that it was a woman standing there, one of the mules from the other room. He had his gun aimed at her chest but didn't fire. Instead, he watched Rev. Jim come up behind her, grab her around the neck, and pull the gun out of her hand.

Dead-Eye turned and whirled back to the three men behind him, getting to them before they had a chance to pull out their stash guns.

"Everything cool?" he said to Rev. Jim.

"Like ice," Rev. Jim answered, shoving the mule into the room. "But what do we do with the Three Stooges?"

"Have the mule help you find some rope," Dead-Eye said. "We'll tie and gag the whole bunch and go out through the roof exit."

"Boomer's already on the street," Rev. Jim said. "Mrs. Columbo's the only one still in."

"She'll be out soon," Dead-Eye said. "And so will we."

"Which means I'm the only one who got screwed," Rev. Jim said.

"How you figure that?" Dead-Eye asked.

"I cleaned all their windows," Rev. Jim said. "And never got to see a nickel."

"People always take advantage of the handicapped," Dead-Eye said. "Get used to it."

. . .

BOOMER AND MRS. COLUMBO WALKED with their arms linked toward the car parked at the corner.

"We can't leave that prick in there with that baby for too long," Mrs. Columbo said, hatred in her voice.

"Pins put in a call downtown while you were still up there showing off your legs," Boomer said. "Edward's going to be taken down in about half an hour."

"You should have an undercover team on sight until the others show," Mrs. Columbo said.

"The two guys in suits across the street," Boomer said. "They'll make sure nobody runs in or out."

"Good work," she said.

"I try," Boomer said.

"I'm on their list," Mrs. Columbo said. "I leave for Maine tomorrow night. A woman's supposed to meet me at the airport."

"We'll have somebody meet her first," Boomer said.

"I told you my plan would work, Boomer," Mrs. Columbo said, beaming. "Admit it. You wouldn't have thought of this. You probably would have just gone in there and shot up the place."

"I'm limited in what I can do," Boomer said, reaching for his car keys. "And I don't think Eddie would have been as interested in *my* legs."

. . .

LUCIA STOOD in the center of the airport hangar, her back to the black Learjet. She was surrounded by eleven armed men. They were all young and brazen and were led by a tall man with a shaved head that gleamed under the glare of the hangar lights.

His name was Wilber Graves.

A thin, long-haired assistant in jeans, black polo shirt, and black pumps handed each of the men manila packets filled with background information on the Apaches—photos, home addresses, dates of birth. The men took the folders and kept their eyes focused on Lucia, dressed seductively in a black knit halter top, thigh-high skirt, and open-toed black pumps.

"There are seven names in the folder," she said, her eyes moving from face to face with mannered ease. "They are to be handled."

"How soon?" Wilber asked, standing behind Lucia, his voice a deep baritone.

"As soon as you find out what they know about us." She answered without turning to look at him.

"Are you suspending operations until we finish the job?" Wilber asked.

"No," Lucia said. "All cargo still moves."

"Don't let these people worry you," Wilber said in a voice filled with confidence.

"I don't let *anything* worry me," Lucia said, stepping closer to Wilber, watching as his blue eyes scanned the length of her body. "I let other people worry. People like you, Wilber."

"I won't disappoint you," he said.

"That's good to know," Lucia said.

Lucia walked away, her thin heels clicking against the thick cement floor. Wilber and his team watched her go, waiting for the Learjet to be fueled and take them toward their date with the Apaches.

16

MRS. COLUMBO SMILED over at her husband, Joe, as she piled an armful of clothes into a tan overnight bag. He was resting on the bed, hands behind his head, a paperback novel open across his chest.

"How's the book?" Mrs. Columbo asked.

"You haven't read it, have you?" Joe asked. "You know how I hate when you tell me how things end."

"No," she said, laughing. "I haven't read it."

"It's pretty good," he told her. "In fact, I think with this one, even you would have a hard time guessing the ending."

"What's the plot?" she asked, folding her clothes neatly into the bag.

"People are found dead at a big research hospital," Joe said, sitting up in the bed. "No one can figure it. They come in for a simple operation. They come out a corpse."

"It's probably somebody who works for the hospital," Mrs. Columbo said with a shrug. "What kind of research do they do?"

"Mary, I'm begging you." Joe clasped his hands together. "Let me have just this one book. Let me get to the end and not know."

"What kind of research?" she said, sitting on the edge of the bed.

"Cancer," Joe said, resigned to his fate.

"The head administrator," Mrs. Columbo said. "Tell me about him."

"Straightforward and honest," Joe said. "Cares about the hospital and the people who work there. You're off base if you think it's him."

"Was the administrator a surgeon before he quit to run the hospital?" Mrs. Columbo asked.

"I suppose," Joe said. "I have to go back and double-check."

"That's your man," Mrs. Columbo said, standing and walking over toward a bureau. "*And* your killer."

Joe stared at his wife, trying to fight the temptation to pick up the book. He closed his eyes, took a deep breath, and went to the last chapter.

"I'm gonna grab a shower," Mrs. Columbo said. "Let me know how it turns out."

She came out ten minutes later wearing a white terry-cloth robe and combing her wet hair straight back. Joe was leaning against a wall on the far side of the bedroom.

"So?" she said.

"I'm giving up mysteries," Joe said. "That's my last one. From now on, it's romance novels for me."

"Like *those* endings are hard to guess," Mrs. Columbo said.

"Remember when I took you to see *Chinatown*?" Joe asked. "Halfway through, you knew John Huston was her husband, her brother, her uncle, whatever the hell he was to her. You *knew*."

"Honey, it's my *job* to know," Mrs. Columbo said, walking over and stroking his face. "Remember?"

"It *was* your job, Mary," Joe said quietly.

"Oh, Joe, let's not have this conversation again, please. I've got too much on my mind right now. If it's still bothering you, we'll talk about it when I get back."

"We were going to take Frankie up to Maine the year you got wounded," Joe said almost wistfully. "We'd made the reservations and everything. Now here you are, going up all by yourself."

Mrs. Columbo stood frozen in her place. Her eyes narrowing in on her husband. "Joe," she said slowly, "who told you I was going to Maine?"

"I don't know," Joe was suddenly flustered. "You must have mentioned it earlier."

"Who told you, Joe?" Mrs. Columbo held both her place and her gaze. "Who told you about Maine?"

"Does it matter?" he asked.

Mrs. Columbo's upper body shook slightly, her face was flushed, and her eyes were lit by rage. "It matters a great deal. Do you know what flight I'm on too?"

"I want it to stop, Mary," Joe said, ignoring the question. "It's too dangerous. You're going to end up getting yourself killed."

Mrs. Columbo sat on the edge of the bed. She was trying to think like a homicide detective, but the emotional rush was too strong. "Do you know what you did, Joe?" Mrs. Columbo asked. "Do you have any idea?"

Joe came over to her side and knelt down before her. "I was trying to save the woman I love," he said. "That's all I did."

Mrs. Columbo reached down and held his face with her hands. "But you didn't," she whispered. "You put us all at risk."

"No one's at risk if you stop it now."

She shook her head.

"There's too many out there against you," he said. "You can't beat them."

"Who did you go see?" Mrs. Columbo asked. There were tears in her eyes now. "Who told you about us?"

"Deputy Inspector Lavetti," Joe said after a long silence. "He was a big help to me after you got wounded. Somebody for me to talk to now and then."

"And you told him about me and the Apaches." It wasn't a question. It was the quiet, firm statement of a homicide detective.

"I thought he was somebody I could trust." Joe now wiped at his own tears.

"He's a dirty cop, Joe." Mrs. Columbo reached down to hold her husband in her arms. "There's no way for you to have known that. But he went out and did what any dirty cop does. He called the people who pay him and told them who we were."

"I didn't go see Lavetti because I wanted you caught." Joe buried his head in his wife's robe. "I went because I was scared I was going to lose you."

"You were never in any danger of losing me, Joe," Mary said quietly. "I put my years in with you and I did it for only one reason. The only reason worth doing it—I loved you."

"And do you *still* love me?" Joe asked. He stared into his wife's eyes, searching for the answer before he heard it.

"You have to deal with what you did," Mrs. Columbo answered. "And what you did was lay a death warrant on the whole team. You have to stand for that."

"That's the cop answer," Joe said. "I'm looking for the wife answer."

"It's the same answer," Mrs. Columbo said.

. . .

BOOMER SAT BEHIND the wheel of the dark Buick, window down to let in the moist spring air, looking across at Mrs. Columbo's house. Though he was never much of a smoker, he wished he had a cigarette. He settled for two slices of Wrigley's doublemint instead, chewing each piece slowly, rolling the foil into a ball and dropping it into the empty ash tin.

Boomer was a fastidious man who liked to do things in orderly fashion. He was one of the few action cops whose paperwork was always properly filled out and submitted within hours of an arrest. He hated surprises and he despised mistakes, and now here he was, sitting in the middle of both.

Boomer looked up when he heard the front door slam and saw Mrs. Columbo race down the steps, an overnight bag in her hand. She stepped around the front of the car, opened the passenger-side door, and slid in. Boomer kicked over the engine and pulled out of the spot.

They didn't say a word until they reached the Midtown Tunnel tolls.

"It was Joe," Mrs. Columbo said.

"What was Joe?" Boomer asked.

"He's the one you're going to be looking for." Mrs. Columbo tried hard not to burst into tears. "He went to see Deputy Inspector Lavetti and told him about us."

"He say why he did it?" Boomer asked softly.

"Because he loves me," Mrs. Columbo said, turning her face to the passing traffic.

Boomer shifted the car away from the toll lines and pulled it over to the side of the road, inches from a red brick wall. He looked over at the cars heading into the city, his mind filled with too many unanswered questions and little time to get them resolved. He now had an enemy in the one place he never thought he needed to worry about—inside NYPD headquarters. He spit the gum out the open window and ran a hand across his tired eyes, for the first time starting to wonder if forming the Apaches was a risk worth taking. In their short time together, Boomer realized how vulnerable the unit was— prone to error, open to the unsuspecting nature of clandestine work— their individual strengths as active cops weakened by their wounds and the passage of time.

"He's not like us, Boomer," Mrs. Columbo said. "He's got more heart than brains."

"How much do they know?" is all he asked.

"They know I'm going to Maine."

Her face was sad and tired, the lights from the toll booths highlighting the fine features and running mascara. Boomer had always had warm feelings toward Mrs. Columbo. More than warm, if he was honest with himself. He admired the woman almost as much as he did the cop. There was always a relaxed ease to their friendship, with mild hints of sexual attraction.

"No," Boomer told her. "They know you *were* going to Maine."

"You can't call this off," she said, grabbing his arm and holding it tight.

"It's too dangerous. They'll be there waiting."

"We've spent our lives going into places where people have been waiting," Mrs. Columbo said. "Why should Maine be different?"

"Because they'll be waiting for *you*." He turned to her, wanting so much to put his arms around her and protect her. But he didn't. He just held the look and let it speak for him.

For all his bluster, Boomer Frontieri had a tough time connecting with women. Maybe it was his background. Maybe it was shyness, or, worse, fear. Or maybe he just didn't want to make a mistake. Whatever the reason, he could never share his emotions with any woman he cared about. It had left him alone, without a wife, kids, or semblance of a real life. It was an emptiness that pained him even more than his wounds. For Boomer Frontieri there wasn't any choice. He *had* to continue his private war with Lucia Carney. It was all that kept him alive.

Mrs. Columbo put out her hands and held Boomer's face in them. "Then *you* be there, Boomer," she said in a soft voice. "And make sure nothing happens to me."

He said nothing for a long time. Then all he asked was "You got another plan worked up?"

"Don't I always?" she said.

. . .

THEY SAT AROUND the table at Nunzio's, their food growing cold as they listened to Mrs. Columbo tell them about her husband's betrayal and Deputy Inspector Lavetti's deception. No one moved and no one other than Mrs. Columbo spoke. She laid it out for them like a cop, sparing no details or facts in the telling.

As they listened they all realized what it was they were hearing. The Apaches were into more than a fight. They were in a war with an enemy eager to take them on. And now their names and faces were known.

"Any of you want to walk from the table, this is the time," Boomer said after several moments of silence. "The truth is, if we had any brains at all, we would *all* walk away. Face the truth and deal with it."

"What is the truth?" Rev. Jim asked.

"That we are what we *know* we are," Boomer said. "Which is a big difference from what we *think* we are."

"We've always known that truth, Boomer," Geronimo said. "We

said yes to this knowing we were only half of what we used to be. Nothing's changed. Our destiny remains the same."

"Nobody in here is eager to die," Pins added. "I know I'm not. But we always knew they would figure out who we were sooner or later. We've just got to make sure we're better prepared than they are."

"They know who Mrs. Columbo is and what plane she's on," Dead-Eye said. "What they don't know is what she's going to be doing. Way I see it, we still hold the surprise card."

"We can put it off," Boomer said, impressed with the unity of the group. "Give everybody a chance to think about it some more."

"I've done all the thinking I need to do," Rev. Jim said. "It's time to go to the dance."

"Let's just figure out a way to get Mrs. Columbo in and out of there," Dead-Eye said. "*Alive.*"

"The same holds for you, Nunz," Boomer said. "Lucia's got your name too. You want to walk, now's a good time."

"I'm where I want to be," Nunzio said. "In my restaurant."

Boomer stared at each of them, looking for a dent in their resolve. He came away empty.

"Okay, then," Boomer said with a smile. "What the hell. Let's hear Mrs. Columbo's plan."

"How about I make some coffee first," Rev. Jim said, getting ready to stand.

"I'll make the coffee," Nunzio said, putting a hand on Rev. Jim's shoulder. "My stomach still remembers your last batch. It was strong enough to kill."

"Maybe you should make that a part of your plan," Dead-Eye said to Mrs. Columbo.

· · ·

DEAD-EYE SOAKED IN the hot water of the ceramic tub, soap bubbles covering everything but his head. The heat from the water warmed his tired body. He had his head against the tile wall. A wet hand towel had been folded and slapped over his eyes.

Eddie crept quietly into the bathroom, removed the towel from his dad's eyes, and used it to stroke the sides of his face. Dead-Eye looked over at him and smiled, always amazed at how closely the boy he loved so much resembled his own father.

The boy reached a small hand into the water and came out with a palm full of bubbles, wetting the sleeve of his Snoopy zip-up pajamas.

"I'm using your bubble bath," Dead-Eye said. "That okay with you?"

"You can get some in your eyes and it won't burn," Eddie said. "But don't get any in your mouth. Okay?"

"I won't," Dead-Eye said with a smile.

Eddie walked the length of the tub, dragging his hand through the water, making motor sounds with his lips. When he turned and came back up toward his father, his pajamas were wet to the length of the sleeve, four fingers cupped across the front of his face to hide the giggles.

"Take your jays off and come on in with me," Dead-Eye said, sliding the zipper down to the edge of Eddie's right thigh.

Dead-Eye waited until his son stripped off all his clothes and then grabbed him around the chest as he moved feet first into the tub. Eddie eased himself gently into the water and rested his head against his father's chest, breathing quietly, watching as the bubbles floated off to his side.

"Do you miss Grandpa?" Eddie said after several slow moments.

"Very much," Dead-Eye said, running a hand through his son's hair. "He was my best friend. Even though he wasn't always the easiest guy in the world to talk things over with."

"Like when you told him about being a policeman?" Eddie asked.

"That was *not* the best of days to talk to Grandpa," Dead-Eye said. "He was pretty upset."

"He told me you were a great policeman," Eddie said, gazing up at his dad. "But he didn't know why you wanted to be a great policeman."

"That's the Grandpa we all loved," Dead-Eye said.

"Would Grandpa be happy you were a great doorman?" Eddie asked, squeezing water out of a closed fist.

"I guess," Dead-Eye said, leaning his head back against the tiles and closing his eyes. "I think he'd have been happy with anything I did so long as it was honest work."

"Would Grandpa be happy you're an Apache?" Eddie said, still playing with the water.

Dead-Eye lifted his head and opened his eyes, looking down at his son. "How do you know about that?" he asked.

"I heard you and Mommy talking," Eddie said. "I was in my room. Sleeping."

"Try sleeping with your eyes closed next time," Dead-Eye said. "You won't hear as much."

"So?" Eddie said.

"So what?"

"Would Grandpa be happy?" Eddie sat up and looked at his father. "About you being an Apache?"

"Yes," Dead-Eye said, running a hand down his son's back. "I think he would have been happy."

"I'm happy too," Eddie said, turning his attention once again to the now-lukewarm water to play with what was left of the bubbles. "Now there's just Mommy left to make happy."

"Let's take it one war at a time," Dead-Eye said.

"Which one first?" Eddie asked.

"The one I can win," Dead-Eye said.

. . .

REV. JIM SAT on the park bench, his legs stretched out, hands inside his pants pockets. It was dark and the buzzing streetlamp above offered little light. He pulled a hand from his pocket and ran it alongside the bench, feeling the chipped wood, the names carved in it, the rusty screws holding it in place. It was where his mother had sat on the night she died, waiting to pay off a drug dealer with borrowed money. He hadn't been back there since that night. Rev. Jim wanted very much to cry and shout out his mother's name. But too much had been ripped out of him over the years. He had no tears left to shed. Instead, he sat in the silent darkness and kept his hand over the wood of the place where a woman he loved once sat.

. . .

PINS WATCHED THE eight-year-old boy grab a bowling ball from its slot, crouch into position, and throw a hard spin down the center of the lane. Pins smiled as the ball curved its way to a strike.

"All right!" Andrew said, pumping a fist in the air. "I'm going to beat you tonight, Pins. I just know it."

"We'll see," Pins said with a smile. He stood up, took a high-five from the boy as he walked past him, then reached for his ball.

There were many boys who made use of the open afternoons at the alley, but none more so than Andrew. The boy didn't talk much, reluctant to bring up a home life that revolved around drugs, beatings, and shouts in the night. Besides, Pins knew all he needed to know without asking. Andrew was there to bowl and to forget. So was Pins.

Pins reared back and tossed a strike down lane six. "Still think you're going to beat me?" he asked Andrew.

"I *know* it," Andrew said.

"Want to bet on it?"

Andrew cast his eyes down to the shiny floor. "I can't bet you," he said in a low voice. "Got no money."

"It's not a money bet," Pins said.

"What kind, then?"

"I'm going to be gone for a while," Pins said. "I need somebody to look after the alley for me. Make sure things don't get out of hand. Interested so far?"

Andrew's face was lit with a smile. "Yeah," he said. "You know it."

"Now, *if* you win," Pins said, "*if* you beat me, I'll pay you to look after the place. But if you don't, then you work the place for free."

"That's a sucker bet," Andrew said, strutting to the floor and reaching for a ball.

"Only for the loser," Pins said, sitting back down and smiling up at the happy boy.

He and Andrew bowled late into the warm night. Outside, the happy shouts of Andrew's first victory over Pins could be heard echoing down the emptiness of deserted streets.

. . .

GERONIMO SAT IN the steam room, a white towel draped around his waist, the medallion his mother gave him hanging around his neck. He let the steam wash over him, the sweat flowing down his body like a waterfall, his eyes closed. It was a ritual cleansing for Geronimo, a warrior about to go off and do battle. He knew his time had come, his destiny near enough for him to touch, and it brought a smile to his face. It was the way it was meant to be. He no longer needed to fear being found crunched over a broken computer terminal surrounded by dust and a blank wall, his heart filled with a sad weight. Instead, Geronimo would meet up with the device that waited for him. A device that would challenge his spirit and bring life back to his soul.

Geronimo removed the medallion from around his neck and rested it on the wooden slab by his side. He no longer needed its protection. His way had been found.

17

MRS. COLUMBO WALKED toward the black van, a bundled latex-
covered doll held close to her chest. The van was parked off the side of
a hill, hidden by a thick cover of trees, ten miles north of Camden,
Maine. Four armed men stood around the rear doors, polished shoes
scuffing against the sandy ground. Two others sat in the front seat,
windows rolled down, their faces up to the sun, necks leaning on
headrests. A black Cadillac was parked at an angle next to the van, its
four doors open to the late-night breeze, the three men inside
checking and cleaning the clips on their semiautomatics.

The outskirts of resort towns were the favored exchange spots for
Lucia's crew. Dealers and mules could come in and out, do business
openly, and not garner any attention. The towns were accustomed to
large numbers of visitors traveling, staying for only days or even hours
before heading back home. It was easy to blend in.

It was even easier, as Lucia quickly discovered, to buy inexpensive
condos on resort properties and utilize them as work bases and

show places for prospective clients. Brokers especially were warm to investors who closed deals with cash. Lucia Carney owned seven such condos, all purchased in someone else's name, each located at a five-star resort situated within a long drive or a short flight to a central drug distribution city. In such places a mule and her team could blend in with soccer moms, golf-crazed dads, and scrambling toddlers, and just as easily disappear from view.

It was, without question, a perfect setup.

Mrs. Columbo's heels chipped against the corners of the tiny pebbles beneath her feet, kicking up small pockets of dust. She stared up at the van and could see the packets of cocaine, stacked high in the rear, all nearly glowing in the reflected glare of the Cadillac's lights. She walked slowly, hemmed in on one side by a short, gray-haired man holding a revolver, and on the other by a sour woman who had met her at the Portland airport, identifying herself only as Angela.

They had made the drive from Portland to the outskirts of Camden in less than an hour, riding in silence, Mrs. Columbo alone in the backseat of a Mercedes 450SL, occasionally looking down at the doll in her arms that luckily no one had yet asked to see.

She and Boomer had made it through LaGuardia with the help of two friends, former cops now working for the FBI, who waited for them by the checkpoint, flashed their shields, unfolded a few sheets of doctored documents, and ushered them through separately, bypassing the X-ray detectors, which would have been sure to spot the cargo in Mrs. Columbo's arms and the guns in Boomer's satchel.

She and Boomer sat three rows apart on the small plane and avoided eye contact throughout the flight. The passenger seated to her right, a square-shouldered woman dressed in head-to-toe L. L. Bean, had asked to peek at her sleeping baby.

"I don't think that would be a good idea," Mrs. Columbo told her, the harsh tone of her voice and the cold snap to her eyes backing the woman away. "She's a light sleeper."

Mrs. Columbo spent the rest of the flight with her head back and her eyes closed, running through all that had happened over the past few weeks. She had done a zero to sixty, going from an ex-cop with a sour disposition to a key member of an illegal unit bent on the takedown of a cocaine queen. In the process, Mrs. Columbo found herself on the verge of a messy divorce, marked as a target by an on-the-pad cop, and now jammed inside a too-tight seat holding a prop baby stuffed with eight sticks of dynamite timed to kick in less than three hours.

It was exactly where she felt she belonged.

. . .

Boomer was first off the plane, rushing past the handful of people waiting at the arrival gate, their eager faces searching for friends and relatives. He stopped briefly in front of Mrs. Columbo's grim-looking party, brushing against the short man's tan leather jacket, eyes connecting for the briefest of moments before he made his way to the car rental booth.

"Your plane was late," Angela said in tones as sharp as the cut of her skirt.

"If you've got a beef," Mrs. Columbo said, shielding the baby from Angela's line of vision, "the pilot should be coming out in a couple of minutes. Give his ear a bend."

Angela's lips curled into what for her could have passed as either a smile or a sneer. As she whirled away, it was clear that she expected Mrs. Columbo and the silent man in the tan leather to follow close on her floppy heels, which they did.

"She a real bitch or just acting the part?" Mrs. Columbo asked her escort.

"Believe me, my wife is for real," the quiet little man said in a voice befitting his size. "It would be foolish for *anyone* to think otherwise."

"I guess you'd be the one to know," Mrs. Columbo said, and she shook her head as the man now walked at a faster pace, trying to catch up to Angela.

. . .

Geronimo and Pins were a quarter of a mile up from the black van, hidden by clumps of trees and a circle of large rocks. Pins had his back to the movement down below, legs folded under him, headphones on, picking up the conversation coming to him from the wire he had run down the prop baby's back. Geronimo put down his small binoculars and checked his watch.

"They smell anything yet?" he asked Pins.

"Not anything that I can pick up," Pins said. "But these guys make their moves with looks, not words."

"Boomer and Dead-Eye should be here in about three minutes," Geronimo said.

"And how long before that doll blows?" Pins asked.

"Six minutes," Geronimo said, lifting two bolt-action rifles and recoil pads from a large black case by his sneakers. He handed one of the rifles to Pins. "Worry about the ones by the van," he said. "I'll take the team in the car. That leaves Boomer with the two around Mrs. Columbo."

"That car looks parked too close to the van," Pins said. "What if the dyno blows them both?"

"It shouldn't," Geronimo said. "Not if Mrs. Columbo centers the doll under the van the way I showed her. Besides, on top of that, I left thirty seconds for Rev. Jim to move the car away."

"Next time don't be so generous," Pins said, checking the night-scope at the center of his rifle. "You'll only spoil him."

Geronimo looked up at Pins and nodded. "Thought I'd throw him a break," he said. "Just this once."

"Kindness is weakness," Pins said, resting the front of the rifle between branches of a tree, an open box of .375 H&H Magnum shells by his feet, headphones resting low on his neck.

"So's missing your target," Geronimo said, lifting the rifle and taking aim from behind the large shadow of a boulder.

. . .

"I STILL DON'T LIKE our end of the plan," Dead-Eye said, sitting on the edge of a rock, four locked and loaded semiautomatic handguns spread out around him.

"If we go down to shoot it out, one of us is sure to buy it," Boomer said, pacing around the dirt, rocks, and twigs. "Pins and Geronimo can clip only so many off the back ridge. Rev. Jim's gotta get to the car and Mrs. Columbo's got enough to worry about with a fuckin' bomb in her arms."

"I don't think Pins has ever pulled the trigger on a rifle," Dead-Eye said. "Which makes the odds very good that if he clips anybody, it's gonna be me."

Boomer leaned against the rock and stared at Dead-Eye. They were a thirty-second run from the black van. They could see Mrs. Columbo and the heavy guns surrounding her, and they could feel the others hiding, their guns prepped, ready to take aim and clean out the Apache team.

"How many more than we can see do you think are out there?" Boomer asked, chewing on a thin twig.

"Hard to tell," Dead-Eye said. "But if they came looking for a total wipeout, I'd say about six more guns. Six more very good guns."

"They're gonna expect us to shoot," Boomer said. "They're gonna be lookin' for us to come down with full loads."

"Wouldn't you?" Dead-Eye said.

Boomer nodded and then smiled over at Dead-Eye. "We got a minute thirty, then," Boomer said, "to go down and do what they would never expect."

"Which is what?" Dead-Eye asked, sliding off the rock and reaching for his guns.

"Ask them to surrender," Boomer said.

. . .

THE MAN IN THE SUNGLASSES walked slowly toward Mrs. Columbo, carving knife in his right hand. She had both hands wrapped around the prop baby, one of them hidden beneath the sheets of a thin cover blanket, fingers holding a .38 Special.

"I need the kid," the man said in a slow-motion delivery. "I'll cut him in the backseat and make the transfer. Then we can all get the hell out of here."

When Mrs. Columbo didn't move, he walked closer and held out his left hand. "I need the baby *now*," he said.

Angela and the man in the tan leather jacket both turned and looked at Mrs. Columbo, their eyes filled with a mixture of anger and suspicion.

"What's your problem?" Angela asked. "Get on with it. Give the baby over to Carl."

"I was expecting to get paid *before* making the handoff." Mrs. Columbo was surprised at how calm she was able to sound.

"And you can expect to be killed if you don't make it now," the man in the tan leather said.

Mrs. Columbo looked down at the prop baby in her arms. "Good-bye, sweet thing," she said in soothing tones, a warm smile stretched across her face. She looked up at the man in the shades and then over at Angela and her husband. "You get attached," she said to them. "You wouldn't understand. It's a mom thing."

Mrs. Columbo kept her smile as she twirled around Angela and tossed the prop baby under the center of the black van, turned, and pointed her gun right in the woman's face. "All of you," Mrs. Columbo yelled without moving her head, her eyes focused on Angela's stunned gaze, "listen to me! You got about a minute before that van blows and kills us all. We can shoot it out or we can get out. I'm gonna let the lady here make the call."

Angela moved her eyes away from Mrs. Columbo and the muzzle of her gun long enough to see Boomer and Dead-Eye coming down the side of a sloping hill, guns at their sides. Rev. Jim had slipped out from behind a bush and was already near the Cadillac, a .38 Special cocked and pointed her way.

"You were ready to kill a few seconds ago," Mrs. Columbo said to her in a low voice. "Now are you ready to die?"

"What do you want?" Angela asked, the words lacking the edge they once carried.

"Let the van blow," Mrs. Columbo said. "And let us leave with the car and the money that's in the trunk. You and your people can scatter."

"And if we don't?" her husband asked.

"Then what the bomb won't kill," Mrs. Columbo said, "the guns behind you and above you will. And you still lose the drugs and the cash. But I'm sure Lucia will appreciate the effort."

"Forty-five seconds!" Boomer shouted from behind them, his gun pointed at no one in particular. "This ain't somethin' that needs a lot of thought."

"You will die too," the man in the leather jacket shouted back at Boomer. "Along with all of us."

"There's one big difference," Boomer said to him. "I don't give a shit."

Angela looked over at Mrs. Columbo one final time. "What about you?" Angela asked her. "Do *you* give a shit?"

Mrs. Columbo smiled and edged the barrel of the gun closer to Angela's cheek. "What do you think?" she said.

Angela lifted her arms slowly above her head. It was all the men around her needed to drop their weapons and run from the van.

"Let's get in that car," Boomer yelled, following Dead-Eye to the Cadillac, Rev. Jim already behind the wheel.

"She will find you," Angela shouted out after Mrs. Columbo, watching as she removed the gun from her face and ran to join the others. "She will find all of you."

"That's what we're counting on," Mrs. Columbo shouted back.

· · ·

SHE WAS IN the backseat of the Lincoln, her window rolled down, Dead-Eye next to her, Boomer and Rev. Jim in the front, dust from the back tires kicking up white puffs of sand clouds all around them. Angela and the rest of Lucia's crew were scattered up hills and down side paths, leaving an array of guns in their wake.

Geronimo and Pins stared down at it all, nestled safely on a rock on the ridge above.

"Now," Geronimo whispered to himself.

He didn't flinch as the loud explosion split the black van and rocketed it skyward, sending dust, metal, debris, and cocaine filtering through the air. Red, orange, and yellow flames were reflected in Geronimo's eyes, the heat of the blast and the strength of the strong steam air washing over him in one swooping wave of destruction. He smiled down at the site in complete admiration. Respectful of its force.

. . .

LUCIA CARNEY STOOD in the bedroom of her Sedona condo, staring out at the fourteenth hole putting green, the light of a full moon filtering in through the shuttered glass. The thick white lace drapes were drawn to the edge of the porch windows and the blinds were slanted up. She wore a silk bathrobe slit down the sides, open in the front, and smoked a cigarette. She was deep in thought and didn't hear her husband, Gerald, walk into the room. He crept up behind her, drunk from an evening out with investment cronies, and wrapped his right arm around her waist, softly rubbing her naked flesh.

"Miss me?" he muttered into her ear.

"No," Lucia said, her eyes still on the putting green, her mind several thousand miles away, picturing a lost shipment of cocaine and cash.

It wasn't enough for those bastard Apaches to blow six hundred thousand dollars worth of her untapped coke to the wind. They had to heap on an additional insult by driving off in one of her new cars, which was holding two hundred and fifty thousand in hundreds in the trunk. A sum that, she had discovered only hours earlier, had been donated in her name to child abuse centers in three states.

Gerald began to nuzzle the side of her neck, his hands lifting and groping the bathrobe in the clumsy manner of a man who should have stopped three drinks into the night.

"Go to bed, Gerry," Lucia said, unmoved by her husband's actions.

"That's the plan," he said, his head resting on the edge of her shoulder. "You and me."

Lucia pulled away from her husband and her view of the putting green, jamming the end of her cigarette into an ashtray on top of a marble end table. Gerald stripped off his blue jacket and undid his matching tie, smiling at his wife, his body juiced by the sight of her bare skin visible under the sheer robe.

He blocked her path as she tried to move past him, his right hand caressing her breasts. "Whatever you want," he said to her, a broad smile on his face, fingers pulling at her nipples. "That's what we'll do."

Lucia stared at Gerald, wondering why she had stayed with him as long as she had. By now she already had more money than he did and had learned as much about investing as he was ever going to be able to teach. On top of which, she had all his contacts and could just as easily go directly to them to further expand her portfolio.

"Get naked," she finally said to him. "And turn down the lights. I'll be out in a minute."

Lucia walked away, closing the bathroom door behind her, leaving Gerald waiting. He undressed quickly, twice stumbling over his pants, and eagerly slid back the satin sheets of the king-sized bed that dominated the room. He propped up two pillows and laid his head down, the ceiling above doing a slow spin, his body feeling light from all the booze. He turned his head and smiled when he saw Lucia come out of the shadows of the bathroom light, naked, clutching her robe in one hand.

She moved like a serpent up and down the contours of his body, working him with her tongue and hands, listening to him moan with pleasure, neither one uttering words. She knew when to stop and switch, spreading her legs on top of him, straddling him, her long hair draped in folds around her face and back. She slowly inserted him inside her, rocking her body in gentle, rhythmic motions, running her hands up and down her own body. Gerald continued to moan, his eyes closed, biting down hard on his lower lip.

Lucia leaned her body back, her hair touching the mattress, rocking harder now, one hand gripping Gerald's leg, the other reaching under her crumpled bathrobe, searching for the .357 Magnum hidden beneath its folds.

She lifted the gun and held it out with both hands, her body moving at a furious pace, hungry to bring Gerald to climax.

"I'm coming, Lucia," Gerald muttered, eyes still closed. "I'm going to come."

"And I have to go," Lucia said, bringing a halt to her motion and aiming the gun straight at Gerald's head.

The loud shot from the Magnum brought two of her bodyguards storming through the bedroom door. They stopped, guns drawn, when they saw Lucia, still on top of her husband, half her body wet with his blood, bone chips, and brain matter.

She turned to look at them, blood dripping down the sides of her face, the hot gun in her right hand. She slid off the bed and walked toward the two speechless men, handing one the gun.

"I'm going to take a shower and get dressed," Lucia said in even tones. "Have someone get rid of Gerald and then get us a private jet to New York."

"How soon?" the one with the gun managed to ask.

"Within the hour," Lucia said, turning to take one final look at her husband.

"Never get boring," she said, walking into the bathroom, ready to turn on the shower's head and wash off the signs of her latest kill.

18

PINS SAT ACROSS the bar from Nunzio, nursing a sweating glass of tap beer. It was early on a Saturday afternoon, two days after the Camden raid, and the place was quiet except for Ella Fitzgerald coming over the jukebox riffing her way through "My Last Affair."

"Freshen that for you?" Nunzio asked, polishing his side of the bar with a white cloth.

"No, thanks. It's still a little early. I'll stick to the one."

Nunzio stared over at Pins and spotted a look on his face that shouldn't have been there. It wasn't so much fear or even concern that was etched across his strong features. It was more the weight of regret, the look of someone who found himself in the middle of a battle he had no business being in. Nunzio always thought Pins was the least comfortable member of the Apache team. The others were harder, tougher, more at ease with the action. Pins, Nunzio knew, was different. He still had too much heart.

In his specialty, Pins hadn't seen as many bodies as the others, was less aware of the ugly side of the street. He liked the team and enjoyed their company, coming to life when they were all gathered around a table, swapping war tales and stupid jokes. He went along with their plans and could be counted on to carry out his role, but, unlike the others, Pins wasn't driven by a need for revenge. He was the only cop, Nunzio felt, who, if given the choice, would take back his commitment and retreat to the quiet sanctity of his bowling alley.

"Okay if I ask you somethin'?" Pins said, pushing aside his glass of beer.

"Doesn't look like you're here to drink," Nunzio said, "and we're not open for lunch. So I figured it was talk you wanted."

"The way things are going," Pins said in soft tones, "it doesn't seem like it's going to end good for any of us. You included."

"Everything's gone your way so far," Nunzio assured him. "You've done some damage, caused the lady a few headaches, and, most important, you got her attention."

"That's right," Pins said. "Those are all the reasons I'm worried."

"Well, you're not wrong there," Nunzio said. "I'll give you that."

"There's a weak link in every team," Pins went on. "I've been around long enough to know that. I don't want to be the weak link here."

"You've held your end," Nunzio told him. "It wasn't your talkin' that got the lady sniffin' in our direction."

"It just seems to come easier to the others," Pins said, his words backed by Ella now singing "Good Morning Heartache." "The action, I mean. It's like they're waitin' for it. Me, I'm always kinda hopin' we just take her down, cuff her, and hand her over to the feds."

"You wanna walk?" Nunzio asked, spreading his hands across the bar. "Might not be too late. Word can spread that you're out just as fast as it spread that you were in."

"Maybe I *will* have another beer."

Pins slid his glass toward Nunzio, who tapped out a refill with a foamy head and reached under the bar for a wooden bowl filled with pretzels.

"They're scared too, you know," Nunzio said. "We all are. And there's good reason to be. Not all of us are gonna make it outta this one alive."

"I know that," Pins said. "Except with them, you can't read it on their faces. With me, you pretty much can. I think that's the difference. It's a look that's easy to spot—by a cop or a shooter."

"They're one up on you, Pins," Nunzio said. "They've been around the action so long, they learned how to hide the look. But that don't mean it ain't there."

"What's your story?" Pins asked, finishing his beer. "Why are you in this? You got a good life here, solid business, steady. You don't need to be in the middle of a war."

Nunzio stared at Pins for several moments, then turned and reached for a bottle of Seagram's and two shot glasses. "Knowin' my story ain't gonna be any help to you," he said, topping off both glasses.

"You don't have to tell me, you don't want to," Pins said. "I was just curious."

Nunzio swallowed his drink in a gulp, wiping his lips with a folded paper napkin. "I got a daughter. Sandy," he said, his voice calm, his body tense. "You may have seen her around the times you been in here. She waits on tables the nights I'm short help."

"I talked to her once," Pins said. "Seems like a nice lady."

"She's a good kid," Nunzio said. "Her whole life, she never gave me any trouble. Married a good guy too. His name was Frank. Irish kid from a hardworking family. He worked two jobs and was going to classes over at Fordham at night. They were crazy in love with each other. Were gonna have a big family and be together forever."

"But they aren't," Pins said.

"Lots of times forever ain't that long a stretch," Nunzio said. "In Sandy's case it was only three years."

Pins rested his hand on top of the older man's. "You can stop there. I think I know the rest."

"I don't think you do," Nunzio said. "They had a baby. A doll of a girl named Theresa. She was only three months old and she already had my heart."

Pins grabbed for the bottle of Seagram's next to Nunzio's elbow and poured out two more drinks. He moved one glass closer to Nunzio.

"August 6, 1972. It was a hot day and hotter night." Nunzio held the shot glass, not drinking. "Nobody could sleep, least of all a baby about to break with her first tooth. Sandy and Frank took her out for a walk. It wasn't just the air they needed. With him workin' and studyin' most of the time, they didn't have all that much time to spend with each other. A walk's a good way to catch up."

Pins could hear Nunzio's voice straining to stay firm.

"They were only ten minutes into the walk," Nunzio said. "It was a clear night and they were holding hands, the baby asleep in the carriage. And then, in a little less than five minutes, everybody's world got a lot smaller."

"They were mugged?" Pins said, hoping the answer was that easy.

"Two guys were standin' in front of them before they even knew it," Nunzio said. "They forced them over into some tree cover. They beat Frankie, beat him bad, lookin' to leave him for dead. And they did things to Sandy I don't need to tell you about."

"What about the baby?" Pins asked, his mouth dry, one hand bunched into a fist.

"Theresa?" Nunzio said. He blinked his eyes twice. He would not let tears fall down the front of his face. "They took her right outta her carriage."

"Jesus Christ!" Pins said. "I'm sorry, Nunzio. I'm so sorry."

"It changed everything, that night," Nunzio said. "Took years to put Sandy back together, bring her to a place where she could come close to leadin' a normal life. And Frankie . . . he never came out of it. Stuck around for a few months and then one morning, got up, got dressed, and got out."

"Where to?"

"Don't know," Nunzio said. "Don't need to know. We all handle our wars in different ways. He's handling his the only way he can."

"They ever get Theresa back?"

"No," Nunzio said. "All my wise-guy contacts. All my cop friends. We all came up empty."

"I don't know what to say."

"Nothin' to say," Nunzio said. "Years go by, you bury it, but you never forget it. And then Boomer comes in here and tells me about Lucia. Now, I know Lucia had nothin' at all to do with takin' my little Theresa away from us. But you know what?"

"Tell me," Pins said.

"She might as well have been the one," Nunzio said. "That's why I'm in. It's why we're all in. To get a taste of even. In our way of lookin' at things, it's as good as you can hope for. You can't ever get back what you lost, so you make somebody pay for it."

Pins stared at Nunzio, his eyes moist, his throat dry.

"I'm just like the rest of the crew," Nunzio said. "And so are you, Pins. Our hearts been carved out by different people in different ways. It's only the taste of gettin' even that keeps us all going forward."

They sat across from each other, sun filtering in through the large front windows, the silence between them welcome and relaxing.

"I'm going over to the bowling alley," Pins said. "Roll a few games. Helps clear my head. Wouldn't mind having company if you're interested."

"You as good as they say you are?" Nunzio asked, the hardness back in his face and voice.

"Probably better," Pins said, smiling.

"What will you spot me?" Nunzio asked.

"I'll give you twenty," Pins said. "We play three games, that's a sixty spot. Highest total wins."

"How much we playin' for?"

"I don't want your money, Nunzio," Pins said.

"You ain't gettin' my money," Nunzio said, walking out from behind the bar. "Now, how much?"

"Ten bucks a game," Pins said. "Twenty if you sweep the three."

"Deal," Nunzio said, rolling down his sleeves and putting on a black leather jacket.

"You ain't a ringer, are you?" Pins said, walking behind Nunzio toward the front door.

"You'll know in a couple of hours." Nunzio shrugged his shoulders and walked out, leaving Pins to lock the door.

. . .

BOOMER AND DR. CAROLYN BARTLETT walked quietly side by side down the south end of Thirty-sixth Street between Park and Madison. It was late on a warm Tuesday night, a cloudless spring night, a mild wind brushing against their backs. Boomer glanced over at her unlined face lit by an overhead streetlight, struck by the simplicity of her beauty and still surprised she had accepted his dinner invitation. He was attracted to Bartlett from the first and admired her for the stance she had taken in defense of Jennifer Santori. He wished he had said something to her about it back then. But, as usual, Boomer let anger stand in his way.

He had driven down to pick her up in front of her office building and taken her over the Fifty-ninth Street Bridge to a favorite Long Island City hangout, where they had feasted on southern Italian specialties prepared to heavenly perfection by the proprietor and his wife. During the course of the three-hour meal, they talked, laughed, easily broke down the barriers thrown between them by their work. They even joined Vincent, a retired cop from Naples, in an off-key rendition of "Amore Mio." Boomer introduced Carolyn to Fernet Branca, an after-dinner digestive with the smoothness of lighter fluid, and he watched with mild wonder as she shot back the drink in one gulp and was able to name three of the herbs used in its making.

They drove back into Manhattan in comfortable silence and she seemed amenable when he suggested that they park the car and walk for a bit. He curbed up next to a fire hydrant, tossed an NYPD permit across the dash, and walked over to hold her door open.

"Are you still allowed to have one of those?" she asked, pointing to the permit.

"No," Boomer said.

"Do you follow the rules on *anything*?" Carolyn asked.

"No."

Carolyn slid a hand under his arm and moved herself closer to his side. "I'm glad you called."

"I owed you," Boomer said. "I ran a little rough on you about Jenny. Wrote you off as another bleeding heart. I should have known better."

"Is that an apology?" she asked.

"It's as close as I get to one," Boomer said. His eyes locked on Carolyn. "But don't go getting used to it."

"I won't."

"You know, I talked to Jenny's dad the other night," Boomer said. "He told me she's starting to come around and that you've been a big help to her and the family. I appreciate that."

"Is that the only reason you asked me out?" Carolyn said, stopping in front of her brownstone.

"No, that wasn't the reason," Boomer said, turning to face her. "That was just a damn good excuse."

"What other reason, then, would you have to ask me out, Detective?" Carolyn asked, running a soft hand against the hard features of Boomer's face.

"Would you buy it if I said I didn't want to eat alone?" Boomer asked.

"No," Carolyn said.

"How about if I told you I wanted free medical advice?" Boomer said. "Would that one work?"

"No," Carolyn said.

"How about if I told you I've thought about you every day since we met?" Boomer said, leaning closer to Carolyn. "And that I picked up the phone a dozen times to call you but didn't because I'd've bet money you'd say no. Would you believe any of that?"

"There's a good chance on that one," Carolyn said.

Boomer leaned closer and kissed her, holding Carolyn tightly in his arms, her hair brushing against his face. Her lips were soft and her breath was as warm as the light wind coming up off the East River. He held on to her for as long as he could, engulfed by the peaceful night and the passion of her kiss. They stood under the streetlight, the pains and fears of their jobs shoved aside for this brief moment.

"Now you know my real reason," Boomer whispered, sliding his face alongside Carolyn's, his strong arms still holding her slight frame.

"And now you know why I said yes," Carolyn whispered in his ear.

"I haven't felt like this in a long time," Boomer said, forgetting what lay ahead, concerned only with the present. "A *very* long time."

Carolyn lifted her head to look at Boomer, cupping her hands around his face. "Come up with me," she said. "But there's something you should know before you do."

"You're married," Boomer said. "And your husband's asleep on the couch with a gun in his hand."

"Besides that," she said, laughing and leading him up the brownstone steps.

"You don't have any Fernet Branca," Boomer said, following her.

"And I *never will* either," Carolyn said, reaching into her shoulder bag for the key to the front door.

"That's as good as my guesses get," Boomer said, standing behind her, arms around her waist.

She shoved the key in the latch, opened the door, and turned around to face Boomer. "I'm afraid for you," Carolyn said, losing the smile. "I don't want anything to happen to you."

"I don't want anything to happen to me either," Boomer said, holding the door open with one hand.

"I'm pretty sure I'm going to fall in love with you, Boomer. And it would be very nice if you were around long enough to see it happen."

"I'll be around as long as you want me to be," Boomer promised. "You've got nothing to be afraid of."

The smile returned to Carolyn's face as she wrapped her arms around him. They stepped into the foyer, let the door shut quietly behind them, and moved up the stairs toward Carolyn's second-floor apartment.

The peaceful spring night was theirs to call their own.

. . .

THE BLACK LEXUS was parked across the street. Wilber Graves sat behind the wheel, smoking a Cuban cigar, a grin on his face as he watched Boomer and Carolyn walk up the brownstone steps.

"Our friend has himself a woman," Wilber said to a young man seated on the passenger side of the car.

"Do you want me to deal with it now?" the young man asked.

Wilber looked over at him and spread his smile. "You have no sense of romance, Derek," Wilber said. "Let the lovers have their night. Let them have something to remember. This way, when we reach for them and let them feel our touch, the pain will be that much harder to forget."

"How soon, then?" the young man said.

Wilber took a long drag from his cigar, filling the front of the car with smoke. He took half of it back in his lungs with a deep breath. "The cop will have his way tonight," Wilber said. "And come the morning, we will have ours."

19

DEAD-EYE WAS ON his third turn around the Central Park reservoir, building up his lung capacity, trying to get back reasonably close to the pace he'd kept in the years before the elevator shoot-out. He was taking long strides, heavy beads of sweat soaking through his blue NYPD running gear, the center of his chest burning with a pain he willed himself to ignore. His legs stabbed at him with sharp bolts, his back muscles twitched in spasms, his stomach churned out its acid.

And still Dead-Eye ran.

The shooting had altered Dead-Eye's life in so many ways, but the physical changes were the hardest. His diet now consisted mainly of fruits, fresh-cut vegetables, and fish. He attacked his local gym three mornings a week, lifting and pulling for three hours at a heavy clip. The longer his workouts went, the more intense his pain grew. And despite stern warnings from a concerned battery of doctors, Dead-Eye made it a point to hit the track.

Four mornings a week, four miles at a time.

It couldn't make him whole again, nothing could do that, but it helped keep him sane. When he ran, regardless of weather or time of day, Dead-Eye always brought himself back to younger years when he raced along the Brooklyn piers next to his father. He was never able to beat him, but he always managed to finish the course, no matter how tired. During their daily runs, Dead-Eye's father had imparted to his son the two rules he held absolute: Give everything you do an honest effort and never give up or give in.

It was the only way Dead-Eye knew how to live. Even with a body that was scarred and ravaged.

He was coming around a hard curve now, trees and brush to his right, the clear waters of the reservoir to his left. He checked the stopwatch in his hand. Forty minutes and two more miles to go. He picked up his pace, looking to finish in thirty-five.

The two men came at him from behind, and he never had a chance. They jumped out from behind a thick row of bushes, slammed Dead-Eye up against the chain-link fence, two guns drawn, both held against his chest.

The man on his left was decked out in a dark designer jogging suit. The other one had on a black leather jacket over a thin black turtleneck and a pair of tailored blue jeans. Dead-Eye waited for them to talk, his breathing still heavy from his run.

"Your little bullshit game is over as of today," the man in the jogging suit said. "You walk away from it now and we'll forget all about the crap you pulled."

"You go back to your friends and tell them that," the one in the turtleneck said, a touch of a lisp to his words. "Tell 'em this is their last fuckin' chance to leave the table alive."

"Give me a nod so I know you understand what we're tellin' you," the jogging suit said.

Dead-Eye stared at the two of them and slowly nodded his head, beads of sweat falling onto the dark dirt by his feet.

The man in the turtleneck reached a hand into the side pocket of his leather jacket and brought out a color Polaroid. He held the photo close to Dead-Eye's face.

"This is your boy, am I right, cop?" the man asked.

Dead-Eye didn't move. But his eyes flashed anger. They had gone beyond touching a cop. They were touching family. He knew now there could never be any turning back. Lucia and the Apaches were alike in only one respect. They were both in this fight to win. And, Dead-Eye realized, looking at Eddie's picture, that the only winners were going to be those who were left alive when the fight was over.

The man in the sweat suit snapped open a black switchblade and watched as his partner slid Eddie's photo over its sharp point. He smiled at Dead-Eye, flashing the photo and the knife. There was a large X drawn in felt tip crossing over his son's face.

"This might hurt a little," he said.

He stuck the knife and the photo into Dead-Eye's right arm.

Dead-Eye's knees buckled and his arms shook. The knife wound awoke every sharp pierce his body had ever felt, from bullet to blade. His lungs screamed for mercy and he swallowed back a mouthful of bile. He gave in to the pain, wanting nothing so much as to fall to the ground and rest his head on the dirt track. Wanting so much for it to stop.

But Dead-Eye didn't fall. He looked out through a blurred vision knowing he now had the one thing he needed to get even. He had the faces of the two men etched across his eyes.

"You go back to your friends," the man in the jacket said. "Tell 'em about our little meeting. Find out how serious they are about dying."

"And it ain't just them that goes down," the other man said. "It's everybody attached. Sons, daughters, wives, husbands, even your fuckin' pets."

The man in the sweat suit pulled the knife blade out of Dead-Eye's arm and held it out for him to look at. "Take the picture," he said, smiling. "Keep it for his scrapbook or his coffin. I'll leave it to you to decide."

He watched the men cross over a steep ridge, walking in slow strides, their backs to the sun, guns holstered at their sides. Dead-Eye waited until they disappeared from sight, then he bent down and picked up his son's photo. He held it in both hands, blood from the stab wound running down his arm, across his fingers, and dripping onto the picture. He leaned the weight of his back against the fence, his face up, his eyes closed, reveling now in the sharp pain he felt. He stayed there for close to an hour, listening as clusters of other runners came charging past, puffing their way through a morning drill. He was sweating, willing the pain to come on stronger, knowing he would need the strength of that pain to fuel his anger further and carry him through to the end of his task.

With his arm still leaking blood, Dead-Eye wiped the flow of sweat from his face and checked the timer on his stopwatch. He then shifted his feet and picked up where he had left off. Dead-Eye continued down the reservoir path and finished his run, holding his son's photo crumpled in his right hand.

The pain his only comfort.

· · ·

GERONIMO AND REV. JIM STOOD against the railing and watched the field of eight horses canter by. The sixth race at Belmont Park was about to start. With racing programs folded open in their hands and small pencils hooked over their ears, they were trying to decide which horse to wager on.

"Number three just took a shit," Rev. Jim said, scanning the program for the horse's name. "That's always a good sign."

"You can't go by that," Geronimo said. "They're horses. All they *do* is shit."

"Catapult," Rev. Jim said, circling the name on the program. "Even his name sounds fast. And he's down at six to one. I'd say he's good for a win, place, and show. You want in, or what?"

"You have to have a sense for the horse," Geronimo said, staring out at the rest of the field. "You need to know how far he'll go for the win. If his heart has the courage it needs."

"We're not askin' for him to *fly*, Geronimo. This ain't a spiritual thing workin' here. We just want him to go a mile around a fast track, win by a nose, and pay for our lunch."

"He won't win unless he *wants* to win," Geronimo said. "No matter what *we* want."

Rev. Jim rested the program against his thigh and looked over at Geronimo. "Just between you and me," he said, "are you really serious about this Indian shit you talk or are you just fuckin' with everybody's head?"

"I would be dead without that Indian *shit*," Geronimo said. "It's all I had to hold on to all those months in the hospital. There was no hope. There was only dread. If anyone knows that feeling better than me, it's you."

"I couldn't talk for months after the fire," Rev. Jim told him. "If I could have talked, I would have asked for somebody to put a bullet in my head. There's a lotta ways a guy could go out and buy it. Having your skin burn away ain't the best of 'em."

"I wanted to leave," Geronimo said. "Take my pension and head for the Southwest, bury myself in the culture."

"Why didn't you?" Rev. Jim asked.

"The people I have there see me as this brave cop," Geronimo said. "To them I am invincible. A warrior who can't be felled. I couldn't go back to them in the shape I was in."

"That why you joined up with Boomer?" Rev. Jim asked. "To go out on your own terms?"

"We choose our way of life," Geronimo said. "I want to be able to choose the way I die. I don't mind going down against a device, but not the way it happened to me. Not with a grenade tossed into an open crowd. I always pictured being alone with a bomb and letting my destiny decide."

"You might get your wish," Rev. Jim said. "From the looks of it, there ain't gonna be a shortage of fireworks."

"I'll be ready," Geronimo said.

Rev. Jim pulled out a crushed pack of Marlboros, shook one loose, and put it to his lips. He searched his pockets for matches and came up empty. "You wouldn't have a light?" he asked.

Geronimo unzipped his flak jacket and reached for a lighter in the front pocket of a checkered hunting shirt. Rev. Jim looked over at the inside flaps of the jacket, each slot packed with sticks of dynamite. "You care to explain that?" he asked in astonishment.

"Ever since I became an Apache," Geronimo said, smiling, "they're my American Express card. I never leave home without 'em."

"You know why you're part of this team?" Rev. Jim asked, turning his attention back to the track. "You're just as crazy as the rest of us. That's why you must have been a great cop. You gotta be crazy to be a great cop."

"Are we crazy enough to beat back Lucia Carney?" Geronimo asked.

"She's probably thinking we are," Rev. Jim said. "She's got to figure by now we're not in this for the money. And there ain't anybody around gonna pin any medals on us if we *do* bring her to a crash. So what's our end? She don't know. And that should give us a little bit of a lead."

"If she only knew the real reason," Geronimo said. "That we're just walking dead men looking for one last battle. To bring peace to our souls."

"There you go with that Indian shit again," Rev. Jim said.

Geronimo smiled, looking at the pack of horses race past him toward the finish line. "That Indian shit just saved you a few bucks."

"How you figure?" Rev. Jim asked, craning his neck to see how the horses finished.

"You're looking in the wrong direction," Geronimo said. "There's Catapult over there, bringing up the rear. Like I said, he just didn't have the spirit of a warrior."

"Havin' a shitty jockey on his back didn't help any either," Rev. Jim said.

They walked away from the rail and eased their way up toward the bleachers. They sat next to one another, spending the rest of the afternoon under the sun of a fast track, winning and losing money, laughing and eating the kind of food neither was supposed to consume. Enjoying a brief day of calm.

· · ·

BOOMER STARED at the crushed photo of Eddie. The blood on it was caked and the felt-tip mark smeared. The rest of the Apaches sat around the circular table, Nunzio pacing behind them.

"He's your kid, Dead-Eye." Boomer's voice was soft with concern. "These are crazy fucks we're moving on, and killing kids doesn't seem to upset them all that much. So I'll let you call the play."

"Eddie and Grace are taken care of," Dead-Eye said in a calm, even tone. "Now let's worry about us. Lucia sent me a message. Sent us all one, really. I think we should send one back."

Boomer looked around the table, studying each Apache in turn. That felt-tip X scrawled across little Eddie's photo might as well have been drawn on every one of them. It was a call-out, a street move, a push by a criminal to force a cop to take a step back. Most cops would fade away. A few would stand their ground. But the ones Boomer chose as Apaches knew only one way. To move forward and attack.

"One hour, then," Boomer said, standing and moving away from the table. "Tenth Street and Avenue A. Nunzio'll lay out the plan. I'll see you there."

"Where are *you* going?" Mrs. Columbo asked.

"To pick up a wrecking ball," Boomer said, closing the front door of the restaurant behind him.

. . .

BOOMER AND MRS. COLUMBO SAT in the front seat of a yellow multi-gear Caterpillar rig. A half-ton wrecking ball hung from an iron hook, swaying lazily in front of them. Both wore white hard hats and heavy construction gloves as the machine slowly inched its way through late morning traffic. Boomer had eased the dozer out of a Lower East Side construction site whose foreman owed Nunzio a few hard favors, grinding gears as he moved the rig past crumbling tenements.

"Are you sure about this?" Mrs. Columbo asked, feeling out of place sitting so high above the traffic.

"You mean letting you ride shotgun? It's a risk, but worth a roll."

"Not that, dorko," Mrs. Columbo said. "I was thinking more about your little idea of demolishing a building in downtown Manhattan in broad daylight."

"It's as good as any other idea I've had," Boomer said.

"That sure helps ease my mind," Mrs. Columbo muttered.

"Besides, it gives you and me a few minutes to talk." Boomer cranked the shaft back into neutral, looking up past three cars at a red light.

"About what?"

"Your husband."

"He's off limits, Boom."

"He made a wrong move going to Lavetti," Boomer said. "But he did it for the right reasons. He was worried about you, so he reached out for somebody he thought would help."

"He could have talked to *me*." Mrs. Columbo turned away to watch a small boy bounce a Spauldeen against a red brick wall.

"Well, you ain't all that easy to talk to sometimes," Boomer said. "Like most cops."

"I can talk to you," Mrs. Columbo said, still looking at the boy and the ball, her voice distant and quiet.

"I'm a cop *and* your friend," Boomer said. "That gives me a leg up on a husband."

"You're saying I should go back with him?"

"You've got a life with him, Mary. And a son."

"It's not much of a life," Mrs. Columbo said. "And I'll always have my son."

"Just think about it," Boomer said. The light turned green and he moved the rig forward. "That's all I'm saying."

"It could have been me and you, you know." Mrs. Columbo still wasn't looking at him. "It wouldn't have taken much. To tell you the truth, I'm kind of surprised it never was."

"I am, too." Boomer glanced over at her. "But you know, sometimes the could-have-been leaves you with a better feeling. We would have had ourselves a few good months, maybe even a couple of years. But we wouldn't have made it past that."

"Thank you, Ann Landers," Mrs. Columbo said.

"You and me, we know each other more than fifteen years now and we can still talk to each other like this. But if we were married, we probably wouldn't even be *looking* at each other. And both of us packin' guns. I'm telling you, it could've gotten ugly."

"Real fast," Mrs. Columbo said with a laugh.

"Plus, you're a better shot," Boomer said.

"Most wives are," Mrs. Columbo said. "Cop or not."

"That's why I'm still single." Boomer signaled to make a left turn.

"So, you gonna tell me about her?" Mrs. Columbo asked. "Or do I have to get all my info secondhand?"

Boomer nearly rammed the ball end of the dozer against the back of a Dodge Dart. "Remind me to pistol-whip Nunzio next time I see him."

"He couldn't help himself," she said. "I squeezed it out of him. I *was* a homicide detective, remember?"

"I went out on a date," Boomer said. "Not a hit."

"And . . ."

"*And* I had a great time. *And* I'm gonna see her again. *And* that's all I'm gonna say for now."

"Why?" Mrs. Columbo said. "You turning shy on me all of a sudden?"

"No," Boomer said. "I'm anything but shy."

"Then why won't you tell me about her?" Mrs. Columbo asked, grabbing on to Boomer's right arm.

"Because we're here," Boomer said.

. . .

GERONIMO RAN UP to the driver's side and jumped onto the side panel runner.

"Rev. Jim and Pins in place?" Boomer asked.

"They're on each end of the avenue, rerouting traffic," Geronimo said. "And they're not all that happy about it."

"Why?" Mrs. Columbo said. "They've got the easiest job. Next to mine."

"They're back in uniform." Boomer laughed. "I got two sets of blues from a friend down at the Chinatown precinct." As Mrs. Columbo covered her mouth with her right hand, joining Boomer and Geronimo in the laugh, Boomer asked, "Building empty?"

"I went with Dead-Eye and checked through every floor," Geronimo told him. "Nothing in there except for a couple of attack dogs that we cleared out and enough cocaine to make every junkie in the city smile for a week."

"Why no guards?" Mrs. Columbo wanted to know.

"She doesn't need any," Boomer explained. He turned the dozer so the wrecking ball faced the front of the building, the street now empty of all traffic. "Any dealer or junkie even thinking of making a move on her would be too scared to touch the place. Even with nobody there, that building is more secure than Fort Knox."

"Until now," Mrs. Columbo said.

"You bet your sweet little ass until now." And with that, Boomer shifted the gears on the rig forward.

Geronimo grabbed on to a yellow pole alongside the large front wheel, signaling Dead-Eye away from the front entrance with his free hand. Dead-Eye smiled and nodded, walking closer to the dozer, waving Boomer forward.

"Aim for the center of the building," Dead-Eye yelled, his hands cupped around his mouth. "That way you're sure to knock something down."

"Listen to him," Boomer muttered, moving the rig at full throttle. "All of a sudden he's Fred Flintstone."

Boomer brought the rig to a halt as soon as it jumped the curb. He rammed the gears into park, then began to shift and pull the wrecking ball crank toward the boarded-up first-floor window.

"I guess it would be a waste of time asking if you've ever run a machine like this before," Mrs. Columbo said, watching the ball sway from side to side.

"Total." Smiling, Boomer eased the shaft forward and watched in awe as the ball crashed against the prewar facade of the building.

The first loud hit brought brick, wood, and dust particles tumbling to the ground. Geronimo and Dead-Eye stood on opposite ends of the building, gold shields hanging from leather straps around their necks, huge grins on their faces, holding back small clusters of passersby.

Boomer turned in his seat and looked over at Mrs. Columbo. "You wanna give it a shot?" he asked. "Unless you think you're not strong enough."

"Move it over, old man," Mrs. Columbo said, standing in her seat, waiting for Boomer to slide down from the rig.

"Try not to kill anybody," Boomer told her.

Mrs. Columbo cranked the gear forward, moving the wrecking ball away from Boomer and toward the left side of the building. "Clear the decks," she shouted as the ball hit with a louder crash than the first blow, breaking through to the gut of the tenement, dismantling its center foundation and bringing two floors down with an enormous thud.

"Here we are, demolishing a fucking building during lunch hour," Boomer shouted over to Dead-Eye. "And what don't we see *anywhere*? A cop."

"It must be true, then," Dead-Eye said. "They're never around when you really need them."

"Not even a brown shirt to write up a violation," Boomer said, scanning up and down the avenue. "I mean, shit, we've gotta be breaking *some* traffic law here."

"It doesn't matter." Dead-Eye shrugged. "We've never paid for a ticket in our lives." After a pause he asked, "Who filled you in on the building?"

"It's on the DEA scanner sheet," Boomer said. "And it matched up with the information I got from our guy downtown."

"Everybody knows the places, but nobody makes a move," Dead-Eye said.

"That all changed today," Boomer said.

They watched Mrs. Columbo maneuver the wrecking ball against the building for the last time. It teetered on the verge of a total collapse, then it all fell in one massive heap, caving inward. A cloud of dust flowed out to the street, and sounds of distant horns and sirens could be heard.

Dead-Eye walked through the debris, stepping over crushed rock, splintered wood, darkened packets of cocaine, and a nest of dead rats. He stood over a small mound of red bricks and put a hand inside his jacket pocket, coming out with the crumpled, marked-up photo of his son. He leaned over and placed the picture under a cracked edge of one of the red bricks, then stood up, turned, and walked toward his fellow Apaches.

"That's just in case Lucia has any trouble figuring out who blew up her stash," Dead-Eye said.

· · ·

CAROLYN BARTLETT LET the hot water run over her body, still tired after an arduous day of coaxing information out of reluctant patients. She had taken on her daily run with relish and looked forward to her post-shower addictions—a low-cal dinner, reading through several chapters of a historical romance, Bach on the stereo and, sometime within the next hour, hearing Boomer's voice coming over the phone by her bed.

She had been reluctant to get emotionally involved with someone so closely linked to one of her patients, especially a man such as Boomer Frontieri. By falling for Boomer, who openly worked outside the boundaries of the law to get what he felt was justice, Carolyn also shattered a promise she had long ago made to herself: Never date a cop, retired or not. But here she was, in less time than it took to fill out a case file, as involved with Boomer as anyone could expect to get.

Carolyn turned the water off, slid the shower curtain open, and reached for the thick white towel folded on the marble sink. She wrapped it around her body and notched it in place. She picked up the silver hairbrush her grandmother had given her on her sixth birthday and ran it through her long wet hair. She wiped a hand across the steam-drenched medicine cabinet mirror and checked her face. The stress of her work had yet to add wrinkles to her skin, but Carolyn knew those days would soon be close at hand. She smiled, remembering Boomer leaning over her and telling her she had the soft, pure face of an angel. She hoped he would always feel that way.

She walked into the living room, slid a tape of Bach into her stereo system before heading into the kitchen to check out which Lean Cuisine special she should feast on. She slipped a chicken and broccoli on a bed of white rice into her small oven and set the cooking timer to forty minutes. She was padding back, in bare feet, toward the refrigerator to pour herself a glass from a half-empty bottle of Orvietto Classico, when she saw the shadow against the living room wall.

Then Bach went silent.

Carolyn could see the telephone from where she was standing, the red message light flashing on the answering machine, and figured it to be her only move. Her mind racing, her thought processes marred by fear, she ran blindly from the kitchen toward the phone. She made it as far as the end table. A dark-gloved hand grabbed her by the hair and pulled her back. She felt hot breath on her neck and grizzled skin scratching against her face.

"He's not at home," Wilber Graves said to her. "He's out. With his friends."

"What do you want?" Carolyn asked, trying to keep a calm voice and a level breathing pattern.

"I want everything the cop calls his own," Wilber said. *"Everything."*

A few moments later Carolyn stood in front of the telephone, the towel stripped from her body and thrown to the floor. She was fully naked, her hands bound tightly behind her with chicken wire, the tip of a Spanish-made red-handled switchblade pressed against the side of her neck. Wilber rubbed Carolyn's body with his free hand, moving gloved fingers in a slow motion up against her firm breasts, down the contours of her stomach, over the front of her thighs. Occasionally, he slipped a finger inside her vagina.

"You won't believe this," he said to her. "But I really wish I didn't have to kill you."

"Why are you waiting?" Carolyn asked. Her eyes stared straight ahead, trying to will herself to another place, a safer one, where men didn't kill on whim or orders and where a woman could listen to Bach, read a book, and wait for someone she loved to call and tell her so. She could smell the Lean Cuisine dinner burning in the oven, too many minutes past done.

It almost made her want to smile.

The phone rang at seven minutes past eleven.

The first ring jolted her, the tip of Wilber's knife edging in deeper, cutting into the side of her skin, drawing blood. Wilber removed his hand from Carolyn's waist, picked up the phone, and placed it against her ear. He let her hear Boomer's voice on the other end. Wilber smiled at her as he moved the phone away and cradled it on the side of his neck.

"Hello, Detective," Wilber said into the receiver.

"Where's Carolyn?" he heard Boomer say.

"She's snug and warm right here in my arms," Wilber said. "I have to tell you, you have excellent taste in women. That's surprising in a police officer."

"Anything happens to her . . . "

"Something *is* going to happen to her, Detective," Wilber said. "We were just waiting for you to call before it does."

"Let her go!" Boomer's shout could be heard well beyond the range of the receiver.

"I will," Wilber said. "I promise you that. But first, would you like to hear her say good-bye?"

Wilber pressed the receiver against Carolyn's ear.

"Speak to him," he told her.

Carolyn closed her eyes and took a deep breath, the knife pressing against her neck. "I love you, Boomer," she said.

She never felt the cut. Her head turned light, the room spun around her in slow circles, the front of her body went warm with blood. Her legs weakened and sent her to the floor, a slight moan coming from her lips as her head touched down on the wooden planks.

Wilber hovered over her and watched her die, calmly ignoring Boomer's frantic shouts into his end of the phone.

"My name is Wilber Graves," he said into the phone once Carolyn had taken her final breath. "I've just killed a woman who loved you, and it was my pleasure. Good-bye, Detective."

Wilber placed the phone back on its cradle, took one more look down at Carolyn, and closed the knife. He turned the stereo back on to Bach, went into the kitchen, and turned off the oven before he walked out of the apartment.

His work for the night at an end.

. . .

BOOMER WENT to the wake, where the coffin was sealed, and to the funeral, held under the angry rain of a late spring day.

He had been fast on the crime scene, arriving within minutes of the precinct sector car. The two young officers hovering around the apartment had been decent enough to cover her naked body with a white sheet stripped from her bed, a sheet he and Carolyn had slept under together. Boomer pulled it back and stared down at the woman he had grown to know so well in such a short time. Her lips and nails were already starting to pale, her clear skin taking on the waxy color of the dead. The open wound still gurgled blood. Her eyes were closed, her mouth curved in a twisted smile. Boomer crunched down and leaned over to kiss Carolyn's still-warm lips. He reached for the edge of the white sheet and slowly lifted it past her face. He zippered his jacket, stood, nodded to the two officers, and left before the meat truck arrived.

At her funeral, Boomer stood out, a stranger among family, sitting in the back row of a candlelit church, listening to the faces who had shared decades with her talk about their memories. He only half listened, his eyes staring down the curved arms of the aisles at the closed oak coffin air-locking the body of a woman who had died for no reason.

Boomer pictured Carolyn's easy smile and allowed his mind to drift off, to conjure up images of the life they might have had together. These images—places they would visit, dinners they would share—were fleeting.

The time for romance was over.

Other images took hold.

Boomer had never met Wilber Graves, but he knew him well. Hard-edged and soulless, a gun for hire whose thrills were fed watching a human being bleed a life away. He would soon meet up with Wilber Graves and it would end as it was destined to end, with one man standing above the other.

He and the Apaches had started the war. Lucia and her crew were now making their move. People would die. Most were deserving, some might be innocent. To win, the Apaches could no longer see themselves as ex-cops out to right a wrong. They had to dig deeper, search harder, strip away their layers of weakness and humanity, and face their foes on an equal footing.

Boomer knelt in the pew, head buried in his hands, and prayed to the God in the room to give him the strength he needed.

To destroy his enemies.

The enemies who erased Carolyn Bartlett from the center of his life.

Boomer dropped two red roses in Carolyn's open grave, then stared blankly as four workmen guided the coffin down into the open pit. The heavy rain washed over his head and down the sides of his neck, but he stayed until there was no one left by the graveside. He didn't exchange any words with Carolyn's family, nor did he offer words of sympathy to the assembled women dressed in short black dresses and veils that hid reddened eyes. Boomer could think of nothing to say that would help ease their painful burden.

So he stood there quietly, head bowed, hands folded under dark and ominous clouds, letting an angry rain lash away at the guilt he carried in the caverns of his heart.

Behind him, hidden under the heavy leaves of an old tree, Nunzio and the rest of the Apaches stood in silence.

. . .

THE APACHES WERE SITTING in the back room of Nunzio's, waiting out the rain. There was an amplified energy to the room, the sense that the next hours would determine everyone's fate.

They were all there except for Pins. His tardiness was out of character. He was usually the first to arrive. Maybe he had decided to roll a few extra games before the action kicked in. Boomer had yellow surveillance folders spread out in front of him, an illegal gift from a friend in the Washington office of the Secret Service. He had been hunting Lucia Carney for the past eight months on a money-laundering scheme.

Boomer, hands on his chin, not looking up, said, "Nunz, throw Pins another ring. This ain't a day to call in sick."

"I just tried him," Nunzio said. "If he's at the alley, he's not pickin' up."

"Anybody hear from him today?" Boomer asked, scanning the faces around him.

"I talked to him last night," Rev. Jim said. "He knew we were meeting and he knew what time."

"It's not like him," Mrs. Columbo said, sipping a decaf espresso. "He's not the kind to blow off a meeting."

A young waiter in a white jacket and thin black tie peeked into the small, crowded room. "Excuse me," he said, "I don't mean to bother."

"Whatta ya got, Freddie?" Nunzio asked.

"A phone call," Freddie said. "Just came in. The guy didn't stay on all that long."

"What'd he want?" Nunzio said.

"Told me to ask if any of the guys were up for a night of bowling," Freddie said.

"He give a name?" Boomer asked in a cold voice.

"Wilber Graves," Freddie said.

. . .

BOOMER AND THE APACHES stood in the center of lane six, shrouded in darkness. The only light in the alley was a heavy-watt spotlight shooting down from the back of the bar, beamed on the bowling cage. Pins was tied to the cage, thick cord rope binding his arms and upper body to the iron mesh. His face was swollen, one eye puffy and closed, blood trickled out of his mouth and nose. He was on his knees, his feet tied by wire, his head held up by a rope around his neck tied to a thin steel beam. Strapped to Pins's chest were a dozen thick sticks of dynamite, a timer in the center clicking down from an hour's limit. Six different-colored explosive wires were entwined around his chest, legs, and arms.

The entire bowling cage was wired and set, three separate devices timed at various intervals.

Boomer and Geronimo walked over to Pins. Mrs. Columbo and Rev. Jim stood behind them. Dead-Eye was searching the rest of the alley, two guns drawn.

"I didn't see them," Pins said, talking through swollen lips. "They came up from behind. There were three of them. I guess I screwed up."

"You didn't screw up anything," Boomer said, taking a wad of tissues from Mrs. Columbo and wiping blood off Pins's face. "You just breathe easy and leave the rest to us."

Geronimo stripped off his jacket and sweater, tossing them in an empty lane. He took a knife from his back pocket, got on his knees, and started to run the blade along the wire lines.

"What do you see?" Boomer asked, sweat starting to flow down the small of his back.

"Six numbers," Geronimo said. "Each attached to different wires. Two strings of wires are dummies. The chest timer is coded to blow in eight minutes, but that could be a decoy. And there's two separate sticks up above, latched to the rope around his neck."

"Can you break this?" Boomer asked.

"I need somebody to go to the car and get my kit outta the trunk," Geronimo said.

"I'll do it," Rev. Jim said, waiting as Boomer tossed him the keys.

"After that I figure you should all get the hell outta here," Geronimo said, "and leave me to my work."

"Can you break this?" Boomer asked again. "I want an answer, Geronimo."

Geronimo stood up, turned, and faced Boomer. "Probably not," he said. "But I've got a better chance than any of you."

Rev. Jim came running back in with a heavy black satchel and handed it to Geronimo. Mrs. Columbo stood off to the side, eyes closed. Dead-Eye came up behind her, his guns holstered. He stared down at Pins, his face flush with anger.

Boomer stooped down and leaned toward his friend. "I'm sorry I got you involved in this, kid," he said softly.

Pins managed a smile around the blood. "Not me," he said. "You guys made me feel what it was like all over again."

"Like what was like?" Rev. Jim asked.

"Being alive," Pins said.

And then there was silence. Until Pins tried to speak again.

"The guy that did this . . . " he said, swallowing a mouthful of blood, straining to get the words out.

"Wilber Graves," Boomer said. "I know the name."

"What you don't know is, I wired him."

It took a moment to register. The Apaches stared at Pins in amazement. He managed a nod, and forced a smile. The look in his eyes acknowledged their awe and accepted it gratefully.

"While they were workin' me over," Pins said, "I dropped a line in his jacket pocket. You can hear him on the scanner."

There was silence again.

It was broken by Geronimo.

"Sooner everybody leaves, sooner I can get started," he said. "I don't have all that much time."

Boomer stroked the sides of Pins's face, his fingers red with the young man's blood. The two exchanged a long look, then Boomer stood and left, followed by the other Apaches, each of whom saluted Pins with a closed fist to their hearts.

Geronimo jumped to his feet and tapped Boomer on the shoulder. "If I don't crack the device, I'd like you to do me a favor."

"I don't wanna lose two of you," Boomer said.

"The favor," Geronimo said. "Will you do it?"

"Name it."

"Blow that bitch away," Geronimo said.

· · ·

SWEAT RAN DOWN the sides of Geronimo's arms and face. He was inching along on his knees, working slowly beside Pins, scanning wires, operating as much with gut as he was with knowledge.

"I'm gonna give the blue wires a snap," Geronimo said.

"What's that gonna do?" Pins asked.

"If we're lucky, not a thing," Geronimo said. "And it'll leave us one less device to worry about."

"What if we ain't so lucky?" Pins said.

"We won't know it," Geronimo told him.

Geronimo took a deep breath, squeezed the tip of his hand pliers over the blue wire, and snapped it apart. Beads of sweat mixed with blood flowed down Pins's face as he gave Geronimo a knowing nod. "I woulda guessed red myself," he said.

"It's a good thing you're the one that's wired and not me." Geronimo wiped at his eyes with the sleeve of his blue Bomb Squad T-shirt.

"How much time left?" Pins asked.

"Why? Gotta be somewhere special?"

"They designed this bomb just for you," Pins told him. "They said you were the best, but not even you could crack what they laid in here."

"You were always the quiet one," Geronimo said. "Wrap a little dyno around you and suddenly I can't shut you up."

"I don't need you to die with me," Pins said. "I can do this alone. I've done everything else that way, don't see why dying should be any different."

"They shoulda taped your mouth shut too." Geronimo was on his back, next to Pins, ready to snap down on a green wire. "Would've made my job easier."

"Boomer, Dead-Eye, the others, they need your help, Geronimo," Pins said. "A lot more than I do."

Geronimo snapped off the green wire, shoved the clipper in his waistband, crawled back several inches farther, and started to remove the wire from Pins's feet. He tossed the wire behind him and inched his way back to the front of the cage.

"Just so you know and it registers," Geronimo said, wiping the sweat from Pins's forehead with the front of his shirt. "There are two things in this life I've never walked away from. A device and a friend."

"Then you're gonna die in here," Pins said. "With this friend and with this device."

"I wouldn't have it any other way," Geronimo said. "Now, that timer is telling me we got ourselves a little less than three minutes. I could snap off a few more wires and hope we stay lucky, or, if you want, I can just kick back and we shoot the shit. Your call, Pins."

"We never did get a chance to talk all that much," Pins said.

"White or red," Geronimo said. "Pick one."

"I still like red," Pins breathed.

"Devices love creatures of habit," Geronimo said with a smile. Then he pulled the clipper and snapped off the white wires. "File that for the next time."

"How many of those wires we got left?" Pins asked.

"Hard to figure. They laid on a lot of 'em. Crisscrossed 'em all on top of it. Most are dummies, only one is lit. So we got that, plus the dyno hooked to the rope around your neck, which can go off of any wire. Best I can do is try to get to the central coil and snap it down, but it would be more a guess than anything else."

"Bottom-line it for me, Geronimo," Pins said. "Where we goin' with this?"

Geronimo laid the clipper down on the shiny floor of the bowling lane. He took off his shirt, wiped the sweat off his body, and sat down. He folded his legs and rested his arms on top of them. He turned and looked over at Pins, drenched in blood and sweat, his legs lifeless from having held one position for such a long time. He took several long, slow, deep breaths.

"The device wins, Pins," Geronimo finally said. "We can't beat it."

"Yeah, we can," Pins said.

"I'm listening," Geronimo told him.

"Don't wait for it," Pins said. "Let it blow on your terms. You're the best at this. So let the best decide when the fucker goes up."

Geronimo smiled at Pins as his right hand reached for the clippers. "Pick your color," Geronimo said.

"I'm a stubborn little bastard. I'm gonna stick with the red."

"Red it is," Geronimo said.

He stood on his knees, one hand grasping Pins's shoulder and the other holding the pliers wrapped around a thin red wire.

"I hope you're not wrong," Geronimo said. The smile on his face faded. Then it came back. Pins met it with a smile of his own.

"Bet on this one," Pins said.

Geronimo snapped down on the red wire and waited for the flash. Once again willing a device to his terms.

. . .

THE FOUR APACHES were jolted in their seats by the loud explosion. They were in Boomer's car, at the far end of the parking lot.

They watched the bowling alley implode. Shards of glass and thick debris flew in all directions. The ceiling caved in, smoke and dust filtered through the air.

Mrs. Columbo gave out a low moan. Rev. Jim was crying and swearing in a rage of emotion. Dead-Eye balled his hands into fists, rubbing them against his legs. Boomer was a mask of stone, the flames reflecting off the darkness of his deep-set eyes. He felt inside his leather jacket, his hand gripping the sticks of dynamite Geronimo had given him. He pulled his hand away and turned the ignition on the car, shoved the gear into drive, and pulled out of the lot.

"Where we going, Boom?" Dead-Eye asked.

"To finish it."

"We know where?" Rev. Jim wanted to know, glancing back at the smoke billowing from the bowling alley.

"We will," Boomer said, looking through the rearview. "Pins wired Wilber. We'll pick him up on the scanner on our way to Nunzio's."

"That where we going now?" Mrs. Columbo asked. Her voice was stoic, almost mechanical.

"That's our first stop," Boomer said.

"And the second?" Dead-Eye asked.

"To pick up a friend." Boomer lowered his foot to the gas pedal, pushing the speedometer past seventy.

"Anybody we know?" Dead-Eye asked.

"Deputy Inspector Lavetti," Boomer said, throwing Mrs. Columbo a quick look over his shoulder and rolling his window up, the night chill too bitter against his face.

"At least it's somebody we can trust," Rev. Jim said, slouching in his seat and closing his eyes to the sounds of the night.

20

THEY STOOD in the center of Nunzio's cramped basement, surrounded by red wooden wine barrels and thick crates marked with a government seal. Several of the crates had been eased open with the flat end of a crowbar. An iron door leading to steps and street level was locked and barred. A series of bare bulbs hung overhead.

"Everything you need, you can find inside the crates," Nunzio said, approaching one and resting a tray loaded with five cups of coffee on it.

"Where did all this stuff come from?" Dead-Eye shook his head in awe. He took a cup from the tray and walked from one crate to the next, his eyes fixed on the astonishing cache of Ingram submachine guns, semiautomatics, grenades, launchers, timers, bullets, vests, knives, and liquid explosives.

"You're not my *only* friends," Nunzio said.

"We need one other thing from you," Boomer said. He passed

on the coffee, instead filling a plastic cup with wine from one of the barrels.

"Tell me," Nunzio said.

"A private plane. With a pilot you trust. We're going to need to move all the equipment out of state and my airport connection can't help me walk in with this heavy a load."

"You want him for the round trip?" Nunzio asked.

Boomer took a look at the Apaches before he answered. "Yes," he said. "We'll be comin' back. One way or the other."

"Where to?"

"Arizona," Boomer said. "Small town, about thirty miles outside Sedona. I'd like to be in the air in about two hours. We picked up Wilber yappin' away over Pins's wire. In between the laugh and the brag, he talked about taking his crew back to Lucia's compound."

"They want to fight you on their turf," Nunzio said. "Why not wait and take 'em out on your own ground."

"We just lost two good cops on our own ground," Mrs. Columbo said.

"You don't even know the layout," Nunzio said. "How many guns she's got, what you're up against. You gonna do it, do it right, Boomer. Don't turn it into a suicide ride."

"This *is* the right way," Boomer said. "It's the way it's supposed to be. Us against them."

"From the phones on that plane we can reach out to all our federal contacts," Rev. Jim said. "Ask 'em to tell us what they know about her spread."

"And then we tell 'em we're going in," Boomer said. "Ask them to follow us out a few hours later."

"How you so sure they're gonna go along with somethin' this crazy?" Nunzio asked.

"They don't have a choice," Boomer said. "They're not gonna blow us out of the sky and they're not gonna rat us out. Besides, half the guys we deal with would kill for the chance to be with us."

"Lucia's expectin' you to go after her," Nunzio said. "That should be worth a thought."

"I think it's time we met," Boomer said. "After all we've been through together."

. . .

Deputy Inspector Mark Lavetti stood under the awning of a doorman building on Madison Avenue, fixing the collar on his brown tweed jacket. He was a handsome man in his early forties, his lean figure topped by a thick head of curly dark hair. He had been a member of the New York City Police Department for twenty-one years and had never recorded a major arrest. He was a test cop, making his steady climb up the ranks by cracking open books in schools rather than cracking heads out on the streets.

He was born with a taste for the sweet life and from his first weeks at the Police Academy was quick to smoke out a pad and how best to squeeze his way in on the action. He took his first envelope while still wearing the grays of a trainee, fifty a week to fill a local dealer in on which probie cops were eager to score free joints and lines, no questions asked. In return, the dealer sold their names to the turf leader of their precinct.

By the time he stood under the awning of the building on Madison Avenue, Mark Lavetti was pulling down twenty-five thousand in cash a month, feeding info to major dealers in the five boroughs. He never went near the money himself, instead using a rotating team of relatives as a pickup posse, letting them move the cash from sealed locker to selected bank and mutual fund accounts.

Lavetti was a master at covering the money trail.

His three-bedroom co-op was in his mother's name. The sporty Corvette he drove when not on duty was owned tire and gearshift by a sister in Mineola. He had a summer home in Woodstock mortgaged to an uncle living in a nursing home. His yearly vacations came courtesy of a cousin who ran a tourist agency.

Despite the rumors floating out of various precincts, the top brass saw Mark Lavetti exactly as he wanted to be seen—a clean cop riding the fast track.

His biggest score had also been his easiest.

Mark Lavetti was on the phone seconds after Joseph Silvestri walked out of his One Police Plaza office. He listened to the sad man tell him about his wife's involvement with a band of disabled cops, assured him all would be kept confidential, then set up a meeting with a main feeder to Lucia Carney's drug business. Outside Gate D at Shea Stadium, Lavetti handed over the six names of the Apaches to a man he knew would want them dead. In return, he accepted a manila envelope crammed with $100,000 in cash.

And he never gave the matter another thought.

Lavetti walked at a brisk pace down Madison, wondering whether to detour over to Lincoln Center to pick up a pair of opera tickets for himself and his new girlfriend, a model who was easily impressed by such things, or wait until after dinner and then drive past. His car was parked at the corner of Sixty-second Street, next to a hydrant, an official NYPD tag in the front window. As he got closer, he noticed a dark blue sedan double-parked close to his car, blocking his exit, the driver nowhere in sight.

He took the keys from the front pocket of his slacks, ready to call in the car and have a truck come tow it, angry he hadn't just parked in the building garage as usual.

"Where you off to tonight, Inspector?" Boomer asked, coming out of the shadows of a shuttered dry cleaners, standing behind Lavetti, both hands in his jacket pockets.

"Who the fuck are you?" Lavetti asked.

"I'm surprised you don't recognize me," Boomer said. "I'm an Apache."

"What the fuck's that supposed to mean?" Lavetti asked. But a shift in his tone betrayed his disquiet.

"You put a price on me." Boomer stepped closer, holding the urge to pull the trigger on the gun inside his jacket. "And on my friends. Somebody started to collect. Two of them died today."

"Are you crazy!" Lavetti said. "Do you know who you're talking to? I'm a cop. A deputy inspector!"

"The two who died were *cops*," Boomer said. "You're just a punk with a badge. But tonight you're in for a treat. I'm going to give you a chance to *die* like a cop."

"I'm not going anywhere with you," Lavetti said, starting to turn and run.

"Then you'll die right here." Boomer pulled the gun from his pocket and pressed it to Lavetti's temple. "On the street, like the piece of shit you are. Either way, I don't give a fuck. It's your decision."

"Where are we going?" was all Lavetti could manage to say.

Boomer turned Lavetti around and cuffed him as he pushed him toward the backseat of the dark blue sedan. "To visit an old friend of yours. And I bet she's gonna be real happy to see you."

"I could have you killed," Lavetti said, glaring at Boomer from the backseat. "One call, that's all it'll take."

"A lot of guys have made that one call, Lavetti," Boomer said, kicking over the engine and peeling out of his space. "I'm still here. And they're all dead."

· · ·

BOOMER AND DEAD-EYE were crouched down, hidden by shrubs and darkness, staring across a golf pond at the heavily guarded three-story house.

"I count at least eight in front," Boomer whispered. "Figure the same number in back. And double that for the ground crew."

Rev. Jim and Mrs. Columbo were stretched out farther up the ridge, Lavetti shoved facedown alongside.

Except for Lavetti, they all wore bullet-resistant vests under their black shirts. On the plane ride over, the four of them had jammed a full arsenal of semis around their hips and waists, loaded up on grenades and ammo, and listened while Boomer laid out what sounded like nothing less than an invasion.

"You really think any of this is going to work?" Rev. Jim asked at one point.

"Are you kidding?" Boomer said. "It'll be a fuckin' miracle if it even comes *close* to working."

"I'm glad to hear you say that," Dead-Eye said. "I was starting to worry."

"With our luck," Mrs. Columbo said, jabbing a thumb toward Lavetti, "he'll be the only one to make it out alive."

"Don't bet on that," Boomer said, staring over at Lavetti, who had stayed silent through the entire flight.

"Run that Greek fire deal by me one more time," Rev. Jim said.

"I'm new at this myself, so bear with me," Boomer said, holding up a white five-foot plastic tube. "But the way Geronimo told it, you air-gun the nitro through the tube and it shoots out above the water, a lot like a torpedo out of a sub. It bounces off the water and right into the house."

"It leaves behind a flame trail," Dead-Eye said. "So you can use it as light too."

"An air gun and nitro," Rev. Jim said. "What could go wrong with that?"

Boomer had alerted his federal sources from the air and bargained himself an hour's worth of attack time. "Don't worry, Tony," he said to a voice at the other end of the phone. "As it is, you're giving us about thirty minutes more than we need. We'll try and leave you nothing to clean up."

Before Tony clicked off the line he said, "I don't know which is better, if we find you dead or alive."

"If you find us," Boomer said, "I'd count on dead."

. . .

LUCIA CARNEY DRANK from a glass of white wine, looking out into the darkness. Wilber Graves stood next to her, a smug smile on his face. She was dressed in a black pants suit, her hair hanging down around her shoulders, a .45 silver-handled semiautomatic lodged against the base of her spine.

"They're here," Lucia said. "Hiding in the shrubs somewhere."

"They won't get far," Wilber said. "Or even close. They'll be dead before they reach the house."

"A shame," Lucia said. "I was hoping to at least meet them. To fly all this way and go to all this trouble, just to end up dead on a golf course."

"There are six men on every floor inside the house," Wilber told her. "Just in case."

"And where will you be?" Lucia asked.

"Where I belong," Wilber said. "Next to you."

Lucia finished her drink and smiled. "Time will decide where you belong, Wilber," she said as she walked past him without looking up.

. . .

"WE HOLD to the plan for as long as we can," Boomer said, looking past Dead-Eye toward Rev. Jim and Mrs. Columbo. "If we make it out, we regroup here and head back to the landing strip."

"Don't I at least get a gun?" Lavetti asked, still stretched out on the ground.

"Know how to use one?" Rev. Jim asked.

"Of course I do," Lavetti exclaimed.

"Then the answer's no," Mrs. Columbo said. "We may be crazy, but we ain't stupid."

"Don't think of yourself as an Apache," Dead-Eye told him. "Think of yourself as a bulletproof vest we don't have to wear."

"It's like havin' my very own shield," Rev. Jim said. He snapped one cuff around Lavetti's wrist, closing the other end on his own. "Wonder how many bullets he takes before I tire of draggin' him around."

"Enough to kill him, I hope," was Mrs. Columbo's answer.

"We ready to do this?" Boomer asked, standing and zipping his jacket.

"No," Dead-Eye said. "But if it means getting out of this heat, I'll give it a shot."

"Dead-Eye and I will walk down the front path like we're invited to a party," Boomer said. "Soon as you can, Rev. Jim, get that Greek fire going across the pond."

"It'll either be flames or me shootin' past that water," Rev. Jim said.

Boomer turned to Mrs. Columbo. "Mary, you get as close as you can and launch those rockets just like we showed you on the plane."

"Don't worry," she said. "If I can drive a wrecking ball down a Manhattan street, I can sure as shit shoot a rocket against the side of a house."

"We all meet inside," Boomer said. "First one to Lucia takes home the prize."

"We're all going to be killed," Lavetti said, panic firmly set in. "She's in there waiting. They're *all* in there waiting. If you turn back now, I can work something out. Have her back off. It's your only way out."

Boomer stepped over to Lavetti and slapped him hard across the face. "As soon as the shooting starts, uncuff yourself from him," Boomer said to Rev. Jim. "He'll be surrounded by his friends."

"See you at the fair." Rev. Jim began dragging Lavetti with him toward the golf pond.

Boomer watched them go, then turned to Mrs. Columbo. He touched her cheek and smiled. "You sure you're gonna be okay?" he asked.

"You worried because I'm the only woman on the team?" Mrs. Columbo asked.

"I'm worried because you're the only woman I care about left alive," Boomer said softly.

"You really know the right time for romance," she answered with a smile. She lifted her launcher and rocket pack and headed off in search of a shooting site.

"That just leaves the two of us," Dead-Eye pointed out.

"You're a smart man." Boomer placed a hand on his friend's shoulder. "How the hell'd you end up with a guy like me?"

"Born under a dark cloud," Dead-Eye told him. "And there's nothing I can do to change it."

"Let's go make some noise, then." They began to walk down the well-lit path, knowing there were eyes on their every step. They turned a slight curve and saw the house, a quarter of a mile ahead.

"They're not gonna let us get much closer," Boomer said.

"I wouldn't have let us get this far."

"Maybe we got it all wrong," Boomer said. "Maybe they don't want us dead."

"That's what Custer thought. Up until that first arrow."

. . .

"WHY ARE YOU waiting?" Lucia asked Wilber, anger in her voice and eyes.

"Can you see them yet?" Wilber asked. "I thought you wanted to see them."

"Enough with your stupid little games, Wilber," Lucia said. "I want to see them *dead*."

"They *are* dead," Wilber said. "They just haven't been told yet."

"Well then, have the men let them know," Lucia said. "*Now.*"

Wilber opened the windows to the terrace, stepped outside, and gave the signal.

. . .

REV. JIM EASED the nitro ball into the air gun, then placed the front tip of the gun inside the opening of the five-foot plastic tube. He and Lavetti were crouched at the edge of the golf pond, directly across from the rear of the house.

"You have any idea what you're doing?" Lavetti asked, desperate.

"Not a clue." Rev. Jim moved both hands slowly, dragging Lavetti's cuffed wrist along.

"It won't work," Lavetti said. "I can tell from your face even *you* know it won't work."

"You're a very negative guy." Rev. Jim looked him over. "Maybe yoga would help."

. . .

MRS. COLUMBO DROPPED the rocket into the launcher pad, her hands, face, and back drenched with sweat. She twisted the base shield to her right and pressed the red button, turning from the launcher. She waited with eyes shut for a blast that never arrived.

"Dammit, Mary," she muttered to herself. "Don't screw up. Not here. Not now."

She peeked over the lid of the launcher and shook her head.

"What a dope," she said, still mumbling, realizing she had put the rocket in backward.

She struggled to pull it out, turned it around, and then placed it back inside the cylinder.

"Please, God," she whispered, her eyes closed. "Please make it work."

. . .

A STREAM OF BULLETS rained down on Boomer and Dead-Eye, pelting the path at their feet.

It was the signal they wanted.

Boomer turned right, Dead-Eye left, each with a grenade in hand, tossing them out into the dark night. After six grenades had blown patches of grass and pieces of men into the air, they each unzipped their jackets and wrapped their hands around the handle of an M-60 machine gun. They stood back to back, pumping bullets in all directions, Boomer leading the way to the house.

They saw the Greek fire before they heard it.

A large ball of flame raced across the rear pond, up onto the back lawn, flush into the house, blowing out windows and walls. Three other blasts followed in quick succession, causing equal amounts of damage.

Mrs. Columbo's missiles found their mark as well.

The first one overshot the main house and blew up the garage. The next two took out five men and half the second floor.

Boomer and Dead-Eye reloaded, kept firing as bullets whistled past. Only one found them, clipping Boomer on his right elbow.

Dead-Eye was running the M-60 like a concert baton, leaving in his wake the moans and thuds of the wounded and dying. Boomer cleared the front of the path, stopping his cascade of bullets long enough only to throw out a few more grenades.

Missiles and nitro blasts lit the sky.

"I guess they know we're here," Boomer shouted.

"Think they're ready to surrender yet?" Dead-Eye asked, spraying two more face down into the grass.

"When we get inside, we'll ask," Boomer said, lighting a stick of dynamite and tossing it toward the front door.

. . .

REV. JIM UNCUFFED LAVETTI, picked him up, and started to run with him toward the house. But Lavetti broke free and drew ahead.

"Wilber!" Lavetti began to shout. "Don't shoot! It's me! Mark Lavetti. Don't shoot!"

Rev. Jim headed off in the opposite direction, around the left side of the pond, running toward the gaping hole in the first floor caused by one of his fireballs, using an Uzi submachine gun to further light the way. He turned to take a look at Lavetti, frantically waving his arms and calling out Wilber's name.

"Hope he finds you," Rev. Jim said.

. . .

MRS. COLUMBO, free of the weight of the rocket launchers and heavy packs, walked quickly down an unguarded rock road and soon found herself by the rear of the house. She smiled as she stepped inside. Wait till Boomer hears about this she thought. He'll never believe it.

. . .

THE DOOR BLEW OPEN and Boomer and Dead-Eye jumped through a circle of fire, guns still spraying bullets in all directions.

"Here's where we split," Boomer said, standing and shooting in the main entry. "I'll take the second floor."

"That leaves the third for me."

"Call if you need me," Boomer shouted, running up the front hall steps.

"Other way around, friend," Dead-Eye said, racing through the kitchen and taking the back staircase.

. . .

WILBER GRAVES MOVED through fire and smoke, stepping over dead bodies, looked out incredulously at Lavetti, standing near the golf pond, shouting his name.

Wilber lifted the machine pistol in his hand, aimed it at the corrupt cop, and waited until he was close enough for their eyes to meet.

"Wilber," Lavetti yelled, blinded by smoke and flames. "That you? That you, Wilber?"

"It's me," Wilber said.

He then calmly pumped three bullets into Mark Lavetti's chest.

The first two found flesh and bone.

The third shattered the bottle of nitro Rev. Jim had slipped inside the pocket of Lavetti's black windbreaker.

The explosion sent Wilber flying onto his back and killed anyone on the back grass who wasn't already dead.

Rev. Jim saw the blast from the second-floor balcony. He shook his head and turned away.

"Some friends you found yourself, Lavetti," he said.

. . .

Mrs. Columbo walked along the wall leading to the second-floor den. Gunfire erupted throughout the house and thick plumes of smoke filtered down the halls, tearing her eyes. She had a .38 Special in her right hand, held down against her thigh. There were scattered bodies and debris everywhere.

She stepped over a black-suited shooter, face down in his own blood, and turned a curved corner, bumping into a tall man with deep lacerations on his face and arms.

"You must be the one they call Mrs. Columbo," Wilber Graves said in a voice revealing his British boarding school education. Graves was born to a life of luxury and had the habits to prove it. But at a young age he had trained his full attention on doing what he liked to do best—kill.

Mrs. Columbo went to lift her gun, but his hand was faster. Graves reached out to hold it in place with a powerful grip. She heard the snap of a switchblade and watched as he moved closer, the fear of the knife stalking her once again, paralyzing her.

She saw the blade come up but could do nothing.

She waited but the knife came no closer. Wilber Graves had noticed her vest, knew the knife in his hand wouldn't penetrate. Mrs. Columbo smiled.

"I'm not making it easy for you, am I?" she said.

"I prefer you didn't," Wilber said, smiling back.

Mrs. Columbo lifted a knee to Wilber's groin and brought the bone of her elbow flush against his nose, breaking it and blinding him with his own blood. He let go of her hand and fell to his knees. She lifted her gun hand and rested the pistol against the top of his head.

"Pull the trigger," Wilber whispered.

Mrs. Columbo made the error every cop dreads.

She hesitated.

She flashed back to the night she was attacked, her body ravaged by a madman's angry knife. She could see the blade swish up and down and felt the pain each time it cracked through skin. She was meant to die that night on that street.

Instead, it would be another man, holding another knife, who would decide the ending to her life.

Wilber Graves shoved the blade of the knife into her knee and twisted it. Mrs. Columbo let out a low groan and dropped the gun. Her left leg went numb and she felt dizzy, holding on to the wall for support. Wilber lifted his right hand and slid her down next to him. He pulled the knife out of her leg, reached behind her to undo the vest. Mrs. Columbo looked at the ceiling, her eyes barely able to focus, her upper body cold, the side of her leg warmed by the flow of blood.

"I'll miss you, Mrs. Columbo," Wilber told her.

"Wish I could say the same," Mrs. Columbo said.

Wilber lifted the edge of her vest and rammed the knife deep into the center of her stomach, sliding it up until he bumped against the muscle of the chest cavity. He left it lodged there, too deeply imbedded to remove. Mrs. Columbo looked at him through glassy eyes, a sharp rush of pain mingled with a soothing numbness. She turned her head to the wall, closed her eyes, and thought about her son.

No one could harm her anymore.

. . .

BOOMER WAS THE ONE who found her.

He fell to his knees, slipping on her blood. He lifted her head and cradled it. She was still breathing, if barely, tongue licking at her lips. She opened one eye and did her best to smile.

"It took this to get you to hold me," she whispered.

Boomer didn't speak. Couldn't speak.

"I told you I could handle the rockets," she said.

He nodded.

"You proud of me?" she asked.

"Yes," he said slowly. "Very proud."

"Means a lot," Mrs. Columbo said.

"I love you, Mary," Boomer said. But those were words she never heard. Mrs. Columbo had already leaned her head back against Boomer's arms and closed her eyes for the last time.

Boomer took off his windbreaker and covered her. He reached over, picked up her .38 Special, and jammed it inside the front of his pants. He undid the Velcro of his vest and tossed it over his shoulder.

Then Boomer stood and walked away from one more fallen Apache.

. . .

DEAD-EYE WAS CORNERED, bullets coming at him from four sides, ripping through the closet door he stood behind. He was low on ammo and couldn't lift his right arm, which had taken two hits from a .44 caliber. There were six shooters closing in, two working pump-action shotguns. He had enough ammo and one good hand left to take out at least two. He took a deep breath and decided to make a rush at the gunmen.

If Dead-Eye was going to go down, it wasn't going to be hiding behind an empty second-floor coat closet.

He jumped from the door, left hand out, gun held at an angle, firing off as many clips as it carried. He hit one of the shotguns in the chest, sending him over a railing. He swirled and took out a suit rushing from behind, and then took a hit himself in the right leg, bringing him down to one knee.

The four moved in closer, prepared to end a battle and a life. Dead-Eye looked at them and grunted.

"Wouldn't have any bullets you could spare?" he asked.

"Just two," the shotgun shouted back. "Both of them going into your fucking head."

"Thanks anyway," Dead-Eye said.

. . .

REV. JIM CAME UP the back steps, two .44 semis crisscrossed in his hands. He pumped three rounds into the back of the shotgun, sending him face down next to Dead-Eye. The other three sprang for cover.

Dead-Eye grabbed the shotgun, pulled the trigger, and took out part of a wall and one shooter. Rev. Jim walked past, dropped a handgun in his lap, and chased the other two down a corner hall, smoke and flames coming out the barrels of his guns. The last two bullets in the chambers left the men down and dead.

"I don't want to hurt your feelings," Rev. Jim said, standing over Dead-Eye. "But you don't look so good."

"It's the heat," Dead-Eye said. "I *hate* the heat."

"Can you walk?"

"Not far," Dead-Eye said.

"Can you shoot?" Rev. Jim asked.

"Just with my left hand," Dead-Eye said. "Right one's gone. At least for today."

"Your one hand is still better than my two," Rev. Jim said.

"You loaded?" Dead-Eye asked.

"Got enough rounds left where we won't embarrass ourselves."

"You'll move faster without me," Dead-Eye said. "Just leave me a gun and go."

"Nobody gets rid of me that easy." Rev. Jim put a loaded semi in Dead-Eye's left hand, a .38 in his waistband, and a .44 bulldog in his right.

"I told you my right arm's no good," Dead-Eye said, forcing himself to his feet. "Can't feel it."

"Your trigger finger numb?" Rev. Jim asked, tossing Dead-Eye's left arm around his shoulders and holding his waist with his right hand.

"No," Dead-Eye said.

"Then why waste it?" Rev. Jim asked.

Dead-Eye and Rev. Jim made their way slowly down the hall, arms linked together, four guns in their hands, spraying bullets in all directions, leaving a line of blood behind them as their trail.

. . .

Boomer stood in the doorway of the second-floor master bedroom, watching Lucia Carney rummage through the center drawer of a bureau, her back to him.

"Nice place you had here," he said.

She turned. From her demeanor, they might have been at a formal dance instead of the middle of a firestorm. "You must be Boomer," she said. "Please come in."

"I *am* in." Boomer held Mrs. Columbo's .38 in his hand.

"I expected to see a larger man." Lucia stepped away from the bureau.

"Firemen are tall," Boomer said. "Cops are short. That's how you can tell us apart."

"You've cost me considerable amounts of time and money, Boomer."

"And you cost me three friends. Somehow it doesn't even out."

"I learned very early on that there's a price for everything in life," Lucia said. "And everyone I've met has one. I just haven't figured out yours yet."

"That's an easy one," he said. "You."

"What?" She moved closer to him.

"*You're* my price," Boomer told her. "When you go down, I'll walk away."

"Your type's not the kind to kill a woman," Lucia said. "Even a woman like me."

Boomer stared into Lucia's eyes and knew there was someone else in the room. He managed to turn just as Wilber's knife was about to shear his back. It flew past the front part of his right shoulder, but its force knocked him up against a wall and sent the gun he held to the floor.

"I've killed your friends," Wilber taunted, his broken nose giving a deep nasal sound to his voice. "And now you will feel the same pain they did."

Boomer waited until Wilber stepped closer, then rushed him, landing against his chest, both men falling to the floor. Boomer held back the knife hand and landed three solid lefts to the side of Wilber's face.

Wilber Graves had firmly pressed a button that should not have been touched. There was an out-of-control rage to Boomer now, fed by the images of Pins, Geronimo, and Mrs. Columbo. He threw punches in a mad fury, breaking his hand against the hard bones of Wilber's jaw and temple.

Boomer beat Wilber until he could no longer lift his arms. He fell over him, exhausted, lifted his head, short of breath, to look up at Lucia, who still stood above him.

He didn't see the knife.

Wilber held it with four fingers and lifted it high above his head, barely able to see out of the slit of his eyes. He dropped the knife deep into the center of Boomer's back.

Boomer let out a sharp yell, and fell face forward. He peered back at Wilber, who was watching, waiting for the cop to die.

Boomer spread his hand out, reaching for the fallen .38. He wrapped his fingers around it, turned at an angle toward Wilber. The killer's face was a mask of red, his eyes vacant and distant as he struggled to his feet.

Boomer inched up to his knees, the pain in his back sharp, and clicked the trigger on Mrs. Columbo's gun. "This is from Mary," Boomer said to Wilber Graves. He fired one shot into Wilber's stomach and watched him crumple to the floor. "And this is from Carolyn." The second bullet went into Wilber's head. The assassin curled into a heap, then never moved again.

Boomer slowly, painfully, lifted himself against the side of the wall, leaving smears of blood in his wake. He walked with stilted, pained steps over toward Lucia, watching her reach behind the small of her back for the gun she had wedged there.

"I've never run into anyone like you," Lucia said, pointing it at him.

"You would have, sooner or later." He inched closer to Lucia, walking on legs he couldn't feel. "There's always going to be somebody like me out to stop somebody like you."

"And how do people like you do that?" Lucia said.

"Any way we can."

Before she could move or respond, Boomer took a deep, pain-filled breath and made a leap for her. Her gun exploded, but Boomer never even felt the bullet ripping into his chest. They both fell to the floor, his blood dripping over her designer clothes. He looked into her eyes, saw the flash of anger, the touch of madness that had made her drug runners tremble. But he wasn't a drug runner.

He was a cop.

Boomer closed a fist and landed two sharp blows against the side of

Lucia's face, knocking her out cold. He then pulled a cigarette lighter from the front pocket of his blood-soaked jeans and clicked it open, staring at the blue flame. He reached behind him and pulled a roll of dynamite from the back of his jeans.

It was Geronimo's roll.

He lit the forty-five-second fuse and shoved the dynamite down the front of Lucia's blouse.

Boomer crawled away from her on hands and knees, the pain so real it had a taste. He glanced at Wilber's prone body for a final time and closed the door behind him with his foot.

He made it halfway down the hall when the dynamite blast took out the entire room and sent him flying toward a corner stairwell.

"The bitch is history, Geronimo," Boomer mumbled, resting his head against a marble step.

. . .

THE THREE APACHES were all on the second floor.

Dead-Eye had his head down, leaning against a wall, weakened by his wound. Rev. Jim sat against a banister, his clothes caked, a bullet rendering his right leg useless. Boomer was spread face down on the tile floor under a pool of blood, Wilber's knife in his back.

They were surrounded by smoke, flames, and the dead. They could hear the sounds of sirens and fire engine horns closing in.

"Hey, Boomer," Rev. Jim said.

"What?" Boomer said without lifting his head.

"I don't wanna upset you or anything, but there's a knife stickin' out of your back."

"I needed a place to hang my hat," Boomer told him.

"Good thinkin'," Rev. Jim said.

As they waited in silence for the rescue squads to come and clean up, Dead-Eye turned to his right. One of the wounded shooters was crawling for his gun.

The shooter looked at Dead-Eye, his hand around the pistol handle. "Hey, nigger," the shooter said, straining to lift the gun. "Don't you ever miss?"

Dead-Eye curled the .44 he held in his left hand and squeezed off one round, hitting the shooter in the center of his forehead, dropping him dead.

"No," Dead-Eye said, leaning his head back against the wall.

"Ask a stupid question . . . " Rev. Jim said.

The laughter of the wounded Apaches echoed through the shell of the burning house and floated out across the ruins of a fallen drug empire.

The ones they said could never be whole again had achieved victory.

EPILOGUE

Every man has his own destiny. The only
imperative is to follow it, to accept it, no
matter where it leads.

—Henry Miller, "The Wisdom of the Heart"

January 1983

Boomer sat at the head of the small table, sipping a cup of tea, watching Dead-Eye and Rev. Jim go deep into a game of chess.

"Is that as boring to play as it is to watch?" Boomer asked.

"Yes," Rev. Jim said.

"So why play it?" Boomer said.

"We don't have any checkers," Dead-Eye said.

The physical healing was almost complete.

Boomer and Dead-Eye had spent a month in an Arizona hospital. Rev. Jim was set loose after two weeks, during which he managed to fall hard for one of the night nurses. They each had to endure painful daily physical therapy sessions, which by now were a given in their lives.

As expected, there had been no legal complications from the attack on Lucia's compound. The feds were more than eager to grab credit for the takedown of Lucia Carney and her crew. The Apaches watched the press conference on a TV in Boomer's hospital room.

"If they could only bust as good as they bullshit," Rev. Jim said, turning off the set, "there'd be no crime."

They never did get to the private plane that waited for them three miles east of the compound. Instead, they drove out of Arizona in a rented convertible. Along the way they stopped to visit with Geronimo's Native American adviser. The old man listened with bright eyes as they told him how Geronimo had died—a brave warrior, unafraid and proud.

"We'll miss him," Boomer told the old man. "He was a good friend."

"There's no need," the man said in a voice filled with strength. "His spirit lives and travels alongside you. And alongside those who will follow you."

"The only thing following us these days are flies," Rev. Jim said.

The old man smiled and nodded. "No one chooses their road," he said. "Especially the brave."

When he got back to New York, Boomer headed straight for Mrs. Columbo's house. He sat at the small kitchen table across from her husband and son. He pulled her shield from his pocket and handed it to young Frank.

"She'd want you to keep this for her," Boomer said to the boy.

Frank held the badge and stared at it. "It's all she cared about," he said, his voice choking. "Being a cop."

"You're wrong about that," Boomer said. "She cared about you. A lot."

"Did you love her?" Frank asked, looking up from his mother's shield.

"Yes," Boomer said, looking right back.

"Did she love you?"

"Yes," Boomer said. "But not in the way you're thinking. Not in the way she loved your father."

"What way, then?" Frank asked.

"She loved me for what I *did*," Boomer said. "She loved your dad for who he *was*. There's a big difference."

"I don't see it," Frank said.

"You don't have to see it now," Boomer said, standing. "But one day you will. And I hope I'm around when you do."

. . .

THEY HAD RETURNED to the predictable boredom of their everyday lives.

Dead-Eye was back on doorman duty, working a building on East Sixty-fifth Street. In his free time he played catch with Eddie and took long drives with his wife.

Rev. Jim went into construction, taking charge of the crew Nunzio had hired to rebuild Pins's bowling alley. The old man thought he could turn it into an afternoon retreat for the neighborhood kids.

Boomer busied himself with daytime stops at movies, museums, and libraries. His nights, as always, were spent at Nunzio's.

. . .

DEAD-EYE MOVED a knight against one of Rev. Jim's rooks, swiping it from the board.

"That's it?" Boomer said. "Fifteen minutes you stare and wait and that's what you do?"

"Couldn't get to his queen," Dead-Eye explained.

"People in comas have more laughs," Boomer muttered.

Nunzio walked over, dragging a chair, holding a cup of coffee.

"There's a call for you," he told Boomer, sitting down to watch the game. "Before you take it, tell me who's ahead here. I don't want to break into their concentration."

"If you get an answer," Boomer said, "I'll buy dinner for the table."

"I'm winning," Dead-Eye said.

"I'll have the steak special," Rev. Jim added.

Boomer pushed his chair back and headed for the phone by the bar.

"Who is it?" he asked Nunzio.

"Wouldn't say."

"Why not?"

Nunzio shrugged. "Maybe he's shy."

Boomer came back to the table in less than five minutes. There was a glow to his face and in his eyes. Dead-Eye, Rev. Jim, and Nunzio all stared over at him.

"You gonna tell us?" Dead-Eye asked. "Or do we play another game?"

"How much longer till you finish this one?" Boomer asked.

"We can stop anytime," Rev. Jim said. "If we've got a good reason."

"Wanna take a ride with me?" Boomer asked.

"Where to?" Dead-Eye said.

"See a guy who's in a little trouble," Boomer said. "He thinks maybe we can help."

Boomer looked at his three friends, and, as the smiles formed on their faces, he nodded.

"I ain't ever gonna get that doorman's pension," Dead-Eye said, pushing the chessboard aside.

"Maybe they'll let you keep the suit," Rev. Jim said, reaching for his cap. "It looks good on you."

Nunzio sat at the table and watched the Apaches walk out of his restaurant into the frigid afternoon of a winter's day. He watched them leave to be what they had always been.

Cops.

ABOUT THE AUTHOR

LORENZO CARCATERRA is the author of the autobiographical memoir *A Safe Place* and the *New York Times* bestseller *Sleepers*. He is currently at work on his new book, *Shadows*.

RANDOM HOUSE AUDIOBOOKS

Lorenzo Carcaterra's

APACHES

is available on cassette from
Random House AudioBooks.

Running time: 3 hours, abridged • on 2 cassettes

AT YOUR BOOKSTORE or call TOLL FREE 1-800-726-0600.
*When calling or ordering by mail, please indicate tracking code: 026-89

Please send me the following AudioBooks by Lorenzo Carcaterra:

Apaches (abridged, 3 hours)   _____ @ $18.00 = _____
ISBN: 0-679-45927-8

Sleepers (abridged, 3 hours)   _____ @ $18.00 = _____
Read by Joe Mantegna • ISBN: 0-679-44750-4   (Quantity)

                                       Shipping/Handling*   = _____

                                       Subtotal   = _____

                                       Sales Tax (where applicable)   = _____

                                       Total Enclosed   = _____

*Please enclose $4.00 to cover shipping and handling (or $6.00 if total order is more than $30.00).

☐ If you wish to pay by check or money order, please make it payable to Random House Audio Publishing.

☐ To charge your order to a major credit card, please fill in the information below.

Charge to   ☐ American Express   ☐ Visa   ☐ MasterCard

Account No._____ Expiration Date_____

Signature_____

Name_____

Address_____

City_____ State_____ Zip_____

Send your payment with the order form above to:

Random House Audio Publishing, Dept. CC, 25-1, 201 East 50th Street, New York, NY 10022.
Prices subject to change without notice. Please allow 4-6 weeks for delivery.

For a complete listing of Random House AudioBooks, write to the address above.